An Accidental Courtship

M.A. Nichols

Books by M.A. Nichols

Generations of Love Series

The Kingsleys

Flame and Ember

Hearts Entwined

A Stolen Kiss

The Ashbrooks

A True Gentleman

The Shameless Flirt

A Twist of Fate

The Honorable Choice

The Finches

The Jack of All Trades

Tempest and Sunshine

The Christmas Wish

The Leighs

An Accidental Courtship

Love in Disguise

Standalone Romances

Honor and Redemption

A Tender Soul

A Passing Fancy

To Have and to Hold

A Holiday Engagement

Fantasy Novels

The Villainy Consultant Series

Geoffrey P. Ward's Guide to Villainy

Geoffrey P. Ward's Guide to Questing

Magic Slippers: A Novella

The Shadow Army Trilogy

Smoke and Shadow

Blood Magic

A Dark Destiny

Table of Contents

Chapter 1

Greater Edgerton, Lancashire
Autumn 1817

What rhymes with divine? Design? Combine? Entwine? Brushing the soft end of the quill against his chin, Parker Humphreys stared off into the vast nothing as his poetic genius scoured for the right word. Fine? Straightening, Parker dipped his nib and scratched out that option beside the growing list.

"Oh, what a creature of the divine, with eyes of brightest green; the finest of the fine," he mumbled to himself as he scratched the words across the paper. A particularly large droplet splattered the bottom, the ink smearing as he tried to salvage it, though there was little point. Parker stared at the words and scowled as he studied his poor attempt.

How did Byron, Shelley, Shakespeare, and the rest manage it? It was difficult enough finding the proper words to describe what he wished to say, let alone organizing them into a couplet.

Slicing the offending bits off with a pen knife, Parker crumpled them up and tossed them into the empty fireplace. At this rate, there would be a paper mountain ready to be burned when the maid lit the fire for the night. With a sigh, his elbow leaned on the desk, his forehead resting against his hand as he stared at the now blank sheet and reconsidered this course of action.

Why did he think that his first attempt at poetry would do anything to earn Miss Rosanna's affection? It was like a lad wishing to translate Ovid the first time he sat down to study Latin. She was so far beyond his reach, Parker needn't add wretched poetry to the list of failings.

But Rosanna Leigh deserved lyrical ballads expressing the extent of her loveliness. She certainly inspired it, reminding Parker of the mythology of old when the goddesses of love and beauty cursed foolish mortal maidens for being more appealing. Miss Rosanna certainly could win such a contest with those eyes as green as a summer field, all vibrant and alive.

Oh, that was rather good.

Parker snatched his quill and tried to write it down, but the words slipped from his grasp, leaving him with, *"Her eyes are like grass."* Another sigh, and he slumped down again. Miss Rosanna had her pick of men, and he was going to approach her with jumbled compliments and awkward affection?

Gathering his strength, Parker straightened again and stared at a fresh sheet of paper. Faint heart never won fair lady and all that. But it would help if he didn't insist on trying to win hers by resorting to awful poetry. Surely, if he spoke plainly, Miss Rosanna couldn't help but feel the depth of his affection—how often she swept into his dreams, leaving him with restless nights. No ball or party seemed complete without her there. Her very presence made the sun shine bright and the very air smell sweeter.

Parker winced and frowned at the blank page. A letter was certainly the better course, but he would have to avoid such mawkish sentiments. A man with seven and twenty years to his credit ought to be able to express himself without resorting to compliments that were more at home in a melodrama.

Straightforward and to the point was best. Leaning over the paper, Parker pressed his quill to the page and gave his thoughts free rein.

...

If there was a lady who despised love letters, Rosanna Leigh didn't wish to meet her, for she could not think of anything better than having a missive secreted to her. The skitter of anticipation that sprouted from the mystery surrounding the sender's identity was intoxicating; to say nothing of the tokens that usually accompanied such things. Even if she were to be buried beneath a flood of post, Rosanna doubted she would feel any different.

Even if the lovesick swain had horrid taste in gifts.

Tucked inside the folds of her latest offering was a length of ribbon, which would be quite useful to adorn her hair, bonnet, and perhaps even a gown—if it weren't pale blue. It was a color that many a lady wore, delicate and maidenly as it was, which was one of the many reasons Rosanna would never do so. One could not stand out in a crowd if one looked like all the rest. To say nothing of the fact that it did not compliment her eyes or complexion. Far too frosty a hue for her.

Seated before her dressing table, Rosanna held up the present next to her hair, turning her head this way and that, but she could not imagine any styling that would make the color appealing. Truly a wretched choice.

Turning her thoughts to the letter in her hand, Rosanna frowned at the handwriting, which matched her newest suitor's dreadful taste in ribbon color. The author must've been suffering from a fit whilst he wrote it. Surely he could've asked a friend or hired a clerk to scribble down his words and thereby presented himself in a more favorable (and elegant) light.

Rosanna scanned the page, which held the usual compliments. Her fine figure, lovely hair, and general perfection were highlighted, but it was the signature at the bottom that held her attention. It took several tries before she deciphered the scribble, and she grimaced.

Dr. Parker Humphreys?

With a sigh, she rose from her seat and tucked the ribbon back into the letter before crossing to the fireplace, her hand outstretched and ready to drop it. And stopped. Her sister might like the ribbon. At the very least, Prudence would find a use for it.

Tossing the packet onto her sister's bed, Rosanna strode from the room.

Whitley Court boasted many fine rooms. Beyond the family's private bedchambers, there was the parlor, the salon or drawing room (depending on who was speaking), the library, and the nursery. Quite a wealth of spaces in which the Leighs might dwell, yet despite that abundance, the majority of the family had invaded Prudence's quiet corner of the library. Never mind that Francis's bonnet decorating was better suited for the parlor or that Benjamin would find the nursery a better battleground for his toy soldiers or that the drawing room was entirely free of the drafts Grandmama feared so greatly.

Even Katherine made herself known in the library; the piano echoed from the parlor, the notes clanging and pounding with more force than Herr Mozart ever intended. Prudence stared at the ledger and winced, silently pleading for her sister to find the G-sharp.

Soldiers scattered across the floor, and Benjamin hooted, his little fists raised high in the air. Only a few more hours until Nurse Johnson returned from her half-day. Prudence took a deep breath, though it did little to help her ignore the boy's cacophony.

Leaning over the ledger, Prudence scanned the lines, her quill ticking off the figures as she tried to focus her thoughts on the household accounts. For the briefest moment, she considered escaping to Papa's study; only he was allowed in that room, but he was not in residence and was unlikely to return before dinner. The thought was fleeting and pointless, but Prudence considered it all the same; perhaps it might grant her a respite.

Movement in the doorway drew Prudence's attention, and Mrs. Hammond swept into the room with a book and pencil in her hand.

"Might I speak with you about the menu, miss?" said the housekeeper with a bob.

Prudence glanced at the ledgers and frowned. "Might you speak with my mother?"

"I fear she's feeling poorly."

Drawing in a breath, Prudence held it for a count of three before nodding. "Of course."

Mrs. Hammond dragged a chair from Francis's table in the center of the room and placed it beside the console table that served as Prudence's makeshift workspace. Then the housekeeper launched into a description of the recipes she suggested, referring to her notebook and making the appropriate marks next to the dishes as Prudence directed.

"Oh, not venison stew, Prudence," said Grandmama, glancing up from her book with a frown.

"Would squab pie suit you better?" asked Prudence.

"Certainly," replied the elderly lady before turning back to her novel.

And that was the precise moment that Francis thought an opinion on her bonnet design was of utmost importance and called for Prudence to say whether the green or pink ribbon suited the style better.

"You'd best ask Rosanna. She has the better eye for such things," said Prudence. But before she could return her attention to Mrs. Hammond, Benjamin ran up with a soldier in hand, begging his eldest sister to sit and play with him, and only hefty promises of the vast war they would wage later put the boy off.

"Perhaps we ought to discuss this in the drawing room," said Prudence, leading the housekeeper away from the noise and distractions. They passed a maid on the stairs, and she stopped the girl. "Jane, please take a pot of the tisane to Mrs. Leigh along with a few of the biscuits she likes. I fear she's not feeling well at present."

With a bob, Jane hurried off to do as bidden, and when Prudence was safely ensconced in the drawing room, she reveled in the moment of silence before turning her attention to Mrs. Hammond once more.

"The squab pie for Thursday, I think." Turning her thoughts through the dishes they'd already decided upon, Prudence rattled off a few sides and desserts that would suit while Mrs. Hammond scribbled away.

"I think that'll do a treat," said the housekeeper with a nod. "But might I suggest asparagus rolls as well? It's a shame not to use them as much as possible when they're in season."

"That does sound delicious—"

The drawing room door, which had been firmly shut, swung open, and the muted sound of Katherine's piano music boomed as Rosanna breezed in. "Here you are, Prudence. What do you think of my reticule? Isn't it fetching?"

"I do not know why you would ask my opinion on the matter," replied Prudence with a huff of amusement. "Francis is far more fashionable."

But Rosanna waved that away. "Because you tell me the truth and shan't lie to please me. I like it, but I am not certain it goes with my gown."

With pinched lips, Prudence studied the article, though a closer inspection did little to recommend it.

"Hideous. I don't know why netted reticules are so popular—especially when they have more holes than substance. Anything small will fall right out, and the craftsmanship is tolerable but hardly spectacular enough to overlook such a deficiency. Your green silk one would complement the peach in your gown far better."

Rosanna huffed and frowned at the offending reticule. "You are entirely correct as always, Prudence."

Turning on her heel, her sister moved to the doorway and called out for the maid.

"Jane is fetching Mama a tisane," said Prudence. "She is feeling poorly."

Rosanna did not go so far as to roll her eyes, as such a thing was hardly becoming, but her lips pinched into a tight little mew that somehow managed to be both vexed and adorable at the same time.

"I suppose I shall be forced to fetch it myself," she said with a sigh.

"Oh, the great struggles you bear," replied Prudence in a dry tone, drawing a smile to her sister's lips.

Then, with a dramatic hand to her forehead, Rosanna feigned a swoon. "Not that a complaint ever crosses my lips."

Rosanna straightened and turned an assessing eye on her sister. "Prudence, why aren't you dressed properly? We must leave immediately if we are to arrive at Miss Latham's at the appointed time, and you cannot go out in such a plain day dress."

Turning to Mrs. Hammond, Prudence gave the house-keeper her final orders and left her to her work. Then, facing Rosanna once more, Prudence waved her sister's protest away. "There is so much to do around here that I haven't the time to go with you. And there is little use in going to the shops when I haven't any pin money to spend."

"Nonsense." Rosanna waved an airy hand. "We have servants to do the work, after all, and Papa can give you a few coins. Please, Prudence. Everyone will be devastated if you do not join us."

"Hardly. Miss Latham only invited me to please you—"

"That is not true, Prudence, and you know it," replied Rosanna with a frown.

However, it was entirely true. No invitation was extended unless it included both Leigh girls, but Rosanna's name always preceded Prudence's, no matter that she was the younger of the two.

"Regardless, I have far too much to do, and if I am to attend the assembly tonight, I must dedicate myself to my work this afternoon," said Prudence, leading the young lady from the drawing room and back down towards the parlor where said work awaited. "I have to attend to the household accounts and inspect the linens, as they need replacing, and then there are Benjamin's lessons, and I've promised Katherine to help her with piano as well. And with Mama feeling poorly, I shall have to see to her."

Taking her sister by the arm, Rosanna pulled her to a stop just outside the parlor. "You do too much, Prudence. Surely you ought to do something amusing today."

"I am going to the assembly tonight—"

"More than that. Let Mama manage things for once."

Prudence scoffed, giving her sister a raised brow.

"Or at least wait until tomorrow," Rosanna amended.

"When another long list of things requires my attention?" Smiling, Prudence leaned in and bussed her on the cheek. "Go, have fun on my account."

Though Rosanna frowned at that pronouncement, she turned on her heel and made the arduous trek to their bedchamber to fetch the proper reticule. Prudence stood in the hallway and tried not to watch as her sister hurried back down and bundled herself up for an afternoon of revelry, and she fought to keep her heart from sinking as the front door shut behind Rosanna.

Chapter 2

Feeling forlorn was ridiculous. Prudence had been entirely honest with Rosanna; not only was there much to be done but accepting an invitation that had been extended out of pity or obligation was not how she wished to spend her afternoon. From their earliest days, Rosanna had refused any invitation that didn't include her poor elder sister as well, so people knew better than to attempt it, but having accepted many of those pity invites over the years, Prudence knew better than to expect anything more than polite tolerance and general apathy whilst the others tittered about all the gossip and goings-on of Greater Edgerton.

Then the ladies were bound to come across a gentleman and practice their coquetry—something Prudence was certain she would never master, especially when compared to the prodigious talent found amongst Rosanna's set. Being reminded of that fact hardly made for an enjoyable afternoon.

So, Prudence ought not to feel so heavy of heart. Yet the noise emerging from the parlor and library picked at her, and no matter how she attempted to return to the household accounts, she couldn't muster the fortitude to do so. Turning on her heel, she climbed the stairs, crept past Mama's bedchamber, and snuck into her own, closing the door tight behind her.

Prudence leaned against the door and sighed. Just a few minutes of quiet. That was all she required.

One deep breath and then a second, and she'd nearly convinced herself that she was restored, yet when she imagined returning to the chaos downstairs, Prudence remained frozen in place. Crossing the bedchamber, she dropped onto her bed, sinking into the pillows. Something crinkled, and she felt the tell-tale prick of something beneath her, but she remained where she was for a moment before finally deciding that her discomfort outweighed the effort it took to remove it.

Rolling, she freed the letter, turned the envelope over, and stared at the address. The author's handwriting was atrocious. Despite staring at the label, Prudence couldn't decipher the initial between "Miss" and "Leigh." Unfolding it, she found a length of ribbon that was a stunning shade of blue, as bright and rich as a summer sky. Prudence didn't need to read the signature below (assuming she could even comprehend the scrawl) to know this was a love letter intended for Rosanna.

Yet she couldn't tuck it away. Lying on her side, Prudence held the paper, her eyes slowly tracing the letters. With practice, it grew easier to comprehend the author's penmanship. She would never admit to anyone just how long she lay there, reading and re-reading the details of his ardor. This was not a grand poem like so many employed; instead, Dr. Humphreys wrote bluntly of his affection and the many ways in which he admired his lady love, both her beauty and her kindness.

It was unlikely the gentleman had ever noticed the elder Miss Leigh. Prudence was far more aware of menfolk than they were of her, after all. However, like any young person who traveled in similar circles, she had danced with the gentleman a time or two and shared the odd conversation. Though not amongst the flashiest of beaus, Parker Humphreys was a good man and well worth catching.

If Rosanna bothered to give him the opportunity.

With seven and twenty years to her name, Prudence Leigh was no young ninny of a girl, easily swept into flights of fancy. A lady with unremarkable features and a figure that left much to be desired learned at a young age not to pin her hopes on a gentleman falling madly in love with her upon first sight—especially with Rosanna Leigh standing nearby to provide an unflattering comparison.

Prudence sighed and dropped the letter, rolling onto her back. If there was anything unflattering in her situation, it was that thought. Neither Leigh sister held the blame for the unfortunate turn of fate that gifted the younger of the two with the sort of beauty that had inspired the tale of Helen of Troy, leaving the elder unable to ever shine on her own.

The bedchamber door burst open, and Prudence jerked upright to see Mama sweep into the room, the lace of her mobcap flapping in her hurry.

"My dear, where is your sister? I must speak with her at once."

Prudence stood from the bed and smoothed her skirts, thankful for the interruption. "She is out with Miss Latham. They've gone shopping and plan to attend the assembly together—"

"Oh, yes, I had forgotten," said Mama with a sigh. "I shall have to speak to her about it there."

"You are going?" asked Prudence with raised brows.

Mama waved that away. "The tisane you sent did the trick. I am feeling quite restored."

"Then might you look at the household accounts—"

"Oh, good heavens, no," replied Mama with a shake of her head that had the frills of her cap bobbing. Then, pulling a lace handkerchief from her pocket, she dabbed at her forehead. "I am feeling much better, but I fear my megrim will return in a trice if I strain my eyes. And both of us needn't labor over such tedious tasks when you are so perfectly suited to manage it all, Prudence. You are so good with the sums, and I fear I am entirely useless with such things."

Mama's gaze fell to the scrap of paper lying on the bed where Prudence had abandoned it. "And what is that?"

Turning to the mirror at her sister's dressing table, Prudence checked her hairpins. "The latest love letter for Rosanna. Jane must've placed it on my pillow by accident, and I didn't realize the mistake until after I read it."

Though not the entire truth, it was close enough that her conscience felt no prick of guilt at the slight fib, for that had been her intention. Even if she hadn't kept her curiosity in check. Besides, Rosanna wouldn't care two figs about whether Prudence had or hadn't.

"For Rosanna? What nonsense, Prudence," said Mama, lifting the letter to examine it. "It is addressed to 'Miss P. Leigh.'"

"I assure you, it is an R, not a P, Mama."

"Stuff and nonsense, my dear." Hurrying to her daughter's side, she pointed at a line. "'Your eyes are lovely to behold...' Rosanna has many lovely features, but of the two of you, your eyes are much finer than hers. Hers are too pale—the faint green is hardly noticeable except in the right circumstances—and yours are such a deep and rich brown. Quite striking."

Prudence's hands stilled their work, and her throat tightened. If she were to claim any vanity, it would be her eyes, which the proud little part of her had often thought very becoming. However, she'd never heard her mother say as much before.

Only when she trusted herself to speak did she point out the obvious flaw in her mother's argument. "I thank you for that compliment, but I shan't be so easily swayed. As no man has ever complimented my eyes, it is clear who Dr. Humphreys intended."

With a sharp huff and a frown, Mama hurried back to the bed and picked up the discarded ribbon. "Did he send this with it?"

"Yes," said Prudence, and then she added with emphasis, "*for Rosanna.*"

"This proves it, my stubborn girl," said Mama, gripping the ribbon in her fist and shaking it at the heavens with a beaming grin. "Your sister would never wear this shade. I do not think she even owns a blue gown. And it is one of your favorites. Blue suits you to a T. No sensible beau would send Rosanna such a gift."

Coming up behind her daughter, Mama tucked an edge of the ribbon into Prudence's dark locks and met her daughter's gaze in the looking glass with a challenging raise of her brows. "I will admit that the script is a little unclear, but it was left on your pillow and contains a gift so perfectly suited for you and entirely unsuited for your sister. How many signs must you receive before you accept that Dr. Humphreys was writing to you?"

The length of silk truly was becoming in Prudence's hair, the light hue playing nicely against the rich brown tresses; it was the reason why she loved the color so much. While she remained there, examining herself in the mirror, Mama rushed to her wardrobe and pulled out the gown intended for tonight's festivities.

"Come, and tell me it is a coincidence that your ball gown for tonight is that precise shade," said Mama, holding it up before Prudence—and, bless the lady, she was correct. Though Prudence intended to wear a darker blue robe atop it, the underskirts matched the ribbon to perfection.

"And how could Dr. Humphreys know what I'm planning to wear?" replied Prudence, her voice far weaker than she'd intended it. Her heart stirred at the thought; she tried to keep it under tight control, but Mama's arguments kept growing, supporting that forlorn hope she'd felt the moment she'd opened the love note.

"That is the easiest thing, my girl," she said with a scoff. "Suitors bribe the servants for such information all the time. How do you think he got the letter on your pillow in such a covert manner?"

Prudence stiffened and gaped. It was no secret that servants gossiped, but the thought of Jane disclosing anything about her for a few coins sat sourly in her stomach.

Then Mama took her by the hand and shook her head. "Don't fret, and do not let on that you know. All beaus require some assistance in courtship, and would you begrudge Jane some extra coins? And her divulging your gown's color is hardly a capital offense—especially when it yields such wonderful results."

Mama's argument was quite sound. Of course, it helped to see the lovely ribbon twisted up in her hair, looking ever so perfect next to the gown. If this was the sort of secret Jane shared with Dr. Humphreys, Prudence couldn't be upset. No, the jittery feeling coursing through her veins was not of the unpleasant variety.

"Oh, my dear, do not turn away from such an opportunity," said Mama, fairly dancing on her toes as she squeezed Prudence's hand. "I know your father and I focus much of our time and energy on Rosanna, but only because her marriage is so integral to the financial security of this family. With her beauty, she is bound to make a prime match, but that does not mean we do not care what happens to you."

Reaching over to pat Prudence on the cheek, she gave her daughter a pitying smile. "I wish your father would've provided you and the rest of your sisters with more than a pittance for a dowry, especially as you haven't Rosanna's natural allures, but with the property tied up in an entail, we have little choice in the matter. I have often fretted and prayed over your future and hoped you might find a gentleman to marry, and now, I am positively giddy at the prospect!"

Turning to the door, Mama called out in a voice that boomed far louder than a lady of gentle breeding (especially one plagued by megrims) ought to utter, "Jane!"

And quick as a flash, Mama was back at Prudence's side and pulling her to the center of the room. Circling her, the lady studied her daughter with an assessing eye. "It is a shame your hair despises curls, for having one draped artfully over your shoulder would soften your features."

"But the assembly is some hours away, and I have work to be done—"

"Hush, Prudence, and leave it to me," said Mama with a narrowed gaze as she cocked her head to the side, apparently comparing the image in her head to the flesh-and-blood lady before her.

Footsteps sounded outside the room, and Mama shook free of her musings and said in a low and rushed voice, "And do not say a word about the letter to Jane, or you shall spoil it. We shan't deny her these little ways to pad her pocketbook, and your beau needs a spy in our household if he is to woo you properly."

The next moment Jane appeared in the doorway and bobbed a curtsy, and her mistress swept her into a whirlwind of face powders, hairpins, perfumes, and so many other things Prudence had never bothered with, for it was little more than attempting to make a silk purse from a sow's ear. But Mama would not be dissuaded.

Especially when Prudence lacked the fortitude to mount a proper battle.

Dr. Parker Humphreys. Being neither wealthy, flirtatious, or overtly handsome, the gentleman was not one to garner much praise or devotion, but then, neither was Prudence, so it mattered not one whit. However, Dr. Humphreys seemed a good sort—enough so that Prudence's heart couldn't help but beat a rapid pace.

A beau. The thought was inconceivable, yet Prudence couldn't deny Mama's logic that the letter was, in fact, intended for her. Years of watching Rosanna's dressing table overtaken by bouquets, tokens, and notes pledging undying affection had left Prudence feeling as though such a thing would never occur in her life. Few gentlemen had ever shown an interest, and even that had not happened in some years.

But tonight, Prudence had an admirer.

Chapter 3

A joyful life was full of simple pleasures. One needn't circulate amongst the finest society and attend the greatest parties to find contentment. Such sentiments ought to be soothing, but Rosanna couldn't help but stare out at the assembly room and imagine the ones in London and Bath, all arrayed to perfection. Great swaths of flowers filled the space and an entire orchestra was ready to play until dawn. Ladies dripping with jewels, and a host of gentlemen with ten thousand per annum.

But Greater Edgerton tried its best. The fact that their town boasted assembly rooms was a minor miracle, but with their industry thriving, it was little wonder that the masters and tradesmen had banded together to build this social epicenter a few years ago where business and society could be conducted side by side. To say nothing of the marriage-minded young people, eager for the opportunity to strut and preen before their prospective spouses.

Not that Rosanna needed to do so, but she enjoyed the spectacle.

Batting her fan, she peered out at the group gathered round her. Gentlemen and ladies all vied for attention. Mr. Gundry did all he could to attract Miss Crewe's gaze, while her focus was fixed on Mr. Hutton, who was entirely oblivious to anything but himself, while Miss Morton sought any male who dared to hold still long enough for her to bat her eyelashes. The whole thing was rather amusing.

"Mr. Potts, would you be a dear and fetch me some punch?" asked Rosanna.

The fellow straightened and fairly sputtered as he dipped into a low bow. "It would be my honor, Miss Rosanna."

Holding back a chuckle at the overdone gallantry, Rosanna sent him off with a flick of her fan, and the hole Mr. Potts left in their circle was quickly filled by Mr. Turley, who squeezed past Mr. Snowley to gain the place, though the latter wasn't about to be thwarted and none-too-gently elbowed in beside the fellow. Despite their jockeying, neither could secure a set with her as all had been claimed. Punctuality and forethought were virtues, were they not? And it wouldn't do to entertain tepid beaus.

Winded, Mr. Potts returned with more than a few splashes of red staining his glove along the edge of the glass, and he gave the usurpers narrowed looks. Rosanna felt like laughing, but she hid it behind a sip of her drink as the others silently battled for their place by her side.

Rosanna turned away from the fools and studied the room. Though simply arrayed, it was spacious and seemed all the vaster for the light blue walls. The dancing had not begun, but the sound of tuning instruments promised the festivities would begin soon. Her feet longed for a dance, and she let that joyful energy thrum through her, bringing a smile to her lips.

But the sight of a new arrival had her shoving her glass at one of the gentlemen and hurrying towards the doorway.

"You are here at last!" said Rosanna, bussing Prudence on the cheek. "I feared you would remain at home, determined to tackle every last chore the household had to offer."

"Ridiculous. You know I have been anticipating tonight," replied Prudence, her eyes not fully meeting her sister's as her lips curled with a secret smile.

Rosanna leaned back and eyed her sister. "My, you look splendid."

Head ducking, Prudence tried to hide a blush but was only minutely successful. "You are too kind."

But Rosanna shook her head, studying the lady in earnest. Where Prudence usually employed simple twists, her coiffure was a riot of braids and ribbons providing the texture and visual interest she couldn't achieve with curls (to Prudence's great consternation). The gown she'd chosen was her most flattering, the light blue of the underskirts contrasting nicely with the dark blue robe lying atop it, and both shades complemented her fine eyes to perfection, bringing out the richness in their shade. True, her sister's features were far too sharp and her figure too slender to ever be fashionable, but something in her bearing softened those hard edges tonight.

In short, Prudence looked as fine as she'd ever seen her. Perhaps not an obvious beauty, but it glowed from within, and Rosanna couldn't help but wonder what had come over her sister.

"You really do look marvelous, Prudence. It seems your time was well spent at home—"

"Rosanna, darling!" Mama swept in, stepping between the pair and taking Rosanna by the arm. "You shall never guess the news I heard today."

"I am glad to see you are faring better, Mama," she replied, casting a look around the lady to catch Prudence's eye; they shared a quick look of exasperation before Rosanna returned her attention to their mother.

"How can I be anything but splendid when Mrs. Hubberts confided to me a very great secret? It seems a Mr. Daniel Courtney—a gentleman of some consequence and position—has come to stay with his dear friend Mr. Atherton. They were school chums and have maintained the connection throughout the years, and he is to stay for a full month in their home."

Mama hardly paused for breath during that quick recitation of the situation, and Rosanna was quite certain what was to follow.

Dropping her voice to the barest of whispers, the lady added, "He is a bachelor worth four thousand a year, and he spied you out riding the other day. Apparently, he was quite taken with you and is attending tonight with the sole purpose of making your acquaintance. Isn't that delightful?"

Rosanna laughed. "He will have a hard time of it, for I am already promised for every dance."

With a frown, Mama waved that away. "A minor detail. There is no other bachelor tonight so worthy to stand up with you. If you have to throw over some other man, then so be it. You must catch Mr. Courtney."

Stomach sinking, Rosanna hoped that silence might induce her mother to follow suit, for she didn't care to hear the all-too-familiar refrain that had haunted her every step since childhood.

"You must think of your sisters, my dear."

Those words were an omen of what was to come, and with a sigh, Rosanna steeled herself for the lecture.

"You know how much we depend on you—how much they depend on you," said Mama with a frown. Leaning close and lifting her fan to block her mouth as she spoke (lest anyone at the assembly had learned to read lips since the last social function), she drew her brows tight together.

"Your father and I prayed for a son to break the entail and provide properly for you girls, and your brother is a godsend, but he arrived far too late to do you or your sisters any good. Most men require security—not promises of a larger dowry once Benjamin comes of age. With your face and figure, gentlemen will overlook that flaw, but your sisters are not so blessed."

Rosanna refused to look at her sister, lest Prudence think she held even an ounce of such a belief. She longed to silence Mama, but the lady would not be stopped as she continued her dire predictions for her daughter's future.

"We've been waiting for a gentleman who is good enough for you, my dear, and we have found him. With this strong alliance, you can aid your sisters in their matrimonial endeavors. You and Benjamin are our only hopes, Rosanna. Do not disappoint us."

As there was nothing to say to such a pronouncement, Rosanna merely smiled and released herself from her mother's hold with a few vague assurances that she would meet with the gentleman if he wished for the acquaintance.

"I will keep a weather eye for Mr. Courtney and tell you the moment he arrives," Mama added, hurrying away to do just that.

Prudence seized the moment and her sister's arm, and the pair meandered along, while Rosanna refused to meet any young man's gaze lest he think it an invitation to plague her at present. Her sister remained at her side, and that quiet strength focused on Rosanna, though there was little else to say on the subject that they hadn't said before.

That was simply Mama. It was how she had always been, and she was unlikely to change one jot in the future. There was no good in hoping for anything different.

Prudence held onto a smile, and Rosanna tried to follow suit; it wouldn't do to make that horrid interlude even worse by giving more fodder to the gossip hounds. But as they wandered along the edge of the assembly, Prudence's expression lightened.

Some spark glowed within her that couldn't be dulled—even when Mama had just proclaimed Prudence and the rest of the Leigh sisters a hopeless bunch without the promise of Rosanna's hypothetical well-connected and wealthy husband. And there was something more to that lift of Prudence's lips than her usual smile. Contentment shone through her.

"I did have a wonderful afternoon," replied Prudence in a low voice. "Quite surprising, in fact. I do not know what to make of it."

Rosanna cast a glance up to the ribbon woven through Prudence's locks and smiled to herself, quite happy to see the gift had given her sister such pleasure. "I see you like your new ribbon."

"Oh, it is marvelous," whispered Prudence, pulling her sister to a stop as the musicians began the first bars of the music, warning the dancers to find their partners and take their places. "I have an admirer."

Sucking in a quick breath, Rosanna forced herself not to gasp or dance up on her tiptoes like a Bedlamite. "That is marvelous! Who is he?"

Prudence cast a glance around, and Rosanna did the same, though she was searching for any sign of Mr. Ridlington, hoping he would not be so prompt and steal her away before she got the whole of the story. Certain that no one was overhearing them, Prudence met her sister's gaze and smiled, the whole of it filling her face.

"Dr. Parker Humphreys."

Her sister could hardly speak as she was smiling so much whilst she relayed the story of the letter and ribbon, and outwardly, Rosanna appeared as calm as a glorious summer day, but inside, her thoughts stormed about like a winter tempest. Had she simply treated Dr. Humphrey's ridiculous love note with more care, this wouldn't have happened, but now, she found herself firmly stuck in a mess. She battled through the cacophony, struggling to lay hold of some idea to aid her, but shock held her firm in its grip.

A flash of Mr. Ridlington had Rosanna dragging Prudence in the opposite direction, for she could not bear an interruption at present. Promise or not, she must do something for her sister.

Chapter 4

"I cannot believe it, Rosanna. I had all but despaired that any man would declare himself in any fashion, let alone in such a perfect and personal manner," Prudence whispered, her eyes sparkling with more light than the chandelier above. "My heart is ready to leap out of my chest. What shall I say or do? I haven't your skill for flirtation. Please advise me!"

There were many times in Rosanna's life that she had felt the sharp sting of guilt. One could not reach six and twenty years of life without having at least a passing familiarity with the sentiment. But seeing Prudence's whole expression filled with a mix of delight and dread, so fully convinced that Dr. Humphreys loved her, Rosanna felt as though a hot knife had sliced into her chest and carved out her heart.

Prudence was such a contented creature, giving no sign that her lack of beaus troubled her at all, but at that moment, Rosanna saw the truth. One could not be so eager for a gentleman caller if one was apathetic towards courting, and Prudence was fully invested in the possibility Dr. Humphreys presented.

The air sat heavy in her lungs, and Rosanna struggled to form words. Her smile remained in place only by the strongest assertion of willpower, and she cursed her slow wits for not seeing some way to keep Prudence happy without her discovering the truth. In a flash, Rosanna pictured what would happen, and though her sister would likely act as though it was of no importance, she knew the truth would crush Prudence.

Yes, it was her mistake, but need she be the one to destroy Prudence's hope? Life demanded so much of her sister; could she not give something back? It was not as though Dr. Humphreys was otherwise occupied: Rosanna had no interest in the fellow.

"Aloofness is your best course of action." The words flew from Rosanna's lips, and she stiffened, her smile growing brittle. "Behave as though it is of little matter to you. Men cannot help but be intrigued by a challenge."

Prudence's brow furrowed. "I do not know if I can. It is not in my nature."

Seizing upon that idea, Rosanna felt her heart settle right back into place. Here was her answer.

"True, but neither is flirting," replied Rosanna. "And unless done well, the gentleman is apt to grow bored if you are eager."

The knit in her brow deepened, and Prudence worried the edge of her lips. "As you have more experience with such things, I would be a fool to argue with you."

Taking her sister by the arm once more, Rosanna patted it with a sigh. "You are best served by going about the assembly as though you are not waiting for him specifically—"

"Rosanna!" Mama burst into their conversation with all the eagerness of a lapdog, her eyes wide and chest heaving, though she attempted to hide it as she took hold of her daughter. "Mr. Courtney has arrived. Come, you must be introduced."

Giving Prudence a significant look, Rosanna turned to her mother. "If he wishes to be acquainted, he shall have to come to me. I am not going to scurry about the assembly to curry his favor."

"I should hope not."

The decidedly masculine voice came from behind Rosanna.

She knew without looking that it would be the mysterious Mr. Courtney, and her breath caught in her throat for the slightest moment before she turned to face him. The gentleman in question gave her a jaunty raise of his brow. Then, turning to Mama, he asked for an introduction, which was freely (and quickly) given.

During all of this, Rosanna pretended not to study him.

Mr. Courtney wasn't the most handsome of men, but that was probably for the best if the rumors of his fortune were true; a man shouldn't possess fine features and a healthy bank account, for it was entirely unfair to the other gentlemen, just like that wretched Miss Lucinda Chambers. She may not have rivaled Rosanna in her physical attractions, but the lady was deemed quite pretty, and doubly so for her dowry of twenty thousand pounds. No one person should be so blessed.

But Mr. Courtney held himself with the confident bearing of one used to getting his way, and Rosanna gave him a cool appraisal and turned back to face her party. That earned her a huff of a laugh from him and a slight gasp from Mama.

"As I was saying before we were interrupted," said Rosanna, glancing at Prudence.

"Is it like that, then?" teased Mr. Courtney.

"If you wish for something more, you must ask for it, sir. I shan't beg for your company," replied Rosanna, giving Prudence yet another arch look. Hopefully, her sister was paying close attention.

"Then I suppose I must beg for a set, Miss Rosanna."

That was when Mr. Ridlington—praise the gentleman—finally discovered where his intended partner had absconded and drew up before her. With a bow, he held out his hand. "I believe I have the honor of this dance, Miss Rosanna."

Giving Mr. Courtney a vague glance from over her shoulder, Rosanna added, "As you see, I am not available, sir."

"Might I claim the next?" asked Mr. Courtney, and she smiled to herself. Though the fellow attempted the same aloof tone, his eagerness peeked through, growing more pronounced with every rebuff.

"I am afraid I am claimed for every set," said Rosanna, stepping forward to take Mr. Ridlington's arm and giving that gentleman a smile that demonstrated far more pleasure than she felt at the interruption (though the expression was turned just enough for Mr. Courtney to see).

Coming around to face them, Mr. Courtney bowed to Mr. Ridlington. "As a visitor to your fair town, surely I ought to be granted the opportunity to stand up with the lovely Miss Rosanna Leigh, sir."

Rosanna's promised partner opened his mouth as though to argue, but Mr. Courtney met the gentleman's gaze, conveying a silent challenge that was akin to the warriors of old, beating their swords against their shields, bellowing for their opponent to step forward—albeit far more passive and polite. However, it was effective, and Mr. Ridlington blanched, offered up a mumbled apology to Rosanna, and scurried away.

Coward.

Mr. Courtney bowed with a smirk. "Might I claim the honor of this dance, Miss Rosanna?"

"After behaving in such a boorish manner?" she asked with a frown.

"If I were to do any less, I wouldn't be worthy of escorting such a beauty around the dance floor."

For all that Rosanna planned on remaining aloof, Mr. Courtney's words distracted her from her instructive purpose, and she couldn't help the twitch of a smile that tickled her lips. But she covered it with a sigh and took his arm, giving Prudence one more significant look before Mr. Courtney led her away.

Her conscience stirred a bit, knowing all too well that tears would soon fill Prudence's eyes, but if Rosanna allowed things to take their natural course, she needn't be the author of that sadness. And Prudence would be saved the embarrassment of discovering her mistake. If heartbreak were in her future, the only thing Rosanna could do was to minimize it by saving her that pain.

But perhaps there was another possibility.

Ignoring Mr. Courtney (though the fellow kept sending her looks as they took their place on the dance floor), Rosanna considered the predicament in a new light. Perhaps there was more she could do. With a few well-placed compliments and nudges, perhaps Dr. Humphreys might transfer his affection to Prudence, leaving the lady unaware of any mistake.

Surely that was better than telling her sister of the misunderstanding.

And dear Prudence deserved a beau.

Yes, this was just the thing.

***

Waiting was an easy thing in the abstract, but in practice, being forced to sit patiently was quite a feat. Prudence remained in her usual position, standing to one side of the gathering while watching the dance, and the one blessing of this anticipation came from the fact that the reward at the end was far more pleasant than what she usually obtained. This time, there were no vain hopes that a gentleman would appear to sweep her into a dance, for there was guaranteed to be one that wished to stand up with her.

Whether or not she wished to be courted by him was still to be seen, but the possibility was alive and flourishing.

Forcing herself not to stand on her tiptoes to gaze over the crowd, Prudence held fast to her composure. Her eyes watched the dancers shift about, moving between positions, and in the midst stood Rosanna, looking as bright and glorious as the burning candles, her golden gown standing out amongst the rainbow of blues, pinks, purples, and greens, though she still looked quite as apathetic towards Mr. Courtney as she had when he'd first approached.

Mama hurried over, her eager steps flitting across the floor. "My dear, what are you doing here? Dr. Humphreys won't know where to find you."

As Prudence had a prime view of the doorway and spied the gentleman entering with the other latecomers, she didn't think her position was a poor one, but Mama dragged her towards him.

"No, Mama," she whispered. Although Rosanna's words of wisdom rang in her head, Prudence's fear held her in place as much as that advice. Approaching anyone was daunting, let alone a potential beau. Even if Dr. Humphreys had been clear in his feelings, it still felt far too bold.

"Don't be silly. You must encourage him."

"I am wearing his token," she whispered, glancing about, though no one overheard. "What more ought I to do? Surely it would be prudent to allow him to approach. Rosanna said I ought to remain aloof."

Mama sighed and shook her head. "That is well and good for your sister, but not all lovers are the same. Some require more encouragement."

Prudence studied the man in question, though he'd yet to spy her. She'd always considered a stockier frame to be far more appealing than a lanky one, but that slimness suited Dr. Humphreys. She couldn't say why precisely—perhaps it was the calm manner in which he bore himself—but she fancied his appearance from the tips of his polished shoes to the top of his curly mop of brown hair.

And the brightness of his blue eyes contrasted so beautifully with his coloring, rather like the length of ribbon he'd given her.

With a furrowed brow, she considered her mother's advice. "I suppose that is true. I had hoped wearing his token would be enough of a sign that I welcome his attentions, but I suppose with his letter being so blunt and forthright, he might require a more direct response."

"No, you goose." Holding fast to her daughter, Mama gave her a look Prudence was all too familiar with, for she had received it so many times since Rosanna burst into the world with her golden hair and bright smiles, destined to outshine her elder sister. And Prudence grasped her mother's meaning, though the lady still felt the need to state it outright.

"You do not have Rosanna's allures, and thus cannot hope to have her success while employing the same games. It is far too risky an approach, and even with her beauty, she may end up a spinster if she isn't cautious. Her time is running short, and gentlemen like Mr. Courtney will only put up with so much coquetry before they surrender and search for easier prey. Do not follow her example. You must put some effort into capturing Dr. Humphreys or he may slip the hook."

"Thank you, Mama," replied Prudence in a dry tone.

"You are welcome, my dear," said Mama, giving her daughter a smile and a squeeze of the arm, as unaware as ever of any humor other than the most direct and obvious.

Prudence tried not to let the words affect her, for she had heard such sentiments often enough, but for all that she had felt like a fresh summer rose a moment ago, now her petals drooped in the heat. But then, there was little point in bemoaning reality, for it did no good. Rosanna Leigh may be the family beauty, but Prudence had many talents and abilities—a wealth of reasons to be grateful—and it wouldn't do to curse her luck for having been denied that one trait.

And as much as it stung to hear the truth put so bluntly, Prudence felt a stirring of gratitude for the logic. She knew better than to attempt Rosanna's tricks in landing a beau, but as her sister's advice had meant Prudence needn't do anything but wait for Dr. Humphreys to approach, it had been far too appealing. Being bold enough to wear his token was hardly an appropriately strong response to Dr. Humphreys' lovely letter.

"Thank you, Mama," said Prudence again, with far more earnestness than before, for the lady was quite correct. Straightening her spine, she stepped away from the comfortable and quiet corner and strode through the crowd with her head raised high.

Chapter 5

Tucking his hands behind him, Parker tried not to sigh or frown. Such petulant displays weren't becoming of any adult, but especially from a man attempting to win the favor of someone so beyond his grasp. However, his heart sank like a rock in a pond, and it took all his strength of will not to let his disappointment show. Any beau of sense knew Miss Rosanna's dances were claimed in a snap, and if one had any hopes of snatching one up for himself, one had to arrive at the assembly promptly.

However, illness and injury refused to acknowledge Parker's work hours, forever plaguing his life with the most inopportune timing, and Mr. Johnson's leg would not set itself or await his return from the assembly. Not comfortably, at any rate.

And so, poor Parker Humphreys was relegated to the edge of the gathering, watching his love from afar. The faintest of hopes allowed him to dream that she had saved one for him, but such subterfuge and deceit was not in Miss Rosanna's nature, even if she wished to stand up with him for every set.

The lady in question danced with some fellow Parker didn't recognize, and he comforted himself with the thought that she seemed unimpressed with her partner, though like the tender soul she was, Miss Rosanna gave little sign that she wished the fellow far from her side.

But she hadn't worn his ribbon tonight. Parker's heart sank as he scoured her hair and gown, hunting for any sign of that delicate blue—but its absence signified nothing. Ladies were known to choose gowns and jewelry long before the night of a party, ball, or assembly, and no matter how much he'd wished to see that sign of her affection, he hadn't expected her to alter her toilette for his sake.

Parker clung to that hope, for it was far more pleasant than acknowledging the possibility that Miss Rosanna had rejected his meager offering. Even with her small dowry, the young lady could marry as she wished, for many a wealthy man sought beauty over finances, having already secured the latter on his own.

And Miss Rosanna was a sight to behold. Her golden gown highlighted the perfection of her fair coloring, enhancing her natural shine rather than overshadowing it, as it would with so many ladies. Having watched his sisters battle with curling papers and hot irons, Parker suspected the curly coiffure was entirely natural, and it was gathered up in an effortless swirl he was certain had taken no more than five minutes and a few odd hairpins.

To say nothing of her lips, which required no rouging to draw the eye. Then there was the pale richness of her complexion, which some might compare with cream but had far too much of a glow to be associated with that lifeless white. Refusing to be demure like so many of her sex, Miss Rosanna embraced life with a hearty joy that could melt the frostiest of hearts, that pure sweetness of temper shining in her pale green eyes—

A clearing throat disrupted Parker's perusal of that beauty, though his gaze refused to tear itself away from Miss Rosanna until the interruption spoke.

"Dr. Humphreys, how good to see you tonight."

Blinking, Parker forced his attention away from Miss Rosanna and found Miss Prudence Leigh standing to one side. Her eyes met his straight on, and she had a rigid posture and stiffness to her shoulders that rang with confidence and strength, though the flush of her cheeks made him wonder if it was feigned—though Parker didn't know why his instincts thought so.

"Good evening, Miss Leigh," he replied with a bow. With only a slight pause, Parker recalled his manners. "It is a pleasure to see you."

That response earned him a brilliant smile, and Parker found himself once more staring at a lady tonight, though this time steeped in confusion rather than admiration. In quick succession, his thoughts tried to grasp why his greeting justified such a pleased expression. It had only been a bit of politeness. Hardly worth such a reception.

The lady said nothing more, and Parker grasped onto the first thought to enter his mind. "Are you having a grand evening?"

"Quite grand," she said with even more enthusiasm, and Parker was left studying her once more.

As they had all lived in Greater Edgerton for some time, he was familiar with the Leigh family, but that did not make him a bosom friend. He'd stood up with Miss Leigh a few times (as was befitting a bachelor hoping to get in the good graces of Miss Rosanna), but that had not given him any grand insights into the lady's personality; however, what he did know of her indicated she was not the sort to grin so blatantly—and at nothing.

Miss Leigh was a stalwart sort. Sensible. Perfectly amiable but not entertaining. Certainly not like Miss Rosanna, who found joy in everything. The poor elder sister was overshadowed in every facet—in face, figure, and felicity. A fact that was made clearer by the silence that stretched out between them.

Casting his gaze around, Parker searched for any rescue, but there was none to be found.

This was Miss Rosanna's sister, and everyone knew they were a matching set; the quickest way to earn Miss Rosanna's ire was to treat her elder sister poorly. So, he'd best stop standing there, gaping like a halfwit if he wanted to make any progress.

"Would you care to dance?" he asked, and once more, she beamed as though his words meant the world to her.

What was happening?

Miss Leigh took his arm, and they moved to join the dancers, but Parker fairly stumbled over his feet at the sight of the familiar blue ribbon.

This wasn't possible.

Perhaps Miss Rosanna had lent it to her sister for the evening; Parker hadn't expected her to alter her toilette entirely to match his love token, and likely the sweet young lady had offered it to her sister, as it suited her dress and coiffure nicely. Yes, that was all.

Miss Rosanna was fiercely loyal to Miss Leigh.

"That is a lovely ornament," he said as they took their places among the dancers. But before Parker could probe further into the matter, the lady met his gaze with expectation shining in her eyes.

"A kind gentleman gave it to me," she replied, with a look that was likely meant to be flirtatious or coy, but it was lost on Parker, for his attention was fixed on the pounding in his chest. His ears rang with his heartbeat, and time slowed, the movement around him stilling until he was certain he was going to be trapped in this wretched moment for millennia.

There was no way to misinterpret her meaning or brush it aside as a minor misunderstanding. Miss Leigh thought his declaration of love had been intended for her.

The music struck up, and though he moved manfully alongside the other dancers, his feet shuffled to a beat no one else could hear, forever chasing the musicians' notes and never catching them. Parker's skill was minimal at the best of times, and at present, it felt as though he were tripping on everything and nothing. All the while, Miss Leigh smiled at him, sending him longing looks as they progressed through the dance.

His letter had been clearly addressed to "Miss R. Leigh," and in their few interactions together, Parker had never shown any preference for the lady at his side. Anyone with eyes knew it was Miss Rosanna who held him captive. What man wouldn't be entranced by her beauty and sweetness of temper?

What was he to do? That one question pounded against his skull, but Parker alternated between staring at the lady before him and scouring the crowd for a glimpse of the one he wished was standing there.

Conscience demanded he tell Miss Leigh the truth. Surely that was the best course of action. A simple explanation and the whole misunderstanding could be laughed away. That was the right thing. The good thing. The only course he ought to take.

But by doing so, he would crush Miss Leigh's heart. That thought alone gave Parker pause. It wasn't difficult to imagine how the lady would feel if he confessed all at that very moment. While some might wave the miscommunication away as a mere trifle, Parker doubted this wallflower would feel so sanguine about it. His own cheeks heated at the thought of her mortification.

Her pleasure over his letter and token was clear for anyone to see; for all that she attempted to remain demure, her eyes revealed the truth. Miss Leigh wished him for herself.

Parker sifted through his thoughts, which were more scattered than his steps. Matters were not helped by the fact that Miss Leigh kept sending him looks that made his cravat tighten around his throat.

"Is something amiss?" she asked with furrowed brows as they passed each other.

The steps moved quickly, and Parker could hardly concentrate on them and his present situation, and converse with Miss Leigh. He remained silent until their part in the dance paused, dropping them face to face as the others moved around them.

"I fear it has been a taxing day," he said.

Miss Leigh frowned, her eyes filling with sympathy. “Is something amiss with a patient?”

The blood in his veins felt like liquid fire, coursing through him, and his hand reflexively moved to loosen his cravat—though he stopped himself before he tugged the thing free.

Honesty was best, wasn’t it?

“I…” But Parker’s words were strangled in his throat. “…One of the families I tend to has a child who has fallen ill. He is on the mend, but I fear serious damage was done to his lungs. He shall have a difficult life ahead of him.”

They turned, and Parker’s face was blocked from view long enough that he allowed himself a frown. That was true enough, though he hadn’t intended to tell her that. Fixing a strained smile on his face, he turned once more to face her. Miss Leigh watched him, and he had never considered just how much emotion a set of brows could convey; hers were pinched together tight, magnifying the sorrow in her gaze.

“No matter how much you do, you cannot heal everyone,” she said. “The child is saved, and that is something to celebrate. You do not know what the future holds for him, and fretting over it will do no good.”

Parker wished she hadn’t spoken, for each sympathetic word added more weight to his guilt. Here he was, stumbling over his words and his blasted feet while trying to plot some way to be rid of her, and Miss Leigh was being kind. And far too sweet. If she showed even the slightest bit of discontent, Parker could simply tell her the truth, but each tender display only emphasized the fact that she would take it far too much to heart.

“You do seem out of sorts tonight,” she said as her gaze searched his expression. “If you need to return home, I will not be offended.”

And Miss Leigh’s expressive eyes supported those words but added a subtext that Parker would be a fool not to see. She wanted him to remain. Very much.

“I am afraid I ought to do just that,” he said.

Despite her shoulders falling the slightest bit, Miss Leigh nodded. "Of course, Dr. Humphreys. Sometimes after a trying day one needs quiet and solitude, and you shan't find that here."

Why did she have to be so gracious? Parker's mouth dried, and his cravat closed around his throat like a vise as sweat beaded at his temples. Offering up his arm, he led her out of the dancers and bowed low, and though he knew he ought to extend some nicety, he couldn't speak. When he straightened, he immediately turned towards the exit, his feet itching to run far from here.

But a hand on his arm stopped his escape.

Turning, he faced Miss Leigh again. Her posture was a touch stiffer, her smile a little strained as she sucked in a deep breath.

"But perhaps you might call tomorrow?" The moment those words left her lips, she clamped her jaw shut, her eyes dropping away as a flush of pink colored her cheeks. But before he could answer, Miss Leigh waved an airy hand and added, "Or whenever you are available, Dr. Humphreys. If you would like. Perhaps."

As Parker couldn't manage a single word at that time, he merely nodded (what else could he do) and bowed. And then made his escape.

Chapter 6

What to do? Those three small words ushered in a wealth of other concerns, troubles, and unknowns, haunting Parker as he escaped into the night.

Autumn tinged the air, filling it with the promise of winter to come. After the heat of the summer months, these first steps into the cold felt all the chillier, and though Parker had only been inside the warm assembly rooms for a short period, he welcomed the bite. Tromping along, he kept his gaze fixed on the ground, for he did not wish to get swept up in conversation by some well-meaning passerby. He wasn't capable of chatter at present.

Greater Edgerton was growing at a rapid pace, and though many bemoaned the loss of the rural feel of the place, Parker was quite grateful for the development that saw the installation of cobblestones along the main streets. His shoes thumped against the pavers, tapping out a beat alongside his heart while his mind swept through his course of action.

What to do?

There were few options available in this situation, which ought to have made the answer easier to discern. However, each was attached to a myriad of consequences, each of which was bound to cause pain.

Passing by his home, Parker trudged through the streets, studying the ground at his feet as though it held the answer to his questions. He needed to move, but no matter how much distance he put between himself and the assembly rooms, the question plagued him, not giving him any answers or respite.

Parker's body thrummed with pent-up energy, and his legs were tiring far quicker than his thoughts. Turning his feet towards assistance, he trudged along in search of respite.

Thankfully, his sister's home was quite a distance away, giving Parker plenty of time to work it out on his own. Unfortunately, it did no good, and he arrived at Pembrooke Place none the wiser. He was quickly admitted and led into his brother-in-law's study to find the fellow seated beside the fireplace, his feet propped up on an ottoman and a book in his hands.

"I thought you had grand plans tonight," said Robert, not bothering to glance up from his reading.

"That is the trouble," said Parker with a sigh as he took his usual seat opposite. "Is Eleanor not at home? I had hoped to speak with you both."

Robert tossed his book onto the spindly table beside him. "She couldn't bear the thought of missing out on the dancing."

Parker stiffened, casting his thoughts back to the assembly, though he couldn't recall seeing her. Granted, he'd been rather occupied.

"In her condition?" he asked.

There was no answer to that question. Or at least none of the verbal variety. Though reclined in his chair, Robert seemed strung taught like a violin's string.

"She assures me she can still manage it, but you of all people know that Eleanor will do what she wishes to do," murmured his brother-in-law with a frown. Before Parker could say a word in response, he added, "But what has you darkening our doorstep when you'd intended to spend the evening wooing Miss Rosanna Leigh?"

Shakespeare had once said brevity was the soul of wit, and that must be true, for his retelling took no more than a few words, and it set Robert laughing as though Parker's life was some grand comedy to be cackled over.

"I do apologize," said his brother-in-law, though his tone and expression held no contrition. "That is quite the dilemma; however, I cannot say I am entirely surprised. With your handwriting, it is a miracle they didn't think it was addressed to the youngest Leigh daughter. Or the maid."

That brought forth more laughter, and Parker sank into his chair with folded arms as he waited for the fellow to calm himself.

"And what am I to do?" asked Parker when his poor excuse for an advisor was sensible enough to answer.

"Tell her," replied Robert. "Honesty is the best course of action. If she is as sensible as she seems to be, Miss Leigh will understand."

With a huff, Parker frowned. "If it were that simple, do you not think I would have done so already? You didn't see Miss Leigh's expression when she approached me. She is enamored. And it doesn't help matters that she shares her sister's sweetness of spirit. There I was, acting the fool, and she was so concerned about me. Though she wanted me to stay, she bid me farewell without a word of reproof because I claimed I was needed elsewhere."

Simply recalling her expression was enough to make Parker's heart constrict. "The whole situation is just a simple mistake, and I doubt she'd hold it against me if I told her the truth, but it will mortify her. Surely I can free myself in a gentler manner. Something better than blurting it out during a dance."

Robert's brows lowered in consideration. "And breaking Miss Leigh's heart will hardly endear you to Miss Rosanna."

Parker stilled, staring wide-eyed into the distance for a long, silent moment before he groaned and curled forward, rubbing at his head. "I hadn't even considered that."

There was a sympathetic grunt in response, though Robert said nothing else—not that Parker was listening, for his mind swirled with the implications. Kneading his temples, he wished he had a cup of his willow and lavender tisane; it was unlikely to have any effect on the building megrim, but it might dull the persistent ache.

"So, if I approach Miss Leigh and tell her the truth, it will bruise her feelings and paint me as a cad, and Miss Rosanna would never consider the suit of a fellow who has hurt her sister. But if I remain mum, I shall raise the hopes of Miss Leigh and make myself unavailable to Miss Rosanna." Parker paused, and added with a heavy sigh, "I am doomed."

"And all because you refuse to write sensibly," added Robert with a dry tone.

That deepened Parker's expression into a proper scowl, but his friend and brother-in-law was entirely unrepentant. "And this is why I was hoping to speak to Eleanor. You are no help at all."

Robert huffed. "If you think your sister won't find great delight in your dilemma, then you are a fool."

Slumping into his chair once more, Parker sighed heavily. "True. However, I hoped she'd have some idea of how a fellow can shake free of a lady without causing harm."

"I doubt even Eleanor can muster that sort of magic," replied Robert, reaching for his book once more. "If Miss Leigh is as keen as you say she is, there is no way to wriggle out of the situation without causing some level of hurt or embarrassment. She has clearly accepted your suit, so you are left with breaking her heart or courting the wrong sister, which will inevitably lead to heartbreak as well."

Parker straightened, his eyes snapping to his brother-in-law, though the fellow was staring at his book. "That is brilliant."

Robert glanced up from his page, his brow furrowed.

"If I wish to make a clean break without causing her harm, I must simply help her to see that we are ill-suited for each other," said Parker.

Robert tossed the book aside with a scoff. "That is probably the worst course of action you can take. Better to be honest—"

"But it is honest." Parker shoved aside the shudder in his heart that recognized the falsehood and amended his statement. "In a way, at least. Miss Leigh and I aren't suited, and it isn't dishonest to encourage her to come to that conclusion on her own. She will break with me, and I will be free to pursue her sister."

"And you think you will be appealing to Miss Rosanna after her sister has tossed you aside?" Robert's tone was incredulous enough that he needn't emphasize it with raised brows, but he did.

Parker waved that aside with a flick of his hand. "That may be problematic, but if I am careful, there is no reason I cannot give Miss Rosanna a favorable impression later. A more direct course of action is guaranteed to fail. At least this gives me the possibility of winning the day while causing the least amount of harm."

But Robert shook his head. "You speak as though this is the start of a grand romance rather than the tragedy it's destined to become."

"I do not like the situation in which I've been placed, but I am trying to make the best of it," he replied, shifting forward in his seat. "I am neither handsome nor wealthy, Robert. I have a comfortable practice, but I hardly have enough income to marry, and certainly not enough to give her the life to which she is accustomed. With the deck stacked against me already, I must tread carefully or I will destroy what little hope I have left."

His brother-in-law opened his mouth to reply, but Parker hurried to add, "What would you do to secure Eleanor? Heaven knows you spent years waiting and working to get my parents to soften towards you. How many times were you forced into unpleasant positions? Yet you refused to surrender, Robert. Surely you can understand my determination."

That shut the fellow's mouth once more, though his expression was neither contemplative nor acquiescent. Robert's lips and brow formed a hard line, which was not unusual for his brother-in-law, but there was something in his gaze that Parker couldn't identify, and his heart hung heavy in his chest at the sight of it.

"I am not proud of my course of action, Robert, but it is the only way to spare Miss Leigh's feelings—to say nothing of my endeavors towards Miss Rosanna. If fate smiles upon me, the former will be none the wiser, and I can try again with the latter."

"As it seems you've made up your mind already, I wonder why you want my opinion on the matter," said Robert, taking his book up once more.

Parker sighed, not wanting to admit the truth, though it rang through him. Wishing for his brother-in-law to eagerly support the venture was foolhardy—Robert was not one to embrace deception—but it would've been nice to have it all the same.

"It is the best course," said Parker. The words were true enough, but for some reason, his heart only sank further at the thought.

"Then do it," replied Robert with a dismissive tone as he began to read again.

Rising to his feet, Parker gave a vague farewell and strode from the room. He really ought to have waited for Eleanor to return home; she would've understood Parker's decision as society was filled with polite falsehoods. If one wished to succeed in the world, one had to adopt a bit of the actor's spirit.

And this was hardly a deception. It was simply allowing Miss Leigh to come to a natural conclusion on her own.

This was the proper course.

Chapter 7

A fortnight was not a long time. It was hardly more than a blink, passing by before one was even aware that the days were gone. But to a child, fourteen days was interminable, destined to stretch on for eternity. Parker hadn't been one for some time and had long ago learned the virtue of patience, but it seemed what was true of children was also true of sweethearts. The past fortnight had marched along with all the speed of a snail.

This waiting might've been necessary, but that hadn't made it any easier for Parker.

Now, he stood on the Leighs' doorstep, and the servants seemed determined to make him linger even longer, as they were in no hurry to answer his knock.

There was no reason to fret. None at all.

Having avoided Whitley Court and the Leighs for such a period, Parker suspected Miss Leigh would be ready to throw him over the moment he stepped into their house. Surely such a tepid display of sentiment had cooled her eagerness. All that was needed now was an awkward conversation, and Miss Leigh would have to come to the proper conclusion.

Simple.

Parker clung to that hope as he was finally granted entry and stepped into the parlor.

Mrs. Leigh was the sort of person who gathered friends, collecting them like naturalists collected butterflies or rocks—though as Parker glanced about the room, he noted she preferred far less diversity than a true connoisseur. Her guests were all precisely the sort of people one found in every ballroom and parlor in every corner of this country, with conversations, fashions, and manners all echoing one another as no one dared to deviate from what was expected.

Miss Rosanna's throng showed more variety than her mother's, but between the pair, the parlor was filled to the brim. A morning call ought never to take more than a half an hour, and the Leighs' parlor was a prime example of why that unspoken rule was a necessity: others must leave before new visitors could be admitted.

And standing in a corner was Miss Leigh. If the other Leighs were collectors, this lady was an observer, her gaze scrutinizing their visitors with as much fascination as a scientist stumbling upon a new species.

Parker steeled his nerves and crossed the room, reciting in his thoughts all the subjects he'd decided upon. There was a fine balance between being irritating enough to drive Miss Leigh away without bruising her pride or ruining his reputation, but Parker was certain he could manage it. Just one morning call, and Miss Leigh was certain to find him unsuitable.

Then the young lady met his gaze, and though Parker affected his most vacant and disinterested expression, her smile blossomed, stretching wide across her face, leaving no one in doubt of her feelings. He gave her a stiff bow, and her grin never faltered as he joined her in the corner. The world buzzed around them, but Miss Leigh beamed, proving that the adage "absence makes the heart grow fonder" had an element of truth to it.

Bother.

Having given this moment plenty of thought, Parker had a myriad of things he could say to her to dampen that fire burning in her heart, but when faced with her bright expression, his tongue tied itself in knots. Each seemed too cruel or critical, and one of the main purposes of this charade was to avoid bruising Miss Leigh's feelings. He couldn't bring himself to give voice to any of them.

And so the chatter around them filled the silence, while Miss Leigh stared at him. Her lips tightened, her grin growing stiff as her brows lowered. Yet still he remained quiet, unable to decide on anything he might say to further his cause.

Then an idea struck, bringing with it his salvation. Perhaps he needn't say a thing at all. Awkward silence was a fine deterrent. What lady would wish to keep a beau who could not carry a conversation?

Tucking his hands behind him, Parker affected a pleasant smile and nodded at her.

"And how are you this afternoon, Dr. Humphreys?" she asked.

Parker waited for a full count of ten before saying, "I am well."

Miss Leigh watched him with a furrowed brow, and he said nothing in return, though he was certain she was waiting for him to reciprocate. His skin itched as they stood there, and the lady's gaze begged him to speak, but Parker forced his lips shut. This was the best course.

Shifting in place, Miss Leigh looked around as though searching for something. When her eyes snapped back to his, she added, "And your family?"

"Quite well."

Parker cursed himself for speaking so quickly. He ought to have stretched the silence out a moment or two. Rocking on his heels, he forced himself not to fidget. With a room full of people talking and laughing, the noise surrounding them only highlighted the quiet between the pair.

Miss Leigh's gaze grew more troubled, her expression falling further with each failed attempt to engage him in conversation. His silence clearly had her out of sorts, but that did not stop her from watching him intently, and Parker's chest constricted. His eyes drifted to the floor and fixed upon the toes of his shoes, but he felt her attention on him.

Parker turned his gaze to the room, hoping to find something that might distract him from the itching at his collar. But the parlor was like any number of ones he'd visited before, with plenty of seating, a fireplace highlighted on one side with an elaborate white mantle and mirror placed above it, and paintings of landscapes and long-dead ancestors hung on the walls. It was entirely unremarkable and unable to hold his attention for long—especially with Miss Leigh's gaze fixed on him.

Tugging at his cuffs, Parker tried to shift his tailcoat back into place, but it still felt wrong. Or perhaps that was just the prickling running along his skin. This was for the best. He tried to remind himself of that, but his eyes kept darting to Miss Leigh's crestfallen expression.

"What..." Miss Leigh's question drifted off, and her fingers twisted together; when he glanced at her hands, she gave him a fleeting smile and tucked them behind her. Straightening, she said, "What do you like best about your profession?"

Parker couldn't help but meet her gaze once more at that odd question. Like all sons of the gentry, he hadn't had a choice in the matter; one followed the path laid out by one's father, which was often dictated by how costly it was to educate the lad and whether the family had any connections in the field. "Liking" had nothing to do with why a gentleman was foisted into an occupation. Parker was simply fortunate that his father thought studying medicine was prestigious enough to warrant the cost of sending his son to school in Edinburgh and boasted a physician friend who was willing to take Parker on afterward.

The fact that Parker enjoyed his profession was a miracle of sorts, and he couldn't think of anyone who had ever bothered to ask such a question. Thankfully, his confusion over the question provided a natural and lengthy pause before he replied.

"Healing people," he said, grasping onto the most simplistic of answers.

Miss Leigh's brows rose with the faintest of challenges, and she huffed. "As that is the whole of your profession, I would hope you enjoy that part. To say nothing of the fact that you would be a monster if you did not enjoy seeing your patients recover."

Parker held back a smile, for it wouldn't further his goals at all.

"What is the most exciting part of your work, Dr. Humphreys?"

His thoughts filled with answers, each of which begged to be spoken—not just to relieve the discomfort of the situation but because he adored the subject. While Parker had planned on being unutterably dull and irritating, he hadn't anticipated that his behavior would work so well on himself. Glancing at the clock on the mantle, he sucked in a sharp breath. Hardly five minutes had passed, yet it felt like ten times that length. There was no way to make a gracious retreat at this point; he must stick it out.

But the silence clawed at him.

Clarity struck at that moment, providing him with a course of action he hadn't considered before. But it might just be his salvation. There was more than one way of being off-putting, and if Miss Leigh wished to know more about his profession, perhaps he should enlighten her.

Chapter 8

Speak, you strange man! Prudence forced all her will into that thought, hoping that somehow Dr. Humphreys would hear and obey. Rosanna coaxed people into conversation with a few well-placed compliments and winning smiles, but Prudence always struggled for words. Friendship was as natural as a wildflower, springing up where it will—not a hothouse plant born from countless hours of pruning and fertilization.

And above all else, Prudence wanted a beau who was a friend.

What good was romance, with all its sappy poetry and tokens of love, if not built on a foundation of true admiration? Mama and Papa were a fine enough example, for though they were cordial enough toward each other, they had little in common. When the years robbed them of their surface attractions, they were left with little but the marriage certificate binding them together. Prudence wanted better.

And so, she stared at Dr. Humphreys, willing him to meet her partway at the very least. There was little hope for them if they were both reticent to speak, and with the last of her verbal kindling placed, Prudence only hoped the spark of conversation would finally catch.

"Though much of my work focuses on maladies rather than injuries, I fear my interests lie more in the latter," said Dr. Humphreys.

"I hadn't thought physicians treated such things," said Prudence. The gentleman stiffened, and she hurried to add, "That is not a condemnation, merely an observation. I don't entirely understand the point of physicians if their scope of work is so narrow. With a younger brother who is forever getting in scrapes, I have stopped sending for physicians, for they do the barest of things before sending you to a surgeon-apothecary, who manages the majority of it."

"If I were to settle in London, Bath, or even Liverpool, it would be easy to make a living off doctoring alone, but I fear the division between surgeon and physician is not so clear cut outside the city," said Dr. Humphreys. "It isn't uncommon for gentlemen of my ilk to blur those lines while maintaining the appearance of respectability."

"As all the mills in the area require surgeons more than physicians, it is wise of you to adapt."

"Which is all the better for me, for there are many aspects of the surgeon-apothecary's work that are fascinating." Dr. Humphreys tucked his hands behind him and added, "I spent a fair amount of time with the surgeons during my education, so I have skills enough on that front. Though I am not as quick at amputations as those I observed in Edinburgh, I am better than most of the surgeons in town because of my training."

"Quick?" Prudence blinked at that, for she hadn't considered speed of the foremost concern.

Dr. Humphreys nodded. "I manage the whole thing in about twenty minutes, though I know many surgeons in Edinburgh that can do it in less."

"Less than twenty minutes? How quick are they?" asked Prudence.

"From the first incision to the final stitch, ten minutes."

Raising her brows, she tried to imagine just how such a thing was possible, but she hadn't the foggiest notion. Medicine was not something people usually discussed with ladies, which seemed an oversight, as they were the head of all medical treatments in a home.

"And why is such speed necessary?" Perhaps she ought to turn the subject to something cheerier, but Prudence couldn't help the curiosity prodding her to ask the question.

"Blood loss," he replied. "Any longer, and the patient is apt to perish. As it is, my time is far slower than it should be."

Though the majority of the guests lingered close to Mama or Rosanna, a few ladies stood nearby, and their darting glances toward her made it clear that her conversation with Dr. Humphreys had been overheard. The others' conversation had been lively enough, but it died quickly as her own began in earnest. Freeing a handkerchief from her reticule, one of the ladies dabbed at her temple as though liable to swoon. Prudence ignored them. If they did not wish to hear such graphic subjects, they could stop eavesdropping.

Banishing the ladies from her thoughts, Prudence turned her attention to Dr. Humphreys again, who was watching her with a considering look. She couldn't interpret the meaning behind it, though she didn't think it was the look of a courting swain; perhaps she ought to have demurred more and spoken of the weather, but this was far more interesting.

But before she could offer up another question, Dr. Humphreys continued.

"Unfortunately, I haven't the facilities to match the speed of the city surgeons. Beds are too soft, allowing the patient to shift. Dining tables can do in a pinch, but the families do not care for me to work there, and they are often the wrong height, making it impossible to get the proper leverage and strength behind the saw. And though I can muster some assistance when needed, they are hardly the trained dressers I require to aid me in the matter."

"Dressers?"

"The surgeon's assistants. To hold the patient down and keep them from thrashing. Among other things." Dr. Humphreys watched her closely as though expecting her to require some smelling salts, but Prudence didn't flinch.

"Cannot the patient's family or friends aid you?" she asked.

"Such things require a strong stomach, and most do not have the fortitude. They are a hindrance more than a help."

And with that, the good doctor launched into a description of the procedure, detailing the many unpleasant things the dressers and surgeon must do to save the patient. The eavesdropping ladies grew ashen and fled to the farthest side of the parlor, and though Prudence couldn't say that she enjoyed the thought of sawing through bones, this was the most fascinating conversation she'd had in some time.

Dr. Humphreys did not spare her sensibilities. He spoke to her like an equal, someone with enough grit to handle such unpleasant things in the world. Prudence banished graphic images of the procedure from her thoughts (for they did make her the teeniest bit queasy), but she hung on his every word as Dr. Humphreys expounded upon the details of his profession.

As Mama was a frequent patient and Rosanna wasn't suited to assist in the sickroom, Prudence had taken the role of the Leigh family healer. Though familiar with some of the common ailments and maladies that struck the household, she hadn't had the opportunity to broaden her understanding beyond what one would find in a book about household management or the sparse list of instructions that had accompanied the family's medicine chest, which had been written by some Leigh ancestor. Thankfully, Prudence's skills hadn't needed to be expanded beyond the basics, but hearing an expert expound on the subject was fascinating.

"I can see why it is a struggle to find proper assistance. It is difficult to see someone I love in such pain," said Prudence. "Do you not find it distressing to cause such pain?"

The gentleman frowned, blinking as he studied her. "It isn't pleasant, but it is necessary. Amputation is always a last resort, and when we reach that moment, I am their only chance of surviving."

"Yet still I cannot imagine it being a pleasant thing for you to do."

Dr. Humphreys shifted, his gaze falling away from her. "It is more difficult to think of what their lives will be even if I do save them. Most are counted among the lower classes, where survival is a struggle at the best of times—let alone with a missing limb. In all honesty, it feels as though I am merely prolonging their death, stretching it out into months and years, rather than allowing nature to take its course."

Prudence's brow furrowed, then their all too brief conversation sprang back to her thoughts, and she echoed the words she'd given him that night as well. Sometimes a single assurance wasn't enough, and she was quite willing to give it again.

"As you said, Dr. Humphreys, your actions are a last resort, and all you've done is give them a chance at survival. Whatever comes next is beyond your control, and you have no blame for it as long as you've done your work to the best of your abilities."

He made a pensive hum as his gaze drifted away from her yet again. "I hadn't considered it in such a light before."

Then, meeting her eyes once more, he nodded. "My thanks, Miss Leigh."

Prudence forced herself not to preen. From her experience with men, being capable wasn't a prime consideration for matrimony, yet Dr. Humphreys spoke as though her words pleased him immensely. Which, in turn, pleased her immensely. Allowing only a faint smile through, Prudence held Dr. Humphrey's tone of appreciation close to her heart.

"Even if I were to be granted the opportunity, I would fare poorly in medicine," said Prudence. "The subject is fascinating, but I cannot stomach the thought of performing surgeries nor do I have the patience to spend my days tending to the sick. Even sweet-tempered people can be unruly when they're ill. I adore my family, but when sick, they're terrors! I cannot imagine dealing with strangers in such a compassionate manner when even those I love bring me to the breaking point."

Dr. Humphreys laughed, drawing a few glances their way (including two disgusted ones from the ladies they'd chased off), but Prudence ignored them.

"Yes, I see your problem," he replied when he was able to do so. "There are some who try my patience, but I've developed a few techniques that have helped."

And once more, Dr. Humphreys delved into the nuances of his trade, and Prudence rather wished she had a bit of paper on hand with which to take notes, for she was certain to employ at least a few of them in the future.

The more he spoke, the more the strain eased from the corners of his mouth and his shoulders. For all that he'd seemed somber at the assembly and when he'd arrived at Whitley Court, Dr. Humphreys was a warm and open gentleman, and Prudence suspected that he was just the sort of physician people adored. In her experience, kind and competent was a difficult combination to find in the field, and his passionate discourse on the subject attested that he was blessed with both traits.

Prudence wished she had more to add to the conversation, but she had little knowledge beyond her meager experience. However, she had a myriad of questions, prodding him along, and for once, it was no struggle to keep the discussion flowing. Dr. Humphreys seemed as eager to speak on the subject as Prudence was to learn about it.

"In truth, though many physicians believe children are the more difficult patients, I find them far more enjoyable than their parents," said Dr. Humphreys with a wry smile. "Generally, children only cry and fret when they are in pain. With adults, you can never tell if your treatments are working, for they moan and complain long after they are on the mend."

Laughing, Prudence nodded. "I know precisely what you mean, sir."

Then, casting a glance at Mama, she leaned forward and lowered her voice. “I would much rather tend to my little brother than my mother or father. Benjamin will pop out of bed the moment he’s better, but my parents will languish in bed long after their health is restored.”

Dr. Humphreys laughed once more, his smile filling his face. “True, Miss Leigh. However, I find children more difficult to examine. They refuse to sit still.”

But Prudence waved that away. “That is easy enough. Whenever I need the little ones to cooperate, I give them sweets. Then they are too preoccupied to care about what the physician is doing. You might think about bringing a bit of fondant or marzipan with you—something that is a genuine treat. It is well worth the price.”

“Then I ought to resort to bribery?” he asked with an arched brow.

“Unless it offends your delicate sensibilities.”

Dr. Humphreys chuckled once more, and his smile softened a touch. Prudence’s heart ceased beating. She’d often read that in such moments a heartbeat quickened, but it felt as though the world slowed around her, drawing out the seconds into minutes. If she had been in any doubt before that Dr. Humphreys was a beau worth having, it vanished in that very moment.

Chapter 9

Maneuvering through society was like a dance. Though strung together in different patterns, there were set steps, and even when thrown amongst a new quadrille or country dance, it was simple enough to keep one's feet as long as one was familiar with chassés, balancés, jeté assemblés, and all the rest. And though people liked to think that each gathering or occasion was unique, the reality was that they followed much of the same set of expectations.

And Rosanna Leigh had long ago mastered such things.

A tittering laugh. A few comments about fabrics and gowns. A well-placed gasp at learning a new tidbit (or conversely, an arched brow to mark that one knew that bit of gossip all along). There were the usual "did you knows" and "have you spied" comments, and it required little effort to navigate the conversation whilst her attention drifted to far more important things.

Rosanna chanced a glance towards Prudence and Dr. Humphreys; they remained ensconced together in their corner of the parlor, ignorant of any of the other conversations circulating about them. The first lesson a lady learned amongst society was to school her features (or it should be, though Prudence never seemed capable of hiding her feelings away entirely no matter how Rosanna tried to teach her), and Rosanna was certain no one noticed just how much of her attention was turned to her sister and Dr. Humphreys.

It felt as though a butterfly had taken up residence in her chest, fluttering about without pause. Surely, if Dr. Humphreys was going to reveal the truth concerning his letter, he would've done so before now, yet Rosanna couldn't keep her gaze from darting in that direction again and again.

With a flippant comment about who-knows-what, Rosanna set the others laughing, and she used the distraction to give the pair a more thorough examination. Dr. Humphreys seemed quite cozily situated in front of her sister, and though Rosanna could not ascertain the subject of their conversation, they were turned towards each other, their attentions fixed solely on the other.

Rosanna's lungs filled, and her heartbeat slowed to a manageable pace. Unintentional though it may have been, perhaps she'd done a bit of matchmaking, for anyone watching the pair would think them quite keen for the other's company. The chill that had taken hold of her eased away in a flush of warmth that radiated from deep inside as Prudence laughed, beaming at Dr. Humphreys.

Grinning to herself, Rosanna reveled in the electric jolt that ran through her, filling the whole of her with jittery energy. This was perfect.

Prudence deserved to have an admirer, and the two looked quite well together. Far too often, romance required a guiding hand as many sweethearts had not the good sense to recognize their perfect match when it arrived. Now, Dr. Humphreys had another lady to distract him from his silly infatuation, and he and Prudence needn't ever discover Rosanna's part in their courtship.

"Might I assume that smile is for me?" asked Mr. Courtney.

Rosanna didn't jump, though it was a near thing. Though she'd been somewhat aware of the conversation around her, she hadn't noticed the gentleman's arrival. Thankfully, it was easy enough to cover her surprise by keeping her attention on Prudence. Only after a long moment did Rosanna deign to turn to him.

"Pardon? I didn't realize you were standing there, Mr...?"

With a single look, Mr. Courtney sent the others away, leaving just the two of them on the sofa together. His eyes drifted down the length of her, perusing her in a manner that made Rosanna feel as though they were hidden away in some darkened nook of a ballroom.

Then, with a smirk, Mr. Courtney said, "Such games are more effective when your mother is equally blasé. She fairly scrambled over the other guests to receive me."

"I fear she is not one for subtlety," replied Rosanna with a sigh. "But I would think a gentleman, such as yourself, would appreciate the effort I am putting into the game. You wouldn't care for an easy conquest, would you?"

Mr. Courtney chuckled. "No, indeed. But the effort is hardly effective."

"You assume that I am as eager as my mother, sir," said Rosanna with an arched brow. "But just as you have your pick of ladies, I have my pick of gentlemen."

That wasn't entirely true, as her pitiful dowry was a heavy mark against her, but as that would only dissuade the gentlemen of lesser means, Rosanna considered that only a minor hindrance.

"So, you see, Mr. Courtney," she added, allowing her attention to drift away from him once more, "I shan't merely fall into your arms, no matter how you parade about, acting as though I should."

"I should hope not." Mr. Courtney had a way of saying things that sounded far too wicked for such an innocuous conversation, and Rosanna frowned at him despite the delicious skitter that ran down her spine. "What are you looking at?"

Rosanna turned her gaze away from Prudence, uncertain as to when her eyes had moved in that direction once more, and found Mr. Courtney studying her with far more gravity than she'd seen him display before.

And before she could brush his question away, he added, "Do not deny it. You are skilled at feigning interest, but your attention has not been on your companions."

"If you must know," said Rosanna with a touch of tartness, "I am spying on my sister. She and Dr. Humphreys have been tucked away for some time, and I hope she's made a conquest."

Mr. Courtney's eyes followed her gaze and landed on Prudence. Despite being a man of the world and adept at playing the games society demanded, the gentleman was not quick enough to cover his scoff when he spied the pair.

"And what do you mean by that, sir?" asked Rosanna, her posture stiffening.

With an arched brow, Mr. Courtney replied, "Must you always feign ignorance? I think my meaning was clear enough."

Sucking in a breath, she narrowed her eyes at the blackguard, though his expression did not alter one bit.

"My sister, sirrah, is a fine woman who does not deserve your mockery. Though her features may not be overtly beautiful, her spirit and heart are far lovelier than anything you will find—even in your precious London ballrooms. She is talented and capable as no other lady you shall meet, and even if society's fools cannot see it, her worth is incalculable. Heaven bless Dr. Humphreys for not being so blind."

Each word fanned Rosanna's temper, though she kept her tone low enough that no one else would overhear.

Mr. Courtney tugged his handkerchief from his pocket and waved it with a laugh. "I surrender, dear lady, and I apologize for saying anything that puts you in such a temper. Perhaps I might make it up to you with a drive tomorrow?"

"I am unavailable," said Rosanna with a huff, turning her gaze from him to sneak yet another peek at Prudence. Being hardly one year apart in age, the two had spent most of their lives bound together. Rosanna knew her sister better than anyone else in the world, and she couldn't recall ever seeing Prudence look so content.

"Come now, I am thoroughly chastened," said Mr. Courtney with a smile that was as false as his contrite tone. "Will you hold my mistake against me?"

"I doubt you have ever been chastened—thoroughly or not."

"True," he replied with another wickedly arched brow. "But then, not many would dare to do so."

A weight settled on her shoulders, though Rosanna could not identify its source, and it rested heavily upon her. What would it be like to have Prudence's simple life? To live without constantly measuring each word? Prudence was so below society's notice that there was little she could do to hurt her standing.

Heavy is the head that wears the crown, as they say. And Rosanna felt so very tired at that moment.

"If you are not free tomorrow, perhaps I might steal you away the day after that," he said.

"I suppose," she replied with a sigh, for there was no other response she could give.

Mr. Courtney chuckled and said in a dry tone, "You shouldn't sound so enthused about the prospect or you might inflate my pride."

But Rosanna merely returned that arched brow he was so fond of giving.

...

A chime sounded, bringing with it a niggling feeling that he ought to heed the time, but Parker had no appointments until much later. Batting the worry away, he focused on Miss Leigh, who was expounding on a novel she'd just finished. It was not a work with which he was familiar, though her description of the adventure grabbed his attention, and he made a note to visit the lending library.

And when the final chime ended, Parker came back to himself. His gaze darting towards the clock's face, he tried to recall the precise moment he'd arrived on the Leighs' doorstep, but he couldn't say if it had been a quarter after the hour or straight up. Not that it mattered, for either answer meant he'd been there far too long for a polite morning call.

Miss Leigh stood with that contented smile on her lips and her hands clasped before her, and that was when the full breadth of his mistake struck him. The only person he'd managed to make uncomfortable during their conversation was himself, and even that had been fleeting before they'd waded deep into the verbal thick of things.

And those dark eyes watched him with such unrestrained joy that Parker's throat closed tight as though his cravat was a noose. What had he done?

"What are you two discussing over here?" asked Miss Rosanna.

Fate was a cruel mistress, not only for placing Parker in this wretched situation but for delivering the object of his affection at that very moment. Coming up beside her sister and taking Miss Leigh's arm with a bright smile, Miss Rosanna turned to him.

"Dr. Humphreys and I were discussing his profession—among other things," said Miss Leigh. "However, I fear he was just about to take his leave."

Parker cocked his head, wondering if he'd spoken the words aloud or if the lady was a witch. He knew he ought to say something, but the proverbial cat had, indeed, stolen his tongue, and he could not wrest it away from the blasted beast.

"No, Dr. Humphreys," said Miss Rosanna. "You must stay another quarter of an hour at the very least. I wouldn't wish you to leave so soon."

It was as though she'd dangled a pork pie in front of a starving man. Having envisioned spending the rest of his life by her side, Parker couldn't imagine a more appetizing invitation, and he nearly nodded. But Miss Leigh stood there, equally eager for him to accept.

The two sisters. Together.

Parker didn't think himself a coward, but the thought of being paraded before Miss Rosanna as her sister's beau soured his stomach, and there was no other option but to retreat.

Sweeping into a bow, he avoided looking at either of them as he mumbled excuses about things to do and patients to visit before scurrying to the front door. Parker snatched his hat and gloves from the waiting manservant and hurried away, though he felt both sisters' gazes upon him as he disappeared down the street.

Confound it! The plan had been simple enough and would've worked perfectly if he hadn't been so wound up in the conversation that he'd forgotten his purpose. Or if Miss Leigh didn't have nerves of steel. The lady hadn't even blanched at his more descriptive anecdotes.

That was an unmitigated disaster. And he had no one to blame but himself.

Chapter 10

It was the little things that told the most about a person. Though seemingly insignificant, small actions and words revealed much—all the more so because the person in question rarely realized just how much they conveyed and did not bother to guard against them. Those sensible enough to notice those minor displays could tell much about the other's true nature.

Mr. Courtney's placement of his hand as he assisted Rosanna spoke amply about him. There was a world of difference between a scandalous hold and a mannerly one, allowing a gentleman an opportunity to communicate secretly to his lady. Conventional wisdom said men weren't subtle creatures, but Rosanna knew the truth was that they weren't purposefully so. Mr. Courtney didn't intend to convey the possessiveness in the grasp of her hand, but it was there.

Rosanna stepped down from his gig, and his smile was as smug as ever, but it was that hold of her hand that told her he believed her to be his in all but name. And she didn't know whether to preen from his attentions or to scowl at the impertinence. In the fortnight since they'd met, he'd called on her once, and this was their first drive out together. It would take more than that to secure her—no matter his fortune or how high an opinion he had of his suitability.

"And are you attending that little soirée tomorrow?" he asked, tucking her arm through his as he led her to her front door.

"Which soirée?"

Mr. Courtney huffed. "Do not pretend that this town has such a thriving social calendar that there is more than one offering tomorrow."

"You do take the fun out of this," said Rosanna.

"Not at all," he replied. "I am thoroughly amused."

His tone had all the usual ennui that the London swells were apt to employ, and Rosanna wondered if she ought to point out that though the gentleman believed himself a step above the rest, he followed fashion just like everyone else.

"And why do you wish to know, Mr. Courtney?"

The gentleman stopped on her doorstep and gave her that knowing arch of his brow. "I have been invited but have no interest in attending such a plebian affair, as I doubt there will be any true entertainment offered. However, if a certain young lady were there, I might be persuaded to join her."

Rosanna met his arched brow. "Is that so?"

"Yes, it is," he said, stepping closer and lowering his voice. "I have been assured that though there shall be games aplenty, there will be some dancing of a sort."

"Will there?" she asked in the same low tone.

Mr. Courtney did not bother to voice his question aloud once more. That commanding little smirk made it clear that he was not the sort to repeat himself, but for all his bluster and pride, he stood there, waiting for her reply.

"I am planning on attending Mr. and Mrs. Breadmore's soirée," she said.

"You ought to grace the finest ballrooms in London, not some middling parlor in the deepest reaches of the country," he said. "It is a shame your family does not attend the Season, for you would be quite the star of society, and I would be the envy of every man if I were to have you on my arm."

Rosanna's heart stuttered at his words and the greedy gleam in his eye. Despite having received her fair share of admiration, she found that the covetousness in Mr. Courtney's gaze made her heart thrum. She had to wonder if it wasn't the same sort of power that a man felt when he faced down an opponent in the field of battle and walked away victorious.

"Perhaps I might, one day," she replied with a coy little turn of her lips.

"Would you save me the trouble of chasing away your dance partners and promise me the first set?"

Rosanna huffed and turned away, breaking his hold on her gaze. "It is not in my habit to make such promises before the evening, sir, for it encourages the gentlemen to arrive promptly."

But Mr. Courtney responded to her protest with another challenging raise of his brow. "I do not care what your policy is with other gentlemen. I am no ordinary man."

"Perhaps," she tagged on, giving him a teasing look that made it clear her response pertained to his last statement and not his petition. "And perhaps I might be persuaded to reserve the first set for you. Perhaps."

With a huffing chuckle, Mr. Courtney moved to bow, but before he could take his leave, she added, "Would a not-so-ordinary man wish to join me for some refreshments?"

"My thanks, but I fear I am wanted elsewhere," he said, turning back to his gig. "I am meeting a horse breeder and must leave if I am to make the appointment."

Cocking her head to the side, Rosanna mimicked his arrogant raise of the brow, though with a coquettish smile to soften it. "Is that truly what you would rather do?"

"It is the main reason I came to this backwater little town. Though I have found other reasons to enjoy my stay, I shan't put it off even a minute later," he said with a nod and strode to the gig, taking the reins from the groom. In a trice, he was rolling down the drive and then disappeared into the maze of streets.

Rosanna stared after him with a frown for a long moment.

Then the world settled back into place, forcing her to reality once more, and she sighed. For all that Mr. Courtney was clearly enamored with her (and she refused to doubt that she was the reason he was "enjoying his stay"), having a beau rush off to meet with a horse breeder was hardly flattering. So unflattering that it outweighed any pleasantness she'd felt during their drive.

Glancing at the door behind her, Rosanna strode down the drive. No doubt Mama would pester her for every detail of the outing—it was a miracle she hadn't already rushed the doorstep and demanded her daughter tell all—and Rosanna was in no mood to speak of Mr. Courtney. The lady wouldn't care to hear anything but a glowing report of how the gentleman had tripped over himself to win the lovely Miss Rosanna Leigh's affection.

And she wasn't certain she even wanted Mr. Courtney's heart. A fortune wasn't the only consideration for a suitable husband, after all.

Moving away from the house, Rosanna tried to hold onto her good cheer, but it slipped from her grasp. It felt foolish to allow a little thing to sour such a fine afternoon, but a beau ought to prize her company above horses. Mr. Courtney was staying for several weeks, so surely he could've visited his beloved breeder another afternoon. Or forestalled their drive until he had more time.

Those thoughts followed her along as she wandered the streets of town. Passersby called greetings, and she nodded and smiled, but strangely enough, she felt no desire to stop and chat. Mr. Courtney was such a puzzle, and Rosanna wasn't certain she wished to solve it. Wealthy and of good standing, of course, but he was too used to getting his way, and she couldn't say she liked it.

With her thoughts so full of that gentleman, Rosanna almost missed Dr. Humphreys emerging from a townhouse. The fellow had his medical bag in tow, and his thoughts were clearly occupied as well, for his attention was fixed on the ground before him as he trudged along the pavement. Even when she called after him, he took no notice. It wasn't until the third call of his name that he jerked free of his thoughts and turned to see her.

"Miss Rosanna," he said, straightening. Then, casting a look about the street, he came to her side and greeted her with a tip of his hat. "And how are you this lovely afternoon?"

Yes, the afternoon was quite lovely, indeed. Though there was bound to be rain later, for now the skies were clear and the sun shone in a blaze of glory as only an autumnal sun could. Aided by the golden hues of the foliage, the world was awash in yellows, oranges, and reds, as though the very ground upon which they walked was on fire.

"I am grand," she said, watching the gentleman carefully. Clearly, Dr. Humphreys wasn't bold enough to ask about Prudence directly, and she amused herself by wondering how he would broach the subject. "And how are you?"

"I am well," he said with a nod. "And your family?"

Rosanna didn't bother hiding her smile at that. "They are all very well. We were pleased that you paid a call the other day."

Prudence had spoken of little else, having relayed every word of their conversation. For Rosanna's part, the discussion seemed a bit gruesome, but as it pleased her sister, she wouldn't dare chastise Dr. Humphreys.

The fellow nodded, and he shifted in place but said nothing more. Giving him a surreptitious glance, Rosanna held back a laugh. The fellow was quite a nervous beau, wasn't he?

Nodding down the street, she asked, "Would you walk with me a bit, Dr. Humphreys?"

Straightening, he nodded, a quick, jerky thing, and then they fell into step side by side. Yet still, the reticent physician remained mute. Gleaning information from him would be more difficult than from Prudence, who was determined to deflect any matrimonial speculation concerning her Dr. Humphreys with a quick, "We have only just begun to court."

The whole thing was far too sanguine. And false. Her sister may not admit it, but even a fool could recognize the truth.

Prudence beamed whenever the subject arose, her steps fairly skipping as she moved about the house, and her gaze shone with the lovesick dreaminess of the first throes of love. No other man had ever captured her sister's affection so, and Rosanna wouldn't turn aside an opportunity to stoke the fire, so to speak. Or glean titillating details that were bound to make Prudence swoon all the more.

Chapter 11

"It was good of you to visit the other day," said Rosanna as they stepped around the passing people and wandered deeper into the town.

"It was my pleasure," replied Dr. Humphreys.

And then nothing.

Men were such fools. Always needing a little help to get anything done properly.

"You and my sister had quite the discussion," said Rosanna. His gaze jerked to her, and he stumbled over an uneven paver. She hurried to add, "Though it sounds a bit ghoulish to me, I assure you she found it very enlightening. She even hurried off to the lending library to see if she could find some better books on the subject. Prudence manages all the home medicine, you see, and she is now determined to strengthen her knowledge. I wouldn't be surprised if she continues to pester you about it."

Dr. Humphreys cleared his throat as he guided her around a group of ladies chatting in the middle of the path. "Yes, she mentioned that she was the keeper of the family medicine chest."

Fiddling with the edge of her shawl, Rosanna glanced at him from the corner of her eye. "It must be nice to share such interests. I must admit I am entirely envious she was able to have such a stimulating conversation during a morning call."

Slanting a look at her, he gave her a faint smile. "Don't your swath of admirers ply you with interesting discussions?"

Rosanna huffed. "An ornament needn't speak of anything but frivolous things."

Having spent her time amongst society, she knew better than to speak without thinking, but the words emerged before she could stop them. Perhaps if she had not just said farewell to Mr. Courtney, Rosanna would've guarded her tongue better, but the lingering memory of their conversation tainted her words with far more honesty than intended.

Matters weren't helped by the stark contrast it presented to the conversation Prudence and Dr. Humphreys had shared. Her sister's beau spoke to her of things with substance, as though he cared for her opinion. Their words mattered.

Dr. Humphreys slowed a touch, his gaze swinging towards her with a furrowed brow.

"Think nothing of it," said Rosanna, waving it away with the sort of bright laugh that men expected.

"I am afraid I can think of nothing else," he replied in a low tone. "You are not merely an ornament, and if any man treats you so, he is not a man worth knowing."

"You are kind to say so—"

"Do not brush my words aside, Miss Rosanna," he said, pulling her to a stop. Others passed around them, giving them only a cursory glance before drifting on their way. "You are a good lady, and do not deserve to be dismissed or treated as though you have little value."

Dr. Humphreys spoke with such earnestness that Rosanna couldn't help but hold his gaze, though his own often darted away.

"You hardly know me, sir."

"We may not have spoken much, but that does not mean that I do not know who you are, Miss Rosanna." He shifted in place, moving his medical bag from one hand to the other. "You are a kind daughter and sister—"

"As are many women."

Dr. Humphreys shook his head, meeting her gaze directly with a furrowed brow. "Do not devalue your kindness, Miss Rosanna. You have enough status to be a dictator in society, like so many other ladies, yet you are welcoming and gracious. You do not amuse yourself by tormenting those with less beauty or grace. Society ignores your sister, but you use your position to ensure she is welcomed alongside you, granting her far more acceptance than she would find on her own. Those are not little things, Miss Rosanna."

Her brows rose at the emphatic tone in his voice and the determined look in his eye; everything from his words to his posture begged her to believe him, though Rosanna couldn't comprehend why this near stranger believed her so praiseworthy. Everyone's compliments directed towards her were fixated on the surface enticements she possessed, ignoring entirely the soul beneath. Yet Dr. Humphreys spoke as though it were an indisputable fact that Rosanna Leigh was something more than a fashion plate.

Scouring her memories, she drew forth only a few interactions, and none of them seemed remarkable. Rosanna felt a flash of heat (though thankfully her cheeks did not color) at the thought that she couldn't recall a single thing he'd written in his letter. Had it carried such tender assurances?

Rosanna continued along, and she tried for an airy tone. "Pay me no heed, Dr. Humphreys. I fear you caught me at an odd moment."

"I think I caught you in an honest moment," he replied. There was a short pause before he murmured, "It doesn't have anything to do with Mr. Courtney, does it?"

Waving a dismissive hand, Rosanna forced a laugh. "Oh, he is like any other man of consequence and fortune. He is interested in a pretty wife who will fawn over his long-winded tales of his business conquests and sporting adventures. I am merely a tad jealous that my sister has a beau who enjoys speaking *with* her and not *at* her. As I said, pay me no heed, Dr. Humphreys."

An unnamable burden settled on her chest as she considered just how blessed Prudence truly was, and it had been Rosanna's own doing. It served her right for being so quick to dismiss that love letter. For all that Dr. Humphreys thought her kind and considerate, he wouldn't believe so if he knew the full extent of her sins.

His hand brushed a light touch against her arm, and Rosanna drew to a stop as the gentleman came to stand before her.

"You shouldn't settle for anything less than a man who values you, Miss Rosanna. You are more than merely your beauty. You are a prize worth winning—even if you were the plainest of women."

Rosanna's breath caught as his eyes held hers, infusing his words with an earnestness that Mr. Courtney would likely scoff at, but she couldn't doubt Dr. Humphreys meant each one. Her mind replayed that moment when she'd cast his letter aside and wondered how different things would be if she'd bothered to read the thing.

In a flash, Rosanna imagined herself standing with Dr. Humphreys in her family's parlor. Of course, they wouldn't be discussing anything so morbid, but it would be just as pleasant. She couldn't think what that would be, precisely, but standing in Prudence's slippers, Rosanna saw herself coyly smiling at the good physician.

Which was the exact moment she recalled the truth of her situation, and her ribs constricted as though squeezing her heart. It was Rosanna's actions that had thrown Prudence and Dr. Humphreys together, and there was little point in bemoaning the mistakes of the past. No matter how enticing that was.

"You are too kind, Dr. Humphreys," she said, clearing her throat. "I can see why my sister is so enamored with you."

Perhaps that was the wrong thing to say, but a heavy dose of reality was precisely what this situation required. Prudence was the perfect physician's wife; she was so very capable. If Rosanna wondered why men spoke to her about nothing of consequence, the answer was clear enough. What did she have to offer them? Of the two Leigh sisters, Rosanna was the beauty—Prudence was everything else.

Dr. Humphreys cleared his throat and turned away. "Do you care for reading, Miss Rosanna?"

With a nod, she grasped onto that subject, regaling the fellow with all the various things she'd learned from the latest *Lady's Monthly Museum*, including a detailed account of the latest installment of *Motherless Mary*, which had grasped her attention from the very first page.

"My mother indicated there was quite a rousing description of the current state of affairs for the country in that issue," said Dr. Humphreys.

"I fear I am a poor scholar," said Rosanna. "I suppose I might find such things interesting if I understood more of what was happening, but I fear my schedule doesn't allow me much time to indulge in such pastimes. I am far too busy."

"I imagine your social calendar is quite full," he replied, stopping before a townhouse. Glancing at the door, Dr. Humphreys gave her a pained smile. "And I fear that mine shan't allow me any more time to escort you about. This is my next appointment."

Rosanna cocked her head and gave him a warm smile. "And I cannot entice you to throw them over?"

Dr. Humphrey sucked in a deep breath. "Unfortunately, illness does not disappear when I have the opportunity to escort a pretty lady about. I cannot throw over my responsibility."

With a sigh, Rosanna nodded, though her shoulders fell as he climbed the stairs without a backward glance and was ushered quickly into the home. But then, a sick patient was vastly more important than a horse breeder.

Turning on her heel, Rosanna walked away, her steps far lighter than before.

Chapter 12

There were few opportunities for physicians to advertise themselves, and though Parker flirted with the bounds of propriety by dabbling in less gentlemanly aspects of the medical field, there were some lines even he could not cross. All the gentry's heirs were forced into professions of some sort, but to behave as though one made a living rather than inheriting it was gauche, and the men of Parker's class were forever caught in the battle of earning their bread without appearing to do so.

No dirtying one's hands with money. Such behavior was beneath a gentleman. Never mind that a gentleman must eat as readily as the working man.

Advertising in the newspapers was not a possibility. Even hanging a sign from his home was crass. So, Parker was left with social engagements and word of mouth, both of which were slow-moving and inconsistent income generators—enough so that Parker couldn't reject any invitation. Especially such a prestigious one as the Breadmores'.

Michaelmas in Greater Edgerton was more than a single day. Though the town boasted more of an industrial bend than agrarian, they celebrated the harvest time with as much enthusiasm as their farmer ancestors, ushering in the forthcoming winter as though it would be their last. Whilst the assembly marked the beginning of the merriment and the Harvest Festival signaled the end, the days between were stuffed with parties, dancing, games, and picnics (if the weather held). And many didn't consider the holiday complete without Mr. and Mrs. Breadmore's harvest party.

However, such merriments were rarely very merry for Parker as it was more about rubbing elbows with potential patients, which was beyond exhausting. It didn't help that his thoughts were far from furthering his financial goals.

Being on the edge of town, the Breadmores' home was larger than the usual townhouse with space aplenty for entertaining—which was for the best, as the entire building was occupied for the night. Only the private bedchambers and the servants' areas were left alone, with the others filled with games and food, and even a bit of light dancing in the drawing room (though it allowed only a dozen dancers).

Parker wandered the house, though his feet kept taking him back to the grand entry because they did not understand that appearing so eager would not aid his suit. After such a successful interaction with Miss Rosanna yesterday, he must approach tonight cautiously, but knowing that and putting it into practice were two vastly different things.

He really ought to be cozying up to Greater Edgerton's elite, but his feet kept dragging him to the Breadmores' front door.

Miss Rosanna had spoken with him. Smiled at him.

But despite his heart yearning to build castles out of that relatively short conversation, Parker forced himself to view the interlude with an honest eye. He didn't think it too proud to say that the young lady had welcomed his company and viewed him with favor. Miss Rosanna had even seemed eager to keep him from leaving.

With his heart threatening to leap out of his chest, it had been impossible to concentrate on the conversation, but Miss Rosanna had seemed to enjoy the interlude, and she'd been her usual earnest and kind self. A silly grin stretched across his lips as his gaze unfocused, his thoughts turning back to those pleasant minutes they'd spent together. Miss Rosanna. If not for the reminder about her sister, Parker would consider the moment perfect.

At least it had provided him with better insight as to how to solve that little conundrum. Miss Leigh required a distraction.

"Anglesey!"

Parker's greeting pulled the passing gentleman to a stop. "Humphreys—I hadn't noticed you standing there. I didn't expect to see you tonight."

"Yes, things have been quite busy of late, but I made certain to clear my schedule. As long as no one falls ill, I should be free to remain the whole evening," said Parker with a smile.

Mr. Anglesey laughed. "I don't think I've ever heard a physician pray that his patients remain well. You'll put yourself out of business."

"I'd rather my services were never required, but as long as there are people, there will always be a need for physicians," replied Parker. "But I am very glad to see you."

With raised brows, the gentleman replied, "Is that so?"

"There is a young lady I would like to introduce you to."

"You shan't impress your Dr. Humphreys by being so eager," said Rosanna, her tone rife with laughter. Prudence tried to ignore this, but it was impossible, for her sister held firm to her arm, keeping her from hurrying from room to room as they searched for the gentleman. Every time Prudence quickened her pace, Rosanna gripped her tighter, forcing her to slow.

"Don't be a hypocrite. You cannot claim indifference when you are eager to see if Mr. Courtney attends after he claimed no desire to do so," said Prudence.

"Mr. Courtney will attend," replied Rosanna with all the confidence of one who knew her suitors would never stray. But there was a hint of something in her tone that gave Prudence pause.

"You do wish for him to attend, don't you?"

Rosanna sighed as she led them past a group of gentlemen, ignoring their invitations to join them. "He is a catch."

"However...?" prompted Prudence.

"However, I wish he wasn't so dull. He only speaks of himself and his interests. And his compliments are far too shallow. Nothing like your Dr. Humphreys."

Prudence frowned at that, but Rosanna waved it away. "I shan't allow myself to be snared by Mr. Courtney unless I wish to be, so do not worry yourself, dear sister. You ought to focus on how to be coy with your beau. You are liable to lose him if you rush about the party, hunting for him."

It was logical and all too infuriating.

Why must she feign an indifference she didn't feel? If Dr. Humphreys was startled by her admiration, then he was not the man for her. But then, his feelings may not run as deeply as hers did, and being too forceful in her attentions may scare him away. But why did they need to arrive at "love" at the same time? No couple reached that pivotal moment in unison, so what harm was there in being honest with her feelings?

Not that Prudence loved Dr. Humphreys. Not yet, at any rate. Love adjacent, perhaps. Certainly admiration. And there was a generous portion of eagerness that came with it.

But Rosanna knew men better than she, and they were a fickle lot. So, Prudence forced herself to examine the Breadmores' decorations and the entertainments. Their home was one of those lovely buildings that was not as imposing as the grand estates nor as pokey as many of the townhouses. The rooms were too snug for such a large gathering, but with the party divided between so many spaces, it gave the evening an intimate feel despite most of Greater Edgerton's society being in attendance. It was like having a dozen smaller parties all existing parallel to each other.

Dr. Humphreys was not in the parlor.

As much as she tried to ascribe to Rosanna's way of thinking, Prudence couldn't keep her gaze from darting from face to face, searching for that head of curly brown hair. And oh, those bright blue eyes. Dr. Humphreys was not a handsome man by most standards (though by no means unappealing), but those eyes made up for any surface deficiencies picky ladies might find.

Swept up in recalling just how bright his gaze was when they'd spoken together, Prudence nearly missed the moment when those eyes met hers.

Running her free hand down her skirt, she wondered what Dr. Humphreys would think of such a simple dress. The color was a lovely cream with a simple cut and skirt, broken up by the intricate stitching done across the overskirt; however, it was the same color as the fabric, making the effect far more subtle than spectacular. Only the thick blue ribbon at her waist broke up the gown, but the colors complemented each other and her brunette locks to perfection.

In any other circumstance, her appearance would be acceptable. Perhaps even pretty. But at her side, Rosanna was a riot of flounces and cord-work, winding around the hem and enveloping almost the whole of her gown. The pink was no delicate shade; it was bold and eye-catching, as were the jewels she'd borrowed from Mama's hoard. Raising her free hand to her throat, Prudence felt for the ribbon that was tied there, ensuring the bow was not askew.

But those thoughts seized as Dr. Humphreys stood before them, sweeping into a bow.

"Dear ladies, it is a pleasure to see you tonight," he said as he straightened. "Miss Leigh, there is someone I would like you to meet."

Then, stepping away, he motioned for another gentleman, who came forward with a bow as Dr. Humphreys made the introduction, giving special emphasis to the elder of the Leigh sisters. Prudence felt a blush coloring her cheeks and forced herself to breathe, but it was far more difficult than it ought to be. For once, Prudence wasn't an afterthought.

Of course, the giddiness of the moment was not helped by the fact that Dr. Humphreys was introducing her to his friends. A gentleman did not do so casually.

"It is my pleasure to meet you, Miss Leigh," said Mr. Anglesey, his eyes bright with a smile. "Dr. Humphreys has spoken of little else since I arrived, and I have been anxious to meet such a paragon of women."

There was no helping it then, for Prudence was blushing like a schoolgirl. "I am certain he was too generous in his praise."

"Never," said Rosanna, squeezing her arm. "If anything, you do not receive enough."

Glancing at her sister, Prudence didn't know what to say, though her complexion was doing a fine job of conveying her feelings on the matter. But before she could think of a reply, she saw Rosanna's eyes dart to the left and widen.

"What is the matter?" whispered Prudence.

"Mr. Courtney has arrived," she said with a sigh. "I do not know what to do about the gentleman, and I do not wish for him to commandeer all my attention tonight."

"You must join me and Mr. Anglesey for a few rounds of cards," said Dr. Humphreys, stepping forward to shield Rosanna and offering up his arm.

"Most definitely," said Mr. Anglesey.

Rosanna quickly transferred from Prudence to Dr. Humphrey's arm, allowing his height to keep her mostly out of sight. It made sense that he would aid her; it was a gentlemanly impulse, and there was no need for Prudence's heart to pang as the pair moved away together. Yet as she took Mr. Anglesey's arm, she couldn't help but feel as though she was being left behind.

The foremost pair led the way, and Prudence's eyes lingered on Dr. Humphreys and Rosanna together, but she refused to allow herself to consider just how closely the two were standing together. Or the fact that Dr. Humphreys never once looked back to see if she and Mr. Anglesey were following.

Chapter 13

For all that medicine was a science (which denoted that there were clear solutions to problems), far too often, it was guesswork. Parker's medical books weren't recipes that could be followed to earn him an expected outcome. Bodies were too varied, and what worked for one was not guaranteed to work for another. More often than not, experimentation was required.

And his dilemma with Miss Leigh was much the same.

Parker's first attempts had not achieved the desired result, but that did not mean there was no happy resolution for them. He was rather surprised he hadn't thought of finding her a new beau before. Miss Leigh would still have a sweetheart, and Parker would be free.

Mr. Anglesey was a much better catch. Besides having a much more robust income, he was a capital fellow. Always ready with an earnest smile. Amiable, gracious, and one of the best men Parker knew. Mr. Anglesey was just the sort to see Miss Leigh's worth. To say nothing of the fact that he was eagerly searching for a wife and quite ready to fall in love.

And Miss Leigh had much to recommend her. Her wit was not the sort that flowed freely, sprinkling every conversation with tittering laughter; it was sly, sneaking up and hitting with more power because of its dry delivery. Though nowhere near as lovely as Miss Rosanna, there was something in Miss Leigh's smile that was quite alluring. In all honesty, the lady might be considered rather pretty if not for the unparalleled beauty of her sister providing an unflattering comparison.

If Parker needed any further proof that his plan was brilliant, he now found himself cozied up to Miss Rosanna with the four of them situated at a card table. Miss Leigh and Mr. Anglesey studied their hands while Miss Rosanna kept smiling at him from behind her cards, teasing him and his partner about their poor performance. Which was not Miss Leigh's fault. Parker was a fine player, but whist required one's entire attention, and his was divided between the beauty at his side and his matchmaking schemes.

He laid his card atop the trick. Miss Leigh was kind enough not to groan, but Miss Rosanna and Mr. Anglesey had no such compunction, crowing over his poor play as they secured the final points of the game. It truly was a pitiful performance on his part, and when he sent Miss Leigh an apologetic look, she merely grinned as though it mattered little.

"I have been meaning to ask you: have you taken my advice?" she asked him when his gaze lingered a little too long on her.

Parker's brow furrowed. "Concerning?"

"Using sweets to bribe your young patients."

"What is this?" asked Mr. Anglesey. With sparkling eyes, the gentleman glanced between Miss Leigh and Parker as the lady quickly recited the tale.

"It is fine advice, and though I've taken it to heart, I haven't treated any little ones in the time since you suggested it," said Parker as Miss Rosanna dealt out another hand. "But I have enough confections in my medical bag that my patients are liable to think I prescribe sugar as a heal-all."

"I find it cures many an illness," said Miss Leigh. "Perhaps your grown patients will fare better if you include a bit of sugar with all your visits."

"I certainly would make myself more popular," replied Parker.

Miss Leigh held his gaze, and it struck him how vastly different the two sisters' eyes were. Where Miss Rosanna's were a green so pale they were almost gray, her elder sister's were brown. Though the latter might seem mundane and commonplace, there was a richness to the hue and a depth to the color as to almost make the color indistinguishable from her pupils. And though that might make them seem cold or empty, hers were quite warm and full of life.

Straightening, Parker pulled his gaze away from her. Forgetting himself was becoming a common occurrence around Miss Leigh, and he needed to keep his wits about him. Especially when his gaze fell on Mr. Courtney, who appeared in the doorway to search the guests within the room before striding to their table.

"Miss Rosanna," he greeted with a bow before tossing vague greetings to the others. "I do believe you promised me a dance."

The young lady sorted through her cards, glancing at him from over the top. "I believe I gave you no more firm response than, 'Perhaps.'"

Mr. Courtney watched her with narrowed eyes. "Will you stand up with me tonight?"

Parker's expression hardened as he studied the gentleman, though Miss Rosanna batted away the hard tone with a wave of her hand.

"Ask me later, Mr. Courtney. I was just about to stand up with Dr. Humphreys."

And then the heavens smiled upon him, for Miss Rosanna's gaze turned to Parker, lingering on him for a long moment before meeting Mr. Courtney's once more with a challenging raise of her brow. Was she choosing a lowly physician over an heir to a fortune? The answer seemed ridiculous—positively impossible—but there was no mistaking the dismissal she gave Mr.

Courtney or how she met Parker's gaze with a conspiratorial look.

Miss Rosanna chose him!

It was a good thing Prudence's nerves hadn't allowed her to eat much at supper, for her stomach soured as she watched her sister toy with Mr. Courtney. Despite her cold reception, Rosanna held the gentleman's gaze with the sort of heat and allure that Prudence could never achieve even if she had even a tenth of Rosanna's loveliness. It was condescending yet inviting, both teasing Mr. Courtney with promises of more while dismissing him.

Prudence frowned; she couldn't say she liked the fellow, but he didn't deserve to be tossed about like a child's plaything. She prayed Mr. Courtney would choose the wiser course, but the intrigue in his gaze testified that he was as big a fool as any man who couldn't help but chase a pretty face.

That was unkind. Rosanna was not merely a pretty woman; she was vivacious and intriguing. Even if she had been born without any outward attractions, Rosanna would've drawn in the menfolk by sheer force of personality.

Prudence was merely out of sorts. She couldn't say she knew Dr. Humphreys well enough to read his moods, but something was amiss. Despite having sought her out in conversation during their last interlude, he kept her at a distance now, even dragging poor Mr. Anglesey along, though Prudence suspected the gentleman would rather have continued wandering the party.

"Do excuse us," said Rosanna, rising to her feet as Dr. Humphreys sprang from his seat, offering her an arm and whisking her away.

Mr. Courtney watched them as they walked away before drifting off in another direction. Only a heartbeat later Mr. Anglesey took his leave as well, abandoning Prudence at the card table, which was precisely the opposite of what she needed at present. Her thoughts were not a safe place.

"Are you finished with your game?" asked a lady, and Prudence popped up from her seat.

"I apologize. I was woolgathering." As she stepped away, the others took the now empty seats, leaving her to wander the party alone.

Few paid her any heed, leaving Prudence without any distractions. The strains of music followed her, and she tried not to pay attention to when the dances began or ended, but she was keenly aware of when Rosanna's dance concluded.

Yet Dr. Humphreys did not return to Prudence's side.

At least, not in any meaningful manner. The gentleman arrived long enough to speak a word of greeting before insisting she meet another of his acquaintances. A lady might find it flattering that he was so determined to introduce her to all his friends, but Dr. Humphreys promptly abandoned her again with a relative stranger. As all his chosen companions abandoned her not long after, Prudence was left to seek Dr. Humphreys out. And then the cycle repeated itself.

Even the most confident of ladies couldn't help but feel uneasy about these exchanges. Prudence had anticipated an evening with her beau, but that was not to be. Perhaps it was better not to live in each other's pockets, but she'd hoped for some time with him. And for him not to flee at every possible opportunity.

Prudence forced air into her lungs as the world pressed in on her. She would not allow this to overcome her. She would not. But the twisting of her stomach told her the truth even when she did not wish to acknowledge it.

Did Dr. Humphreys not wish to be alone with her? Not that anyone at a party was "alone," but it was easy enough to indulge in private conversations. Yet he had kept as much distance from her as a gentleman could without leaving the party altogether. As much as she tried to paint his behavior in a favorable light,

Prudence couldn't ignore all the many ways he maneuvered away from her.

Playing their previous conversation through her thoughts, she tried to find some reason why he was doing so. Once they'd settled into a conversation, Dr. Humphreys had seemed keen to speak with her. Prudence didn't think she had imagined that. Yet clearly, he no longer wished to associate with her.

What had she said? What had she done? Prudence had believed that her appearance was what kept gentlemen at bay, but here was one whose interest had been piqued from afar, only to reject her when he came to know her.

Prudence's breaths came in heavy pants, her eyes stinging as she considered that wretched fear for far too long. Her throat tightened as she played through the conversation, searching for any sign of what she had done wrong. Surely she could make it right again.

But of course, he had grown bored with her.

Dr. Humphreys may not be wealthy, but he had a decent income and was only bound to do better as the years passed. He was charming and, though not dashing, his features were pleasant. And his heart was so kind and good.

So many physicians were forced into the role by their families and had not the temperament or passion to make it their calling. They prescribed too many concoctions, were often sour, and, despite asking their patients to enumerate their troubles, they listened to only one word in ten. Prudence may not have witnessed him in action, but she couldn't imagine Dr. Humphreys giving anything but the best of care and his full attention.

And Prudence? She was the Leigh family workhorse. The one everyone relied on, to be certain, but she was given little other thought. Clomping around society like a Clydesdale, valued for what it could do but not admired for its grace or beauty like the Thoroughbreds.

Doubts swirled like inky blackness all around her, drawing Prudence deeper into the whirlpool. With each, her shoulders fell, her heart squeezing tight as though trying to disappear into itself. And just as the current threatened to pull her under, a lifeline dropped into her hands, giving her a dose of clarity.

Her beau had been equally puzzling during their first interaction, but that was due to concern over his patient. Dr. Humphreys approached his work with his whole heart, and difficult days bled over into other aspects of his life. And hadn't he spoken earlier of some of his worries for his troublesome patients?

For all that she thought herself a logical creature, Prudence could be quite the fool at times. Here she was, ignoring the most obvious answer in favor of doubting and denigrating herself. With a deep sigh, she shook loose her shoulders and straightened.

Dr. Humphreys had suffered a troubling day. That was it. Nothing more.

Chapter 14

Fate was not always kind. Her cruelty had landed Parker in this trouble in the first place, after all. Then she had compounded her sins by ruining his previous attempts to set things right. But for once, Mistress Fate decided to smile upon Parker Humphreys.

Tonight could not be more perfect. Though Miss Rosanna was now occupied by others, he'd secured an entire set with her. Having watched her dance with others before, he'd known she was graceful and elegant on the dance floor, but being partnered with her was an entirely different experience from merely pining from afar.

Being a physician required a healthy dose of practicality, and thus Parker couldn't delude himself into believing Miss Rosanna was ready to welcome his suit, but something in the looks she sent his way told him her heart was warming to him. Not that she would entertain such thoughts while he was "courting" her sister, but in all their years being socially adjacent, Miss Rosanna had never noticed him. Gaining her attention now was a victory of the highest order.

The cold journey home tonight would be warmed by the memory of Miss Rosanna smiling at him, her gloved hands clutching his; no doubt her fingers were softer and gentler than the silk that encased them tonight.

He had presented Miss Leigh with a dozen viable beaus; one of them was bound to suit better than an awkward physician whose heart was engaged elsewhere. Truly, his plan couldn't have been more successful had it been ordained from On High. Perhaps it had been. Surely the Almighty wished them to be happily wed to the proper spouse, and there was none more proper for him than Miss Rosanna.

Standing to the side of the dance floor, Parker watched as Miss Rosanna moved about the figures. With so little space for dancers, she ought to have made way for others, but the gentlemen would not be put off; once she'd stepped into the drawing room to dance, she had not been given a moment's peace. The poor thing.

Turning, the young lady caught his eye, and she smiled. Parker's heart stopped.

For all his dreaming, that practical part of him couldn't quite believe it would ever happen. Yet there it was. Finally, Miss Rosanna was aware of him. This wasn't how he'd wanted it to unfold, but Parker supposed the mistake with his letter had brought about the desired result in the end.

"Dr. Humphreys."

The quiet voice barely carried over the quartet playing with all the volume of a much larger orchestra, the dancers' footfalls punctuating each beat like drums. Parker turned to face Miss Leigh, but his gaze swept the gathering, searching for another possible beau in case the others hadn't done the job.

"Good evening, Miss Leigh," he said with a nod and a smile. "Might I fetch you a glass of punch? Or some refreshments?"

Parker turned away, but she grabbed his arm, holding him in place.

"Please do not leave," she said, her tone matching her hold on his arm. Miss Leigh's gaze fell to her hand, and she blushed, dropping his arm. "I feel as though we've hardly had time to speak, and I was hoping for at least a few minutes of your time."

With a strained smile, Parker nodded and stretched his neck surreptitiously, though it did nothing to ease the tightness of his cravat. He forced his hands to remain at his side, for he longed to tug it open.

"Of course, Miss Leigh."

She stood there, watching him with such bright eyes, but Parker didn't trust himself to speak a single word: best not to give her any reason to set her cap at him.

A movement from the other side of the room drew his attention to Mr. Gundry. The fellow was enamored with some young miss (Parker couldn't recall whom), but she did not return his affection, making him free for the taking. If anything, he was a jolly fellow, bound to entertain Miss Leigh.

"How was your day? Not trying, I hope," she said.

"Not at all," he replied, tucking his hands behind him and glancing at Mr. Gundry as the gentleman wandered the room. If he came any closer, Parker could easily draw his attention here.

"Then the Faxons are on the mend? They've been on my mind often of late."

Her words snapped Parker's attention back to the lady before him. She watched him with a furrowed brow, her gaze pleading for a good response. Parker couldn't help but smile—not only for her kindness in remembering them but for her genuine concern.

"I am happy to inform you that they are much better, soon to make a full recovery." Parker's smile grew as Miss Leigh's rigid posture eased at that announcement.

"I am glad to hear it," she said, a smile lightening her expression. "Might I inquire which of your remedies did the trick?"

"It is often impossible to know which of the plasters and tisanes did the trick, especially as it is often a combination. However, I feel certain it was..." Parker's voice drifted off into silence as he realized just how comfortable he was with falling into a discussion with Miss Leigh. She was so easy to speak to, but doing so only added to their troubles.

Parker nodded towards Mr. Gundry. "There is a gentleman I would like you to meet—"

"Please don't." Miss Leigh seemed to shrink before him; though she tried to keep her shoulders up, darkness filled her gaze. She closed her eyes, and Parker watched as a wave of calm swept over her. When she looked at him once more, it was with a will of iron straightening her spine.

"Have I done something to offend you, Dr. Humphreys? Is that why you wish to foist me off on others?"

Her words buried into his heart like a knife, and Parker swore he heard Mistress Fate's laughter echoing through the room. But before he could say a word (though he knew not what that would be), Miss Leigh continued, her words rushing forth.

"If your feelings have changed, sir, I understand. I treasure the letter you wrote me, but that does not mean you are irreparably bound to me. At times, we think we know what our heart wants, but once a closer acquaintance is formed, our desires change. There is no shame in that."

Despite her strength, Miss Leigh's voice wobbled at the end, and she winced, closing her eyes.

Heat flushed through Parker until it felt as though his skin could light a fire with the barest touch. He'd treated many a fever before, and he felt more flushed than even those on death's door. It was as though every eye in the room was pointed towards him (though no one paid the pair any mind), and Parker couldn't help but shrink beneath their judgment.

All this time, he'd congratulated himself on his brilliance, thinking that Miss Leigh was none the wiser and his mistake would disappear into the ether, never to be revealed. Instead, he'd driven this poor lady to assume that the fault lay with her and that his feelings—once bright and burning—had evaporated after a short and pitiful courtship.

Heat swept through him, leaching the strength from his limbs, and Parker wished he could simply slip away from the crowd and forget all about love letters and courting. Noise rang in the air, making it impossible for Parker to think, though he knew no amount of logic would resolve this in the happy fashion he'd imagined.

They say the road to hell was paved with good intentions, and this moment proved that proverb.

Had one of his sisters' beaus done this, Parker would've drawn and quartered him, and the bounder would've deserved every bit of agony. More so because if he'd simply put his pride aside and spoken with Miss Leigh at the very first instance, the issue would be done and over—with a little embarrassment, to be sure, but nothing unforgivable.

With Miss Leigh's gaze fixed on him, pleading for some explanation, Parker knew he had taken a terrible situation and made it all the worse. Though it had been in part to spare her, far too much of his motivation had revolved around Miss Rosanna.

Robert had been right, and Parker had been a fool.

"I need to speak with you," he whispered, casting a furtive glance around. "But not here. Perhaps I might call on you tomorrow?"

Miss Leigh stiffened, and her cheeks paled.

"There is no need to draw this out. I comprehend your meaning, sir, and I free you from any obligation concerning our..." Waving a hand between them, she allowed the words to drift away as she inched towards the door.

But Parker followed after her. Miss Leigh's gaze clung to the ground, refusing to meet his. He hadn't thought the lady fragile, as she seemed the most stalwart woman he'd ever met, but she backed away from him, shrinking within herself as though bending beneath the weight of the world.

Surely there was something he could say to heal this. Not all wounds were salvageable—he knew that all too well—but surely there was some verbal tonic or remedy that might help salve her injured pride.

"Please, it is not what you think."

Shaking her head, Miss Leigh attempted a smile, but her lips quivered. "Your feelings have changed, Dr. Humphreys. I understand. There is no need for us to speak further on the matter."

Without knowing it, the lady had handed him an answer to his troubles. A way for him to avoid the consequences of his decisions. Though it was clear Miss Leigh was pained, he knew she was too good a soul to hold his change of heart against him. Parker could walk away now with little ramification.

Miss Leigh had just broken with him, after all. This was exactly what he'd hoped for.

But in those schemes, he hadn't intended for her to bear the pain of rejection. Miss Leigh did not deserve to shed a single tear over what had passed. For all that his honor had supported a little deception, Parker's insides wrenched and twisted themselves into knots at the sight of her pain turning inward, shouldering the blame for his fickle feelings.

If this ruined his chances with Miss Rosanna, so be it. Parker could not let things stand.

"Miss Leigh, I did not write that letter for you."

Chapter 15

There was only one missive Dr. Humphreys could mean. Yet knowing that did not keep Prudence from mutely blinking at the gentleman. Surely there was a mistake.

Ears were known to play tricks. A creaky floorboard that was not a murderer sneaking about the house. A noise on the breeze whose origin could never be ascertained. A call of a bird that sounded right beside oneself but was, in actuality, a fair distance away. Though this "confession" was far more complex than any of those examples, one could not always trust what one heard.

Dr. Humphreys' eyes pleaded for forgiveness, his posture and agitated movements adding weight to his words. But one's eyes could not be believed anymore than one's ears. One's senses were fallible things, and she struggled to give weight to hers.

"Pardon?" she asked. When Dr. Humphreys repeated himself, it left her in no doubt that she had heard him correctly. "But it was addressed to me. It was on my pillow."

The arguments meant little, as they did not alter the fact that the intended recipient was not herself, but Prudence couldn't think what else to say.

"I do not know what happened, but I delivered the letter to your house with specific instructions to give it to Miss Rosanna, and I addressed it to 'Miss R. Leigh.'"

For all that she had protested her mother's assumptions when that wretched letter had appeared in her life, Prudence couldn't let go of that belief now that it had woven itself into her view of the world. Dr. Humphreys had wanted her. He had. But though she tried to hold firm to that reality, it unraveled in her hands with each of the gentleman's emphatic denials.

Merciful heavens. Or rather, not so merciful heavens.

How had this come to be?

"I am so very sorry," he whispered, stepping closer. "I didn't mean to make things worse, but I didn't know what to do. I had hoped to free us both without causing you distress. I never meant to cause you pain, Miss Leigh. I give you my word. This was just an unfortunate misunderstanding that I should've addressed the moment I realized what was happening."

Pressing a hand to her stomach, Prudence tried to calm the roiling mess brewing inside her as her heart grew leaden, sinking like a rock in a pond. Her memory dredged up their interactions of late, and in quick succession, she viewed them anew. Tingles swept through her, bringing with them a wave of heat that turned her cheeks a cherry red.

Dr. Humphreys had been trying to shake her loose all this time, and she'd thrown herself at him again and again. Her insides rebelled, threatening to spill forth. She couldn't breathe as memory after memory assailed her, casting every wonderful moment in a new light. What a fool she'd been!

Prudence stepped away, her gaze fixed on the rugs at her feet, unable to raise her eyes above the others' shoes. They were staring at her. She felt all those mocking eyes, watching her. They'd known the truth. Everyone had. What gentleman would choose Prudence over Rosanna? The idea was laughable.

With seven and twenty years to her name, she ought to have known better than to believe Mama.

And still, Dr. Humphreys drew closer, speaking in low

tones guaranteed not to carry to the others, though Prudence was certain they were all aware of her foolishness. He spouted apologies, and her lungs heaved, struggling for breath but unable to find relief. Her eyes burned, and she glanced about for an escape, but she couldn't bring herself to look up for fear of seeing all the attention focused on her.

"Prudence, what is the matter?" asked Rosanna.

Squeezing her eyes shut, she prayed that this truly was a figment of her overheated imagination, but when Prudence deigned to glance in that direction, she caught sight of her sister's pink skirts approaching.

"Are you unwell?" she asked, taking hold of Prudence's arm and pressing a gloved hand to her forehead. "Goodness, you are flushed. Dr. Humphreys, perhaps you might take her on a stroll in the gardens—"

"No!" Prudence jerked away, stepping two paces away from the pair. Pressing a hand to her forehead, she straightened, though she still couldn't bring herself to look around. Then, lowering her voice, she asked, "Did you know, Rosanna?"

"What are you on about?" asked her sister, the question rife in her tone.

Oh, how Prudence wished she didn't need to speak the words. If not for her frantic heartbeat thumping in her chest, she might ignore that niggling question, but the rapid pace rang like a drum in her veins, demanding she speak.

"Did you know that Dr. Humphreys' letter was meant for you?"

Rosanna huffed. "What a thing to ask. Don't be silly, Prudence."

Her eyes slid closed, and she inched farther away. When she looked at the world again, Prudence forced herself to meet her sister's gaze. "That isn't an answer."

And it wasn't, but though Rosanna excelled at controlling what she displayed to the public, Prudence knew her sister too well to mistake a lie when she heard it. There was no single clear sign—simply a sense developed from spending so many years side by side.

Rosanna had lied to her.

Parker stood like a statue, staring at the Leigh sisters as his addled wits attempted to grasp the shift in the conversation. Miss Rosanna hadn't known the truth of this misunderstanding. Had she known, surely she would've spoken to her sister, rather than encouraging the match.

"Why didn't you tell me?" whispered Miss Leigh, a slight quiver in her tone.

"I thought you might like his gift. I didn't think you would assume the letter had been for you. It was addressed to me," she said, hazarding a look at Parker, and that was enough for him to see the truth in her gaze. Turning back to her sister, she hurried to add, "When I realized you'd mistaken the letter for your own, I wanted to tell you, but you were so pleased to have an admirer."

Miss Leigh covered her eyes. "I am not a child who cannot accept the truth for what it is, Rosanna!"

"I thought you two might suit. In that case, you needn't ever discover your mistake," she replied, her voice lowering until Parker wasn't even certain he heard it—but with another guilty glance in his direction, she confirmed what he'd feared.

Miss Rosanna Leigh had rejected his suit and fobbed him off on her sister as a bit of charity.

Ice swept through him, far colder than anything winter could produce. Parker felt frozen in place and so brittle that even a slight touch would shatter him. And all the while, Miss Rosanna kept sending him sympathetic looks, but it was like placing a plaster on a gaping wound. She had rejected him and given his token of affection to another.

As there were no more words to offer Miss Leigh (and Parker didn't trust himself to speak), he gave a curt bow and strode away, not slowing as he fetched his things and disappeared into the night. The wind nipped, tugging at his hat, and Parker strode on. Entirely alone.

"Please listen, Prudence—"

She had enough sense not to shout back at Rosanna, but it was a near thing. Yanking free of her sister, Prudence poured her heart into her gaze as she glared at Rosanna; she didn't trust herself to speak, but her eyes declared her feelings clear enough.

Turning away, Prudence sought the door, looking up just long enough to find its location before staring determinedly at her toes. She didn't need to see the people staring or laughing.

There went the silly Prudence Leigh, who dared to think a man might choose her above her sister. Despite never having spoken to the gentleman above a few scant words, she believed him to have fallen madly in love with her from afar. Bewitched by her beauty.

Rosanna attempted to follow but either surrendered or was set upon by her pack of adoring gentlemen. Prudence didn't know. Nor did she care. She was simply grateful to be allowed to escape in peace, and she hurried down the stairs and quickly collected her things. Her dancing slippers weren't fit for walking home, but she couldn't remain there. Pulling her cloak around tight, she stepped out onto the doorstep and spied a figure hurrying off into the darkness.

Dr. Humphreys.

Prudence's cheeks burned brighter. Despite her path lying in the same direction, she turned away and chose a circuitous route. Thankfully, Whitley Court was not far from here, so even doubling the distance was not so great a burden. Especially as it allowed her to avoid that man.

As her path drew her away from the house's lanterns, darkness wrapped around her. Glancing up at the sky, Prudence found a wall of black. It was vast and unyielding, swallowing up the light of the stars and moon and leaving the world beneath shrouded in shadow. It was a good thing she knew the path well, or she might find herself lost.

Though at that moment, Prudence couldn't say it truly was a good thing. Arriving home meant facing the world. Soon, Mama would return and demand to know all the details of what had happened. Then the tsking and hand-wringing as the lady fretted over her daughter's dim future.

A spinster. What other path was there for one such as Prudence Leigh? The weight of that thought pressed down on her, and her footsteps felt heavy along the lane. It was as though the very air around her echoed with the truth. With no beauty or dowry of note, Miss Prudence was good for nothing. For all her virtues and abilities, a man would rather have an ornament like Rosanna than a workhorse like Prudence.

Perhaps she could fool herself for a time and say outward appearances meant little, but it was impossible to hold onto that lie when the world reiterated the truth again and again. It was ingrained in their greetings, which always included superficial praise surrounding one's gown, coiffure, or appearance. And outward changes were always the first to be complimented or commented upon after a long separation.

Even when people meant well and claimed all women were beautiful in their own right, it reinforced the fact that attraction was paramount. No one ever said all women were amusing, delightful company, creative, caring, or wise. No, they were all aesthetically pleasing. If looks didn't matter, then the message would simply be that some are average, some are not, but it mattered not one jot either way.

Why else would they fixate on that message if outward appearances were unimportant?

"Isn't your sister divine?" Prudence had heard variations of that question her entire life. Beyond charisma and lovely features, Rosanna boasted little talent. Yet people praised and petted her, as though she were an angel from on high. The beautiful Leigh girl.

Plain Prudence Leigh, for all her skills and usefulness, was not worth noting.

Chapter 16

Casting aside her cloak, Rosanna hurried up the stairs. Mama called after her, but there was no good to be had in continuing that conversation, and if Rosanna didn't hurry to their bedchamber first, Mama might take the prerogative to check on Prudence. At best, the lady would wring her hands over her daughter's lost prospect. At worst, she would spend the time alternating between pitying Prudence, for her deficiencies, and herself, for struggling to find her eldest a proper husband.

When Rosanna reached their bedchamber, she paused and gathered herself before inching open the door. The maid had stoked the fire recently, which was good, as there were no candles lit. Though it was difficult to see in the darkness, Rosanna thought she spied Prudence curled up in bed.

Thank the heavens. With a sigh, she carefully shut the door behind her. She would need to call Jane to help Prudence out of her gown, but if they worked quietly, there was no reason to disturb her sister's slumber. As much as there were things that needed saying, it was better done in the light of day, after a good night's rest.

Creeping towards her dressing table, Rosanna reached into her hair, feeling for the pins that were holding her locks aloft.

"You needn't sneak about on my account."

Prudence's voice jolted Rosanna, and she whirled about, her hands flying to her mouth to stifle the shriek. Pressing a hand to her chest, she tried to calm her racing heart.

"I didn't realize you were awake," she said, turning to the bed.

Prudence remained curled on her side, her eyes staring off into the fire. She said no more. Coming to the bed, Rosanna tried to sit beside her sister, but Prudence made no move to give her space. Her expression was empty, and it was as though Rosanna were staring at a ragdoll cast upon a child's bed.

Nudging aside her sister's foot, she sat on the edge of the mattress. "I am so sorry for what has happened."

Rosanna's heart cracked, and though she longed for the words to describe the pain, she was no wordsmith. Seeing her sister so listless and broken strengthened her torment until it throbbed through her. Reaching for Prudence's foot, she gave it a squeeze, which drew her sister's gaze to her, though her eyes were blank and unfeeling.

"I arrived home as quickly as I could," said Rosanna.

"I imagine it took some time to bid farewell to everyone." Her voice was as empty as her gaze. "You wouldn't want to leave unexpectedly and disappoint all your admirers."

Rosanna stiffened, though her sister didn't seem to notice. "Mama refused to call for the carriage."

Prudence huffed and turned away. "Yes, and I am certain you begged and pleaded with her to hurry home so you could sympathize with your poor spinster sister—who is so desperate for a husband that you must toss her your castoffs."

Throat tightening, Rosanna blinked back a sudden sheen of tears. Her eyes pricked, and she tried to keep herself from falling to pieces, but Prudence's blunt words struck her heart with blinding force.

"Please, Prudence. I hate it when you say such things about yourself," she whispered, and there was no more fighting the tears that slipped out and rolled down her cheeks.

Something in her sister's gaze shifted, as though her eyes truly focused on Rosanna for the first time since she'd arrived. Sitting up, Prudence leaned into her sister, and Rosanna drew her arms around her.

"I am sorry, Rosanna. It is unfair of me to speak to you in such a manner."

"Oh, I deserve many hard words," she murmured, leaning her head against Prudence's as they snuggled together. "Had I simply been brave enough to tell you the truth the moment I realized your mistake, I would've saved you a world of heartache. And for that, I am sorry."

Straightening, Rosanna met her sister's eyes. "I swear to you that I only allowed it to go on because I truly thought that something might come of it. Had I known what would happen, I would've never encouraged you."

Prudence drew in a sharp breath, and her chin trembled. "I—"

But her word broke, and her hand flew up, covering her mouth. Seeing her sister break eradicated the last of Rosanna's fortitude, and she joined in Prudence's tears. Holding her sister tight, Rosanna wished for something she could do to protect that poor, broken heart, but the damage had been done.

"He is a fool for not seeing that you are a prize," said Rosanna. "Heaven knows you are a far better person than I am."

Prudence sighed and pulled away, but before she could protest too strongly, Rosanna took her by the hands and squeezed them, forcing her sister to meet her eyes.

"You are so talented, Prudence. You play the piano and sing beautifully. Your paintings and drawings are superior to most. You read all sorts of books—and more importantly, you understand the massive things. You balance the accounts, oversee the servants, manage Mama and Papa with little trouble, teach Benjamin and the girls their lessons, and do all sorts of things. I have spent my life watching you tackle new tasks with ease, mastering them with far more speed and ability than most."

"And it all means nothing because I am homely," replied Prudence with a huff.

"Don't you dare say that!" Rosanna's lungs heaved, and she struggled to keep her tears at bay to get out the words. "I shan't allow you to speak about my sister in such a manner. You are not homely! And I may be pretty, what of it? I long to be useful, but I can never match your skills. Do not denigrate what you have to offer the world, Prudence. I would give up every ounce of my beauty and admiration to be so blessed."

Giving a watery scoff, Prudence accepted her sister's embrace once more, leaning her head against Rosanna's shoulder. The sound made it clear that she gave Rosanna's words little weight, but then, Prudence didn't understand just how true they were. An ornament was pretty, but who wished to be one?

Before those thoughts took hold of Rosanna, Prudence gave another shuddering breath as she fought against her tears. Leaning her cheek against the top of Prudence's head, she held her sister tight.

"I am sorry he is a fool, and I am sorry that I added to your heartache. I am sorry," she whispered again and again, and never had Rosanna meant her words so much. She only prayed Prudence believed them.

...

With the fire banked, the embers were hidden from view, leaving the bedchamber shrouded in darkness. Only the faint hint of orange flickering from beneath the ashes gave any sign that the flames still smoldered, ready for the servants to revive them once more come morning. A faint line of light along the edge of the curtain warned that the house would soon be stirring, but Prudence prayed the night would linger on.

Silent tears wet her pillow, and she fought against her jagged breaths, which threatened to rouse Rosanna once more.

How much the world had altered in only a few short hours. And now, Prudence was staring into the dark, wondering what this day would bring. Mama would not allow the subject to be dropped, of that Prudence was certain. No doubt the lady wanted to comb through the details, picking apart the death of Prudence's fleeting romance like a carrion bird. The rest of her siblings didn't know what had passed (though they were bound to ascertain that from Mama's lamenting). Papa wouldn't care, except to make a passing comment or two about a missed opportunity.

Prudence hadn't often thought her solitary state an enviable one, but had she been in Rosanna's shoes, there would be endless calls from friends to offer condolences, which would only serve to open the wounds again and again. That she needn't suffer that public humiliation was something of a blessing.

Of course, had Prudence been in Rosanna's shoes, this wouldn't have happened in the first place.

Pulling her thoughts to a halt, she considered that. There were too many variables in life to know for certain what would or wouldn't happen, but of this much Prudence was certain: she did not want to haul this pain around with her.

Contentment was not a simple thing to achieve, and happiness was even more difficult. Melancholy was easy, for life presented plenty of reasons to be miserable. Simply allow the wound to fester until the hope of healing was gone, and wallow in the pain.

But a single thought took hold of her heart, growing in strength and ferocity as the hours ticked away—Prudence didn't want that life.

She was no young miss anymore, allowing herself to drown in such self-deprecation. She had navigated those waters long ago and arrived on the other side a little wet and worn, to be certain, but she'd made her way through the storm. It had been so long since she'd had to guard against such moments that she'd almost missed the signs as the winds began to blow.

But the lifeline guiding her ashore was an old friend, and she clung to it now.

Looking within, Prudence dredged her thoughts for all those things she adored about herself. They came slowly at first, but as she laid hold of each and held it close, more came on its heels. She was talented. Intelligent. And though it was easy to overlook being capable, she knew her family wouldn't survive without her assistance; their finances would be overturned in a trice, and they'd be ruined if not for her. That was no small thing.

Prudence Leigh was a fine woman regardless of whether or not anyone else recognized it. She knew her worth and would not allow herself to set one more toe into those stormed-tossed seas.

Her heart rested heavy in her chest as she considered just how readily she'd handed her sense of self to another. True confidence was not some house of cards, toppled by the slightest breeze, and she had allowed her foundation of stone and iron to crumble simply because a man proved false.

It took far more time than she liked to admit before she could breathe easily again, but she did. Despite the uncertainty of what the future would bring, Prudence knew her place in the world. Better still, she accepted it.

Her sphere of influence may be small, but those within it were better with her than they were without her. Her life had value because she gave it meaning and purpose, rather than relying on the praise others gave her. Not everyone could be beautiful and vivacious, but that did not mean her offerings to the world were worthless.

And she would not allow anyone—not even herself—to make her doubt it ever again.

Chapter 17

Even as a child, too much of Prudence's time had been spent "managing" (as Rosanna put it) her mother and father. The older she grew, the fewer hours she had to devote to her pastimes. But there were moments when playing or drawing was not merely something pleasant to do but a necessity.

Assuming she could get Katherine to surrender the piano long enough.

Thankfully, the stars had aligned to allow Prudence a moment of peace today. The world around her faded to nothing as she lost herself in the world John Field created. Though Mama despised the Irish musician (for she did not comprehend how such a backward country could produce anyone of true brilliance), Prudence adored his work.

The notes tripped along in a delicate fashion, conveying far more emotion and spirit than the work of Hummel or Mozart. The music flowed from her heart into her fingers, filling the air with sounds that reminded her of brilliant summer days spent sitting amongst fields of wildflowers while the breeze made the grass bob up and down. Or a forest creek winding its way over rocks and under fallen trees. It spoke of simple things.

How she longed to hear the sonata performed with the entire orchestra. Having worked on it for some months, she knew the piano part, but Prudence had never heard it with the full orchestra playing alongside. She could only imagine what it would sound like all together.

The final note lingered in the air, and she longed to remain in that very moment with the music filling her soul. It was as though she were apart from the world, in a realm of light and love.

Applause shattered the illusion, thrusting her back into reality, and Prudence turned on her bench to see Benjamin bouncing on his toes, clapping.

"Brava," said Mama with a smile, before turning back to her youngest and holding up a toy soldier that looked newer than the rest. Prudence stopped herself from asking about the addition to his troops, for there was no good in voicing a question she knew the answer to, and she was in no mood to argue with Mama over the expense. Benjamin's army was large enough to take France.

"Oh, you are a capital general, my dear boy," said Mama as he stomped on the soldiers; thankfully the bits of metal were sturdy enough to take the abuse. Casting a glance at Prudence, she smiled. "He truly is the most brilliant of children, don't you think?"

Prudence had no response to that, so she turned back to her music. Running her fingers across the keys, she wondered if she ought to begin learning a new piece, but with the magic of the moment broken, it was unlikely she would recapture it.

"You know, you really ought to spend more time instructing Katherine," said Mama. "The poor girl tries so very hard to match your skill, but she doesn't have your talent."

A shift of skirts drew the room's attention to the young lady in question, who sat at the far side of the parlor, hugging her book to her chest. Prudence tried to send her sister a sympathetic look, but Katherine did not look up from her lap.

That was when Prudence finally noticed just how many of her family had joined her here. Yes, the parlor was the center of the home and often at least one or two of them could be found there, but today everyone except Papa and Rosanna had invaded Prudence's musical escape.

With a sigh, she gave a forlorn look at the piano. Her respite was over.

"Don't be missish, Katherine," said Mama with a shake of her head. "It does no good to inflate one's ego. Better to be honest about one's ability, and yours is middling at best. Perhaps with Prudence's assistance you might be something more than that."

Mama snatched up a biscuit from a plate on the table beside her and handed it to her son with more declarations about his prodigious abilities on the battlefield. Sitting in the armchair beside her mother, Francis reached for one, but Mama frowned.

"No man wants a portly wife, dearest. You poor girls have far too many obstacles before you. It's best not to add to them." For once, the lady refrained from speaking every thought in her head, but Prudence heard the implication clear enough. Mama glanced at her eldest daughter. Fidgeting with her skirts, the lady shifted in her seat.

Prudence turned to the piano and gathered her sheet music, tucking it firmly into the portfolio where she kept all the loose pages. She felt her mother's attention on her, and she moved quicker, closing up the instrument before standing to leave. But she was not quick enough.

"It is a tragedy," said Mama with a heavy sigh. "Dr. Humphreys seemed so keen. It would've been such a blessing to have secured a match for you. I suppose there is little hope now."

Those final words had been a common refrain over the past several days, and Prudence still didn't know if the hope Mama referred to concerned Dr. Humphreys particularly or Prudence's marriage prospects as a whole. Only a fool would ask such a question when she wasn't certain what the answer would be. Prudence moved towards the door (attempting to both hurry and not draw attention to the fact that she was doing so), but she was not quick enough to avoid the forthcoming comment.

"I blame myself, of course," said Mama with a heavy sigh.

Pausing at the threshold, Prudence stared at the hall and the escape it presented, but as much as she longed to take it, she turned back around and faced her doom. "That is ludicrous, Mama."

But the lady was shaking her head before Prudence had finished speaking.

"Who else should hold the blame but I?" Mama's brows knitted together, her eyes filling with such anguish as she rose and swept her daughter into her embrace. Her words trembled, and Prudence closed her eyes, praying for strength. "It was I who encouraged you to think the letter was for you."

"Everyone holds a little blame, Mama. It is ridiculous to claim the whole of it." Prudence led her mother back to her seat, but the lady remained standing.

"I shouldn't have pressed the issue. I shall never forgive myself for that." The last of her words were broken by a delicate tremble of her voice, and Mama patted her daughter on the cheeks. With a wistful frown, she added, "I prayed so hard you would grow into your looks, and that hasn't happened. I just wanted to believe that a gentleman had finally taken notice of you. I cannot bear the thought of you becoming a spinster. There is nothing worse in life, and I do not want it for you."

Prudence refrained from shoving Mama back into her chair, and thankfully, the lady sat down herself—though not before snatching her daughter's hand. With a few more words, she mourned the loss of Dr. Humphreys and Prudence's impending doom. But most importantly, her own failures.

For all that Prudence had ample experience managing Mama's moods, it required more emotional fortitude than she possessed at present. She couldn't spend one more moment listening to Mama's empty expressions of sorrow over her shortcomings as a mother that rarely acknowledged guilt over the proper things or in the proper manner.

"Mama, please. I must get to my work," she said, tugging her hand free.

"Of course," she said, dabbing at her eyes with a lacy confection of a handkerchief. "You are such a good girl. Always taking care of your dear family. You would make such a good wife."

But before Mama could start down that path once more, Prudence turned her attention to Benjamin, drawing their mother's gaze to the battle commencing around her feet.

"Oh, that is a brilliant move, Benjamin," Mama said with a smile.

Prudence moved to the door once more, hoping for an escape, but before she was two steps towards it, Katherine appeared before her, blocking her path. At times, it was difficult to recall that her younger sister was a grown woman with nineteen years to her credit, but at present, the young lady stood before Prudence with a rigid spine and a commanding look, as though facing down an enemy.

Pushing her spectacles up her nose, she opened her mouth to speak, but Mama frowned.

"If you insist on wearing those wretched things, do not play with them. You are not a child."

Katherine's brow furrowed, a sour look pulling down her features. Sparing her mother only a passing glance, she stepped closer and whispered to Prudence, "Would you please accompany me into town? I would like to purchase some new sheet music, but I haven't your eye for it."

Prudence resisted the urge to pinch her nose, though it was a near thing. "I would love to any other day, but I fear my schedule is full."

"Then tomorrow?"

The firm set of Katherine's jaw told Prudence that her sister wouldn't be cast aside. "Perhaps we might discuss it next week."

"But—"

"Katherine, please. I do wish to help you, but not at this very moment." And with that, Prudence moved to the door once more, only to stop at the sound of Grandmama's sharp voice. Glancing over her shoulder, she spied Mama handing yet another sweet to Benjamin.

"You are spoiling the boy, Gertrude," said Grandmama Cora, without looking up from her book.

"Nonsense," said Mama, stiffening at the disapproving tone. "Benjamin deserves sweeties."

"And when he grows as portly as you fear Francis will be?" replied her mother-in-law.

Mama scowled, and Prudence sighed, waiting for yet another disagreement to arise between the two ladies. Would she be forced to spend her afternoon negotiating peace? But thankfully, Mama's vanity came to the rescue, and she considered the boy, who munched away on his treats while destroying the opposing forces.

This battle was naught but one in the war between the two ladies, and there was no ground to be gained from wading into the fray, so Prudence took the opportunity the distraction presented and hurried to the door. But just before her hand touched the doorknob, it swung open, and she found herself toe to toe with Papa.

Chapter 18

"Just the person I was looking for," said Papa, but when he spied the hubbub behind Prudence, he stepped around her and swooped into the parlor with a bellowing call of, "Benjamin, my boy!"

"Papa!" The child threw himself at his father, latching onto his leg like a monkey. And soon, Papa was marching about with Benjamin laughing as he bounced along on the top of his father's foot.

Standing there as her father lavished attention on his son, Prudence tucked her hands behind her and thought through her list of tasks for the day. Her excuse to Katherine had not been fabricated, and she had dawdled at the piano for far too long already.

Only after Benjamin was well and truly riled did Papa stand and sweep Prudence out of the parlor without sparing a glance at his wife or the rest of his family. Guiding her through the house, he gave no hint of what this business was about until they were tucked in his study, the door firmly shut behind them.

"I need to speak with you concerning Dr. Humphreys," said Papa, motioning for her to sit as he rounded his desk. Prudence froze in place like a statue for a heartbeat before she sank onto the chair.

"There is nothing to discuss. I am not happy about what has happened, but I hold no ill will towards him—"

"Not that. Though I was quite unhappy to hear of that trouble." Papa paused and straightened with a frown. "Ought I to speak to the young man about that letter business?"

"Gracious, no." Prudence kept from shouting it. Thankfully, her father seemed as pleased with her answer as she was when he abandoned that notion.

"It's about that fellow and your sister."

As Prudence was already quite rigid in her seat, there was no way for her to straighten even further, though she felt that statement thrum through her, forcing every muscle to attention. "What of them?"

Papa leaned on his elbows. "Do not pretend you haven't noticed."

"I assure you, I am in earnest. After Rosanna rejected his suit, and with his behavior of late, I would think there is nothing between them."

"I do hope so," he said, leaning back into his chair and resting a hand against the arm, drumming his fingers against the wood. "However, I fear something is brewing."

Prudence's hands twisted in her lap, and she rubbed at her chilled fingers. "Rosanna already made her feelings concerning Dr. Humphreys clear when she rejected his suit."

"Their behavior during the Breadmores' party was remarked upon. It's a miracle Mr. Courtney hasn't noticed. Or perhaps he appreciates a bit of competition," added Papa with a furrowed brow. "Wealthy men are a silly lot and are as ready to double their efforts to win a lady someone else wishes to claim as they are to toss her aside when no one pays her any mind."

A familiar timbre filled Papa's tone, and Prudence held back a sigh as the gentleman allowed his thoughts to wander back to his youthful follies and the path it had set him on. Unfortunately, the silence that followed allowed Prudence's thoughts to drift to the question at hand.

Was Rosanna setting her cap at Dr. Humphreys? Gossip was too fickle a thing for Prudence to trust it, but that she couldn't immediately dismiss Papa's assertion spoke volumes. Hadn't she marked some strange partiality between them? Or rather on Rosanna's part, as Dr. Humphreys' was well-documented.

Swallowing to clear her throat, she forced the conversation forward, dragging her father from his thoughts. "I doubt it, Papa, but even if it were true, what would you do about it? Rosanna is not one to be dissuaded once she has set her mind to something. If you push her, she will cling harder to him."

"My thoughts exactly, Prudence. Which is why I need you to distract them."

Silence lingered after that pronouncement, and Prudence stared at her father, uncertain if she was understanding his clear, comprehensible English.

"Pardon?"

Papa waved a vague hand about. "Keep a close watch on them. Do what you can to ensure they are never alone. If you see Rosanna speaking with him, insert yourself into their conversation. Distract Dr. Humphreys with those medical conversations you both enjoyed so much. Rosanna will be bored to tears or revolted. Then turn her attention to Mr. Courtney. He's a far better husband for her than that physician."

The air in her lungs froze, and Prudence struggled for breath. "You cannot be serious."

"And you cannot be so naive," he replied with a frown. "Besides Benjamin, Rosanna is our only asset. She has the beauty and manners to catch herself someone far better than a lowly physician. Frankly, Mr. Courtney is not good enough for her: Rosanna could land herself a nobleman if given the opportunity."

Prudence's eyes darted to the ground, and her jaw tightened until her teeth ached. "We do not need nobility, Papa. We need economy. Mama spends more on tea than all the servants' salaries combined. You insist on wax candles when tallow would do just fine—"

"The odor is atrocious, my dear!" replied Papa with the sort of horror reserved for scandalous elopements or deaths in duels. "Do you have any idea how unbearable it is to sit in my chair, reading by the light of tallow candles? The light is poor and within an hour, I reek like an abattoir! I indulge in that one luxury—"

"What about your library?" asked Prudence, gesturing to the fortune lining the walls. Once she had attempted to tally all the money tied up in these books, but she'd given up when the figure doubled Mama's tea bills. Lending libraries could easily keep her father in books at little expense, but he was forever adding to his private collection.

"A man must have an occupation, and improving my mind is mine."

Prudence hid a wince, but there was no point in bemoaning her rash tongue. It had been a misstep to mention the books, for they were his pride and joy. It was said that actions spoke louder than words, and Prudence knew better than to examine too closely how easily Papa spent money on his library whilst bemoaning his inability to provide for his family.

But she refused to retreat now that the subject of money had been broached.

"How about the fact that we regularly dine as though we are hosting the elite of Greater Edgerton?"

Papa gaped. "Would you have us starve?"

"We needn't dine like kings every night," she replied. "And you never say no to Mama and the girls when they ask for more money for frocks and shoes and frippery. Thankfully Katherine and I do not care for such things, or we would be beggared!"

Leaning forward in her chair, Prudence held her father's gaze. "We are not paupers, Papa. You and Mama needn't speak as though we are. If we employed a little economy, Papa, we could provide fine dowries for Katherine and Francis."

She knew better than to include the elder Leigh daughters.

Neither Rosanna nor Prudence had any need for that, though for entirely different reasons. If she had not been able to entice a beau with mediocre looks, she had no interest in luring in gentlemen who only wanted a wife for her dowry.

But Papa scoffed and shook his head. "You know better than to rein in your mother and sisters. They shan't be curtailed with their fashions and frivolities. Besides, if God wished me to economize, he wouldn't have given me Benjamin. Once he is of age, we shall break the entail and provide for Katherine and Francis—"

"That is fourteen years from now, Papa. Katherine is out, and Francis will soon follow. Any assistance he might give them will be too late."

"Yet again, my dear, you show how little you understand the way the world works," he said with a patronizing smile. "Marriages are formed all the time based on the promise of funds to come through inheritances. This is no different. The entail will be broken, and then, you shall all have a windfall."

"By selling off bits and pieces of Whitley Court until there is nothing left."

Papa huffed and waved her away. "No more of your dire predictions, my dear. It won't take much to set everything to rights."

Though she couldn't remember her grandfather, Prudence knew the gentleman had been astute: entails were set in place to protect property from frivolous sons and grandsons. Bile churned in Prudence's stomach as she considered the future that might come for Whitley Court when Benjamin reached his majority and helped their father to break it.

Rising from his seat, Papa took Prudence by the hand and pulled her to her feet.

"Distract Dr. Humphreys and guide Rosanna towards Mr. Courtney. Then all will be set to rights in a snap," he said with a warm smile, as though the things he asked were naught but a trifle.

"She will choose who she chooses, and I am uneasy at the

thought of meddling with Rosanna's beaus."

Papa sighed and shook his head as though Prudence's objections were little more than an inconvenience. "I am suggesting this for her good, my dear. Do you believe Rosanna will be happy to live a life of economy? Her best chance of happiness is with a Mr. Courtney—not a Dr. Humphreys. If you care for her well-being, you would do best to step between her and disaster. It shouldn't take much to distract her from this flight of fancy."

Prudence tried to swallow, but her throat clamped shut. Her heart rebelled at admitting the whole truth, but as Papa refused to be swayed in any other way, she allowed the words to flow.

"I do not think I can face him, Papa," she said with a shake of her head. "I would be very happy never to see Dr. Humphreys again, let alone speak to him. I cannot bear the thought. Please—"

"Now, don't be missish, Prudence," he said, leading her towards the door. "For all that you speak of us sacrificing our little pleasures, you refuse to make yourself uncomfortable to secure your sister's and your entire family's future."

The air fled her lungs once more, leaving Prudence unable to speak as her father led her away and deposited her at the study door.

"Hush, my dear. This is for the best. There is no need for us to bother with tallow and tea and all the like. We each have a role to play in the family, and at this moment, I need you to help your sister fulfill hers. There's a good girl."

Papa beamed at her, looking at his eldest as though she were the single bright thing in this dark world. "The Chorleys' shooting party is this afternoon. Rosanna and Mr. Courtney are to attend, along with half of Greater Edgerton. You must go as well and ensure that if Dr. Humphreys attends, he'll be too occupied to notice Rosanna."

Then he closed the door, leaving her standing in the hallway. And with all the bits of that broken heart, Prudence prayed Dr. Humphreys would not be there.

Chapter 19

Whenever people praised autumn, they described the foliage, the crisp air, or the sport to be found in it, but to Parker, it was the worst season. People often complained about the fickle and finite nature of weather, and never was that more relevant than in the autumn. One day it was hot. The next cold. Frost arrived in the morning and melted away by afternoon. One had to prepare for everything from a balmy summer's day to a frosty winter wind.

And though the changing colors were lovely for a time, it was a season of death and decay, which was far too morose for his liking. The green world faded to brown, and then one was left with the bare trees and ground, praying that snow would soon arrive to cover the scenery in something more appealing than mud.

To say nothing of the fact that autumn was bursting with activity. Social calendars were filled with parties and gatherings galore, never easing until the harvest time was well and truly over. As though preparing for the long stretch of winter months, in which the snow made it difficult to pay calls and host parties, society threw itself into celebrating autumn with far more fanfare than the season deserved.

Parker might enjoy all the festivities if not for the fact that the unpredictable weather meant an increase in chills and fevers, which meant house calls morning, noon, and night.

And a physician was as much a politician as he was a purveyor of tonics and tisanes. The wealthy of Greater Edgerton had a few physicians from which to choose, and gatherings were paramount to maintaining his income. A little flattery and a few well-placed conversations, and he might gain the most coveted of all patients—the wealthy hypochondriac, who viewed visits with his physician and taking medicines as a hobby.

There was nothing finer than having one or two amongst his patients, for they sent for the doctor far more often than was required, leaving little for him to do during such visits but share a cup of tea and alleviate fears that the imagined spot was the black plague or smallpox.

It may sound a bit mercenary to anyone outside the profession, but Parker knew too well how easily such people were manipulated by unscrupulous physicians and apothecaries. He'd "treated" far too many who were truly made ill by others, and Parker never gave them medicines they didn't need nor fed their delusions.

As such calls made the patient happier and the physician richer, it was a mutually beneficial arrangement.

Unfortunately, it meant Parker had to attend these wretched functions, even when he'd rather be anywhere else. Which was how he found himself tramping about the woods, pretending to stalk pheasant or grouse or whatever blasted bird he was supposed to be hunting. With his rifle pointed to the ground, he trudged through the undergrowth and wondered what the likelihood was that any living creature was still nestled in this wood.

Guns blasted around him, and the forest rang with cheers as various groups brought down the birds in flight. Parker hardly noted the movement around him, focusing on placing his feet so he didn't end up face-first in the mucky leaves. With each squishing step, he cursed himself for having come here.

This was such a ridiculous venture. He would've been better served staying at home; skulking around by himself wasn't growing his list of patients, and he wasn't in the mood for socializing.

Of course, it might help matters if Parker admitted that his coin purse had nothing to do with his accepting the Chorleys' invitation. Miss Rosanna had been his only consideration, and he couldn't risk offending his hosts by canceling now that the truth of that wretched letter had come out. Even if his future with that young lady was as dead as the poor game birds falling around him.

At least he had the hunting to keep him occupied. If this had been a ball or a card party, Parker would've been forced to see the Leigh sisters from afar and stew in his regrets and shame. Here, he could do so in relative privacy.

A crack of a twig had him turning in place, though he kept his rifle lowered as his eyes sought the culprit. And a good thing, too, for Miss Rosanna stood there, looking like a mirage conjured from his fantasies.

"I am no ptarmigan," she said with a laugh.

Was that what they were hunting? Cocking the gun open, he removed the shells and placed them in his pocket with the other unspent rounds. Parker nodded, though he had no idea what he might say to her.

"I am surprised you came, sir."

Parker frowned and forced himself to look at her long enough to see whether a sour expression accompanied that statement, but she looked at ease. Like the other ladies, she was dressed in fashions that were a tad ridiculous in the forest but entirely appealing to the creatures the ladies hunted. The green pelisse suited her eyes, bringing out the faint hue, and of course, it suited her light curls to perfection.

"We do travel in many of the same circles, Miss Rosanna. You may not have noticed me, but I was well aware of you." Parker forced himself not to cringe at that; nothing like making himself look like a desperate fool to cement his place as the worst beau in the history of courtship.

Miss Rosanna ducked under a low-hanging branch and around a thick tuft of grass, and when her foot wobbled, Parker was there to steady her before he realized he had moved.

"Thank you, sir," she said with a bright smile. "I feel I should apologize for not having noticed you sooner. I suppose it is often the case that one does not notice something until it's brought to one's attention, and then one cannot help but see it everywhere."

Once she was on solid ground again, Parker released her and nodded, stepping away. "That is not uncommon."

The words were sour in his mouth, for he hated the thought that he had gone so unnoticed by her. Parker supposed it was the curse of the overeager beau. Such a man always hoped the lady in question noticed him in any fashion and always dreaded the thought that she didn't.

"I am glad to have a moment to speak with you, sir."

Parker's gaze jerked upward and found her smiling at him. "Concerning?"

Miss Rosanna blushed, ducking her head away as she turned towards a path that cut through the thicket. "Would you join me on a stroll? I hate to interrupt your sport—"

"Not at all," he said, draping the gun over his left arm and following after her. Miss Rosanna stumbled again, and he drew up next to her and offered his free arm. Then tried to crush the happy flutter in his heart when she took it so readily.

"I owe you an apology," she whispered.

Though Parker pretended to focus on the path ahead, his attention was fixed on her. He felt he ought to say something, though he didn't know what. For a moment they wandered along in silence, following the path aimlessly. Parker had thought they were deep in the forest, yet it wasn't long before the sounds of lawn games, clinking china, and laughter caught his ears. A flash of lawn between the trees testified that the others were just beyond a thin wall of woods.

A dainty furrow pulled at her brow. "You wrote me that lovely letter, and I cast it aside because of my pride."

Parker opened his mouth to respond to that, and she squeezed his arm and hurried to add, "It isn't that I thought myself so very high above you..."

Miss Rosanna's cheeks pinked, and she dropped her gaze to her boots. "I suppose I did. But the truth was that I didn't know you. I didn't realize how earnest you were. I often receive empty tokens from men who only want someone pretty on their arm like some matrimonial prize."

Those words sparked a flame in his heart, the old longing springing to life as though it had never died. Parker refused to let it take hold, but he couldn't help but hope that her words indicated something significant. Surely expressing regret over her dismissal of him was a good sign, wasn't it?

"You are a prize," he said, forcing his thoughts back to the conversation at hand. "But that is not the reason I wished to court you."

Pulling him to a stop, Miss Rosanna faced him. "You are always so kind to me. Why?"

Parker's brows rose. "Ought I to be unkind?"

"Certainly not, but you seem so certain that I..." She sighed and turned her gaze to the surrounding wood, not seeing the trees or golden foliage falling around them. "You have such faith in me, and I do not know what I have done to deserve it."

"Any man who doesn't make you feel as though you are the finest of ladies doesn't deserve you."

She huffed and smirked before turning back down their chosen path. "Gentlemen are quick to say such things. I am beautiful, lovely, and—"

"You are so much more than that."

Chapter 20

With her at his side, Parker tried to focus on the scenery and not the words that hovered just beneath the surface. "What I've told you in the past is true, Miss Rosanna. You are no mere ornament. You are kind and generous to your family and friends. Though everyone pets and praises you to no end, you are not the spoiled princess you could be."

"Believe me, Dr. Humphreys, I am spoiled enough."

Parker's lips quirked up in the corner. "And you are humble enough to admit that. If you wish to be more than a man's trophy, you can choose to be so, Miss Rosanna. Do not settle for anything less."

Pulling him to a stop once more, Miss Rosanna faced him down yet again, her brows knitted together as she held his gaze. "Other than my sister, you may be the only person who sees anything beyond my surface. You almost make me feel as though I am as good, kind, and wise as you seem to believe me to be."

Parker stared into her eyes, thinking about how many times he'd longed for just such a moment with her. Of course, in those instances, Miss Rosanna hadn't tossed aside his love letter without a second thought. But could he blame her for assuming his motives were as vain and frivolous as all the other gentlemen who vied for a prize rather than prizing the lady she was?

Ought he to say something that might press his suit? At any other time, he would've taken hold of her hand and pressed a kiss to her knuckles, or asked if she would go on a drive with him. Parker didn't own a carriage, but that didn't matter; surely he could pilfer his family's gig.

But her sister's spirit hung between them, and Parker didn't know how to proceed.

Before he could think to say anything, Miss Rosanna stiffened, her lovely eyes blinking rapidly as she shook her head, which made the golden curls bounce. "And see what a goose I am? I came here to apologize to you for abusing your heart so, and all I've done is speak of myself. That is unpardonable."

"None of us are perfect, Miss Rosanna. Even you," he replied with a grin.

"True, but you speak as though I am an angel among men when I am anything but." And before Parker could question that assertion, she bit down on her perfectly pink lip and frowned. "I am vain."

"I have met many vain people in my life, and I assure you, Miss Rosanna, even if you did tend towards that shortcoming, it is not to a large degree."

The young lady shook her head again and sighed. "Only because I am so very good at hiding it. I am so petted and praised that it is difficult to keep one's pride from puffing into some great, hulking thing."

Parker motioned for them to continue their walk through the woods, and she followed the prompt, though her gaze remained unfocused as she stared at the golden foliage surrounding them.

"Did you know that I paint?" she asked.

"I haven't had the pleasure of seeing—"

"It is no pleasure."

Parker huffed. "I highly doubt that."

"Monsieur Blanchet would disagree, as would anyone with a modicum of artistic talent."

Then, before he could ask who that philistine was, Miss Rosanna continued, "A few years ago, the Downings hosted an artist in residence for a short time. They claimed it was for him to refine their daughters' skills, but everyone knew it was a show of status and wealth. They always were desperate to elevate themselves."

Waving that addition away, the lady returned to the original point at hand. "They hosted a large showing in which they invited all the young ladies to submit work to be displayed. I chose a little watercolor landscape, and I was so very proud of it. The young ladies were to stand by their pieces so that people could question them concerning the subject and techniques, and I spent the evening being praised to the skies. Judging from the comments, it was easy to think that mine was far greater than even Monsieur Blanchet's."

Miss Rosanna sighed, her shoulders dropping. "Then the man of the hour arrived. He gave me a few trite words that were hardly complimentary, and I ought to have left it be, but I pressed him, wishing for the same admiration I had seen on everyone else's faces that night."

"And he did so, and the evening was a grand success," interjected Parker with a wry tone. The jest slipped out before he could think better of it, and he had only a heartbeat to worry about its reception before Miss Rosanna turned her gaze to him and met that with a silent laugh in her eyes.

"Certainly. He prostrated himself before my artistic offering," she replied in a voice that matched Parker's. Then, with another sigh, she shook her head and turned her eyes back to the path ahead. "He said that my subject was insipid and, though I captured it with some ability, I had no true talent."

"That seems unnecessary—"

"Do not judge him too harshly, Dr. Humphreys. He was baited into speaking bluntly, for I refused to accept his gentler assessments. And he only said that which I knew in my heart," she said with a frown. "For all that people praised and honored my prodigious talent, I have eyes. And growing up with someone as talented as my sister, it's impossible to remain blind when my talents are always compared to hers."

Parker tucked his hands behind him, and he considered that. "That—"

"But that is not my greatest sin," she admitted with a wince. "The truth is that I haven't allowed myself to paint again. I deny myself something I enjoy, simply because my efforts are so pitiful. Some compliments were from people wishing to win my good opinion, but how many were from people secretly laughing at me? I cannot bear it. See what a vain fool I am?"

"I am not your confessor," he said, glancing at her from the corner of his eye, though she was far too preoccupied to notice. "You may think to scare me away by reciting all your shortcomings, but I assure you it will not. I do not expect you to be perfect: none of us are. What is important is whether or not we choose to do better today than we did yesterday."

Pulling him to a stop once more, the young lady watched him with wide eyes for a long moment. "You truly believe that?"

"I wouldn't say it if I didn't."

Another long pause as she studied him. "Your faith makes me truly believe I am capable of being so much more."

"I should hope so. For you are."

Ducking her head, Miss Rosanna huffed again. "And here I go, continuing to speak only of myself."

"You are far more interesting than I am," replied Parker.

Miss Rosanna laughed and swatted at his arm. "I doubt that. You seem exceptionally interesting, sir."

Parker glanced at the place she had touched, and he struggled to keep the confusion from his expression, but a question immediately sprung to his mind, crashing into his thoughts with the delicacy of a runaway horse. No matter how ridiculous it seemed, he couldn't cast it aside. Especially with Miss Rosanna looking up at him with such a sweet smile on her lips.

Was she flirting with him?

"Do you plan on attending the harvest festival?" she asked, her light eyes brightening.

"I usually attend with my twin sister, Eleanor, but as she married not long ago, I fear she's occupied with her new husband and has no time to traipse around the fairgrounds with her brother."

Miss Rosanna tucked her hands behind her and smiled sweetly at him. "I was hoping to attend as well, though I have not fixed a time. Or with whom I shall attend."

Parker blinked, his mouth drying as he considered the lady before him and the pretty picture she made. Surely she was not suggesting that he should ask her. The idea seemed ludicrous. Perhaps he wouldn't have thought twice about such a situation a few weeks ago, but now, it was akin to a miracle. And Parker's life did not feature many of those.

"Rosanna, there you are," called Miss Leigh.

Four simple words, yet everything inside Parker seized.

"I have been searching for you, high and low." Miss Leigh's tone was tight as she appeared at her sister's side, slipping her arm through Miss Rosanna's with a brittle smile. "Mr. Courtney has been asking after you."

And with that, the lady eviscerated the last of Parker's good mood. No matter how strong his fantasies, even he could not ignore the gaping divide between him and the wealthy Mr. Courtney.

Miss Rosanna cast him a sympathetic smile that helped to heal some of the damage done, but before she could speak, Miss Leigh hurried to add, "Mrs. Chorley assured me she had a mount Mr. Courtney could borrow for the day, and he is very interested in exploring a bit, and you are by far the best guide he could find for a ride."

Parker gave the lady a bow. "Miss Leigh—"

But a flush of pink in her cheeks had his sentence dying on his lips. Her gaze darted near him but never touched him directly, and Parker shifted in place, reaching for his cravat, though a good tug did nothing to ease the tightness there.

Parker cleared his throat. "Miss Leigh, I owe you—"

"Rosanna, please," she whispered, pulling at her sister's arm while studiously not looking at him.

But Miss Rosanna ignored her sister and turned to him. "I am hoping to gather a group of friends to attend the harvest festival. Would you be so good as to join us?"

Though he was aware of Miss Leigh watching him closely, Parker couldn't help but beam at the invitation. Miracle, indeed.

"I would be honored, Miss Rosanna."

The young lady beamed at him—him! And Parker's smile broadened.

Miss Rosanna's eyes danced with merriment, a blush stealing across her cheeks. "Wonderful—"

"Come," murmured Miss Leigh, tugging her sister away.

And with that, Miss Rosanna and her sister ventured down the path, and though Parker longed to follow after the two of them (for two vastly different reasons), he allowed them to retreat. No good would be had from pressing his suit too quickly with Miss Rosanna. Caution was required, but their conversation allowed his fretful heart to ease a little and embrace patience.

Miss Leigh, on the other hand, was a different kettle of fish. One that required a more direct solution.

Chapter 21

Dry leaves rustled as her skirts dragged over them, but despite the distance they placed between themselves and Dr. Humphreys, Rosanna's thoughts remained at his side. For all that the good doctor claimed her to be merely a maiden with feet of clay, she couldn't help but feel as though her failings were vast, indeed. For it was that very vanity that had allowed her to cast aside the fellow with little thought in the first place; how quickly she'd judged herself far better than the gentleman, rejecting his suit without giving him a proper chance.

Rosanna considered herself a happy person, more apt to view the world with a heart full of joy than so many of the realists in the world. But that dear organ was filled with something far more substantial at present. It was a sensation she'd never felt before. Strong yet tender, it swelled in her chest.

Dr. Humphreys' words played in her thoughts once more as Prudence tugged her along. His praise felt far more real than any she'd ever received before. More meaningful. Rosanna chanced a glance over her shoulder, and Dr. Humphreys held her gaze until they disappeared.

The forest thinned around them, and the canopy of trees opened into the lawn. In the distance, the ladies and some of the gentlemen entertained themselves with boules, battledore and shuttlecock, and any number of lawn games. Off to the side stretched blankets with picnics scattered across them, and though Rosanna thought the air too chilly for sitting about, she couldn't help but imagine enjoying a picnic basket with a certain gentleman.

"Were you flirting with Dr. Humphreys?" whispered Prudence. Though her sister did not look at her, the accompanying frown was too pronounced to miss even in profile.

"He is a good man, Prudence." Rosanna's lips turned downward to match her sister's as she considered all she knew about the gentleman. "I truly believe he is grieved by what has passed. He meant no harm."

"That has no bearing on my feelings at present."

Rosanna dug in her heels, forcing Prudence to a stop, and pulled her arm free. "Doesn't it? We were having a pleasant conversation, and you inserted yourself into the conversation and fairly dragged me away. I am upset about what happened between the two of you, but I truly do not think he is a villain."

"I am not angry with Dr. Humphreys—"

"Poppycock. You hardly looked at the man."

Prudence's lips pinched together, her rigid posture giving Rosanna's words credence. "Every time I do, I am reminded of my folly. So, yes. I do struggle being near him. But I am not angry with him, and that has no bearing on this. What are you doing with him and Mr. Courtney?"

Rosanna sucked in a sharp but silent breath, forcing herself to remain calm, despite Prudence's gaze boring into hers.

"And do not feign ignorance, Rosanna. I know your games too well. You cast Dr. Humphreys aside—"

"I misjudged him!"

"Whether or not you did is immaterial. Once more, you have several gentlemen all vying for your attention, and rather than choosing and cutting the others loose, you are toying with them all, and it is time for you to stop the games."

Rosanna gaped. "I do not toy with men. They chase me about, and I do not allow them to catch me. I have made no promises, so I am doing nothing wrong."

"Spare me your excuses! I have seen this too many times. Whether or not you choose to believe it is immaterial." Prudence paused, turning her back on her sister and taking a deep breath. For her part, Rosanna could only stare at her unflappable elder sister and gape at the outburst.

"That is unfair of you, Prudence—"

"Ah, here you are," called Mr. Courtney.

Never had Rosanna despised a man more than Mr. Courtney at that moment. The gentleman stepped around Prudence on the path and stopped before Rosanna, sweeping into a bow.

"I hope I am not interrupting," he said with a challenging grin that simply begged for a saucy retort.

"You are, Mr. Courtney," said Rosanna.

His expression only brightened further, and Rosanna's lips couldn't help but quirk up in response. But that flutter of humor died a quick death when her gaze drifted past Mr. Courtney to Prudence, who stood just behind him. Her dark eyes were half-lidded, watching Rosanna with what might be deemed a blank expression if not for the irritation emanating from her gaze.

And Rosanna couldn't help but notice that her instinctive reaction to Mr. Courtney strayed too close to the accusations Prudence had just leveled at her. Was she toying with him? It wasn't as though she knew Mr. Courtney enough to decide whether to keep him or turn him aside. How else was a lady to know without a bit of flirtation?

"Would you be so kind as to join me for a ride?"

"Who said I wished to ride today?" Rosanna gave him a narrowed look while sending a frown inward as those all too comfortable and teasing words emerged.

Mr. Courtney gave her a long perusal, his gaze lingering long as it swept over her. Rosanna couldn't help the flush of pink that stole across her cheeks; no woman could withstand such an appreciative perusal from such a fine specimen of manhood.

Then, drawing closer, Mr. Courtney held her gaze and murmured, “Again, Miss Rosanna, if you wish for me to believe your coquettishness, you ought to be more consistent with your objections.”

Rosanna arched her brow. “Meaning?”

“That you ought not to claim you do not wish to ride when you are wearing your riding habit,” he replied while his eyes sparked with mirth.

Lips pinched together, Rosanna tried to keep her chagrin from peeking through, though it was a lost cause. With one final attempt to salvage her pride, she added, “And since I am wearing my riding habit, that must mean I am desperate to ride out with you.”

Drawing nearer, he lowered his voice, and the warm tone skittered along her skin, drawing up gooseflesh. “It is clear in every half-hearted protest you give.”

“And you believe yourself to be subtle?” replied Rosanna with a lift of her chin.

“I never intended to be,” he replied, offering up his arm. “Ride with me.”

Rosanna would have far preferred that last statement to include more of a question than a command, but with Mr. Courtney’s warm appreciation still thrumming through her, she had no choice but to take the proffered limb. The pair walked through the crowd, arm-in-arm, and Mr. Courtney nodded at people as they passed, his posture all puffed up as he gazed upon the admiring throng with a superiority that only a fool would miss. He strutted along as he led her to where the horses awaited the riders.

Releasing her long enough to inspect the mount, Mr. Courtney ushered her towards a docile mare who looked more eager to graze than gallop.

“I thought you wished to go riding,” she said with raised brows. “My childhood pony had more spirit.”

That earned her another of his amused glances as he merely considered Rosanna. "You wish for a rousing romp, then?"

Goodness, he could make even the simplest statements sound wicked, and though Rosanna knew she ought not to encourage such roguish behavior, she couldn't help the skitter of anticipation that ran down her spine. His eyes alone could teach Rosanna a thing or two about flirtation, for she fought against the blush stealing across her cheeks. She would not preen from his admiration. She would not.

They stood there, silently considering each other for a long moment before he led her to a beast with far more spirit; the horse pranced in place, eager to be out exploring the fields around Greater Edgerton. With a single glance, Mr. Courtney asked if this mount met Rosanna's approval, and she lifted her chin and stepped forward, taking hold of the reins.

Before she could step towards the mounting block the grooms had brought for the ladies, Mr. Courtney took hold of her and lifted her into the saddle as though she weighed no more than a dried leaf. Settling her skirts with all the care of a lady's maid, Mr. Courtney held her gaze and winked.

Rosanna couldn't help the blush that time, though she covered it by shifting in her saddle and arranging the reins in her hands.

Mr. Courtney merely chuckled and stepped away, his gaze never leaving her. "If you are half so fine a rider as you are a dancer, I will be the envy of every man."

Smile faltering, she stared out at the green before them as her companion took his seat and led them from the gathering with the puffed-up vanity of a preening peacock. Had Mr. Courtney spoken those words even an hour ago, Rosanna might've felt a flutter of anticipation, but with Dr. Humphreys' compliments still warming her heart, she couldn't help but notice how shallow Mr. Courtney's were in comparison.

"And so, you wish to ride with me to make the other gentlemen jealous?" she replied, the words souring her tongue.

"What of it?" he replied with a laugh. "Are you saying you weren't speaking to that physician to rouse my jealousy? You should choose a better fellow next time if you truly wish to inspire envy."

Rosanna frowned. "Dr. Humphreys is a good man and does not deserve your scorn."

Mr. Courtney sobered, though his grin was far too close to a smirk to convey any true repentance. "No doubt he is a paragon."

Slanting another of his heated glances in her direction, Mr. Courtney smiled, sending a warm flush across her skin. "But then, I suspect you prefer a sinner over a saint."

Chapter 22

Miss Rosanna Leigh was no picture of perfection nor angel among men. Thankfully, that worked in Prudence's favor because the young lady was too busy with her own concerns to notice her sister inching away. Rosanna meant no harm, but that didn't lessen Prudence's discomfort when she manipulated men's affections, and Prudence didn't need to be party to it.

Making her way along the edge of the gathering, she searched for a refuge. The Chorleys had been kind enough to provide chairs for any who wished for a proper seat rather than lounging on the ground, and though Prudence appreciated that attention to detail and would far prefer availing herself of that comfort, they were arranged in a fashion that encouraged others to gather nearby.

She couldn't bear the thought of speaking to anyone at present.

At the farthest side sat a lonely and unoccupied blanket that was unfortunate enough to be in the shade. Though such a situation would be highly prized during the hot summer months, the autumnal picnickers hunted for any patch of sunshine they could find to keep themselves from being prematurely chilled. Whilst not the most comfortable location, it suited her needs perfectly.

With each step, her heart sank lower. When she dropped into her chosen seat, it was as though the weight pulled her down, dropping her with more force than intended. All the while, the image of Rosanna and Dr. Humphreys played through her mind.

Despite everything, the gentleman harbored feelings for her sister. Still.

When one was not blessed with outward attractions, one must compensate with a winning personality, and though Prudence never expected to outshine her sister, she had thought that her gifts (paltry though they may be) might give her some appeal to a gentleman. If one ever held still long enough to notice her.

Whether by his own doing or fate's cruel sense of humor, Dr. Humphreys had been forced into conversation with her. A pleasing one at that. Or at least, Prudence had thought it so. The subjects had been interesting, the debate was lively, and the thing as a whole had been quite engaging, flowing along with the sort of natural grace one found when both parties were equally invested.

Prudence hadn't imagined that.

Tucking her skirts around her, she tried to find a comfortable position, but she had never understood the appeal of sitting on the ground. One's legs were bound to fall asleep within a few minutes, and there was nothing against one's back to allow one to repose enough to relieve the pricks and tingles. But it served as a decent distraction from her thoughts. Unfortunately, the moment she settled once more, there was nothing else to divert her attention from that ever-present weight that rested in her heart.

Rosanna never wanted for friendship. Never wanted for praise. Never wanted for admiration. The world seemed a simple and joyous thing to her because it was. Shadows didn't dare taint Rosanna Leigh's sunny world, but they leached into Prudence's, darkening the day into a bleak and stormy thing.

Prudence worked hard to keep the household running, but Rosanna was the one they doted on. She had cast Dr. Humphreys aside, and still, he tripped all over himself to win her favor when she gave him the slightest encouragement despite having enjoyed Prudence's company. Her chest burned as she considered all the blessings that had been heaped upon Rosanna's head, giving everything to that blessed young lady whilst leaving nothing for her sister.

All those emotions swirled within Prudence, twisting and roiling about her insides, but she embraced the pain, for she deserved it. Rosanna was her sister, and Prudence loved her dearly. The young lady was imperfect, but she had a good heart and was well worth pursuing for more than merely outward attractions.

Was it any wonder that Rosanna was a tad entitled? Prudence did as much as she could to keep Benjamin from succumbing to their parents' adoration, and it was a miracle Rosanna was not swanning about the place when their parents had done everything to feed their dearest daughter's pride.

With a sigh, her shoulders drooped as she stared at the blanket. Her fingers traced the lined pattern of the cotton, and her eyes followed the movement, glad to have something to turn her attention to, however unimportant.

Gripping her cloak tight around her, she cursed her shortsightedness. Anyone with sense knew autumn weather was impossible to predict. Despite the sun blazing in the morning, the afternoon might turn chilly, yet Prudence had chosen a lighter covering that provided little warmth in the chill breeze. Of course, the shade didn't help matters.

With a shiver, she burrowed into her cloak and turned her attention to the goings-on of the picnic. It wasn't a useful diversion, but it was better than nothing. The Chorleys' party was best defined by a single word: chaos.

Games abounded with ladies and gentlemen rushing about in a gale of laughter that was far more boisterous than befitted such a pastime. Riders came and went, their horses snorting and pawing the ground as the poor creatures longed for something more than ambling sedately about the countryside. Hunters emerged from the forest, their dogs rushing around their masters with great birds lolling out their mouths. The truly lazy sat in chairs and on blankets, availing themselves of the plentiful (though uninspiring) food.

Perhaps she might send for the carriage, and leave the family to her merrymaking. Dropping her gaze once more to the blanket below her, Prudence sighed. Escape was impossible. And slipping once more into the dark recesses of her mind, she traced the pattern of the blanket beneath her.

"Pardon me, Miss Leigh—"

Prudence was jerked from her thoughts, her muscles tensing as her gaze snapped up to meet Dr. Humphreys. Standing just to one side, he avoided her eyes and cleared his throat.

"I apologize for intruding…" he began, shifting in place. "I didn't mean to startle you. I…"

With wide eyes, she watched as he hemmed and hawed, constantly moving his weight from one foot to the other.

Then, lifting his arm, he offered up a blanket. "You looked chilled, and I asked Mrs. Chorley if she had an extra one lying about." With a shrug, he added, "I didn't want you to catch cold."

Prudence stared at the blanket and then at the gentleman once more before taking it from his hands and wrapping it about her shoulders. Though thin, it was heavy enough to stave off the breezes, and her shivers quickly subsided.

"Thank you," she murmured.

But Dr. Humphreys shook his head, holding up his hands as though to ward off her words. "It is the least I can do."

Prudence gave a vague huff of agreement and burrowed into her blanket, her gaze resting on his boots. Yet Dr. Humphreys remained there before her, shifting back and forth as though ready to bolt. The rational part of her mind knew she ought to say or do something to set him at ease, for that was the kind thing to do, but her charitable reserves were empty at present.

So, the gentleman stood there for several long and uncomfortable moments before he finally spoke. “I owe you an apology. Or rather, a better one.”

Kicking at the ground with the toe of his boot, he sighed and shook his head. “I wanted to speak with you privately, but your servants refused me entrance to your house. I suppose I ought to honor that and leave you be, but my conscience won't allow me to pretend as though nothing has passed.”

Prudence remained wrapped in her cotton cocoon, not meeting his eyes and instead studying his feet as he continued to shift in place.

“I was a coward,” he said with a sigh. “When I realized the mistake, I should've spoken the truth immediately, but I knew it would embarrass you. I couldn't bear the thought of causing you pain.”

With a huff, Prudence finally looked up at him, smirking, though he didn't meet her gaze. “You didn't want to hurt your chances with Rosanna by embarrassing her sister.”

That drew his eyes to hers, his brows knitted together as he held her gaze. Prudence saw the denial come to his lips, but he paused, his posture relaxing as he considered that.

“I won't say I hadn't considered that,” he admitted with a shake of his head. But turning his earnest gaze to her, he added, “But my primary concern was always your feelings and a desire to keep you from embarrassment. Had I immediately spoken out, perhaps I might've spared us all. However, I will say that I was so startled during the assembly that I couldn't think how to respond, and after that, it was too late to avoid anything but catastrophe.”

Dropping his gaze once more, he shook his head. “I don't know if I can ever forgive myself for the grief I have caused you. I can only confess that I had hoped you would discover on your own that we weren't suited for one another or that I could find you a better beau, and thus save your pride."

Prudence's mouth opened, but she snapped it shut again before she could speak the thought that came to her lips. Her heart burned at how confidently he stated that they didn't suit; they knew too little of each other to say either way, yet he seemed certain it couldn't be the case.

"I am not here to ask for your forgiveness, but I did wish to explain myself better in the hope that you might find solace in understanding my motives," he said with a frown. "I wish I had some better excuse to offer than my idiocy, but that is all I have."

"Do not discount the importance of motives. It helps to know that your intentions were pure—if misguided." Then, with a chuckle that was anything but amused, Prudence added, "I suppose I ought to be flattered that you thought a gentleman like Mr. Anglesey would be interested in me."

Dr. Humphreys stiffened. "You speak as though it would be an impossibility, but why wouldn't he be?"

Tucking her blanket tighter around her, Prudence turned her gaze away from the obtuse gentleman and stared out at the party. Would this torture never end? She longed to slip into her bed and sleep. Mama was so fond of retiring to her bed for days at a time; perhaps Prudence ought to try that tonic for the soul. Even if it never seemed to do that lady any good.

Clearing his throat once more, Dr. Humphreys continued, "I do not expect forgiveness, Miss Leigh. I simply wished to explain myself. I suppose I hoped it might ease my conscience a little."

"Did it?"

"Not in the slightest," he replied with a rueful tone.

Prudence drew in a deep breath and let it out. "You may not expect forgiveness, but I will grant it nonetheless, Dr. Humphreys. I won't pretend I was unaffected by the deception, but I do believe you meant no ill will, and as much as I would adore nursing a grudge until the end of my days, I haven't the strength to do so. Especially when the gentleman in question brings me a blanket when I am chilled."

Dr. Humphreys gave a vague grunt, as though considering those words, and shifted once more. "That is magnanimous of you, Miss Leigh, and I do appreciate it. However, as I said before, it may be some time before I can forgive myself."

Nodding, she expected him to leave. Rosanna may still be riding with Mr. Courtney, but surely the good doctor would need to spend his time cozying up to potential patients. Yet he remained standing before her.

When she finally raised her gaze to look at him, he tugged at his jacket and fidgeted with his waistcoat. With a raise of her brows, she sent him a silent question, and he gave a hesitant smile in response.

"I was hoping I might join you."

Prudence's brows rose even further.

Drawing in a deep breath, Dr. Humphreys glanced at her and then at the party around her. "I cannot bear the thought of leaving you here all by yourself."

That response left her blinking at him, unable to answer and uncertain if she had understood him correctly. A faint smile lifted the corners of her lips, but Prudence didn't know what to say in the face of such concern.

Dr. Humphreys dug into the ground with the heel of his boot once more and gave a stilted chuckle. "Consider it part of my penitence."

Prudence's smile (what little of it that there was) vanished, and the warmth she'd gained from the blanket and his kindness fled as a cold wind blew through her. It was clear enough that he was teasing, but her fragile heart couldn't handle even that most pathetic of jests. Dr. Humphreys' expression fell, but before he stammered apologies, Prudence rose to her feet, leaving the blanket on the ground.

"I do not need your pity, Dr. Humphreys." Then, striding away, Prudence went in search of a new sanctuary in which to hide.

Chapter 23

Bless the Chorleys! They often hosted a hunting party in the autumn, but Rosanna couldn't think of another she'd enjoyed as thoroughly as this one. The weather was quite fine, with the skies remaining clear the entire time. Though brisk, the air was not bracing, and it encouraged one to move, which was far better than the boiling days in which one could only laze about, waiting for the festivities to end. The skies were so clear, the sun so bright, and the leaves were in that glorious transition between the verdant green of summertime and the oranges, reds, and yellows of autumn.

Yet even with so many fine things to recommend the day, it was thoughts of Mr. Courtney and Dr. Humphreys that lingered in Rosanna's mind as the carriage bore the Leighs away from the Chorleys' estate and into town. Two such fine gentlemen. And so vastly different.

While many thought her foolish for waiting some years before settling down, to her thinking, only a fool rushed into the first offer she received. And Rosanna's patience had paid off, for Mr. Courtney was precisely the sort of beau she'd hoped to find. Though some thought his pride bordered on arrogance, Rosanna thought his confidence was becoming; he was a man who knew his place in the world and embraced it, heart and soul. Of a good family, good standing, and good fortune, Mr. Courtney was the object of every mama's machinations.

Yet he desired Rosanna. No other would do.

The gentleman knew how to use his eyes to his best advantage, and Rosanna felt so light and buoyant around him. As though she could float about on the breeze or dance on a dewdrop. A smile stretched across her face as she recalled some of his more wicked expressions (both on his face and in his words), and she fought against the blush that rose to her cheeks as she considered that coy man.

Yet even as she lounged in those glorious memories, Dr. Humphreys crept into her thoughts.

Rocking with the carriage, she allowed her gaze to follow Prudence's, watching the passing trees and cottages as she considered this unusual development. Dr. Humphreys was the opposite of everything she wanted in a beau. His features seemed more handsome of late, but he was not remarkable in that fashion and never would be. The same could be said of his fortune, and though he was an engaging fellow, he had not Mr. Courtney's magnetism.

Yet still, his words lingered in her thoughts, growing in strength each time she considered the conversations they'd shared.

Perhaps if not for the comparison between the two, Rosanna would not have seen how lacking Mr. Courtney's conversation was—but no matter how engaging and lively the gentleman was, it was Dr. Humphreys whom she longed to speak to again. The former desired her on his arm, but it was the latter who desired her company, viewing her not only as a lovely creature but as a woman of good character.

Her heart stirred within her, wishing she might meet Dr. Humphreys' expectations, which was a rather odd sentiment, as it was usually the men who vied for *her* good opinion. Rosanna's life was filled with admiration; she could not recall a time when she didn't draw attention. In all honesty, she wouldn't think a thing of it if not for the stark comparison of Prudence's forays into society.

Reaching over, Rosanna threaded her arm through Prudence's, leaning close, though her sister's gaze remained fixed on the passing landscape. Leaning her head against Prudence's shoulder, Rosanna mused over that mystery, for she could not comprehend why so many men seemed blind to the eldest Leigh daughter.

Prudence was so talented and so good. Far better than Rosanna ever managed to be. Mr. Courtney's accusation rang in her ears, for though she wished to refute it, she couldn't help but admit that sinners were appealing. Even if she wished to deny it, she couldn't help but acknowledge how much she adored the gentleman's teasing wickedness.

Yet even as her heart sank at the thought of her shortcomings, she found herself considering Dr. Humphreys once more. Rosanna couldn't comprehend why he had such faith in her, but flawed as his belief was, she felt his certainty deep in her bones.

"...I do not expect you to be perfect: none of us are. What is important is whether or not we choose to do better today than we did yesterday..." Was such a thing truly possible? Though it felt like a daunting prospect, she couldn't help but gather that hope close in her heart.

"You seem quite content," murmured Prudence. Her voice barely carried over Mama's; the lady was rambling on about all the goings-on of the party, as though the rest had not been at the same function. As it was more monologue than conversation, it mattered little that the others paid her no heed; no doubt she would find an eager audience in Francis, for a megrim had forced the poor girl to remain at home.

"I had a wonderful day," replied Rosanna in an equally soft tone.

Prudence's jaw tightened, her brow pulling low as she stared at the passing landscape. "Does it have anything to do with Dr. Humphreys?"

Rosanna straightened, her eyes darting to their parents, but the former hardly drew breath as she excitedly detailed every nuance of Mrs. Hamstall's coiffure, which was far too ostentatious for the gathering and would likely send the poor dear to her bed with a head cold since her bonnet was too thin for the weather. Papa disappeared behind the newspaper he'd left behind in the carriage. Neither paid them any notice, and though Katherine glanced in their direction, their younger sister approached most conversations with the enthusiasm of an undertaker.

Turning her attention back to the question at hand, Rosanna used her free hand to smooth her skirts and whispered, "What a thing to ask."

That earned her a sigh and a shake of the head as Prudence tried to pull away (though there was no space in which to distance herself).

Rosanna held fast to her sister's arm and hurried to add, "If you must know, I had a wonderful day because it was lovely outside, and I spent my time in the company of several fine gentlemen and ladies. I have spoken with a few and plan to get together a group to attend the harvest festival. You will join us, won't you?"

But before Prudence could say a thing, Mama cut in, "And what are you two girls going on about? Mr. Courtney was in fine form today."

"He was," replied Rosanna with a smile, though her thoughts turned almost immediately to the far more enjoyable conversation she'd had with Dr. Humphreys. "We were thinking of attending the harvest festival together."

Mama clapped her hands. "Brilliant!"

Rosanna's thoughts drifted to her wardrobe, picking through her pieces in search of the perfect gown for the occasion. Yet there was nothing that would suit. Brows knitted together, she mentally picked apart each outfit, attempting to fit them together in some new way. A bit more ribbon might help her green day dress, but it was far too plain. Perhaps she could add another few flounces to the hem, but everyone would know the gown was in last year's style.

"I think we might want to visit Mrs. Templemore's tomorrow," said Rosanna. "I haven't anything appropriate to wear."

But her broad smile faded when Prudence's gaze jerked to her with a frown. Even without her sister voicing the concern, Rosanna knew what she would say. The expense was unnecessary. She had many gowns to choose from. Reworking a dress was far better than making a new one—to say nothing of the added fees they would pay for the seamstress to make it quickly enough.

Each one of those arguments was entirely correct. Yet even as Rosanna's heart whispered to her that she ought to follow her sister's sage example, she couldn't imagine herself attending the gathering in an inferior day dress. For all that Dr. Humphreys claimed she was no ornament, would he care for her so deeply if she was plain? The answer was clear enough, as it was seated right next to her—on either side, really, for Katherine had followed in Prudence's poor footsteps, being not only plain but bespectacled, and neither of them garnered any attention from the menfolk.

"It is not such a great expense," said Rosanna, glancing at Prudence before turning to her papa.

"You have spent all your pin money," replied Prudence. "And even if you hadn't, the funds wouldn't pay for a new gown. Besides, your wardrobe is bursting as it is."

Rosanna huffed, her brow furrowing as she considered the sister who had the luxury of not caring two jots for what she wore.

"Mr. Courtney is a gentleman used to the finest things," replied Rosanna, fixing her attention on her papa, who had not bothered to look up from his paper. "He will not be impressed if I arrive in a gown from last year—even if I were to dress it up prettily."

"Which is why it is ridiculous to chase after fashion," murmured Prudence with a frown. "Your clothes are forever needing to be renewed—"

"What nonsense," replied Mama with a scoff. "If you took more care with your toilette, perhaps you might have a beau of your own."

Rosanna's cheeks burned bright, though for her own sake as much as for Prudence's; Mama's words mirrored too closely her thoughts moments ago, and seeing the pain flash in Prudence's gaze made Rosanna feel as though she had spoken them instead of Mama.

The lady leaned forward and patted Prudence on the cheek. "I do not mean to be cruel, dearest. You are an incredible woman. It pains me to see you overlooked because you prefer simplicity over fashion. With just a little help, you might turn a young man's head."

But that pronouncement was overshadowed when Papa added, in a distracted tone as his gaze never wavered from the print on his newspaper, "Buy whatever fripperies you wish, Rosanna."

"Oh, thank you, Papa! You are the best of men." And if it weren't for the fact that the carriage was far too crowded for such a maneuver (and that the gentleman wouldn't welcome the disruption), she would've thrown her arms around his neck right then and there to give him a hearty kiss on his cheek.

Chapter 24

Despite the interruption, Papa seemed pleased with Rosanna's outburst, giving her a kindly look from over the top of the newspaper as Rosanna and Mama began planning their shopping excursion. How many gowns did a woman require? But the question was ridiculous to ask, for the answer was always the same—however many Rosanna desired.

Prudence's arm slackened, though Rosanna seemed not to notice, merely holding fast to the limp thing as she described grand visions of muslin and ribbon, destined to infatuate the entirety of mankind. Prudence's heart sank with each jostle of the carriage, and the moment they stopped at the front steps, Mama and Rosanna hurried off to spend their evening pouring over fashion plates and planning out the grandest dress anyone had ever worn to a simple harvest festival.

Katherine remained on the path, watching the pair of them as Prudence emerged. "Might I speak to you?"

"Not this very minute," she replied as she stepped clear of the carriage. "Find me later."

Katherine nodded and pushed her glasses up her nose before following after the others, her shoulders drooping, and Prudence's heart twisted itself into knots. However, her mind was too clogged with other troubles to sort out Katherine's at present. "Later" was all Prudence could offer her sister at present.

"Papa," she called as the fellow strode past, but he didn't slow, and she hurried to catch him.

Before she could say a proper word to him, he beamed at her and clapped a hand on her shoulder. "Excellent work, Prudence. You are a credit to your dear papa. Rosanna and Mr. Courtney spent almost the whole day together, and now they are attending the harvest festival. It shan't be long before he comes seeking a word with me."

Prudence's insides gave an unhappy twist at the thought of her work that afternoon. "About that—"

"Do not fret, dearheart. They are on a good path, and with you distracting Dr. Humphreys like that, he'll be forgotten in a trice."

"I wouldn't say I distracted him."

"Don't be so modest," he said with a grin. Then, with a nod, he turned as though to leave her and the subject behind. Prudence stepped into his path, blocking him from the door.

"That is not what I wanted to speak to you about, Papa," she said. "Rosanna does not need another gown—"

"Not again, Prudence." Papa huffed and tried to step around her, but she held firm. "We are not in danger of ending up in the poor house. We can afford some finery."

Fighting against the hard twist of her stomach, Prudence straightened. "We live within our means, but only just. We have no savings to speak of, and it would take so little for our good fortune to sour if we aren't cautious."

"Oh, now, dear," he said in a patronizing tone that set her teeth on edge. "You needn't be jealous of your sister's wardrobe. I allow her to be extravagant because she knows no better, and besides, it's an investment. If she can catch herself a Mr. Courtney or better, it will do much for our family, so it is wise to allow her free rein with the purse strings."

"But we shall be outside, and you shan't even see it beneath her pelisse—"

"Don't fret, my dear. Your charms may not be as obvious, but they are there and do not need such ornamentation. You're too sensible a girl to need all those frills and sparkles. Such a good, useful creature."

For all that Papa meant to compliment her, Prudence's heart felt as hard and heavy as lead as he patted her on the cheek and turned away, with a jaunty spring to his step, so very pleased with his useful daughter and his investment.

Would they spend their lives forever compared one against the other, with Prudence cast as the unfortunate elder sister, who was "useful" and "sensible" but wholly unremarkable unless she was balancing household accounts or managing the family affairs?

Plodding along, she moved through the entryway and mounted the stairs with all the speed and grace of an octogenarian. Pulling at her cloak's ties and her gloves, she marched to the bedchamber, unaware of anything else going on about her. But when she opened the door, she found their bedchamber in a hubbub as Rosanna was hastily digging through the drawers of her dresser and side table.

"Have you seen the latest copy of *La Belle Assemblée*? I could've sworn I tucked it here somewhere, but I cannot find it," she said in a distracted tone, not looking up as Prudence dumped her things on the bed. "There was this lovely blue frock that I think would be perfect for the festival."

Prudence froze, stopping herself from taking a seat on the mattress to stare at her sister. "Blue? You do not care for blue."

Rosanna laughed at that. "I think I misjudged it. With my coloring, a nice pale blue might be just the thing. It is such a delicate and feminine hue, after all."

Unable to contain herself, Prudence straightened and asked, "Have you set your cap at Dr. Humphreys?"

Pausing in her search, Rosanna stared at her sister with brows raised high up her forehead. "What makes you think I have set my cap at anyone?"

"Do not toy with me," replied Prudence, dropping down onto the bed beside her things. "I saw you with both him and Mr. Courtney."

Rosanna snatched the magazine from her drawer but set it on the bed before sitting beside her sister. "I may flirt, but that doesn't mean I am determined to have either of them, Prudence."

Her actions had seemed contrary to that, but there was an earnestness in her sister's gaze that allowed the pressure in Prudence's chest to ease some.

"Are you still angry with Dr. Humphreys? For if you were, I would cut ties with him—" began Rosanna. But Prudence held up a staying hand and shook her head.

"However misguided his behavior, I do believe him to be a good man." Though a touch irritating and condescending with his ridiculous offers of pity conversations.

With a sigh, Rosanna smiled, and in a low tone, she said, "Despite everything, I like him. He is such a good man and unlike any of my other suitors. He inspires me to be better than I am—though I fall short all too often."

That was easy enough to explain away, for Dr. Humphreys was not one of her usual fribbles who cared only for sporting and drinking. But even as she considered that, Prudence knew there was something more to it. Though she couldn't say she had felt that same influence Rosanna claimed to feel, it was easy to see he was far and away better than Mr. Courtney.

Rosanna's fancy was not surprising, but neither was it wise. Not for their family's sake, but for hers and Dr. Humphreys'. Though Prudence didn't care for Papa's underhanded tactics, there was at least one reason behind his desire to separate the pair that had to do with more than merely securing the Leighs' financial future. Or rather, Papa's reason may have been mere lip service, but it was sensible enough that Prudence couldn't ignore it. Rosanna's dreams for the future did not coincide with what Dr. Humphreys could provide, and no marriage could survive that disparity.

"That is well and good, Rosanna, but have you considered what it would be like to marry a man like Dr. Humphreys? Even if he does well, he won't ever have Papa's income to afford gowns and baubles whenever you wish."

"Do you think me so shallow that I only care about a gentleman's income?" asked Rosanna with a frown.

"Not shallow, but I do not think you understand how hard your life would be. Even with a healthy income, I do so much work to keep our family solvent. As Dr. Humphreys' wife, you may have a maid-of-all-work to manage much of the household duties work, but you would be unlikely to have a nursemaid or governess. And then there are the bills to pay and the household accounts to balance. Do you wish to do that yourself?"

Rosanna's eyes widened a touch, but she laughed it off. "I have said I am not determined to have him, and even if I were, we needn't worry about money. Benjamin will break the entail when he comes of age, and Papa will be free to do as he wishes to provide us with dowries after the fact. That is only fourteen years hence—not a lifetime—and if necessary, I can borrow against that expectation until that day arrives."

Prudence tried not to gape, but Rosanna's plans were so foolhardy that she couldn't think what else to do. As she had so many times since Benjamin had come into their family, she prayed for his sake, if nothing else, that her parents would never resort to selling away their son's future simply because they had not the sense to economize. Though she knew that was a vain hope.

Better to hope that Benjamin would be wise when that day came. Mama and Papa had planned poorly for their daughters' futures, and breaking the entail would only doom their son as well. There was a reason Grandpapa had placed the entail on Whitley Court, and it was not because he thought his son a wise steward over the estate.

Pressing forward, Prudence added, "And then there's the matter of marrying a physician. Would you care to have a husband who may be gone at all hours of the day? Who cannot be counted upon to escort you to parties and such? Who puts his very life in danger to make others better?"

Rosanna rose to her feet and laughed. "I have told you, Prudence. I have not set my cap at any gentleman, so there is no need to fret and fuss about what may never come to pass."

Yet even as her sister placed a kiss on her cheek and hurried off with her newly recovered copy of *La Belle Assemblée*, Prudence couldn't withstand the sinking feeling that weighed her down, and she sank onto her bed.

Chapter 25

Rosanna Leigh was a pigheaded mule of a woman. There was no denying that fact as she stood before the looking glass, turning this way and that to admire her gown. Though the pale blue was not as flattering on her as pink or green, it was clear that she had spent six and twenty years underestimating the color, casting it aside without giving it its proper due. Fool that she was.

It was rather becoming with her eyes, matching the pale quality quite nicely, and it complemented her fair coloring even better than she had anticipated. And as Rosanna considered the vision before her, she wondered why she'd despised it for so long. Granted, it was such a maidenly hue, and Rosanna preferred a bolder shade.

Turning about, she studied every angle and frowned at her coiffure. Jane was such a master with hair (not that Rosanna's natural curls required much assistance), but something was missing. A flower perhaps? But the delicate thing was unlikely to survive long while she wandered the festival grounds. And she wouldn't dare risk losing one of her nicer combs.

For the briefest moment, Rosanna considered the perfect ornament. Dr. Humphreys had intended for her to have the ribbon, after all, and Prudence did not wish to wear it after the whole debacle. It was such a shame to waste it, and the blue would look lovely woven through her ringlets.

But sanity prevailed, making her acknowledge that not only would it bother Prudence and give rise to the belief that Rosanna was setting her cap at the doctor, but it would be too bold a statement. One that would be easily misinterpreted by all parties.

With a sigh, Rosanna turned away. Her bonnet covered her hair anyway, so there was little point in fretting about that small detail, but any woman with sense knew one's confidence came from those smallest of details. Even unseen, ill-fitting stays or a ratty pair of stockings had the power to make one feel disjointed and discomforted.

"Prudence?" called Rosanna. But there was no sound in reply. No doubt the lady was off doing important things although they needed to leave soon if they were to arrive at the appointed time.

Carefully, she placed the bonnet on her head and tied the ribbons beneath her chin. The bow bunched together, and she pulled it loose and began again. With quick tugs, she fluffed the loops and ensured the draped ends rested at the proper length down her torso. Finally, Rosanna twisted the curls at her temple and neck, ensuring that they stuck out from beneath the rim in just the right fashion.

With a grand sweep, she drew on her pelisse and ran her leather-clad hands down the front, parting the green edges to allow the blue gown beneath to peek through. A spencer would highlight the gown better, but the nip in the air demanded something more substantial; suffering often accompanied fashion, but risking one's health and complexion with a chill was foolish.

Striding from their bedchamber, Rosanna called again for her sister, but yet again, there was no response, and she frowned at the empty corridor.

"What am I going to do with her?" she murmured to herself, punctuating the words with a heavy sigh.

Glancing into the rooms as she passed, Rosanna searched the house. Katherine and Francis knew nothing about Prudence's location. Only when she chanced upon Nurse Johnson scurrying by with a steaming teapot did Rosanna guess the truth, and she followed the nursemaid.

Coughs echoed through the topmost floor of the house, and Rosanna's lungs ached at the hoarseness of the sound. With hurried steps, she strode into the nursery and found Prudence seated beside the little bed with Benjamin tucked up tight inside it, his cheeks blazing with a fever. Mama stood in the corner, her handkerchief flapping as she paced the room, dabbing at her eyes and murmuring quiet prayers of healing.

Prudence directed Nurse Johnson to the side table where the family's medicine chest sat open, the various jars waiting to be used. With quick movements, Prudence dropped in a pinch of this and a few drops of that, mixing the cup of tea before taking it to her brother's bedside.

"Ought we to send for the doctor?" Mama asked, a hint of hysteria making her tone shriller than usual.

"It is a touch of fever and a cough. Troublesome but nothing to fret over yet," replied Prudence as she lifted the boy just enough for him to drink a few sips from the cup. "Nothing we haven't weathered before."

"But ever since that fever two years ago, he has been susceptible to even trifling illnesses," added Mama, her footsteps worrying a line before the fireplace.

Prudence glanced at the doorway to see Rosanna standing there and sent her sister a look of such abject exhaustion and frustration that Rosanna knew this was not the first or second time Prudence had said such things.

"You know Prudence is right about such things, Mama," said Rosanna.

"True, true," said Mama with a flap of her handkerchief. "But—"

"Mama, might you speak to Mrs. James about that lavender tincture you like so very much? I am certain it may do wonders for Benjamin," said Prudence.

"Of course, my dear," replied the lady with a vigorous nod before hurrying out of the room in a flurry of lace to seek out the cook.

Once the door was shut, Prudence seemed to breathe again.

"The lavender tincture?" asked Rosanna with a frown as she came to his bedside and sat beside her brother. "He doesn't look like he needs calming."

"No, but Mama certainly does," replied Prudence, giving her baby brother a faint smile.

"I might feel better with a bit of cake," he murmured, with quite a sad and put-upon look.

Rosanna chuckled and tweaked Benjamin's cheek, which drew a chuckle from the lad. Unfortunately, it set him to coughing again, and Prudence quickly administered another few drinks from the teacup.

Once their brother was resting against his pillows again, Rosanna brushed a stray lock of hair from his damp forehead and gave him a wan smile. "You poor mite."

Despite the fevered look in his eyes, he gave her another pleading look. "My throat hurts, but a biscuit might make it better."

"I do not doubt Mama is putting together the finest selection of cakes and biscuits any child has ever known," said Prudence, which made his eyes brighten. Then she turned to study Rosanna's outfit, her brow furrowed. "Are you going out?"

"*We* are, you goose," said Rosanna with a smile. "The festival."

Which was precisely the wrong thing to say, for Benjamin immediately began begging to join them, despite the impossibility. But that was to be expected. His eldest sister's protests, however, were entirely unacceptable.

"I cannot leave Benjamin—"

"What rubbish, Prudence!" said Rosanna with a huff. Then, giving Benjamin a narrowed look, she added, "You just said it was just a touch of fever. Nothing serious."

At which point Benjamin feigned a great and mighty cough, but in turn, it drew forth a natural one, and Rosanna winced at the sound.

"Is there anything more you can do that you haven't done?" asked Rosanna. Motioning to the nursemaid, who stood in the corner, awaiting her orders, Rosanna added, "Nurse Johnson is entirely capable of managing things, and they can send word if he worsens."

Just as Benjamin began to protest their abandoning him, she added, "And we can bring him back some of that Buckbee's apple cake he adores."

Greed gleamed in his eyes as the child quickly calculated his odds of getting Prudence to allow him to join them compared to her bringing her patient back a treat to make him feel better, and being no fool, Benjamin threw in with the latter course of action.

Prudence's brows furrowed as she studied her brother.

"It is only a few hours," said Rosanna. "Please. It shan't be as much fun without you."

The bedchamber door swung open once more, and Mama bustled in, rambling about tisanes. Not one to turn aside opportunities, Rosanna took the lady's arm and led her to the bedside.

"Mama, you must tell Prudence to go with me to the festival."

The lady's eyes remained fixed on her eldest daughter for the longest moment, as though she could not comprehend what was happening. "Leave? Why, no. She cannot abandon Benjamin at such a moment. What if he were to take a turn for the worse?"

"You can send for us at once, and we will return straightaway," said Rosanna. Then, grasping for the one subject that might gain her the advantage, she continued, "I have organized a whole group to attend together."

There was no need to mention any potential beaus, for Mama scented such things as easily as a bloodhound followed a fox. Though there was no one in particular Rosanna wished to pair with her sister, one ought never to squander the possibility that one might present itself. Pricking up, Mama glanced between her son and daughter.

"It is only for a few hours," added Rosanna once more.

"You really ought to go. It isn't wise to forgo any opportunities to mix in good company," said Mama, sweeping towards the bed to usher her daughters towards the door.

With a frown, Prudence allowed herself to be herded in that direction.

"Nurse Johnson will see to everything," said Mama, echoing the assurances Rosanna had given just moments ago.

Standing on the threshold, Prudence finally nodded. "I should fetch my cloak."

"Good heavens, child! What are you thinking?" said Mama with a gasp, her gaze raking over her eldest daughter's gown. "You'll never catch a beau if you do not take more care with your toilette."

"It shan't do any good," mumbled Prudence, though only Rosanna heard it. Drawing close, she took her sister's arm and squeezed Prudence as the two turned away from the nursery with Mama raving about coiffures and gowns.

"She means no harm," said Rosanna, once they were out of earshot.

"True, but that makes it all the more difficult to ignore. If Mama were cruel rather than thoughtless, I could simply brush away her comments. And matters are only made worse by the fact that the gentlemen support her assertions."

Rosanna pulled her to a stop. "What nonsense."

With an arched brow, Prudence huffed. "Is it? I think it is entirely accurate to say I am unattractive when I cannot attract a gentleman."

"You are an incredible woman."

But her sister shook her head and walked away with her shoulders hanging low. Rosanna hurried to stand before her and pulled Prudence to a stop.

"Do not brush me aside. I am entirely in earnest and entirely accurate. You are the most talented woman I know, and you are far kinder, wiser, and more patient than I could ever hope to be," said Rosanna. "You have so much to offer others, and when gentlemen overlook you, it says more about their obtuseness and lack of foresight than it says about your worth. I wish I could be more like you."

Though her words had all the hallmarks of hollow compliments, sounding more like the vain rallying cry that ladies often gave themselves when faced with the bumps and bruises of life that damaged their vanities, Rosanna meant every syllable. And when Prudence stood there, watching her, Rosanna hoped she saw that truth shining in her eyes.

For all that she understood society (or as well as anyone could), Rosanna could not comprehend why there were so many undervalued ladies like Prudence. If she were a gentleman, she would choose from among those indomitable wallflowers, who bloomed amid such difficult circumstances. And it broke her heart to see Prudence's gaze steeped in uncertainty, as though wanting to embrace Rosanna's assurances yet fearing to do so.

Prudence straightened. "Thank you. I am sorry if I have been cross of late."

"You've been understandably cross, dearest." Then taking her place at her sister's side once more, Rosanna led her down the hall. "And thank you for being my sister."

Such small words, yet so much feeling and truth were woven into each syllable, and with a tight squeeze of Rosanna's arm, Prudence smiled, her expression aglow with that same love.

"And thank you for being patient, despite all the reasons I give you to be cross," added Rosanna.

With a shake of her head and a faint smile, Prudence moved to the stairs, but Rosanna steered her towards their bedchamber, her smile growing strained as Prudence sent her a questioning look.

"You may wish to freshen up a touch, dearest. You needn't change into a fashion plate, but you do look as though you've been wrestling with dogs."

Prudence glanced at the looking glass as they strode through the doorway. Her cheeks were red from her exertions, her dress had a few splashes of tea dotting the front, and her hair was tumbling free of her bandeau, making her look as if she had, in fact, wrestled with dogs.

Covering her eyes, Prudence shook her head with a laugh. "I look a fright. You'd best go without me."

"I shan't," said Rosanna, moving to the wardrobe to fetch a fresh dress.

"You'll be late," she insisted, giving her sister a stern look. Unfortunately for Prudence, it was one she had employed far too many times in their youth, and Rosanna had developed an immunity to it.

"Put that on," she said, nodding at the navy gown she'd tossed onto the bed. "It will take only a quarter of an hour, and it'll do those men good to wait upon us. Best not to let them believe we are too eager to see them."

Prudence gave her sister another hard look, though it possessed too much humor to hold any sting, and then they set to work.

Chapter 26

Having never needed to attend the festival's morning offerings, Parker had never witnessed the hiring fair that took place in the early hours of the day. Servants, day laborers, clerks, and all others searching for work had spent the morning doing what they could to find themselves a position amongst the farmers, housekeepers, and tradesmen. It was easy enough to see who were victorious, for they remained behind to revel in the entertainments the afternoon had to offer, whilst the still unemployed drifted away to seek other avenues of income.

Then there were the more practical goods that took center stage during those early hours. The small carts selling fruits, vegetables, cheeses, and other goods rumbled away, to travel the streets in search of better selling locations near the households, for no one attending the afternoon's entertainment wanted heads of lettuce or jugs of milk. The horse and livestock markets remained where they were, but the owners wandered off to find libation or food, leaving their stableboys and farmhands to guard the merchandise until the harvest market resumed the following morning.

Meanwhile, the owners of stalls focused on the afternoon and evening revelers began to ready their wares. The sensible goods were quickly replaced with all the sweets and goodies one expected of a festival, and Parker watched as the air filled with anticipation at the coming attractions and treats.

Mr. Courtney stood to one side, laughing with Mr. Gundry and Mr. Turley, who hung on the fellow's every word, while other circles of ladies and gentlemen all buzzed around them. Miss Rosanna hadn't been speaking in jest when she'd said she was gathering a group, for there were a good twenty people there. How they were supposed to enjoy the festival together in such a crowd, Parker didn't know. But neither did he care as long as she attended.

Unfortunately, his perusal was marked by Mr. Courtney. Such standoffs between gentlemen generally resulted in one of two possibilities. The rival either gave a long, assessing look, as though summing up all the other had to offer (and finding him lacking, of course), or looked away as though attempting to be dismissive. Parker wasn't surprised to see Mr. Courtney adopt the second attitude, for everything he knew about the gentleman suggested someone who held far too high an opinion of himself.

No matter. Let Mr. Courtney think he had won the day. Having gained this much ground, Parker wasn't about to surrender the field of battle, and the victor was still to be determined in this war.

Puffing out his cheeks, he watched the road passing by the fairground, which was little more than an empty pasture the Chorleys had lent the town for the cause—far from the house proper, of course. Most arrived on foot, though a handful of carriages and gigs rolled over to where a handful of grooms and stableboys waited to take hold of the horses, and Parker's gaze tracked each. Unfortunately, so many of them looked similar that it was easy to mistake the Leighs' carriage.

Then a blonde head peeked through the window. Miss Rosanna waved at the group with a call of greeting as they rolled to a stop.

"I do apologize for my tardiness," she said in a flurry of skirts and petticoats. Miss Leigh emerged a moment later, and Miss Rosanna took hold of her sister's arm. "I fear my hair was uncooperative, and I couldn't leave until I was set to rights."

Miss Leigh's cheeks pinked, and Parker frowned at that, but before he could wonder as to the source of her discomfort, his attention was stolen away when Mr. Courtney strode forward and offered up his arm to Miss Rosanna. Impulse demanded that Parker force his way past the demanding fellow and give the lady the option of either of their arms, but sanity prevailed, and he remained where he was.

Of course, that resolve was far more difficult when the blackguard leaned close to Miss Rosanna and whispered something in her ear that set her blushing. Then, with a playful tap of his arm, she took it.

Parker felt like a ship on the ocean after the wind had died, emptying his sails and leaving him bobbing about on the waves with no direction. Not that he had expected her to ignore Mr. Courtney, but the man's behavior was bordering on shocking, and seeing her encourage the fellow made him uneasy. Though he supposed jealousy was expected from a suitor and ought not to be countenanced, he couldn't quite brush the sentiments aside.

Turning in place, Miss Rosanna greeted all her friends, and when her eyes met his, the winds gathered in his sails once more, for her already glowing eyes brightened at the sight of him.

"You came," she said, releasing Mr. Courtney's arm to draw nearer.

"As you see," he replied with a bow, but before Parker straightened, another lady swept forward and took Miss Rosanna by the arm, leading her into the festival grounds. Like ducklings following their mama, the others drifted behind her as the sound of Miss Rosanna's laughter rang through the air.

The rest all grouped in little batches, leaving Parker standing alone. Was there any good to be had in staying? This invitation had seemed like manna from heaven, but rather than an intimate group, she had brought a circus, and with so many about, it was unlikely that he would do more than he had every year he'd attended the festival—watch from afar and hope she noticed him. Like most, he believed himself a good man, but he knew his limits, and watching his love flatter and flirt was unbearable.

Parker considered this conundrum for a brief moment, but before he could think what to do, he spied another lone figure. Despite being surrounded by the crowds and her sister's gaggle of friends, Miss Leigh seemed so very solitary. Perhaps more so because of the cacophony around her, for she stood by herself, examining the stalls as she passed. His heart sat uneasy in his chest at the sight, and Parker's feet were moving before he knew what they were about.

"Might I join you, Miss Leigh?" he asked, as he fell into step beside the lady.

His words seemed to jerk her out of her thoughts, and Miss Leigh's brows knit together as she slid a glance in his direction. With a dry tone, she asked, "Do you wish to? I expected you to be fighting for your place at my sister's side."

Parker scratched at the back of his neck, nearly knocking his hat from his head. Thankfully, no one noticed. "As much as I believe in fighting for love, I also believe the sentiment must be reciprocated. Your sister knows my feelings. If she wishes for more, she must make it clear. I have no interest in fighting through her admiring throng if she does not care enough to seek me out."

Miss Leigh stiffened and halted, her eyes closing for a brief moment before she turned a chagrined look in his direction. "I apologize for being so brusque. Neither you nor my sister deserves such hard words. I am out of sorts today, and I ought to guard my tongue better."

Parker tucked his hands behind him, his expression matching hers. "As I have had a significant hand in why you are 'out of sorts,' it is only fair that I should be made to suffer for it."

With brows knit tight together, she sighed. "I did not mean to—"

But Parker held up his hands to forestall any further apologies. "That was my awful attempt at a jest, Miss Leigh. But it seems as though I have only made matters worse—as I did the last time we spoke. I didn't intend to offend you or make you feel as though my offer to sit with you was born of pity."

He shifted in place. "I had hoped to see you today to offer an apology."

"There is no need," she said, stepping away with her hands raised as though to ward off his words.

"But there is—"

"The business with the letter was my own mistake, and I would rather we just forget it all." Miss Leigh marched down the path, leaving Parker to follow after.

Digging into his pocket, he drew forth the brown-paper package and held it in front of her. "Then do not think of it as an apology but rather a peace offering."

Miss Leigh halted once more, staring at his offering. As she slanted him another furrowed look, Parker tried for a lighthearted air, but at best, he managed a pleading smile.

"I had thought to bring you flowers, but I didn't think you would appreciate them as much as this," he said.

"Because a steady, sensible woman like me does not need such frivolous things?" Her question held more than a touch of bitterness, and the moment she spoke the words, her cheeks flamed, and she shook her head. "I apologize—"

"Not another word, Miss Leigh," he said. "Our conversation will be utterly tedious if we spend all of it apologizing to each other."

For the first time since they'd begun this disaster of a conversation, the lady seemed to truly smile. "I would appreciate it if we could forget what has happened and begin again."

Not allowing himself to rethink the course of action, Parker swept into an elegant bow. "Do pardon my intrusion, miss, and do not think me boorish for being so forward, but my name is Dr. Parker Humphreys, and I would very much like to make your acquaintance."

Sweeping upright once more, he dropped his hat on his head and stood before her, hoping that his jest would not go amiss this time. Miss Leigh watched him with narrowed eyes. Thankfully, there was a hint of a smile that kept him from fleeing.

"I have no one on hand to vouch for my character," he said, glancing at their party, who had drifted far enough away to make the statement true enough. "But I was born and raised in Greater Edgerton before I was shipped off to Edinburgh to become a physician of middling ability. I have since returned home and managed to convince a handful of patients that I am quite skilled, though what I truly excel at is sketching, indecipherable handwriting, and placing my foot firmly in my mouth whenever I am speaking with ladies."

Miss Leigh let out a sharp laugh and covered her mouth as she glanced about, though no one noticed the outburst amidst all the festivities. Parker stood there, watching her, waiting to see what she would do.

Chapter 27

Miss Leigh stood there for a long, unbearable moment, and Parker nearly cried defeat. But then, she swept into a courtly curtsy.

"Good sir, it is a pleasure to make your acquaintance," she said with all the gravity such a silly moment demanded. "I am Miss Prudence Leigh. I had the good fortune to be born and raised in this delightful town, but also the ill fortune to have never ventured beyond its borders. Though my family believes I manage the household to perfection, I am more like the jailor of a madhouse who is inching closer and closer to joining her charges. I would say I am a skilled artist and musician, but unfortunately, I know enough of the world to know that though I am talented compared to most of the ladies about town, I am far from spectacular."

"I find that hard to believe," he said. "I have heard you play a time or two at concerts, and I would call it spectacular."

Miss Leigh huffed, the silly facade fading as she gazed at him. "I find that the more pompous a person is about their creative endeavors, the less skilled they truly are. They tend only to grace small gatherings and are praised because they are compared to other mediocre musicians or artists. My skill has pushed me into wider circles, and amongst those, I know precisely how I measure up. I am talented, but I am nothing compared to those who earn their bread with their instruments or brushes."

"I have found that true of medicine, as well. The puffed-up physicians are not the ones I want at my sickbed. Humility and ability are often intrinsically linked."

Nodding further down the festival stalls, he asked, "Would you mind if I walk with you a bit?"

With a nod, she stepped forward at his prompting, but that was when he noticed the peace offering still sitting in his hand. Stopping her, he nudged the package towards her again.

"We may wish to forget what has passed, but this gift is still yours," he said.

Miss Leigh held his gaze for a moment, but there was clear curiosity in those dark eyes of hers as she considered the gift. Then, with nimble fingers, she tugged at the string and pulled away the paper.

"*Dr. Buchan's Domestic Medicine*?" she read before turning bright eyes to him.

"'Twasn't my doing, Miss Leigh," he said with a vague wave about the area whilst affecting his stranger guise once more. "I found it on the ground and thought it must be yours."

The lady gave him an earnest smile. "You needn't hold onto pretense, Dr. Humphreys. As peace offerings go, it is perfect."

"You showed an interest in home medicine, and I heard you were scouring the lending library for books on the subject. In my opinion, this is the best reference you'll find, and Mr. Brookstone does not have a copy."

Holding it to her chest, Miss Leigh watched him with wide eyes. "I ought not to accept such an expensive gift, but I fear I'm too selfish to refuse it. My deepest thanks. It is perfect, and very apropos at the moment."

"Are you ill?" he said, giving her complexion a quick study, but it was as fine as it ever was.

"My brother woke this morning with a cough, and though it is slight, he is developing a fever." Miss Leigh glanced at her reticule, but it was far too small to hold the book, and her cloak provided no solution. With a quick promise to return it to her when the afternoon was over, Parker placed it back in his pocket for safekeeping.

"Does he have a history of being ill often?"

"No more than any other child, though Mama is always certain it is scarlet fever or the plague," she replied with a huff.

"When you arrive home, administer essence of camphor," he said. "I've found it one of the best medicines to give in the early stages."

Miss Leigh straightened. "I shall do that. Thank you—"

"If we are to agree to stop apologizing, I think we ought to forgo constantly thanking one another for demonstrating basic human decency," he said with a smile as they wandered among the stalls.

"I will when basic human decency is commonplace," she replied in that same weary tone, as though the cares of the world pressed down on her. Parker slid her a sideways look, struggling to study her and keep from colliding with the teeming mass around them.

Miss Leigh had such an air of confidence about her, as though she knew the ills and cares of the world but met them each without shirking—but at that moment, she seemed almost fragile. Not frail, per se, for there was a thread of steel woven through her, but it was as though the heart beating beneath that strength might crack at the slightest touch.

It was such an odd dichotomy, and Parker couldn't help but wonder what had this indomitable lady so at odds with the world.

"Then I must thank you for your recommendation," he said with an arched brow and teasing smile as they wandered past merchants selling their wares. The purveyors shouted out to the passing people, though the food did much to sell itself, for all the scents of spices, fruits, and frying oil practically begged them to stop.

"Recommendation?" Miss Leigh paused at a fritter stall but continued after only the briefest moment.

"*The Abbess*. I confess I only began it because I was desperate for something to read and could find nothing else, but it gripped me as quickly as you said it would."

Miss Leigh's smile brightened, and she turned to him, nearly walking backward as she tried to face him while still marching along the path. "Did you finish it?"

Parker winced. "I may have arrived at Mr. Brookstone's doorstep the moment he opened the lending library to fetch the second volume, and ended up taking it and the third to avoid any more delays."

"It is such a ridiculous and lurid tale, but at times there is nothing better than a bit of the ludicrous. What was your favorite part? No matter how many times I read it, I am still on edge when Marcello sneaks in to see Maddalena, but it is really the Abbess."

"I may have gasped at that moment."

Miss Leigh huffed and sent him a look of such utter disbelief that he couldn't help but smile.

"Perhaps not a gasp exactly, but it was quite shocking," he said.

That earned him a smile, and her eyes sparkled, making Parker grin in turn as they wandered along; their conversation meandered haphazardly much like their feet did, dodging and ducking around the musicians, acrobats, and dancers, who vied for the passing people's coins.

...

The festivities were well underway, with all the tedious affairs of the morning forgotten in favor of excessive drink and food with a world of entertainment at their fingertips. The summer was long over, the harvest finished, and both the farmers and masters were content to roll up their sleeves and celebrate. Of course, most of the people engaging in Greater Edgerton's frivolities had no ties to the harvest, but what town did not celebrate such a time as this?

The group gathered around Rosanna like buzzing bees, each drifting near to point out some attraction. Bunting of every color had been draped above them, as though celebrating their presence, and the sellers in the stalls and carts called for them to spend a farthing or two on their wares.

Rosanna enjoyed the performers the best, for such talents and tricks were not often found in their little corner of Lancashire. At her side, Mr. Courtney seemed unimpressed with the meager offering, but then, London offered far more dazzling entertainment. For all that she tried not to let his opinion sway her one jot, she couldn't help but temper her thrill when acrobats stood one atop the other, stretching up higher than the tents around them, each balancing upon the other's shoulders whilst juggling. But she couldn't keep from gasping when the tallest leapt from the human ladder to land nimbly on the ground without a scrape, his partners following quickly after him.

Yet for all the excitement of the tumbling, Rosanna's attention drifted towards Prudence and Dr. Humphreys standing at the edge of their group, their attention fixed on each other rather than the show. With a furrowed brow, she tried not to watch them, but her gaze drifted back again.

It was nice of him to keep Prudence company. As much as she adored her sister, Rosanna did not understand her at times like these. She was so quick to hide in the background, lingering on the edge of the festivities and leaving Rosanna with the constant worry that Prudence was bored or lonely. It was difficult to avail oneself of all the amusements swirling about her when her sister seemed so unwilling to throw herself into the midst of it.

So, Rosanna was pleased that Dr. Humphreys had taken Prudence under his wing. He was an amiable fellow and would make a capital companion for her. And Prudence seemed to be laughing and smiling quite a bit.

Quite often, in fact.

"Would you like some biscuits and cider?" Mr. Courtney spoke low, leaning in closer than was necessary for such an innocent question, but Rosanna smiled as his breath tickled her ear.

"That would be divine," she murmured.

Holding her gaze in that effortless manner of his, Mr. Courtney took his leave with a swagger in his step that Rosanna couldn't say she liked, precisely. But neither did she despise it.

Miss Davis filled in his place, taking Rosanna's arm as she chattered away about the sights around them, reveling in them with such abandon that Rosanna longed to take part in all the merriment, but her gaze drifted back to Prudence and Dr. Humphreys.

It was good they were spending the afternoon together. It was.

Prudence had gained an amiable companion, and it was only a matter of time before a sensible man like Dr. Humphreys saw her value and snatched her up. Precisely as he ought to. He was a good man and ought to find himself a good woman, and Prudence deserved his affection even more. Not that he was anywhere close to declaring himself—Rosanna doubted he even recognized the possibility yet—but she saw the potential and knew in an instant what it might be with encouragement.

Good and proper. Rather a pleasing outcome after all the wretched business Dr. Humphreys' love letter had caused. Yet all the joy of the moment leached out of her, leaving Rosanna oddly hollow as she spied the pair.

She was so happy for Prudence.

The pair deserved happiness.

"It is such a pleasant afternoon, isn't it?" blurted Rosanna.

Prudence and Dr. Humphreys jumped at her question, jerking around to face her with as much puzzlement written on their faces as she was feeling. Rosanna didn't know how she'd crossed that distance, but there she was, standing before her sister and the lady's potential beau.

"I am thoroughly enjoying myself," said Dr. Humphreys, casting Prudence a smile different from his usual one. There was a softness to it, and it was easy to read the pleasure in his gaze, as though the conversation had been more than merely agreeable. Rosanna's stays tightened until she couldn't breathe.

Good for Prudence. Good for Dr. Humphreys. They were such good people and deserved to find joy in each other's company. Rosanna was so happy for them both.

"We were going to wager on the final smock race." Rosanna fought back a cringe at her tone, which was too loud and quick for the simple statement. "Will you join us?"

"We had been considering watching the magician next," said Prudence. "I heard the show is exceptional this year."

With an exaggerated pout, Rosanna looked up at Dr. Humphreys from under her lashes. "And you would prefer that to a smock race?"

Dr. Humphreys' brows rose as she held his gaze, and Rosanna let her lips drift into a half-smile, the corners curling upwards. At that moment, she felt the world shift as his attention grew more fixed. There was a question shining in his eyes, but it melted away as her gaze trapped him in its power. And he was a willing prisoner. Rosanna felt it, and the knowledge coursed through her, filling her heart to brimming.

"The races are so titillating," giggled Miss Davies. Rosanna jumped and turned to find that the young lady had followed after her. "Quite shocking to see all those young ladies running about with their skirts gathered up. Their legs bare to the world."

Dr. Humphreys huffed and shook his head. "You will forgive me if I do not blush and stammer over such a display, Miss

Davies. In my profession seeing a lady's legs is hardly titillating."

"And these are village girls—not ladies," said Mr. Courtney in a cool tone as he came up beside Rosanna, placing a hand at her back as he gave her the flagon of cider he'd procured. His eyes were as icy as the winter wind, and though a shiver passed through Rosanna, she warmed her gaze. With a flash of an arched brow and the barest of smiles from her, his coolness melted away, unable to withstand her allure.

"Trust me when I say that whether it belongs to a duchess or the lowest serf, a leg is a leg. One's station does not alter the physiology," said Dr. Humphreys. "And even if everyone else enjoys betting, I am content to keep my money in my pocket and not gamble it away."

Rosanna gave a comical gape. "Do not tell me you abstain from wagering? It gives one a vested interest in the outcome."

"If that is the only reason to enjoy the sport, I do not see the point in the thing," replied Dr. Humphreys.

Though no one else was watching her sister, Rosanna noticed Prudence's eyes brightening as she watched the gentleman, the approval clear for anyone to see if they bothered to look at her. Which they didn't.

"Life is to be lived, Dr. Humphreys," said Mr. Courtney. "What point is there if one does not live it to its fullest?"

But it was Prudence who answered that, her brow furrowed. "And why is it that people use that to justify risky behavior and bad habits? Choosing a quieter path is not condemning oneself to a half-life. There is more to this world than chasing after excess and adventure."

"Spoken by someone who has not truly experienced adventure," said Mr. Courtney with an expression that was far more condescending than warm—but if he expected Prudence to be cowed by that, he was a fool, for Rosanna was certain no one could put Prudence in "her place."

Straightening, Prudence gave him a look that held none of the gentleman's haughtiness, for it felt more compassionate than condemning. "And I am certain the same could be said of you, sir. Have you ever experienced the joy of a simple life?"

Mr. Courtney huffed. "There is none to be found in it."

"And there is no joy to be found in living recklessly."

"I disagree."

Prudence gave him a faint smile that was genuine. "And that, sir, is the joy to be had in differing opinions. Do not foist yours upon me, and I shall do the same. If you disagree with my stance, that is your prerogative, but belittling my beliefs does you no credit and does nothing to persuade me."

"Brava," said Rosanna.

With that, Mr. Courtney took her by the arm, and they turned towards where the races were to take place, but when they were a few paces away, he stopped. Mr. Courtney's brow furrowed, his expression growing stormy. With his dark coloring, he looked like a Gothic villain come to life, and Rosanna couldn't help the shiver of delight that ran down her spine as he turned those tempestuous eyes on her. There was a reason that such wretched characters were so captivating, and Rosanna couldn't help but smile at the show of temper.

Stepping closer, he lowered his voice so only she could hear. "Desist in these ridiculous games, Miss Rosanna. I do not take kindly to ladies who try to manipulate me. Flirt again with the physician, and I shall break ties with you. Do not test me on it."

"I wasn't flirting with him," she whispered back, though her sinking stomach testified that it wasn't the entire truth.

"I hadn't meant to," she amended, yet that felt no more honest than her first statement. Had she truly intended to do so? It hadn't been conscious. Not entirely. She didn't think so.

Her gaze darted to the man in question for a heartbeat to see if he'd heard that accusation. But though Dr. Humphreys watched her with a furrowed brow, which deepened as he considered Mr. Courtney, he did not seem to hear the accusation.

"I am no fool, Miss Rosanna, and I shan't repeat myself." Mr. Courtney paused for a moment, holding her in an implacable gaze that demanded obedience. And for all that Rosanna wanted to respond flippantly, there was something in that command that made her giddy. For all that he was a strong-willed man, he was captivated by her. Enough that he felt threatened by a man far below him.

Rosanna's lips twisted into a coy smile as he raised his arm to her. Moving to take it, she was freed from Mr. Courtney's spell when Prudence swept in and took hold of her sister.

"It is my turn to walk with Rosanna," she said as the pair hurried off in search of the smock races.

Chapter 28

Hazarding a glance at Prudence, Rosanna sighed and shook her head as the others trailed after her. "You needn't worry about Mr. Courtney. He is brusque and demanding, but I rather like an authoritative man."

And once more today, her instincts were shuddering and twisting as though recognizing some truth she would not or could not recognize. Mr. Courtney worshiped her. Of that much she was certain, so there was little else to fret about.

Rosanna glanced over her shoulder to see him watching her and added, "Perhaps he is a tad—"

"You mustn't wager on the races," whispered Prudence. Her tone was brittle and her smile a bit too stiff, but they walked arm in arm as though nothing was amiss.

"Pardon?"

"You heard me, Rosanna."

"True," she replied with a wry smile, "but I am struggling to follow the conversation. I had thought—"

Prudence shook her head as a slight frown wrinkled her brow. "You already spent a fortune on a gown that no one can see, and you have no more pin money."

"Papa gave me some before we left," said Rosanna, lifting her reticule and giving it a jingle. "Not that I need it, as Mr. Courtney has paid for everything."

Prudence turned her gaze to the path before them, her expression carefully blank, and Rosanna sighed.

"You fret too much, Prudence."

"Do you truly wish to waste your money on something so frivolous?"

Prudence's words were so close to Dr. Humphreys' objections that Rosanna couldn't cast them aside so easily. Betting was harmless. Truly it was. Despite the cautionary tales of fortunes being lost, most people wagered a little and were none the worse for it.

But clearly, Dr. Humphreys prized caution, and with his praise ringing in her memory, Rosanna couldn't help but wish to be the lady he believed her to be. And Prudence was right, for it was far better to spend her money on tangible things. She could buy several lengths of ribbon or maybe a few new handkerchiefs, rather than waste it on the unlikely chance she might win.

However, those thoughts were disrupted as their group cleared the tents and stalls to see the race course stretching before them. The crowds were thick around the edge, filling in every inch of green. Children even hung from tree limbs to get a better view, and a few of the wealthier patrons were seated in their carriages and atop their horses, watching from afar with opera glasses. But whilst their distant seats were far more advantageous for viewing, Rosanna preferred the thrum of the crowd.

Along one end stood a group of young women, all looking to be in their teens or early twenties. They strutted about, waving to the crowd and warming up their limbs in preparation for the coming race. The announcer at the far end bellowed something that was swallowed up in the tumult. Thankfully, the gentlemen of their group quickly gathered round, clearing a space for the ladies.

Mr. Courtney came up on her right side and took her free arm. "I found a bloke who is offering good odds, and I've placed twenty pounds on the blonde taking it all."

Rosanna followed his gaze and spied the comely lass with golden hair. She stood a good head over the others, giving her a clear advantage with those long legs of hers.

"They say she easily won the earlier heats. She's a scrapper and slated to win, but more than that, blondes are my lucky charm." Mr. Courtney gave Rosanna's golden curls draped around her face a smug look, but she refused to blush.

"Are they?" she asked with an innocent air.

"Very much so," he replied in that low tone of his that had the unfortunate tendency to make her weak in the knees. Navigating the courting arena required competence and strength, and having a gentleman who made her feel like jelly was hardly conducive to success.

Then, turning to their group, Mr. Courtney bellowed out, "I've put twenty pounds on the blonde. Anyone think they can beat me?"

Mr. Davis laughed. "Count me in for a pound on the buxom brunette at the end."

His sister gaped at his description, and though the bounder had the good sense to look a little chagrined at his inopportune words, any embarrassment he might've felt evaporated as Mr. Courtney laughed.

"A pound? Do not wager at all if that is all you're going to stake, Mr. Davis. I had thought you braver than that," he said in a dismissive tone.

"A fiver?" Mr. Davis added with a strained smile.

Mr. Poole clapped the man on the shoulder. "I'll match Mr. Courtney's wager, but on the redhead in the center."

And soon, the gentlemen were calling out amounts and their runner whilst the bookmaker wandered the group, writing down the tallies. It took no more than a few seconds of the surge of energy before the ladies were throwing in with the gentlemen, though with a touch more caution.

"Shameful, ladies," said Mr. Courtney with a laugh, which spurred them to throw in just a touch more, though none of them had enough pin money to match the gentlemen. The air thrummed with energy like in springtime when the world burst into color; it filled Rosanna, pulsing through her with the promise of something wonderful to come.

"I think the blonde will take it all," said Rosanna with a broad smile at Mr. Courtney.

"You do, do you? And how much will you stake on the matter?" he asked with a smirk.

"Rosanna," whispered Prudence. Though quiet, the sharpness of her sister's rebuke startled Rosanna. More so when she turned to find Prudence watching her with a deepening frown.

Turning to her sister, Rosanna let the energy of the moment flow through her. "Don't you feel it, Prudence? I know she will win. It's not a wager when it is a certain thing."

Dr. Humphreys brow furrowed; his expression was so full of righteous indignation that Rosanna's insides twisted.

"Don't get all high and mighty, my good doctor," said Mr. Courtney with a laugh. "It is a harmless diversion."

"Perhaps for those who can afford it, but not everyone has your deep pockets," murmured Dr. Humphreys.

Turning to Rosanna, Mr. Courtney watched her with an appraising look. "And what will you wager on our blonde to win?"

The coins in her reticule were not so great as all that, but the young woman was certain to win, so was it truly that much of a risk? Mr. Courtney looked so assured, his gaze daring her to lose her courage, and Rosanna jutted out her chin.

"I'll put," Rosanna hesitated for the briefest moment before concluding, "twenty."

Prudence gaped, and her eyes widened, but the expression held none of the power the lady intended. It was so sanctimonious, and Rosanna bristled at the accusation in her gaze. But before any further discussion could be had, the rest of the group laid out their bets, and soon the announcer was bellowing something that still did not carry above the tumult. However, as the young women were lining up, it was clear the race was about to begin.

At the finish line stood a tall pole with outstretched arms, serving as the marker for the end of the race and displaying the prize that was to be theirs. The white smock stood out like a beacon, and though Rosanna could not tell from this distance what fabric it was precisely, it was fine linen or perhaps even Indian muslin with extensive embroidering around the neck. Rosanna had quite a few chemises, but this one was fine enough that she nearly wished to join in the race.

A pistol cracked in the air, and the maidens shot forward, hiking up their skirts to sprint across the green. Their bare feet and legs flashed in the sunlight, their hair pulling free of their bandeaus to flap behind them. Rosanna hopped up and down, clinging to Mr. Courtney's hand as their blonde took an easy lead, eating up the ground with her long strides while the others trailed behind her.

But a small brunette darted forward, closing the distance and nipping at the leader's heels. They all streaked across the grass, the crowd pulsing and jeering as they cheered the racers on. The brunette did her best to catch the leader, but she continued to lag just behind. Rosanna shouted with all her strength, certain the blonde could hear her as the racers tore closer to the finish line.

With a burst of speed, the brunette drew up within touching distance, and with outstretched hands, she ripped at the blonde's skirts, jerking the girl off-balance. Rosanna's hands flew to her mouth as she watched her racer tumble to the ground, and though the blonde rose once more, the brunette crossed the finish line.

Rosanna froze in place, her lungs seizing as she realized what had happened. Twenty pounds! Twenty! Good heavens, how was she to pay such a sum?

But it had been a certain thing. Their racer would've won had the brunette not pulled such a nasty trick. That wretched woman! If one could not win by fair means, one shouldn't race at all. Teeth clenched together, Rosanna cursed the girl and all her kin to perdition. Yet even as anger bubbled within, she knew it needed to be directed inward. There were no rules in these races; thus, the brunette's move had been perfectly strategic. And the young woman hadn't forced Rosanna to make the wager.

Shoulders dropping, she caught sight of the bookmaker striding towards their group, all smiles. But then, it was he who benefited most from the race.

"That was a laugh," said Mr. Courtney as he handed over a banknote, ignoring the general devastation skittering through their group.

"That may be a pittance to you, sir, but that is more than many people make in a year," said Prudence.

With a huff, Mr. Courtney shook his head. "You may be named Prudence, but you needn't be so prudish. It is no different than buying theater tickets or a book or any other diversion. I was entertained, so what does it matter?"

"Mind your tone, Mr. Courtney. Speak to my sister with respect," said Rosanna, taking Prudence by the arm and turning away, but then she realized she needed to remain to settle her debts. What she didn't know was how the shillings in her reticule would transform into twenty pounds.

It didn't matter anyway, for Mr. Courtney hurried to stop them.

With another of his disarming laughs, he gave the two of them a grin. "It was a simple jest. There is no need to be so tender about it."

"You ought not to mock those who encourage you to be better," said Rosanna, holding firm to her sister as Prudence glanced between the pair.

"Far better people than you or your sister have tried and failed," he replied. "I am not one to reform, and if you think to try your hand at it, you'd best surrender. The odds are not in your favor, and you've proven yourself a poor gambler."

Then he leaned closer and whispered into her ear, "You needn't fear the bookmaker, my dear. I shall cover the loss."

Rosanna jerked away. "I cannot accept such a gift, sir. People will talk."

She'd spoken with such haste that she did not lower her voice. Thankfully, the crowd was raucous enough that only Prudence and Mr. Courtney heard her, and the former looked all the grimmer for it.

"And what would they say? That I am securing Miss Rosanna Leigh as my wife?"

Her heart grew heavy, and her insides gave a sickening turn as Mr. Courtney spoke so flippantly about her, as though he were purchasing a side of beef.

Rosanna clung to Prudence and responded with an airy tone. "I am worth far more than a twenty pound note."

"Too true, or I wouldn't bother with playing your games."

Feelings were a fickle thing. Though she'd longed to cast him aside just moments ago, Mr. Courtney spoke with enough sincerity that her cold feelings warmed, and they heated all the quicker when he used those handsome eyes of his to such advantage, gazing upon her with an admiration that even the stoniest of hearts could not ignore.

Giving her a curt little bow, he offered up his arm to her once more. "Do not rush off now. I apologize if your feathers were ruffled, but there is no point in leaving so soon. We ought not to let a trifling wager ruin a wonderful afternoon."

"Rosanna..." whispered Prudence, but it was hard to hear her over the din of the crowd and the heartbeat thumping in Rosanna's ears.

With a sigh and a shake of her head, Rosanna released her sister and took Mr. Courtney's arm. "I cannot leave until I see the magician."

Chapter 29

There was nothing quite like having a man gaze upon you as though you were what he desired most in the world, and thoughts of Mr. Courtney had followed Rosanna into sleep, filling her dreams with burning gazes and words whispered in that low tone of his that never failed to send a shiver down her spine. His arms wrapped around her, filling her senses as he leaned close to kiss her.

Loud steps in the hall jerked Rosanna out of her dreams, and she groaned, pulling the pillow over her face. She did not wish to face the world when there were still so many delicious fantasies to play out in her sleep, but no matter how she tried to find a comfortable position, her mind was too alert to slip back into Mr. Courtney's embrace.

Plumping the pillows beneath her head, she stared at the canopy above her. The maid passed their door once more, the floorboards creaking with every step.

"What are they doing out there?" she murmured to her sister, but there was no reply. Turning on her side, Rosanna stared into the shadow of her sister's bed, and the bright white of the sheets thrown back made it clear even in the dark that she was not abed.

Rosanna lay there for a few more minutes before curiosity drove her from her bed. She yanked open the curtains, her eyes squinting against the morning light; then, pulling on her wrapper and donning her slippers, she stepped into the hall. But despite all the activity moments before, there was not a soul in sight now.

Following the noises, she climbed the stairs to the nursery. Coughing cut through the air, hard and deep enough that Rosanna's lungs hurt in sympathy, and her footsteps quickened as she snuck into her brother's bedchamber. The curtains were pulled tight, with only the light of the candles and fireplace helping her to see. Mama sat in the corner, weeping into her handkerchief, and Rosanna's heart shuddered beneath the funereal air choking the room.

"Mama, please calm yourself and fetch us some more of your tincture. You know it is never fixed properly without your oversight," said Prudence, though her gaze remained trained on her brother. She dabbed at his head with a washcloth and directed the nursemaid and kitchen maid to arrange teapots and tinctures about the side tables.

The lady straightened and moved to the door, though it took more cajoling before Mama finally slipped past Rosanna and hurried down the hall. Stepping fully into the room, Rosanna shut the door and came to the bedside.

"Is he worse?" she asked, though it was a ridiculous question when his lungs rattled with every breath, struggling for air as though they were filled with cotton. "He seemed so much better before bed."

"He had a turn for the worse in the middle of the night," said Prudence, her attention never wavering from her brother as she bathed his forehead.

"What can I do?" asked Rosanna, wringing her hands before her. Stepping closer, she reached for Benjamin's cheek, pressing a touch to the fevered skin when Prudence lifted the rag away to dip it once more in the cool water. The poor child panted, his eyes watching his sisters in a fog of fever.

"Mr. Upton just left," replied Prudence. "He said the cough sounded worse than it was."

Rosanna's brows rose, and her vision grew misty. "But he can hardly breathe—"

"I am doing what I can," snapped Prudence, though her frown deepened the moment she said it. With a sigh, she shook her head. "I apologize. I am exhausted, and it will be some time before we shall see if Mr. Upton's remedies do any good."

Glancing at the space their mother had occupied, Rosanna was certain the hours her sister had spent at Benjamin's side had not been easy ones. "Take a rest. I shall watch over him if you will tell me what he needs."

Prudence paused in her ministrations and looked at her sister; Rosanna met the gaze, her own pleading that her sister would listen. Stepping forward, she reached for the rag, but Prudence shook her head.

"It is so kind of you to offer, but I have it in hand. Mr. Upton's instructions were vast and complicated, and it would take more effort to explain than to manage it on my own. I am not so tired that I cannot remain."

"But how may I be of assistance? I wish to help, Prudence."

Benjamin stirred, his head turning towards his eldest sister, and she quickly wetted the cloth and touched his forehead and cheeks again.

"I have it in hand, Rosanna." Then, in a low tone, Prudence added, "You haven't the nerves for the sickroom, and I have my hands full at present."

She set to cooling her brother's brow again and directed the nursemaid to give Benjamin a few sips to drink.

"I am not comfortable nursing, but I am not wholly useless at it," murmured Rosanna with a furrowed brow, though it was close enough to a lie that her conscience gave an unhappy wriggle.

"I did not mean it as a censure. We each have our talents, and this is not yours."

And though Prudence's tone rang with truth, Rosanna

couldn't help the way her shoulders drooped as she considered how short her list of talents was.

"Please give me something to do. Anything." Rosanna hated the plaintive timbre in her voice, but she couldn't help it.

Prudence glanced at her with a furrowed brow before directing the nursemaid to fetch more boiling water. "Dr. Humphreys recommended essence of camphor, but I fear we do not have any in the medicine chest. Perhaps you can run to the apothecary and fetch some. We also need more mustard powder for plasters."

Standing there, Rosanna watched her sister as she directed the servants whilst comforting their little brother, managing all without the slightest slip just like the skilled jugglers they'd witnessed yesterday. And apparently, Rosanna's only use was to go shopping.

"Please, dearest," said Prudence. "I cannot go myself, and the servants are all occupied."

Rosanna nodded, turning on her heel to hurry to their bedchamber. In a trice, she changed, forgoing her usual ministrations. But as she pulled on her cloak and strode towards town, she couldn't help but notice the similarities between how Prudence "managed" Mama when she was making a nuisance of herself and the "urgent" errand she'd sent Rosanna on.

...

Greater Edgerton suited Parker. Though he'd enjoyed a taste of city life in Edinburgh, such places were better for visiting rather than as a permanent residence. For all that this town was busier than many of its country cousins, with its thriving commerce and noisy mills, Greater Edgerton moved at a slower pace than the bustling metropolises. However, he missed the vendors clogging Edinburgh's streets.

A physician learned early to take food whenever he could manage it, for one did not always know how long a case was going to take, when he might be expected at home, or if his patient's family would deign to feed him. However, during his university years he'd had no trouble finding something to tide him over. And Parker's stomach was murmuring like an entitled old biddy.

That was not to say that Greater Edgerton didn't have shops selling meals to hungry patrons, but eating by himself in a restaurant or coffee house was unappealing. Parker didn't mind it at times but preferred quick bites to a seated meal. There were vendors sprinkled on the street corners, but the quality was sadly lacking, leaving Parker uncertain as to whether or not he'd get beef or cat in his meat pie with a crust made of flour or plaster.

There was a particularly fine cart he favored, for it carried the most buttery and light sweet buns he'd ever tasted, with a warm mug of salop to wash it down. However, as luck would have it, he was a good hour's walk from that location, and no matter how tempting it was, it was a waste of time. But then, he had little else to do at present. Parker's scheduled calls were finished for the day, and though there were a few patients he might visit, their cases weren't pressing.

Wandering the street, he pondered what to do with himself as his feet steered him around the people and carts. One possibility lingered in his mind, needling him as he turned his thoughts toward food. It was too presumptive. The Leighs had not requested his professional services, and Miss Leigh was quite capable of procuring medicines and administering them to her brother.

But the idea followed him along until he couldn't deny the impulse any longer. And apparently, his feet had already decided for him, for they had taken him in that direction. Soon he was on the Leighs' doorstep, wondering what excuse he was going to give for poking his nose into their business.

But any such concerns evaporated when the maid opened the door, dropped her gaze to the medical bag in Parker's hand, and beamed at him. "Thank goodness you've come, sir."

Brows raised, he followed the servant through the house, delving deeper inside than ever before. Parker was quite used to having access to personal quarters, but it felt strange in the Leighs' home.

"Did they send for me?" asked Parker with a furrowed brow. That expression only deepened when he couldn't recall the maid's name, though he usually made a habit of learning them, for he spent more time with the servants than he did with the family—excepting his patient.

The girl glanced over her shoulder and winced. "I ought not to have said anything, sir, but Miss Leigh is desperate for aid, and that Mr. Upton only made things worse."

Parker nodded, and his stride lengthened until the maid was struggling to keep ahead of him. In short order, they were in the uppermost reaches of the house, but before the young woman touched the doorknob, the bedchamber door opened and Miss Leigh emerged, a deep furrow marring her brow as her hands worried her skirts. Behind her, a cough rent the air as wheezing lungs fought for breath.

"Dr. Humphreys?" Miss Leigh's brows rose, and she glanced behind him, as though the explanation for his appearance would appear out of thin air.

"I thought I ought to call and see how your brother is doing," he said. "You seemed quite worried about him yesterday."

Miss Leigh's ashen expression testified that her worries had not eased since he'd seen her last, and it was clear from her morning gown and the haphazard manner in which her hair was gathered up in the bandeau that she had likely been up half the night with her patient and likely needed assistance, as the maid had said.

Yet despite that, she shook her head. "That is kind of you, but I wouldn't wish to trouble you—"

"It is no trouble. I find myself without anything to do this afternoon."

"Mr. Upton examined him early this morning, and there is little more we can do for Benjamin," she said with a shake of her head, motioning Parker back down the hall.

"If you wish me gone, then I will go, but I cannot leave you in such a state without offering assistance."

Despite her best efforts, Miss Leigh's gaze blazed with gratitude and relief, those dark depths revealing far more than she likely intended, for again, she motioned him away.

"I sent Rosanna out a while ago to fetch some more medicines, and I am simply waiting for her to return. Then we shall have everything in order. I would hate to impose."

"Despite all the trouble I've caused you, I had thought we were becoming friends." Parker shifted in place and scratched at the back of his head with a free hand. "Or I had hoped we were, at the very least. To my way of thinking, friends cannot truly impose upon one another."

Miss Leigh stilled. She swallowed, ducking her head and leaving him unable to read anything in those expressive eyes, and Parker longed to nudge up her chin so he could see them once more.

"Please allow me to help. Even if it is just until your sister returns." Then, with a smile, he lifted his bag and added, "And I would like to mention that my medical bag is stocked with many of the medicines you require."

A tremulous smile pricked at the corner of her lips as Miss Leigh met his eyes once more, her own far brighter than before. "Thank you, Dr. Humphreys."

"There is no need to thank a person for basic human decency," he replied with a grin.

Miss Leigh gave a halting chuckle, which had an edge of tears to it, though she held herself with that same calm fortitude that resolutely bore any trouble heaped upon her.

"If you insist on handing out your services for free, Dr. Humphreys, it is a wonder you have any income at all."

"You are a special case," he said, nodding towards the door, and Miss Leigh followed the prompt, opening the bedchamber door.

Chapter 30

The doorway was a black portal, striking a stark boundary between the bright hallway and the nursery. Parker could hardly see a thing, despite the handful of candles placed around the bed, and he blinked at the shadows, wishing his eyes would adjust quicker. Without prompting, he stepped around Miss Leigh and moved to the child's side, and even the untrained eye could tell he was in a bad way, though not in such a state that he deserved the wailing sobs coming from the corner.

Ignoring Mrs. Leigh's weeping, Parker took the seat beside the boy. "Hello there, Benjamin. I hear you're not feeling well."

Eyes so very like his eldest sister's opened and peered at the physician, though they struggled to focus. Parker felt Benjamin's forehead. There was an infection of some sort, though thankfully, the lad's neck was not so tender or swollen as to imply something truly concerning. Miss Leigh came to the other side of the bed, hovering nearby but without impeding the examination.

Benjamin let out another wracking cough, followed by a low moan from Mrs. Leigh as she buried her face in her handkerchief.

"You there," Parker called to the maid.

"Yes, sir," she said with a bob.

Parker nodded towards the windows. "Draw open the curtains. I need to see."

"Mr. Upton said that we ought to leave the room dark and warm," said Miss Leigh.

And that it was, for Parker felt like wiping the sweat from his forehead. "If the light does not bother Benjamin's eyes, there's no need to keep it dark, and I need to see."

But it was her mother that replied to that with a shake of her head. "Mr. Upton said to do so. We ought not to go against his orders or Benjamin might be made to suffer from it."

"I assure you I am quite well-trained," said Parker, glancing between the mother and daughter. He didn't wish to go so far as to disparage Mr. Upton, for the surgeon-apothecary was quite knowledgeable, but his learning was tainted by the old home remedies and superstitions.

Miss Leigh needed no further urging. Her mother continued to voice her concerns, her tone growing shriller as she alternated between dire predictions and tears, but in a trice, Miss Leigh called for the candles to be snuffed whilst she walked to the window and drew back the curtains. Everyone inside flinched at the light, but the patient hardly noted the change, and Parker frowned at the brightness of the lad's cheeks.

"What are we to do if he should perish?" murmured Mrs. Leigh, dabbing at her eyes. "Please, Dr. Humphreys, you must save him. We shall be ruined!"

Parker paused with his hands on the edge of the bedcovers, his gaze shooting to the lady.

"We cannot lose him, Dr. Humphreys." Mrs. Leigh's words were broken, and she drew her arms tight around her. "We prayed for a son for so long. Surely the Lord cannot take him now that we have him. We will lose everything."

"Mama," murmured a young lady at her side, and Parker's attention turned to the figure he hadn't noticed amongst the shadows before. Miss Katherine Leigh set down her book and glanced between her mother and Dr. Humphreys. "Benjamin is not at death's door."

"Do be quiet, Katherine!" snapped Mrs. Leigh, sending a scowl to her daughter. "Why do you insist on filling the air with your nonsense? He has the look of death about him, and it is just like fate to give us hope and then snatch it away. Then your father shall contract this pestilence, and we shall lose everything to the dreaded entail—"

Miss Leigh shot from her feet and moved to the corner, saying in a low voice, "Mama, would you please fetch some of that tisane Mrs. Poole recommended? And perhaps you might have Mrs. James make some more of Benjamin's favorite cakes. That would do a world of good."

"Send Jane to do it," said Mrs. Leigh, waving at the maid in the corner.

"You know it shan't be done properly if you do not direct them," said her daughter with a smile. "It is bound to raise Benjamin's spirits if nothing else."

Parker watched the whole thing with wide eyes as Miss Leigh quickly bundled her mother and sister out of the room, managing it with ease. With a look of apology to the maid, she whispered something more in the girl's ear before the door shut tight behind them all, leaving Parker and Miss Leigh alone with Benjamin.

"Nicely done, Miss Leigh," said Parker, but when the young lady sat down once more, there was a hint of pink to her cheeks that he might've thought was fever if not for the scene that had just played out; a strand of hair fell free of her bandeau, and she tucked it behind her ear, unable to meet his gaze.

Parker wanted to say something, but as he considered what it might be, he realized the best thing he could give her was silence; that was the only way in which he wouldn't embarrass her further. Or cast himself in a poor light again.

"It looks like a putrid sore throat. What was done for him?" asked Parker, taking up the abandoned washcloth on the side table to dab at Benjamin's forehead. The child turned towards the cool touch, the strain in his expression easing.

"I gave him a mustard bath and have been feeding him tisanes of meadowsweet and wormwood, and a few grains of fever powder and some drops of ipecacuanha wine as Dr. Buchan directed in his book," she said. "I was afraid to give him more, for he had a bad reaction to it some years ago."

"It can have that effect if given in too great a dose," he said with a nod.

"When Mr. Upton arrived, he applied leeches and then a mustard plaster before giving him a bit of laudanum to sleep," she said. "I wanted to give him essence of camphor, as you suggested, but I do not have any, and Rosanna has not yet returned from the apothecary."

Parker nodded, tucking each bit of information away in his memory. "It is only valuable in the early stages, so I doubt it would do any good now."

Turning his attention to his patient, Parker pulled back the bedclothes. Benjamin shivered despite the heat of the room, and Parker murmured those little comforts that the sick needed in such times, but his gaze was fixed on the mustard plaster applied to his chest.

"How long has this been on him?" asked Parker as he peeled back the edge of the linen adhered to his skin by the mustard paste. From the feel and the redness beneath, it must've been some time ago.

"Mr. Upton insisted he needed it to clear his chest and to leave it on him for twelve hours—" But her words died as the plaster pulled away to reveal Benjamin's inflamed skin. Covering her mouth, she stared at the rash.

"He was correct on the first point, but he should never have told you to keep it on for so long," said Parker as he pulled the rest of the plaster away and tossed it onto the side table.

Yanking open his bag, he pulled out clean linen and wiped the child's skin. Thankfully, Benjamin was too fevered and medicated to fuss over the sting. Miss Leigh leapt from her chair and hurried to a table on the far side of the room. Pulling through her medicine chest, she grabbed a bottle and brought it to Parker's side, offering it up.

"It's a lotion mixed with pennyroyal, marshmallow, and zinc sulfate," she said. "I haven't had much practice in the sick-room with fevers and the like, but Benjamin often suffers from rashes and irritations, and this seems to help."

Parker nodded and took the bottle, rubbing the lotion into the child's chest. Glancing at his bag, he was about to reach for a clean square of linen, but Miss Leigh swooped in and handed it over before he moved.

Turning back to his patient, he continued his examination, and Miss Leigh remained at his elbow. Having managed many an anxious mother before, Parker intended to send her back to her seat, but the look in her eyes simply begged to be of some use, and he handed her his case. With little prompting, she fetched anything he required, quickly anticipating many of his requests as efficiently as any nurse he'd seen before (and in many ways more so).

With eyes darting between her brother and that little black medical bag, Prudence had plenty on her mind. Dr. Humphreys gave clear and easy instructions, allowing her something to do rather than hovering nearby, praying for the best. But even with her thoughts and hands mostly occupied, she couldn't ignore the way her throat clamped tight.

She should've known better. Mr. Upton had been insistent, but Prudence knew her brother and ought to have questioned the apothecary's strong mustard plaster and application. What a fool she was, and poor Benjamin was paying the price.

Dr. Humphreys settled in to wait, and Prudence forced herself not to harry the gentleman. Surely there was something more they could do, some powder or tincture that might ease the fretful cough that rang in the room. But if that were true, Dr. Humphreys would've done it.

Benjamin groaned, and Prudence leaned around the doctor to press a kiss to his hot forehead. She sent out a silent prayer on his behalf, hoping that something they did might bring Benjamin comfort.

"I wish there was more I could do," said Dr. Humphreys with a frown as he watched his patient. "But now, it is merely a matter of waiting to see if our efforts bear fruit."

Taking up the water and washcloth, Prudence returned to her seat and bathed her brother's forehead. With a glance at Dr. Humphreys, she said, "It is kind of you to visit, but if there is nothing else for you to do, you needn't remain here."

Dr. Humphreys' gave her a raised brow. "You wish to be rid of me so quickly?"

The tone was too amused to sting, and Prudence gave him a faint smile in response. "Of course not, but surely you have more important things to do."

"Not at all," he replied. "And my staying will give you and your family some comfort, so why shouldn't I? I have appointments tomorrow, but until then, my time is yours, Miss Leigh."

Straightening, Prudence looked at the fellow, for he truly seemed determined to settle in for a good, long wait. For all that he hadn't been able to do much, it set her heart at ease knowing Benjamin was in far more capable hands.

With too few hours' sleep and the strain of Benjamin's health pressing down on her, Prudence struggled to keep her eyes from brimming. It was ridiculous behavior, but between Dr. Humphreys' fortuitous arrival and all the kindnesses he'd exhibited, she struggled to maintain control. Dabbing at Benjamin's brow, she sent out another silent prayer of thanks for angels who took human form. Perhaps it was a bit ridiculous to think of this very fallible man in such a heavenly light, but at that moment, he was a messenger from on high.

"Thank—" But she cut off that word when Dr. Humphreys gave her a kindly meant but stern look.

"No thanking me for human decency," he reminded her with a spark of laughter in his gaze.

Straightening, Prudence met that with a lift of her chin. “Thank you, Dr. Humphreys.”

Crossing his arms, the gentleman chuckled and turned his gaze back to his patient. To her untrained eyes, Benjamin seemed to be resting better than before, though every breath rattled and strained.

“It is always difficult to watch the little ones struggle,” said Dr. Humphreys, drawing her attention to find him watching her with a sympathetic shine in his gaze. “I would much rather suffer it myself—”

The nursery door opened, and Prudence closed her eyes with a sigh: no good would come through that door.

Chapter 31

"Is he any better?" asked Mama, carrying a tea tray to the table on the other side of the room before hurrying to the bedside while holding her handkerchief to her nose. "His color looks worse."

"It has been only a quarter of an hour—a half hour at the most," said Prudence, holding back a sigh. She ought not to blame Jane for Mama's untimely return; the maid could do little to deter her mistress when the lady was of a mind to do something, but Prudence had hoped for a little more of a respite.

"Oh, my dear boy," said Mama, fluttering about the bed. "If he should die...surely God would not be so cruel."

Prudence glanced at Dr. Humphreys; he had that same pinched look about him as before, and she felt her cheeks heat again.

"You do look a little flushed, Prudence," said Mama. "Surely you have not contracted it as well?"

"I am well, Mama. Simply tired, that is all."

"Oh, of course, my dear," she replied with a vigorous nod. "You've been working so very hard."

Turning towards Benjamin, Prudence distracted herself by

mopping his brow. For all that Mama didn't think he looked any better, the child was calmer, and surely a proper rest would help most of all. Prudence's eyes ached, warning her that she could do with a lie-down as well.

"I assure you we've done everything we can," said Dr. Humphreys.

"Certainly," said Mama, moving around the bed as though seeing her child from a different angle might set her more at ease. Prudence forced herself not to watch the agitated pacing, for it was bound to set her head pounding. "You are so capable, Dr. Humphreys, and Prudence is such an excellent assistant. So good and steady. Just the sort that one wants by their side."

Prudence's cheeks heated once more, but it loosened some of the knots inside her stomach rather than tightened them. She wasn't tending to Benjamin for the praise (and heaven knew Mama wasn't a fine judge of character or worth), but it was gratifying to have someone acknowledge her efforts.

"She has been an excellent nurse," said Dr. Humphreys, drawing Prudence's gaze for the briefest of moments. Their eyes locked, and he gave her a faint smile, which made her blush even further. Thankfully, the room was still warm enough that her cheeks had a natural pink to them.

"I—" But Prudence's words died as Rosanna swept into the room, casting aside her pelisse as she hurried to the bedside with a basket.

"I have what you requested..." Rosanna paused when she spied Dr. Humphreys. With her free hand, she patted her hair, only to discover her bonnet was still fixed in place, and quickly, she removed it and moved to her sister's side of the bed.

Prudence turned away, focusing her attention on Benjamin, for it was far better than acknowledging her sister at present. With the room alight once more, she cast a glance at the clock on the table and the heat in her cheeks spread, settling into her heart. Stepping forward, Rosanna dug a bottle from her basket and held out the requested medicines with a beaming smile as though anticipating some grand show of pleasure.

Only when she was certain of her tone did Prudence ask, "I needed that hours ago, Rosanna. Where have you been?"

Setting the bottle and the basket on the bed, her sister had the good sense to give a chagrined tinge to her smile, but the airy wave and the fact that she could grin in any fashion set Prudence's teeth on edge.

"I crossed paths with some friends," said Rosanna, her brows pinching together. "Your tone made it clear the errand wasn't urgent, so I didn't hurry."

Prudence drew in a deep breath, letting it out through her nose as she dabbed away at Benjamin's fevered skin.

"Foolish girl," said Mama, startling everyone in the bedchamber, for she had managed to remain silent for several minutes. "Your brother needed this medicine, and you wandered around, chatting with your friends? What if he had died because of it? How important would your gossip have been then?"

"Mama..." said Rosanna, standing at the bedside like a gaping statue.

But her mother only huffed. "It is a good thing Prudence is such a good, steady girl. She has been slaving away, tending to his every need while you swan about without a care in the world. I am thoroughly ashamed of you!"

For one bright, burning moment, Prudence's heart lightened; Rosanna's brows rose as though the censure was altogether mystifying, and it was. Prudence couldn't think of a time she'd ever heard Mama chide beloved Rosanna. And why should she? Rosanna was the dear girl destined to save them from penury. Until Benjamin arrived in the family seven years ago, she'd been their only hope for the future.

And now, it was Prudence Leigh who had value in their mother's eyes.

But the truth of the situation crashed down on her like a bucket of ice water, dousing the flame before it had time to grow. What sort of person found joy in her sister being belittled? Having spent so much of her life struggling to accept her inherent value, Prudence knew better than to look to others for such validation. Yet with one small word of praise and censure, Prudence ignored all the hard-won lessons of the past and basked in her sister's downfall.

Her dear sister. Prudence didn't understand how love could be so complicated, for she knew with all her heart that she adored Rosanna. There was no question of that. Yet at times, she struggled to remember it.

Prudence's stomach churned, her hands clenching tight around the wet cloth, and though she knew Rosanna could not read her mind, she couldn't bear to look at her sister, lest she see the truth of her wicked thoughts.

"What were you thinking, Rosanna?" continued Mama. "He might've died, and we would've been ruined. All because of your selfishness."

"Mama!" snapped Prudence, cutting into the conversation and drawing the lady's attention away from Rosanna. Standing, she moved to the tea tray sitting on the table in the corner. Benjamin's toys had all been cleared away, leaving a perfect place for the spread, and Prudence began preparing a cup for her mother. "Here, you must be parched. Sit and calm yourself."

With a nod, Mama took the seat beside the table and drank deeply from her cup before turning her attention to the cakes. Prudence returned to her previous position, mulling over what she might've said to defend her sister, but Mama was not one to be reasoned with. Raising her eyes to her sister, Prudence tried to send her an apologetic look, but Rosanna's gaze was fixed on the rug at her feet.

"I fetched everything you requested and a few more medicines the apothecary recommended," she murmured, motioning to the basket she'd set on the edge of the bed.

Prudence didn't know what to say to ease the timid tone in her sister's voice, for her emotional and physical reserves were well and truly spent.

"Whom do you patronize?" asked Dr. Humphreys with a furrowed brow.

The sisters glanced at him, and though Prudence started to answer, it was Rosanna who blurted first, "Worth & Son."

Taking the basket in hand, he examined the bottles and sighed. "Mr. Worth is far too apt to prescribe more than is necessary, and I fear he has done so again. It would be wise to keep these in your medicine chest, but most are only moderately helpful for putrid sore throats."

Rosanna's shoulders fell even further, her brows drawing together with a sigh. She didn't speak, but she didn't need to; Prudence felt the disappointment and self-reproof rife in her posture and expression.

"Might I be of assistance?" she whispered, drawing nearer to her brother's bed and resting her hand on the footboard.

Rising to her feet, Prudence drew Rosanna away from the others. "Do you know what I would wish above all else?"

With a furrowed brow, Rosanna shook her head.

"Please take Mama and distract her. Keep her from the sickroom."

Rosanna's shoulders drooped yet again, but before she could mount a protest, Prudence hurried on, "I am in earnest. The greatest aid you can offer is to keep her from Benjamin."

Sighing heavily, her sister nodded. "But I can do more."

"There is nothing more important than that, Rosanna, I promise." Allowing just a touch of her desperation in her tone, Prudence added, "She spends her time fluttering about, moaning that he shall die. Besides being uncomfortable for Dr. Humphreys and myself, poor Benjamin can hear all her dire predictions. It is not helping matters, and she will not stay away. It will take all your skill to keep her occupied and away from the nursery."

The few hours of rest from the night before weren't enough to bear Prudence through an already taxing day, and she longed to climb into bed beside Benjamin and curl up beneath the covers. Her eyes burned with every blink, her head pulsing the early warnings of a megrim, yet she felt more at risk of bursting into tears at the thought of her sister and mother nearby.

They meant well. As much as she clung to that belief, it didn't help the strain resting heavy on her shoulders, making every joint and muscle ache as though she were an old and broken woman. More than that, her heart struggled to bear the weight of yet more expectations and emotions swirling in the room. Yet another person who required her to tend to them.

"Please," whispered Prudence. "I need your help."

Rosanna's chin trembled, and she drew her arms around Prudence. In a voice thick with tears, she murmured, "I am sorry for taking so long. I truly didn't mean to. I lost track of the hour and didn't realize how long I had tarried in the shops. I am such a foolish girl."

Prudence's arms squeezed tight around her. "Do not listen to Mama. You know what she is like, and she couldn't be more wrong. You are my favorite sister and my dearest friend, and I wouldn't adore you so if you were merely a foolish girl."

Leaning back, Rosanna gave a weak chuckle. "With such a sterling reference, I must be of the highest character."

"Certainly." Heart aching enough for the both of them, Prudence held her sister's gaze. Those eyes she knew so well. They had shared so much throughout their lives, and despite the turmoil and troubles of the world, Rosanna was always there. A ready companion.

"I do not say it enough, but I do love you." The whispered words made Rosanna's chin wobble, and Prudence struggled to keep her tears from leaking down her cheeks. "And I want to help in whatever way you require. However long it takes."

"Thank you, dearest. And I love you, too," she said, taking Rosanna's hand in hers. Then, leaning closer, Prudence gave her a pained grin. "Now, please rescue me from our mother."

Shoulders upright once more, Rosanna nodded and turned on her heel. Drawing up next to their mother, she said, "Perhaps we might take our tea downstairs, Mama."

"But—"

Rosanna employed that coy little pout that so often swayed men and women to her way of thinking and murmured, "But you promised to help me make over my bonnet. Mr. Courtney asked me to join him on another drive, and I ought to look my best."

Mama's eyes widened a fraction, and she darted a look at Benjamin for the briefest of moments.

"We shall send for you if anything changes," said Prudence, and that drew a nod from Mama.

"You are far more capable than I am, and with Dr. Humphreys, there is no reason I ought to remain," said Mama with a bright smile. Popping to her feet, she took Rosanna by the arm and quickly began dissecting the intended bonnet with the fervor and diligence of one of Dr. Humphreys' professors at medical school.

As the pair wandered out of the nursery, arm in arm, Rosanna sent her sister a smile from over her shoulder, and Prudence waved them off before shutting the door firmly behind them. She longed to sag against the wood, for she was quite certain her legs had not the strength to carry her back to her seat. They surprised her, though, dragging her over and dropping her heavily into the straight-backed chair.

And that was when she noticed that the washcloth was not where she'd left it, and Prudence glanced around with her brow pulled low. Then it appeared at the edge of her vision, and she turned to see Dr. Humphreys leaning across Benjamin to offer it up.

Prudence stilled, everything within her freezing as she met the doctor's gaze, though her courage failed her, leaving her unable to look at him. She didn't need the confirmation (for he had been seated there the entire time), but that glance was enough for her to know Dr. Humphreys had witnessed all of that travesty. The only comfort was knowing that she and Rosanna had spoken low enough that it was unlikely he'd heard anything, even if he was closer than Mama.

Lowering her gaze to Benjamin, she tried to keep her hands and thoughts occupied, but it was impossible when she was so very aware of Dr. Humphreys sitting right there.

Chapter 32

Prudence drew in a breath, steeling her nerves. "I apologize—"

"No need."

With another heavy sigh, she sent Dr. Humphreys a sad smirk. "I am not allowed to thank you for human decency. Am I also not allowed to apologize for uncomfortable moments?"

"When they are not of your making?" he asked with a raise of his brow.

That was true enough, but it did not untangle the bindings squeezing her heart or cool her flaming cheeks.

Dr. Humphreys shifted in his seat, settling into it. "But you should know that I spend much of my time in private quarters during anxious moments in people's lives. I often witness things families would rather be left private."

"Is that so?" asked Prudence, simply because it seemed as though he needed some prompting, though his assurances failed to leave any mark on her heart.

"Quite," he said with a challenging glint in his gaze. "During my time in Edinburgh, I treated a lady who was visiting relatives a few towns over. She was one of those sorts who often felt far more ill than in reality, and she imagined herself on death's door, so she returned home to be nursed in comfort. I was called for and was at her bedside, providing more comfort than healing. Then her husband arrived home."

A smile tugged at his lips, and he paused for a long moment, as though waiting. Prudence couldn't help her curiosity as it tickled at her, demanding she speak.

"And?" she prompted.

"He thought she was still away, so he returned for the evening with his...*special friend.*" Dr. Humphreys' brows rose significantly, his tone speaking the word he didn't need to voice, and Prudence's eyes widened. He nodded, and added, "That would be shocking enough for my patient—if it weren't for the fact that the woman was also his wife's closest friend."

Prudence's mouth gaped, and she drew in a sharp breath. "No!"

"My patient rose from her deathbed like Lazarus of old and chased him about the house, trying to clobber him with the warming pan while the servants snuffed the hot coals spilling forth. It was a miracle the house was not burned to the ground," he said with a laugh. With a wince, he added, "And the husband's *special friend* was dragged out by her hair, leaving trails of flowers and false locks behind her."

"Your poor patient," she murmured, raising a hand to her chest. "I cannot imagine—"

"Do not feel too sorry for her, Miss Leigh," he replied. "Though I do not condone her husband's behavior, like many failed marriages it was not a matter of one being the victim of the other's poor behavior but both being too selfish and uncompromising to find a happy cohabitation. Both he and my patient were well suited in that they deserved one another. Misery loves company."

Prudence chuckled. It was faint and weak, but she did, and the sigh that followed was not so heavy or deep, but she knew her spirits wouldn't lighten until Benjamin was whole again. Turning back to her own patient, Prudence dabbed at his brow and wondered how long it might take for this illness to run its course.

"Then there was a time I overheard a rather spectacular deathbed confession." The statement sounded innocuous, but there was just a hint of a tone to it; like a fishing lure, it dangled before Prudence, begging her to take it.

"I imagine you've heard quite a few of those," she replied.

Dr. Humphreys nodded. "Yes, but they don't usually reveal that the fellow had cut his son and heir from his will in favor of his beloved bloodhound."

That startled a laugh out of Prudence, and when she glanced at the doctor, he looked far too pleased with himself, so she attempted a stern look, but the gentleman looked unrepentant as he began to weave the tale.

...

Waiting was an important ingredient in medicine. Though many of the physicians refused to linger after their treatments were prescribed, the best among Parker's profession knew an important secret to their trade—he was there to aid the family as much as he was there for his patient.

The truth was that despite so many advances in their field, the body was a mystery. Most of the diseases he faced were unknown, and even if an ailment had a name, the cures were varied and haphazard; too many of their efforts were driven by hopes and prayers rather than true understanding. However, having a doctor brought patients and their families peace. Their faith in his abilities was far grander than he deserved, and sometimes hope was all he could offer them.

And that was what kept Parker at Benjamin's bedside.

The boy required no more attention. Parker had done what he could, and the only thing left for a physician to do was pray that this time the body healed itself. And despite the lateness of the hour, Parker remained in his seat.

The door handle rattled, and his gaze darted from the bed to the noise, his brows furrowed. The door crept open, bouncing a little, and then the edge of a tray poked through, and Parker jumped to his feet and hurried over to help Miss Leigh as she fought to get the food tray through the stubborn door.

"Here," he said, reaching to relieve her of the burden. The moment she released it, Parker nearly spilled it on the floor, as it was much heavier than it looked. Miss Leigh bustled past him and directed him towards the table, which had spent the day traveling ever closer to the bedside. The tea things were cleared away, and she laid out a spread that was far more suited to a dinner party than a vigil.

"Why isn't the maid managing this?" he asked with a frown.

Miss Leigh's gaze was just a touch unfocused, her eyes lifting to his in confusion as the words finally registered in her clearly foggy brain. "Nurse Johnson needs a rest if she is to be of any use to us later tonight, and as it is dinner, the maids are occupied."

Why the family thought the maids were better employed in managing their dinner instead of aiding Miss Leigh, Parker could not understand; however, after several hours in this household, he wasn't surprised, either. He said nothing more, merely frowning at the pies, meats, potatoes, breads, and fruits, all of which were far more than any two people could eat.

"If you insist on remaining with us gratis, then the least we can do is feed you well," said Miss Leigh with a smile, though it faded as her attention turned to her brother. His state was precisely as it was when she had left, so there was no use in her asking, though her gaze did so all the same.

"He is resting soundly," said Parker, moving to take his seat.

Miss Leigh nodded and turned her attention to the food, filling a plate precariously high. In quick movements, she laid a napkin and silverware on the bedcover in front of Parker, and before he knew what she was about, she handed over the plate.

"You needn't wait on me hand and foot, Miss Leigh."

"Again, Dr. Humphreys, I will remind you that you have spent hours at our home, watching over my brother and doing everything you can to heal him, to say nothing of the medicines you've administered from your supplies—which I highly suspect you do not intend to charge us for. The least I can do is wait on you hand and foot."

"You speak as though you've been lazing about." Parker's stomach growled at the scent of beef and vegetables smothered in gravy, and Miss Leigh smiled and gave him a pointed look at the food. But Parker gave her a pointed look in return. "Are you not going to eat?"

She shook her head. "Not at present. I can watch over Benjamin while you enjoy your meal."

"You need to eat."

"You are kind, but—"

"But nothing," said Parker, rising to his feet. Bringing over the plate she'd prepared, he forced it into her hands and strode back to his seat. There was no reason the two of them couldn't enjoy a meal at the same time, but if the lady was determined that one of them remained at the ready, then Parker would comply. "As your physician, I insist that you eat first."

"And if I said I wasn't hungry?" But before Miss Leigh could offer up any more of a fuss, a large gurgle erupted from her stomach, testifying as clearly as any witness in court that her words were lies. Her eyes widened, and she pressed a hand to the offending organ while stifling a smile.

Parker chuckled and nodded at the food. Miss Leigh stared down at the plate and then at him, but he was undeterred.

"Eat, Miss Leigh. You need to take care of yourself, or you will be of no use to anyone." Pausing, he gave her a considering look. "In fact, I am ready to prescribe a little sleep. For a quarter of an hour at the very least."

In truth, he thought Miss Leigh ought to have much more than that, but if he could get her to nod off for even a few minutes, that would undoubtedly lead to more. It was unlikely the poor lady had slept much the night before, and it was bound to be another long night.

Miss Leigh opened her mouth (no doubt to argue), but once again, her body betrayed her, and instead of words, a deep yawn emerged. Her eyes widened as she fought against it, and the thing died into a chuckle as she shook her head.

"I suppose I have no defense now."

Rising, Parker snatched the blanket draped across the foot of the bed and moved to her seat. Meeting her gaze with a challenging lift of his brow, he stood there until she relented and lifted the plate high enough that he could drape the blanket beneath, tucking it around her lap. It was too much to hope she would leave her vigil, but as the straight-back chairs had been replaced with far more comfortable armchairs, it would be a decent resting place once he procured her a pillow.

Miss Leigh held her plate level as he adjusted her bedding, ensuring that her feet and legs were wrapped up, snug and proper, and when everything was just so, he squatted beside her seat.

"Please take a rest, Miss Leigh. I can watch over Benjamin for a bit on my own."

"You've already done so much," she murmured, though her eyelids were already drooping precariously.

"And you've done far more than I have," he replied, giving her a faint smile as he straightened a wayward edge of the blanket. "You are an impressive lady."

Miss Leigh held his gaze for several long moments, staring at him as though she could not comprehend his words. The candlelight played off her features, catching the darkening of her cheeks as she dipped her head. Parker had witnessed many a coy blush before, but hers was so genuine that he couldn't help but smile at it.

"You are too kind, Dr. Humphreys."

"I am honest, Miss Leigh. I wouldn't say it if I didn't mean it."

She lifted her gaze just enough to peek at him, her brows furrowed together, and Parker was captivated by the emotions rife in those eyes. Brown was such an ordinary hue; it was the most common color, after all. Yet there was a richness to Miss Leigh's eyes that Parker had never seen before. He couldn't put his finger on a proper comparison, for he couldn't think of another example of such a warm and dark shade.

Parker couldn't look away.

Then a sheen of tears brightened those eyes, and she whispered, "I know you tease me about thanking you, but I am so grateful you are here."

When Parker had entered Whitley Court, her thanks had meant little; such gratitude was commonplace in his profession, for everyone was eager to see him arrive and aid their loved ones. But this declaration meant far more now that he'd witnessed the massive burden her family placed on her sturdy shoulders.

"Then perhaps you will stop trying to send me away every quarter of an hour," replied Parker.

Miss Leigh's lips trembled the faintest bit, her throat working to swallow, and she gave him a little nod. A lock of hair tumbled free of her bandeau, draping across her cheek, and before Parker could think better of it, he reached up and tucked it behind her ear.

"Now, eat and rest. I will watch over Benjamin."

Chapter 33

With heavy footsteps, Rosanna forced herself to climb the stairs; it was far too early in the evening to be so fatigued, but the weariness was bone deep. She often danced until the early hours of the morning with no ill effect, yet this day had required far more fortitude, despite nothing of note happening. But the answer behind that puzzle was easy enough.

Mama was exhausting at the best of times. When she was in a mood, it was infinitely more difficult to manage her, and today was the worst Rosanna had ever witnessed. Thank heavens Katherine was so adept at pestering her, for the lady's attention was now fully absorbed with her at present.

Holding up her candle, Rosanna made her way to the nursery door. As hers was the only light in the hall, it was easy to peer into Benjamin's bedchamber since Dr. Humphreys and Prudence had lit a wealth of candles.

But he wasn't in his chair.

Rosanna's gaze fell to her sister and found the doctor crouched beside Prudence, tucking a blanket about her.

"You are an impressive lady."His words cut through the quiet of the house, halting Rosanna in place as the air fled from her lungs. She'd heard Dr. Humphreys express similar compliments before, but this tone was far more significant. His statement was no flowery speech of undying love, but it was impossible to miss the sentiment stirring beneath it.

Certainty was such an odd thing. Knowing the world was as it should be filled one with strength; one needn't expend energy fretting when the future was known. Yet for all that power, that confidence was a fragile thing. Even the slightest crack and the whole thing tumbled to the ground, leaving one far more fearful in its absence than if it had never existed in the first place.

Five minutes ago, Rosanna would've wagered far more than twenty pounds that Dr. Humphreys' heart belonged to her. Despite all the pain their little misunderstanding had caused, he still gazed upon her with such admiration. Yet those five words saw her foundation begin to disintegrate.

Did Dr. Humphreys fancy Prudence?

How wonderful for her sister. Surely that was a blessing. Prudence deserved to find a good man who valued her as she ought. Rosanna was so happy for her. Such a blessing. A lovely, lovely blessing.

Yet even as she clung to those happy thoughts, Rosanna's stomach sank and her throat clamped tight, making it difficult to breathe. Dr. Humphreys was a good man. Prudence was a good woman. Surely they deserved each other.

And Mr. Courtney was a gentleman in a true sense. With wealth and status. A much finer husband than a simple physician, and he worshiped Rosanna. He was not the sort to be easily distracted from the object of his desire. Yes, a much better choice for her.

Rosanna's heart burned as she considered that, watching Dr. Humphreys and Prudence together, their voices low enough that she couldn't hear—especially when her pulse was pounding in her ears. As it thrummed in her chest, a new clarity entered her thoughts, coalescing as it hadn't before. True, she'd flirted with the idea for some days now, but now, seeing it begin to slip from her fingers, her certainty strengthened.

She wanted Dr. Humphreys for her own.

Mr. Courtney was alluring, but even now, when she recalled Dr. Humphreys' kind words, her heart swelled, filling her with such hope and desire. Mr. Courtney merely admired her, but Dr. Humphreys believed in her, and at that moment of clarity, she knew she wanted the latter more than the former. What woman of sense would choose a grand house over a husband who valued her?

But anyone with eyes could see that something was brewing between her sister and Dr. Humphreys, and that was a happy thing. Such a blessing for Prudence. Rosanna was so pleased for her. She was. Even if it felt as though her lungs had shrunk, leaving her unable to breathe deeply.

Dr. Humphreys remained crouched beside Prudence, taking great care that the blanket across her lap covered her properly, and he gazed at her with a tender smile. Such a wonderful moment. So good.

Pushing open the door, Rosanna ignored the way Dr. Humphreys shot to his feet and Prudence turned away to hide her blush.

"Forgive me for interrupting," she said, breezing into the nursery with a smile. Placing her candle on the bedside table beside Benjamin, Rosanna pressed a hand to his burning forehead. "How is he faring?"

"He is resting quietly for now," said Dr. Humphreys. "But we have a long night ahead of us."

Rosanna nodded. "I thought I would join you two and see if there was anything I might do for you."

Prudence speared a bit of carrot on her fork and took a bite. "That is kind of you, but Dr. Humphreys and I have everything in hand. What I need most is for you to keep Mama out of the nursery."

"She is occupied downstairs, but surely there is something more I can do," said Rosanna, her hand resting on Benjamin's footboard. "I may not be good at administering medicines, but

I could take your place for a bit. Allow you to rest in your bed for an hour or two."

Prudence straightened, the edges of her blanket falling away. "You are kind, but I assure you I am well enough."

"Now you've done it, Miss Rosanna," said Dr. Humphreys with a hint of a smile to soften the chiding. "I have spent the past quarter of an hour convincing her to take a nap in the armchair and had just about lulled her into agreeing. Now, she will patently refuse to rest."

But for all that he spoke with a teasing tone, there was a touch of a furrow to his brow that had Rosanna's stomach sinking. Dr. Humphreys clearly did not mean to scold her, but there was a hint of true frustration in his words.

"I apologize. I didn't mean to cause trouble," said Rosanna, inching towards the door.

"Rosanna, please stay," said Prudence, though her smile was far too brittle to be believed. "I am sorry if you feel I have been ignoring you today, but I truly need your assistance with Mama, and with Dr. Humphreys by my side, your talents are much better served distracting her than aiding us. But if you are weary with that task, please join us for a bit."

Dr. Humphreys rose from his seat and offered the far comfier armchair to Rosanna. Sitting, she straightened her skirts and watched from the corner of her eye as he dragged over one of the hardback seats that had been relegated to the corner of the room. Rosanna's face was turned to her lap, but her attention was fixed on him as she waited to see where he placed his seat. She tried not to smile when he set it at her side.

Silence fell, broken only by Benjamin's ragged breaths and the sound of Prudence's cutlery clinking against the plate. And the faint ticking of the clock. Rosanna tried to count the seconds, but her thoughts drifted away far too often for her to keep track of the passing minutes.

Rosanna shifted in her seat and leaned against one of the arms. "How have you been, Dr. Humphreys?"

The fellow raised a brow at her and slanted her a look. "As I haven't moved from this room since the last time I spoke with you, there isn't much to report."

Rosanna's fingers traced the raised pattern of the fabric, and she shifted once more. "Of course."

No one spoke again, and despite all the little noises in the room, the quiet felt oppressive. That clock rang out with its strident little ticks.

"If you are bored, Rosanna, you could fetch your sewing," said Prudence, as she took another bite of her dinner.

"This may be a solemn occasion, but if we are to be graced with Dr. Humphreys' company, I would much rather take advantage of the opportunity and talk," she replied, turning her gaze to the gentleman at her right side.

"I fear my thoughts are sluggish at present, and my conversation will suffer because of it," he said.

"Nonsense. You are always such a lively companion." Rosanna straightened and turned her knees towards him. "When I was out this morning, I ran into Miss Poole, and it seems that Mr. Heber has gotten himself into quite the trouble with his wife, for he let it slip that she shall be two-and-fifty this year despite her claiming that she is not a day over nine-and-forty. Mrs. Heber overheard and nearly suffered apoplexy in the midst of a card party. Her face was as red as a strawberry!"

Rosanna laughed, though it died quickly when no one else joined in. With a strained smile, she glanced at Dr. Humphreys, who watched her with a furrowed brow, and then at Prudence, whose gaze held more than a tinge of exasperation.

"If you wish to be helpful, you could read for us," said Prudence, nodding at the book lying at the foot of the bed. "I fear my voice needs a rest."

Picking up the novel, Rosanna turned it over and sighed, "*The Victim of Prejudice*? That is such a dull story. I have attempted it twice already and haven't been able to get past the first half of the tale. I cannot comprehend the heroine at all. She is such a strange creature."

Prudence stared down at her plate and said nothing.

Rosanna sighed and shifted again. "I could fetch us some cards, and we could play a game."

"If you wish to play on your own, then do so," said Prudence. "But I haven't the strength or patience to entertain you at present."

Straightening, Rosanna stared at her sister as her cheeks heated. "I hadn't intended for you to entertain me."

Shoulders dropping, Prudence leaned over her plate with a frown. "I apologize. I didn't mean to be snippish. It has been a long day, and as much as I would love to play a card game or gossip with you, I fear I am not in a fit state of mind to do so."

But for all that the words were placating, Rosanna felt the meaning throbbing in her heart. She'd heard Prudence say such things to Mama far too often to mistake it for anything but placation. As though Rosanna were some child needing to be watched over and managed. Her stomach burned as she watched Prudence turn her attention to her dinner.

Rosanna darted a look at Dr. Humphreys and frowned. "Didn't you get our guest a plate, Prudence? He must be starving."

Rising to her feet, Rosanna moved to the table, though Dr. Humphreys gave a half-hearted protest. When she returned to his side, he met Rosanna's gaze, which helped to ease the tightness in her chest. With his eyes holding hers, it felt as though the world shifted back into its proper place. Dr. Humphreys' attention was fixed on her, and though it held none of the quiet passion that so usually filled his gaze, she felt it there, lurking beneath.

"You must take care of yourself, Dr. Humphreys," she murmured, her lips pulling into a coy smile. His own expression lightened, and her limbs seemed to regain their strength; her blood coursed through her veins, sending a jolt through her system. With gentle hands, she set the plate in his lap, her hands brushing against his as he took hold of it. And still, Rosanna held his gaze, her touch lingering as his eyes widened.

He still desired her. That would never change. Rosanna straightened, the heat in her blood filling her as she reveled in that knowledge. A look was all it took.

But ice water crashed down on her as she stepped away and found Prudence watching them, her eyes so full of her heart; Rosanna saw the hurt as clear as day, though the proud Miss Prudence Leigh worked so very hard to hide it. Stomach clenching, Rosanna backed away from Dr. Humphreys, her gaze dropping to the floor as she moved to the door.

Her throat closed up tight, and she struggled to get the words out, but as she reached the door she managed a hurried, "I should see to Mama."

And with that, Rosanna fled the nursery.

Chapter 34

The streets of Greater Edgerton teemed with life and commerce, but Parker ignored it all, navigating around the carts, people, animals, and all the like, as his thoughts tried to grasp the great alterations wrought in his life of late. If it weren't for the fact that he knew the streets by heart, he might've been in danger of getting lost or trampled, and as it was, he had a near miss with a passing carriage. And it was a good thing he'd just completed his final appointment for the day, for he was entirely useless.

And it wasn't the exhaustion that had his feet trudging along as though ankle-deep in mud. Though Parker was no longer a spry lad of twenty, he could manage a sleepless night with little trouble. It was a hazard of his profession, and as he'd been well rested before, the hours he'd spent at the Leighs' home were hardly a burden. Dealing with the family itself was another matter altogether.

Despite his best efforts, Parker's thoughts drew up images of Miss Leigh and her sister, shifting between the two. The stark comparison sat uneasily in his stomach, for the two were entirely different from one another. However, his view of them both was transforming at an alarming rate.

When Parker bothered to notice the world around him, he found himself in a familiar part of town. There was no point in fighting the inevitable, for marching about the streets was hardly doing him any good. With long strides, he crossed the road and let himself through the front door of Robert's office.

To one side sat a desk with a young man scribbling away amongst a mountain of books, which was surrounded by walls of books, as though his employer was some dragon of old who hoarded legal tomes instead of gold. Parker cast off his great coat, handing it to the lad when he rose.

"Is he in?" asked Parker, already moving towards the back of the room where Robert's office door sat. But before the clerk could respond, Robert's voice boomed from the far door.

"Yes, he is."

Striding in, Parker set the door swinging shut as he set down his medical bag and collapsed into the chair opposite his brother-in-law.

"You are in a fine mood, I see," said Robert with a tone as dry as the Sahara.

"I am in a state of endless felicity," replied Parker in kind.

His brother-in-law dropped his quill to the side and leaned into his chair. "You radiate contentment. I see you are making progress with your lady fair."

With a frown, Parker narrowed his eyes. "I called at your home to speak to Eleanor, but she was out and about. So, I came here. I see I should've waited for her."

"You shall have to wait some time. She is rarely there at present. Forever flitting about."

Robert's response was quiet, spoken so low that Parker wasn't certain it was intended for his ears. His gaze was pointed at the desktop but remained unfocused as his brows furrowed. They were laden with a heavy quality that had Parker straightening and studying his brother-in-law. But he didn't know how to broach the subject or even what subject to broach.

"In my experience most expecting ladies are fatigued," said Parker, grasping the only thing he could think to say. "Yet Eleanor is fairly bursting with strength and vitality."

Robert straightened, his eyes snapping from the desk to meet Parker's, and that hint of melancholia vanished as though it never existed. "So, what has you in such a serious mood today?"

Questions lingered in his mind, adding to the growing disquiet he felt every time he saw his sister and her husband together—which was all too infrequent of late—and Parker's mouth opened, the words on his lips. But a hard glint flashed in Robert's eyes, warning him away from that tender subject.

"I think I care for Miss Leigh," he blurted instead. Robert's brows merely rose at that, and Parker clarified, "Miss Prudence Leigh."

Robert's brows rose all the higher, and Parker sighed in response. At least the truth was out, blunt and clear.

"I..." he began, but no words followed. He'd rather hoped that simply starting the sentence might've induced his thoughts to coalesce into something more useful than the tangled web they were at present.

Meanwhile, Robert sat there, watching his hapless brother-in-law with that unyielding gaze of his.

"I paid a call on the Leighs yesterday." Had that only been the day before? Parker's gaze drifted from Robert to stare at a point on the wall as he sorted through the hours, which hadn't, in fact, stretched beyond the usual twenty-four.

"Miss Leigh had confided that her brother was ill, and I was concerned that he might require assistance." Even as Parker began at what seemed to be the beginning of the tale, an unspoken truth niggled in his heart—one he hadn't wanted to admit previously. Concern for Benjamin had not been his motivation.

"What is that look?" asked Robert.

"It is the look of a man who has been struck with a realization that was as gentle as a lightning bolt."

"Not very comfortable, is it?"

Parker ignored the hint of humor in his brother-in-law's tone. "The truth is that I had never paid much mind to Miss Leigh before this whole ridiculous situation arose, and since then, I've had the opportunity to spend more than a few hours in her company. And I rather enjoy it."

Gathering his thoughts, Parker described the time he'd spent with Miss Leigh. The words flowed quicker, and despite his having known the lady for such a short time, there was quite a lot to share. Far more than Parker had anticipated, and once he'd begun, it was difficult to stop. Her conversation was so vastly enjoyable that he found himself lingering on witticisms and observations, though Robert looked far less amused by them than Parker had been when she'd spoken. Clearly, he wasn't delivering them properly.

Then, when his retelling finally arrived at the Leighs' doorstep, Parker's heart burned, his brows twisting together. "The household was in chaos, with no one bothering to help her, rather adding to her burdens in a dozen little ways. Yet she managed it all with skill. It is clear that she is the head of the household in any way that matters, and she bears it without complaint, giving of herself until she is ready to collapse."

Lifting his bag onto his lap, he pulled open the straps and pointed to the interior. "And amidst everything, she took the time to do this when I wasn't looking."

Robert leaned forward to look within, his brows raised. "I'm afraid you'll need to elaborate, Parker. It looks like your medical bag and nothing more."

"She cleaned the entire thing! Polished each instrument and bottle, and then replaced them in such a clever manner that I am hesitant to touch the thing, lest I spoil the organization," he said, staring down into the contents. Parker still didn't know when or how she'd managed it, but his heart burned at the sight of the metal and glass gleaming back at him.

"So, you find yourself enamored with Miss Prudence Leigh because she is capable and a hard worker?" asked Robert with a hint of a smirk.

Parker paused, considering that, his thoughts drifting through those hours they'd worked together. "Do not discount how attractive competency is. Miss Leigh is incredible."

Those last words sat heavily on his tongue, souring them just a touch as Parker considered the greatest revelation that came from all those hours together.

"But how can a man go from loving one lady to another in such a short time?" he asked with a frown. He stiffened as he considered that. "Not that I am in love with Miss Leigh, but surely there is something amiss when my feelings shift from one sister to the other in a matter of hours?"

Robert raised his brows, studying his brother-in-law as though he were one of his clerks overlooking an obvious answer. "Did you love Miss Rosanna?"

"Of course."

That earned him a disbelieving huff, and Parker's expression deepened into a scowl.

"I did love her and love her still. But—"

"She rejected you in such a callous fashion?"

Parker scratched at the back of his neck. "That did not help matters. But love doesn't disappear in a moment or simply because it is not reciprocated. Unrequited love is far more common than the requited variety."

"But you did not truly know her until this past month, and now, you've spent a fair amount of time with both the Miss Leighs. It is little wonder that your heart and opinions might alter."

Setting aside his bag, Parker crossed his arms, leaned back into his seat, and considered that. While he didn't want to think his feelings were so fickle, there was truth in Robert's words.

"Miss Rosanna is a lovely creature, and she has a great capacity for kindness," he murmured. "But she is thoughtless at times. The way she bandied about wagers chilled me to the core. It was unwise, and I think she did it merely to flirt with Mr. Courtney and twit her sister. Perhaps even me. It was..."

Parker's words trailed off, and he couldn't bring himself to finish the thought, though it rested heavily on his heart like a physical weight bearing down on him. Picking through the memories, he tried to reconcile them with the lady he thought he'd known when he'd written that love letter all those weeks ago. But it was like pulling on ill-fitting trousers, and no matter how he maneuvered about, Parker couldn't make them work.

Miss Rosanna was not a wicked creature. She had so many shining qualities, but the more he came to know the Leigh sisters, the more the elder outshined her younger sister.

"I suppose it would be convenient for a physician to have a wife who was skilled at nursing, as Miss Leigh seems to be," said Robert. "Better to choose a sensible wife than a beauty."

Parker stiffened, his brows pulling low. "But Miss Leigh is a beauty. Not in the conventional sense, perhaps, but for all that everyone says her sister is the fairer of the two, Miss Leigh has a quality about her that draws the eye. The way the candlelight plays off the lines of her face as those wayward locks tumble down her shoulders. And her eyes are the loveliest I have ever seen. So dark and rich..."

It was only then that Parker focused once more on Robert's expression and found his brother-in-law watching him with an amused turn of the lips. But that humor faded as Robert studied Parker with that strong gaze that often made others quiver and quake in their boots.

"I have no answers for you because the choice of who you court is yours. All I can say is that you need to be careful before you throw yourself fully into loving anyone." Robert's gaze drifted from Parker, dropping to the desktop as he fiddled with the quill resting there. "Do not rush things. It is far too easy to get lost in attraction and convince yourself that the lady you love is utter perfection. You put it into your head that she is the only one who will do, and one day, you find yourself married to a stranger who is as dissimilar to you as oil is to water."

Silence fell, leaving only the ticking of the clock to ensure the gentlemen that time was, indeed, moving forward, for it felt as though the world around them slowed. Parker stared at his brother-in-law, and for all that he hoped the fellow was speaking in the abstract, Robert's tone was tinged with the sort of regret one only saw from someone who was trapped in a situation of their own making, without any way to escape.

Robert did not meet his eyes, his gaze fixed on the quill as he added, "Love is well and good, but a wife is so much more than a sweetheart. She is a partner in life. The one who will work beside you through the good and bad, who will be there when all others fail you. The best marriages are a mixture of attraction, friendship, and respect, and the least important is the first. It is the most fickle and will eventually fail without a hefty supply of the other two."

That drew Parker up short once more, and he studied his brother-in-law with a furrowed brow and a desperate need to say something—anything—that might raise his spirits. It was impossible to ignore the heavy tone with which Robert spoke and the implications rife within it, and Parker's heart ached for both his sister and her husband.

"Robert..."

Straightening, Robert rose to his feet and met Parker's gaze without flinching, the sorrow of the last few minutes vanishing as though it never existed.

Then, with a smile, he added, "You have a difficult decision ahead of you, Parker, but I am certain you will manage it brilliantly."

Chapter 35

Rubbing the rag across her face, Prudence reveled in the cool water as it kissed her flushed skin. With a quick swipe of her neck, she felt almost human again, but when she straightened and caught sight of her reflection in the looking glass, she sighed. Despite her best efforts, water had dribbled across her bodice, though thankfully, the apron had caught the majority of it.

Strands of hair dangled free of her bandeau, and Prudence tucked them beneath the cotton band, but for every one she secured, another fell free, leaving it a rumpled mess. With another sigh, she tugged the strip of fabric and pulled out her hairpins. Twisting her locks into a quick chignon, she secured them once more and wrapped the bandeau around it, tying it securely enough that she hoped she would avoid having to redo it in a few hours.

Prudence straightened before the looking glass and ran her hands down her front. She'd wasted enough time in her bedchamber and must return to the nursery, but the quiet wrapped around her, making it all too difficult to leave her haven. Rosanna was at Benjamin's bedside, and nothing much could've happened in a quarter of an hour. Surely all was well, and she could remain for another few minutes.

But responsibility was a stern taskmaster. Those who never heeded its demands could go blithely about their lives, doing precisely that which they wanted to do and no more. But for those susceptible to its call, there was no escape. And despite knowing that another quarter of an hour was unlikely to cause any harm, Prudence stepped out of the sanctuary. Though she moved slowly to the nursery.

Unfortunately, that left her mind free to dwell on forbidden, and all too wonderful, subjects. For all that she warned herself not to allow it, Dr. Humphreys entered her thoughts, bringing a smile to her lips as she wandered along.

Fantasy demanded that she throw her entire heart after the fellow, and despite her better judgment, Prudence couldn't help but imagine that heated moment once more when Dr. Humphreys had crouched beside her, tucking the blanket close with such gentleness, his gaze filled with such tenderness. Though a frisson skittered down her spine, for one brief moment, she allowed herself to hope and dream that his actions had been more than mere gentlemanly kindness.

Prudence felt as light as a bird on the wing, fairly floating along the corridor, and Dr. Humphreys' spirit followed at her heels, invading every thought. Every heartbeat. It was ridiculous. She hardly knew the man. But with each moment they spent together, she discovered more and more reasons to admire him.

The upper floor of the house rang with Rosanna's voice, singing a silly little country tune Nurse Johnson often sang for them, and though a little hoarse and halting, Benjamin laughed. Prudence gave a silent word of thanks that her brother was on the mend.

Climbing the last few stairs, she made her way to the nursery and found quite the sight.

Rosanna spun about before the bed, singing of flowers in the garden who had gotten a nip of the farmer's whiskey. The words were the sort that entertained the children with the silliness and allowed the adults to snicker at the deeper meanings the young minds couldn't grasp, and Rosanna twirled around and stretched her features into a cross-eyed grimace that would've had her blushing had anyone of standing seen it.

Benjamin was nestled in bed, his head propped up with a mountain of pillows, but he was smiling at his sister, a halting chuckle on his lips as she danced about. Then his lungs heaved, shaking and jerking as he tried to draw breath. With wide eyes, he fought against the cough, but it grew in strength, and Rosanna paused and stared at the boy while Prudence hurried to his side.

"Where is his tisane?" she asked, gazing at the empty spot on the side table where the teapot had been when she'd left.

Rosanna wrung her hands. "What tisane?"

A burst of fire flared in Prudence's heart, burning through her veins. "The tisane I told you to give him if he had a coughing fit, Rosanna. The one I placed right in this very spot, should you require it."

But her sister merely stood there, wringing her hands and fluttering about the bedside. "I…uhm…"

Prudence sat beside him and rubbed his hands, hoping that touch and the soothing words she murmured might calm him, but Benjamin stared at her with wild eyes as the coughs shook him, growing in strength with his wracking breath. She glanced about, caught sight of the familiar blue pot atop the mantle, and hurried over to grab it up, though the porcelain was stone cold.

Rosanna gripped the footboard and watched as Prudence lifted him to give him a sip. "I gave him something to drink not ten minutes ago."

And something to eat, no doubt, for the boy's shirt was covered in crumbs and splashes of tea.

"This isn't just tea, Rosanna," she murmured. "I told you this pot had his medicine in it."

Stone cold as it was, the drink was less efficacious, but Benjamin's breathing slowed all the same, helping him to relax and allow his lungs to function better than before. Prudence brushed back his hair and pressed a kiss to his forehead as she laid him down once more, his eyelids growing heavy after the exertion.

"He was doing better," said Rosanna. "I wanted to give him a treat."

Prudence's jaw tightened, and she closed her eyes, praying for a bit of patience. But the past twenty-four hours had been so trying—all the more so when she recalled the night before. She didn't trust herself to look at her sister, for when she did, she only saw the image of Rosanna flirting with Dr. Humphreys.

Fire snapped and crackled in her heart as she reached for the rag to mop at Benjamin's brow, though the fever had broken some hours ago. Neither sister had spoken of that incident, and Prudence didn't know what she would say if they did. That heat coursed through her with every heartbeat, and a question came to her mind again and again.

Was Rosanna trying to steal Dr. Humphreys away simply because she could?

With a sigh, Prudence closed her eyes and straightened, tossing the washrag on the side table. Rubbing at her forehead, she forced herself to breathe and banked the embers burning in her chest. That question did not reflect well on either of them. In fact, it reflected worse on Prudence than it did on Rosanna.

Firstly, it assumed Dr. Humphreys had shown partiality towards herself (and his showing pleasure at having a good assistant was hardly a declaration of love), and Prudence knew better than to hope a gentleman so deeply in love with Rosanna would alter course and pursue her plain older sister. Secondly, it painted her sister as a jealous hag, determined to steal away his affection simply because it had slipped from her grasp.

Prudence needed more rest.

"You are a mess," she murmured, brushing at Benjamin's front.

"The cake was delicious," he murmured.

A faint smile tugged at her lips. "I imagine so."

"I can fetch him some new clothes," said Rosanna, turning away from the bedside and hurrying to the chest of drawers on the far side of the room. Pulling open the top one, she dug through it just long enough to ruin the order within before proceeding to the next.

"It's on the right side," said Prudence, turning to watch from over her shoulder. But Rosanna reached in the wrong direction. "No, the other right, dearest. And down in the bottom drawer."

Rosanna crouched down but still pulled open the wrong one, though Prudence didn't know how much clearer she could be in her directions. Dropping her head with a sigh, she rose from the bedside and came over, reaching into the precise drawer she had indicated and pulling out a fresh nightshirt.

"I can assist you," said Rosanna, reaching to take it from Prudence's hands. "He's still too weak to stand for long—"

But for once, providence smiled down on Prudence in the form of Nurse Johnson arriving with fresh linens in her arms.

"We have this in hand, dearest," said Prudence. "What would be the greatest assistance is if you could fetch more of the tisane. It works best if it's hot."

Rosanna glanced at the pot on Benjamin's side table, and her shoulders drooped. For all that she could easily read the disappointment in her sister's gaze, Prudence hadn't the strength to manage Rosanna's bruised feelings. It was enough of a battle to stay upright at present.

Turning away, Rosanna trudged into the hall, and Prudence couldn't help the sigh as the tension in her shoulders eased.

"Come," she said to the nursemaid.

The two worked in unison, quickly stripping Benjamin and getting him into a clean nightshirt and changing out the bedclothes. In a trice, he was tucked back into his bed, a contented sigh on his lips as he cuddled into the pillows. Benjamin took Prudence's hand in his, and his eyes slid closed, though he fought gravity's pull for a minute or two.

Nurse Johnson settled into the corner, taking out her knitting and setting to work on a new set of wool stockings while Prudence took Dr. Humphreys' chair. She paused at that thought and wondered at the mental slip. It wasn't his chair by any means. Prudence had occupied it for hours before the gentleman had arrived, but for most of the last day, it had been his chosen position. Close to the patient, to watch over his fretful sleep.

It gave her a clear view of the one set on the other side of the bed, and she couldn't help but recall that delicious moment they'd shared. It seemed too grand to think they'd had a "moment" of any sort, let alone something of a romantic bend, but Dr. Humphreys' gaze rose in her memory again and again, and she couldn't help but feel—hope, really—that something new had stirred in those blue eyes.

But on its heels came Rosanna's phantom, fawning over him like those desperate debutantes who cast their lures, hoping to catch any male who crossed their paths. And Dr. Humphreys had responded. Of course, he had. Rosanna was so vibrant and lively, and he'd been clear concerning his feelings for her again and again.

Prudence's stomach sank and her heart shuddered as her thoughts drifted back to an old, familiar wound. For as long as she could remember, people had compared the two Leigh sisters. Rosanna was not simply pretty or lovely. Her tresses were gold, and her eyes were sparkling emeralds. A laugh that lit the very air with sunshine. A smile that could stop gentlemen in their very tracks.

On the other hand, Prudence was stalwart. And didn't that just make a lady feel desirable?

Sighing to herself, she frowned as Benjamin's hold slackened around her hand, his muscles relaxing as he drifted into a peaceful sleep. Prudence's gaze rested on his face, those little features she knew as well as her own. And her heart burned anew, filling her chest with an intense but not unpleasant pressure. She struggled to keep her breathing even as she considered the past day.

If given the choice to surrender all the things that made her capable and stalwart for the beauty and admiration she craved, would she? Prudence gently rubbed Benjamin's hand, her touch feathering along his palm and fingers as she studied those dear little fingers.

Perhaps she would never quite erase that longing from deep within that wished for accolades or appreciation, but Prudence couldn't say that she would wish herself different if it meant she must sacrifice the core of who she was. Even sitting there with a sleep-addled brain and her fragile heart beating so close to the surface, she liked the woman she was.

Prudence Leigh was a steady lady. The sort one wanted at one's back. She was keen to help and make others' lives better. She enjoyed a quiet life. Though far from perfect, Prudence was a good person who wanted to be better. And that was no small thing.

If Dr. Humphreys could not see that value on his own, then he was not a beau worth having.

Chapter 36

A thump sounded at the nursery door, and the handle rattled a touch, drawing Prudence's attention. She jumped to her feet to open it. Rosanna stood on the other side, balancing a massive tea tray.

"I had Mrs. James prepare some food for you as well as Benjamin's tisane," she said, coming over to the table and setting it on a clear patch. "You are not taking care of yourself as you ought, Prudence."

Rosanna began shoving the dirty dishes to the side. "And I've asked for Jane to come and clear these away."

The plates stood up in a precarious tower, and Prudence quickly pulled out the utensils, placing them in a pile beside the dishes. Rosanna started another, stacking teacups and saucers up, and Prudence followed after, separating the former from the latter so that they weren't in danger of toppling over.

"Would you prepare a cup for me?" asked Prudence as she caught a stray fork before it plunged to the floor.

Rosanna stiffened and nodded, quickly sorting out the tea things before shooing Prudence towards the chairs. The sisters sat on either side of the bed, and Prudence sipped from her cup, fighting not to wince at the pale brew that Rosanna preferred.

Setting the teacup on the side table, Prudence relaxed into the armchair and watched Benjamin, whose coloring was precisely what it should be, even if an ominous rattle still plagued each breath.

"Do you think Dr. Humphreys will come today?" Rosanna's question seemed innocent enough, but there was something pointed in her tone that had Prudence sliding a glance in her direction.

"He has appointments, and I am certain he has much work to see to after having given us so much of his time." Yet even as she said the words, Prudence's stomach gave a little flutter. For all that Dr. Humphreys had given no assurances, his farewell had held a bit of a promise to it. If she were apt to wager, she would lay money that he would come again this evening.

Gazing down at her rumpled dress, she wished she had something nicer to wear. For all that she had been allowed a few minutes to freshen up, Prudence was in a sad state of disarray, and it might be nice to face Dr. Humphreys with a new gown, even if it was a work dress and apron.

Utter nonsense. There lay Benjamin, still suffering, and here she was thinking about presenting a pleasing image to the good doctor when he arrived. Soon. Hopefully.

"What are you thinking about?" asked Rosanna.

Prudence stiffened, her brows rising. "Pardon?"

Studying her sister closely, Rosanna added, "Just then. You had a rather odd look about you."

Matters weren't helped by the fact that her cheeks quickly heated, and instinct had Prudence ducking away from her sister's watchful gaze.

"That!" said Rosanna, straightening. "What has you blushing?"

For all that thoughts of Dr. Humphreys made Prudence's temperature rise, her sister's question chilled her through. Such an innocent query, and had it been asked yesterday, Prudence wouldn't have hesitated to answer.

Her heart burned with the desire to speak to her sister. Rosanna had always been a wonderful confidant and support, and Prudence couldn't think of another time in which she hadn't shared all with her. But that image of her fawning over Dr. Humphreys surfaced in her thoughts, reminding Prudence all too well that Rosanna's own heart was still in question.

"Please, speak to me," said Rosanna, leaning forward with a twist of her brow. "You have been so silent of late."

"I am often silent," she replied with a smile. "Not everyone is chatty."

Rosanna huffed and held her sister's gaze. "Perhaps, but you are not usually so silent with me. What is the matter? Have I truly upset you? I do apologize for being so foolish yesterday. I thought you wished me gone, so I took my time. Had I known you were truly waiting for the medicine, I would've hurried back."

The words were so earnest that Prudence wondered if Rosanna believed them. Not that she thought her sister so selfish as to withhold necessary medicines in favor of a bit of gossip, but Prudence was all too aware of how unaware Rosanna could be at times. And easily distracted.

A question bubbled into her thoughts, and Prudence watched her sister, wondering if she dared ask it. Or if she truly wanted to know the truth. Would it alter things? Her stomach sank, for deep within, she knew it would.

"Are you sweet on Dr. Humphreys?" The question sprouted forth before Prudence could allow her fears (or good sense) to overtake her.

"He is a good man."

Silence.

"Is that all?" asked Prudence.

Rosanna's gaze was fixed on her lap as she shifted in her seat and smoothed her skirts. "I greatly admire him. He has done so much for our family of late, how could I not?"

The words should've comforted Prudence, and had they been spoken before Rosanna's flirtatious performance last night, they might've. But she knew her sister too well to ignore the gnawing in her stomach.

And did Prudence wish to admit this secret to Rosanna? Harboring fantasies in one's mind was one thing, but speaking them aloud was another. Whatever her instincts may or may not be saying about Dr. Humphreys' feelings, Prudence's own thrummed in her veins, filling her with unshakeable certainty. Her heart was not in question, but only a fool would declare as much when the reception was uncertain.

Yet this was her sister. How many times had Prudence shared the feelings of her heart, despite knowing the gentleman might never reciprocate? All the countless hours they'd spent together, gossiping about their hopeful beaus. The more Prudence thought of it, the steadier she felt. This was her sister. Her Rosanna. Her dearest friend. Her actions last night had been hurtful, but surely that was only because she didn't know the full depth of Prudence's feelings.

"I like Dr. Humphreys," she said, not allowing herself to question the confession. Her feelings suffused each syllable, filling them with far more significance than those simple words conveyed on their own.

Rosanna's brows rose. "You do? After everything that has happened?"

Prudence drew in a deep breath. "I—"

The moment her lungs filled, a tickle shook them, ripping out a cough that had her doubling over. Benjamin's little eyes opened to watch her with a furrowed brow, and Rosanna hurried to her side, patting her on the back, though it did nothing to calm the coughing fit.

"Good heavens!" said Rosanna, straightening and turning about like a dog chasing its tail. She let out a few more exclamations, but Prudence was too busy trying to calm her breathing to notice anything more than the general agitation as Rosanna fluttered about the room.

Nurse Johnson rose from her seat and crossed the room, pouring her a cup from Benjamin's teapot. The liquid was still piping hot, but Prudence forced down a few sips.

"Calm yourself, Rosanna," she murmured. "It is only a little cough."

"Nonsense! You are ill as well." Rosanna crouched beside her and felt her forehead. "You are burning up."

Nurse Johnson followed suit and shook her head. "A little warm, perhaps, but nothing to worry about."

Clinging to her sister's hands, Rosanna nodded towards the door. "We must get you in bed."

"Dearest, please, I am well enough," said Prudence. "It is not surprising that I have a little bit of a cough, but it is not worrisome yet—"

"Let me take care of you," she murmured, her brows pulling tight together as she held her sister's gaze. "I am not wholly useless, Prudence. Everyone else treats me like an ornament, but I didn't think you thought of me in such a light."

"I never said you were."

"But every time I attempt to aid you, you send me off on some errand. I wish to care for you as you so readily care for the rest of the family. Please let me."

Rosanna gazed up at her with eyes so imploring that Prudence couldn't deny her, even if she wanted to. The moment she nodded, it was as though a valve within her loosened, releasing the last of her strength and leaving her drained. It took far more assistance than she would've liked to admit to raise her from the chair, but Rosanna had her quickly bundled in a blanket and marched back to the comfort of her bed.

Chapter 37

In Edinburgh, Parker's days had been long and filled to bursting. A city such as that brimmed with the sick and injured, keeping a physician forever employed. His education allowed him little time to himself, and with what time he did have, his mind was too fatigued to do more than simply exist. Wallowing in self-reflection had been a luxury.

Now, he had nothing but time. Despite having appointments throughout the day and into the night, Parker spent as much time traveling between appointments as he did seeing to his patients' ailments, leaving him trapped in his thoughts as he stalked the streets of Greater Edgerton.

Perhaps it was time to establish a formal office.

Physicians in the city expected the patients to come to them, which allowed them to treat more of the sick and afflicted. Country physicians were expected to make house calls, so it would be a difficult shift, but Greater Edgerton was getting large enough that if he wished to make a healthy income, he needed to stop wasting his time traveling to appointments.

Parker turned his thoughts to that hypothetical, planning out the rooms required and where everything must go. Tromping through the streets, he wove through the townhouses and dodged around the carts and carriages. The crowd and calls of the street vendors blended, the cacophony drifting to the background as his thoughts fixed fully on what his office might be like.

And the diversion worked. For a good five minutes.

What he wouldn't give for some disaster to strike a mill. Something that set the city into chaos and required his full attention. But his patients were surprisingly hale at present, providing him with no distraction from Miss Leigh or his brother-in-law.

He ought to go to Whitley Court, but Benjamin's fever had broken, so there was little danger left to the boy. The Leighs did not require him. However, deep in the pit of his stomach where his more certain instincts resided, Parker suspected Miss Leigh would not only welcome the assistance but needed it. Which was silly, but Parker couldn't rid himself of the feeling.

Of course, that innocent thought caused Robert's voice to resurface, making Parker recall their conversation, which not only stirred his confusion concerning the Leigh sisters but had his heart sinking fast as he considered his sister's marriage as well. Something was not right between the pair, and it was unlikely he could do anything about it. Especially when Eleanor refused to remain still long enough to speak to her twin about her troubles.

Thoughts of Robert followed that, though Parker knew any interrogation would prove fruitless, for his brother-in-law was not one to confide about Eleanor to her brother. Even if Parker was his closest friend.

And quick on that heel came thoughts of Robert's warning about marriage. Which dredged up Miss Leigh. And Miss Rosanna. All of them swirled together like a maelstrom, occupying Parker's thoughts yet never coalescing into anything tangible or useful.

Then, ahead, he spied Miss Rosanna descending from the front steps of a townhouse, and the gales truly began to blow.

Yet in the same instance, clarity struck strong and deep like the boom of the church bells calling its parishioners to repentance. Not long ago, catching even the faintest flash of Miss Rosanna would've sent his heart into palpitations, and while that organ was doing some rather interesting acrobatics at present, none of them were of the pleasant sort. And the sour twist of his stomach served as further evidence that whatever his feelings had been, Parker's current ones were vastly different.

"Dr. Humphreys!" Miss Rosanna's face brightened, those rosy cheeks of hers heating as she called to him from her position, waving at him with all the excitement and vigor he'd so often dreamt of seeing. Of course, those fantasies hadn't included Parker glancing around while quickly tabulating whether or not he could escape.

"How delightful to see you," she said as she came to stand before him. "I was just paying a call on the Nightingales. What has you wandering the streets this fine afternoon?"

Parker hazarded a glance at the gray skies above, and the young lady's gaze followed his. When he met her eyes once more with a questioning arch of his brows, Miss Rosanna laughed.

"So, it is yet another gloomy autumn afternoon, but whenever our paths cross, the day seems lovely, don't you think, Dr. Humphreys?"

Smile straining, Parker cleared his throat and nodded as his gaze darted about. But no one was watching. That didn't mean they were wholly unnoticed, but the conversation was drawing no undue attention. Yet he shifted his weight between his feet and then his medical bag from one hand to the other.

"Certainly, Miss Rosanna," he managed before nodding down the street. "I was going to your home to see how your brother is faring."

That he managed to say "your brother" without stumbling was something of a miracle, for it was certainly not Benjamin Leigh he wished to call on.

With a furrowed brow, he added, "I am surprised you are out and about with everything that needs doing at home."

Miss Rosanna waved that away with a laugh. "Nurse Johnson is quite capable of managing on her own, and I have only been gone a short while. I was to attend the Nightingales' party tonight and had to give my apologies. I cannot attend if I am going to spend the evening caring for my family."

"That is good of you," said Parker, shifting the medical bag between hands once more as he nodded down the street. "But I fear I shouldn't tarry here. Your sister might need more assistance than the nursemaid can offer. Nurse Johnson is better than most, but her medical knowledge is more of the old wives' tales variety."

Sidling up to him, Miss Rosanna took his arm. "Wonderful. As I was planning on returning there post haste, you can escort me home. I would welcome your assistance, as I am taking over Prudence's duties."

Parker ignored the blatant spark of flirtation in her gaze and frowned. "Why?"

"I am quite capable of managing on my own, sir." Miss Rosanna's words held a hard edge to them that he'd never heard her employ before, and Parker glanced at her from the side of his vision. "But as it happens, Prudence is feeling poorly as well, so I sent her to bed."

Parker jerked to a stop and stared at the young lady. "And then promptly abandoned her to call on someone?"

Miss Rosanna cocked her head to the side and studied him with a wrinkled brow. "I had already accepted the Nightingales' invitation. It would've been rude of me to not attend, and I would've simply written an apology, but as Prudence is sleeping and requires nothing of me at present, I saw no harm in going in person, as my last-minute cancellation is quite uncouth."

"I see," said Parker, continuing their march down the lane, though Miss Rosanna kept him walking at a glacial pace. For an instant, he wanted to shake free of her and hurry along, but he reminded himself that this was Miss Leigh's sister. She deserved respect—even if she was ridiculous enough to believe Miss Leigh was resting.

Parker's brow furrowed as he hazarded a glance at Miss Rosanna, who continued to prattle on about the weather, the Nightingales' party, and the gossip she'd gleaned from her "short" visit, which, according to how much information she relayed, must have been close to an hour or more. Even without the growing warmth in his heart drawing him ever closer to her sister, Parker couldn't help but feel his affection for Miss Rosanna decay.

How did the young lady know her sister so little? Or did Miss Rosanna simply prize her desires above others?

From what Parker knew of the younger Leigh sister, he didn't think her selfish or vapid, and despite the change in his feelings, he knew she wasn't devoid of empathy or feeling. Her affection for her sister was genuine, and Parker hadn't imagined the kindnesses he'd witnessed. Miss Rosanna may not be the woman for Parker Humphreys, but that did not mean that the lady he'd loved had been an illusion.

Whitley Court came into view, and Parker sped up the tiniest bit, struggling not to drag Miss Rosanna along. Thankfully, they eventually arrived at the front door, and she ushered him in. In short order, his hat, gloves, and coat were taken, but he refused to wait another moment as Miss Rosanna dawdled by the stack of missives sitting on the salver beside the door.

Parker didn't know which of the bedchambers was Miss Leigh's, but as she was more likely to be in the nursery, he strode up the stairs. An open door had him pausing at the second landing, and he peeked down the hall, but the room was empty with the bedclothes cast back from the bed.

"Jane?"

Though it was weak, he recognized the voice calling from the far end of the hall, and Parker stepped into that bedchamber to find Miss Leigh in her dressing gown, seated at the edge of Miss Katherine's bed, her hand pressed to her sister's forehead.

"Would you bring us—" But Miss Leigh paused as she glanced up at the doorway, her dark eyes widening as she finally saw the figure standing there. The wide-eyed surprise then melted away, her lips stretching into a smile as her expression lightened with such joy that it thrummed through Parker. But then her chin began to tremble, and she looked away, pressing a hand to her reddened cheeks.

Parker was at her side before she could say another word. Taking her by the elbow, he helped her to her feet and tried leading her back to her bedchamber, though she was pulling against him. "You need to lie down, Miss Leigh."

"I cannot," she said, turning back to her sister's bedside. "Nurse Johnson is watching over Benjamin at present, and the maids are occupied with laundry. We're running low on linens, and Benjamin is out of nightshirts. Mama disappeared with Francis to who knows where—not that they'd be any assistance—and Papa has locked himself away in his study, too busy with his books and newspapers to be bothered with helping. Rosanna left for a short visit and has been gone for hours, and Katherine is ill with no one to take care of her—"

"And you have a stalwart doctor at your side to manage everything in your stead," he said, turning her toward the empty bed beside her sister's. It was unlikely he could get her to go any further, so it was better to forgo that battle.

She sat heavily on the mattress, and in a low voice, she whispered, "I was hoping you would come."

"Did you think I would just walk away?"

Miss Leigh didn't answer, though there was a dangerous sheen to her eyes that made Parker want to bundle her in his arms. Her breath hitched, and she nodded as she took hold of his hand and clutched it with far more strength than he would've expected given her weakened state.

Holding his gaze, she murmured, "Thank you."

Never had two words struck Parker so strongly. They were simple and small, but they were steeped in so much emotion, as though Miss Leigh's entire heart and soul were wrapped up in them.

"Nurse Johnson can manage Benjamin, and I shall manage you and your sister."

Miss Leigh's braid was draped over her shoulder, and a dozen little hairs flew free from it. Her dressing gown was rumpled and askew, and her eyes were red with exhaustion, and yet Parker was struck by the sight of her. It was strange and inexplicable, for though he recognized she would be embarrassed if she realized just how disheveled she looked at that moment, Parker thought her undeniably lovely.

Her eyes held his with such passion and feeling that he couldn't help but get lost within them, and he knew that the jests his brother-in-law had made about his liking a useful lady were entirely incorrect. For it wasn't just admiration or appreciation that burned in his heart at that moment. It was attraction.

Which was rather awkward at present, given the situation.

Parker leaned away, giving himself the tiniest bit of clarity as he cleared his throat. "Do not worry, Miss Leigh. I am here, and I will manage everything."

But at that pronouncement, her eyes widened, that sheen of tears thickening as her chin began to quiver in earnest. Biting on her lips, she dropped her gaze away from him, her hands flying to her mouth, but they couldn't stop the sob that broke free.

Chapter 38

Curse her exhausted body and mind. Curse her useless family. Curse Dr. Humphreys for finding her in such a state. Except Prudence couldn't even think that final one with any true vehemence. It was herself she ought to curse more than him. Dr. Humphreys wasn't the one blubbering like a babe simply because of a little comfort offered in a trying time.

Prudence wiped at her cheeks and held her breath, though her shuddering lungs fought her hold. Covering her face, she shook her head and cursed herself anew. Why was she such a ninny? But her heart and mind were worn thin after the last few days, and she had no defenses against Dr. Humphreys and his sweet words.

And then the man stirred her emotions anew by drawing his arms around her, holding her tight as her tears broke free, streaming down her cheeks. He didn't prompt her to remain strong or beg her to stop; he merely held her as she fell to pieces. Her good sense warned her not to do so, but any logic or reason had faded long ago in the torrent of exhaustion, illness, and his kindness.

Laying her head into the crook of his neck, Prudence accepted his solace, for there was no other to be found. Belatedly, she realized she was dousing his jacket, but she was beyond reason, and still, Dr. Humphreys held her close, comforting her as no one had in such a long time. Only Rosanna ever seemed to care about her feelings, and she wasn't here, so Prudence reveled in the peace that permeated his embrace.

When her tears slowed, she remained there for another few shuddering breaths before reality settled once more, bringing with it the knowledge that she had been sobbing all over Dr. Humphreys. Straightening, Prudence wiped at her cheeks again, though he did not move away.

"I apologize," she whispered. "I don't know what came over me."

Gathering what little strength yet remained, she turned a tremulous smile to him and found the gentleman gazing deeply into her eyes. With a gentle touch, he brushed a finger down her cheek.

"I am not feverish," she murmured.

A smile lit his gaze while a hint of it tickled the edge of his lips. "I wasn't checking for fever."

"Oh..." Her words drifted into silence as she stared at him, her brows pulling close together as she tried to comprehend his meaning. Her thoughts ground together like ill-fitting gears in a machine, and Prudence struggled for some sort of coherency, but no matter how she tried to ascribe a medical meaning to his words, the warmth in Dr. Humphreys' gaze and tone belied any clinical translation.

And that was when she realized just how close they sat beside one another. Though Dr. Humphreys had released his hold of her, they were pressed together from hip to knee, their arms entwined. And when had he taken hold of her hand? Surely a lady ought to know the precise moment. Prudence's gaze dropped to it, and she gaped at the sight.

Her eyes darted back to his, widening as she struggled for words. And all the while, Dr. Humphreys' gaze drifted over her features as tenderly as his caress.

"I—" Prudence stopped, blinked, and gaped. "Are you toying with me?"

"Pardon?" Dr. Humphreys stiffened, his brows rising. "Of course not."

"You are in love with my sister."

"I *was*," he corrected. "Or I had thought myself enamored at any rate."

"And now that she has rejected you—"

"That has nothing to do with it," said Dr. Humphreys with a frown. "I had thought we suited each other, but as I've come to know her and you better, I realized I was mistaken."

Prudence's expression matched his. "Ah. You two don't suit because she spends her time flirting with Mr. Courtney. And I have proven myself such a useful creature, a far better choice for a physician."

He leaned back, his brows twisting together as he shook his head. "That is not it at all."

Scoffing, Prudence forced her gaze away from him. "Believe me, sir, I have heard such things my whole life. Rosanna is the attractive one. I am the competent one—"

"Do not put words in my mouth, Miss Leigh," he said in a firm but gentle tone. "I am well aware of how my change of heart might appear to you, and I am ashamed that I have given you reason to distrust my feelings. But the past few weeks have allowed me to know you better, and I have come to care deeply for you. We share a bond of friendship and admiration that I have never felt before."

Oh goodness, how that little word pierced her heart. "Friendship."

"I have always believed the best of marriages are founded on it."

Pressing a hand to her head, Prudence wasn't certain if her head was throbbing because of the current situation or because her horrid body was betraying her, but either way, she just could not remain upright a moment longer. And before she could say a word concerning it, Dr. Humphreys helped her up, pulled back the bedclothes, and settled her into the bed properly.

"Whatever you may think, Miss Leigh, I assure you I am in earnest," he said, drawing the blankets over her.

Prudence opened her mouth, though no words came forth. Granted, she didn't know what to say to such a thing. Especially when tears began gathering once more. Straightening the edge of her bedclothes, his hand drifted to her face again, and Prudence's breath caught at the feel of his fingers brushing her cheek.

"You are fatigued and feeling poorly, so you'd best sleep now," he murmured. "Do not worry, Miss Leigh. I will watch over your family while you rest."

Swallowing past the lump in her throat, Prudence nodded and blinked away her tears.

Dr. Humphreys straightened, his brows arching with the movement. "But this conversation is not finished, Miss Leigh. When you are restored, we shall talk further."

The last of Prudence's good sense evaded her grasp, and she was left with only the baldest of truths. "I won't be any man's second choice."

Dr. Humphreys actually smiled at that, his face lighting with it. "You—"

"I am sorry for the delay, but the Nightingales were so very chatty," said Rosanna as she swept in, cooling the moment like a rainstorm on a hot summer's day.

Prudence pulled the bedclothes to her chin and stared at Rosanna for a moment before her gaze darted to where Katherine slept. Good gracious! What a time to have a conversation!

Her eyes met Dr. Humphreys' for the briefest moment, and her heartbeat stuttered at the determined glint in his eyes. It was as though she could hear his voice in her head, promising her this was not over; then he sighed and turned to greet Rosanna. Prudence struggled not to gape at the sight, for the impatience was so very genuine yet incongruous with the loving letter he'd written Miss Rosanna Leigh not one month ago.

Rosanna hurried to her side, babbling excuses about why it wasn't her fault that she'd been delayed, and Prudence struggled to nod and give all the little assurances required of the moment; her thoughts were entirely fixed on the man standing behind Rosanna, watching Prudence with a gaze that held more affection than mere "friendship."

Success in society depended on one's ability to act. There was a strange sort of subterfuge that came with navigating the maze, but thankfully, it had strengthened Rosanna's playacting skills. So, she stood at the edge of Prudence's bed, gazing down at her sister as though the very world around her wasn't shattering to pieces.

"Whatever you may think, Miss Leigh, I assure you I am in earnest..."

Was it true? Rosanna struggled with the whispered words she'd overheard, but she couldn't deny that Dr. Humphreys must've meant every one of them: he was not the sort to toy with another's affections.

How wonderful for Prudence. Rosanna clung to that thought, though it slipped and wriggled from her grasp like a fish. This was precisely what she wanted for her sister. It was wonderful news. Simply wonderful. Yet Rosanna's stomach twisted and wrenched within her, threatening to cast up all the tea and cakes she'd had at the Nightingales'.

"We shall watch over you," said Rosanna with a nod of her head. "I will do my utmost to assist our Dr. Humphreys."

Then, turning to the gentleman, she added with a raise of her brows, "What would you have me do?"

Dr. Humphreys shifted in place and glanced about. "I have everything in hand here, Miss Rosanna. Perhaps you'd best aid Nurse Johnson."

"Benjamin is on the mend," said Rosanna, waving his suggestion aside. "She does not need me. Surely, with two patients, I can be of more assistance here."

Prudence let out a low sigh likely not meant to be overheard, and Rosanna's heart shrank at the sound and the false brightness in her sister's tone when she said, "It is best if I sleep here with Katherine. It would be very helpful if you could move Francis into our bedchamber for the next day or two."

It wasn't as though that required anything more than Francis climbing into Prudence's bed rather than her own, but the meaning was clear enough. Rosanna was not wanted.

Straightening, her spine grew rigid, and she glanced between the pair, neither of whom showed any sign of wishing her to stay. With a slow nod, she backed out of the room and stepped into the empty hallway. The murmur of voices sounded for a moment before the room lapsed into silence, and Rosanna watched as Dr. Humphreys took his place at Prudence's bedside, his entire attention fixed on her.

Rosanna pressed a hand to her stomach, though it roiled with such violence that she hurried down the hall to duck into their bedchamber. Closing the door behind her, she leaned against the wood and pressed a hand to her mouth as a sob pulled free.

She was happy for Prudence. Of course, she was. Her dear sister deserved to find happiness with a gentleman who valued her. But even as Rosanna clung to those thoughts, repeating them again and again, she couldn't help her heart from cracking at the thought that Dr. Humphreys was well and truly lost to her.

Pushing away from the door, she stumbled towards her bed and dropped down atop it. How did one manage such pain? Tears slipped down her cheeks, and she didn't bother wiping them away. They leaked out, taking with them her strength and vitality, and she felt as though she'd been hollowed out.

The door opened without fanfare, and Rosanna twisted away, brushing at her face as Papa strode in.

"Ah, there you are, my dear." He paused before her and arched a brow. "There's no need to get yourself worked up about your siblings. They are hale creatures. Unlikely to succumb to a trifling cold. And tears are of no use anyway."

"It is hardly trifling—"

"I came to tell you that Mr. Courtney wrote to request a private meeting with me on Wednesday," said Papa, tucking his hands behind him and rocking on his heels. With a smug smile, he winked at her. "I knew you could do it, Rosanna."

"And what is that, precisely?"

"Don't be missish, my dear. You know a gentleman only calls on a father for one purpose. This is quite a coup."

"To catch a gentleman who cannot be bothered to call promptly to ask such a momentous question, choosing instead to wait until next week?" asked Rosanna with a frown.

Papa waved that objection away. "Nonsense, my girl. Mr. Courtney is a busy man."

"Occupied with his horse breeders no doubt. It is a wonder he spared the time to write," she murmured.

"Mr. Courtney has many demands on his time, and we ought to be grateful he is paying our family this great honor. And bitterness isn't attractive, Rosanna. You ought to avoid it when he arrives. Men like him enjoy a bit of teasing, for he enjoys the challenge, but do not push him too far."

Staring at him, she gaped. "But Papa, with illness in the house we should avoid social engagements at present."

"It's hardly social, though it will be an engagement," he said with a waggle of his brows as though his wordplay were especially witty. "Besides, Prudence has everything in hand."

"She has fallen ill as well."

That drew him up short. "Is that so? Then you'd best avoid her at present. It would be a shame for you to catch it as well and spoil your looks for Mr. Courtney."

Rosanna's gape widened, her brows pinching together. "That is heartless, Papa."

"Nonsense, my dear. Prudence understands. We each have a part to play in this family, and on Wednesday, you shall fulfill yours," he said, fairly preening as he rocked back on his heels once more.

She tried to swallow, but her throat clenched, and her heart followed suit; it was as though everything inside her tightened and strained at the thought. Her thoughts spun with things she longed to say, though she struggled to settle on the right one. Though she knew she ought to tell Papa that she didn't care for Mr. Courtney, she knew with equal fervor what his reaction would be if she said such a thing.

They all had their part to play in this family, after all. This was hers.

Then, turning to the door, Papa added, "Your mother will be in raptures to plan the wedding, so be prepared to spend the evening listening to her wax poetic about lace and silk. Heaven help us."

And with that, he strode from the bedchamber, leaving Rosanna alone once more.

Was it any wonder that Dr. Humphreys chose Prudence? She was so talented and impressive, and Rosanna was naught but a decoration. A trophy. A lure for a wealthy man. That was all she was good for. For better or worse, that was her role in this world.

Lying down on the pillow, Rosanna stared sightlessly at the far wall as though glimpsing into the future that would begin Wednesday.

Chapter 39

Exhaustion was a sneaky thing. Inch by inch, it crept into one's life, slowly tainting every hour, then day, then week, making one think fatigue was the standard, and it wasn't until one was forced to slow that one recognized how compromised one's strength was. As much as Prudence liked to believe she managed all her responsibilities with ease, the past days had given her much time in which to reconsider that.

One did not usually emerge from an illness feeling more alert and revived. Despite the usual need to ease back into one's daily routine, once the fever had passed, Prudence found herself with more vitality than she'd felt in months. Perhaps longer.

That was a sobering thought. But true enough. More sobering was to know that without Dr. Humphreys, she wouldn't have been allowed even these few days to focus solely on her health. But despite that startling and all too morose realization, Prudence was smiling.

It took so little to prompt the thing, but it was impossible to school her expression. She'd heard of sickbed romances, and she finally understood the appeal. Was there anything sweeter than having someone take care of you? It was said that actions spoke louder than words, and never was that more apparent than through Dr. Humphreys' gentle ministrations.

As she stood before the linen cupboard, his voice echoed in her thoughts, prodding her to rest. Read in the library at most. But after so many days of sleep and books, Prudence was eager to do something of value, and taking stock of the linens was not strenuous. Holding the register in one hand, she ticked off bed linens, tablecloths, and the like.

Dr. Humphreys had a lovely smile. Perhaps "lovely" was not the proper word, for that implied it was something dainty or delicate, and his was anything but. It took over the whole of his face and shone in his eyes.

Prudence hugged the book to her front and stared at the cupboard, her gaze fixing on nothing as she sucked in a deep breath, letting it out in a sigh worthy of any lovesick heroine from a melodrama. Was there anything else she could do in such a circumstance? Dr. Humphreys had been true to his word and said nothing concerning courtship or his feelings all those hours at her bedside, but that hadn't stopped his gaze from lingering on her. Or the warmth glowing inside his blue eyes.

Her memories of the past few days were hazy at times, struggling to establish the boundary between dream and reality, but he'd been there with medicine or food at the ready when she woke, and it was Dr. Humphreys' voice reading aloud that had lulled her back to sleep. Forever at her side, despite her illness being little more than an inconvenience.

If anything, it was a bit disappointing that she was feeling well enough yesterday that Dr. Humphreys had finally surrendered his place at her bedside, which was entirely too selfish of her, as he had work aplenty to do without hanging about Whitley Court—especially as he still had yet to accept any compensation for his services here.

Straightening, Prudence lowered the ledger and stared at the linen cupboard again. This was the fifth time she'd attempted to count the tablecloths, and she was still uncertain if her final count aligned with the official tally, for every time she attempted it, she was left with a different figure. Shutting the book and the cupboard, Prudence turned away. There was little point in attempting this if her thoughts were so very far from the task at hand.

Humming to herself, Prudence meandered to her bedchamber and tossed the ledger on the side table. She paused at the sight of a brown paper package lying on her pillow; there was an envelope atop it with clear, even letters addressing the parcel to Miss Prudence Leigh, with her Christian name underlined. The handwriting was so crisp that she hardly recognized it, but it still held a hint of Dr. Humphreys' style.

With a smile, she sat on the bed, tugged at the strings, and pulled back the paper to find the first volume of *The Bravo of Venice* by Matthew Lewis, and she couldn't help but laugh. They had spent so much time discussing it the other day, and she hugged it to her chest, eager to share the ludicrous tale with Dr. Humphreys. But the laugh drifted away as her gaze turned to the envelope.

She ought to have opened it first, but Prudence stared at it, recalling the last time she'd found a letter from him. The comparison was not flattering, but she knew it would be as different from his missive to Rosanna as the gift that accompanied it.

Prudence kept the book tucked in one arm and reached for the letter, breaking the seal, and her vision quickly wavered when her gaze fell to the first line below her name.

You are not my second choice.

Goodness. Prudence sucked in a breath at those simple words. They were not the flowery, twisty words he'd used in that other letter, and they held more power because of their directness. She knew it was unfair to compare the two, but having read the first so many times, she knew it almost by heart, and it popped into her thoughts as her eyes drifted through his lines.

Dear Miss Leigh,

You are not my second choice.

I may have been a fool in the past, but there is no other person I would rather have at my side but you. It pains me to know that I've given you reason to doubt my sincerity, but after only a few hours in your company, I began to see the truth. Blind though I may have been, my lovely Miss Leigh, I have long admired you.

Though you scoffed at the thought of friendship being foremost in my thoughts, I assure you that is no little thing to me. Love cannot survive on attraction alone, and I cannot think of better soil in which to plant the seeds of love than friendship. Believe me when I say I now count you among my closest friends.

I shall call today at three o'clock, and if you do not welcome my overtures, you need only send me away. But please, allow me the opportunity to show just how earnest I am. I hope to win your forgiveness and so much more.

Forever yours,
P. Humphreys

Oh, good gracious. Prudence stared at the lines, reading them again and again. And her eyes fell to that casual endearment. "My lovely Miss Leigh." Lovely? Had he said something of the sort before, Prudence would've scoffed, but wrapped in such sweet sentiments, she couldn't bat it away as a bit of folly.

A friend? The word seemed so insipid in such a moment, but her breath quickened as she considered the whole of his meaning and the sentiment in which every word was steeped. When described in such a manner, it certainly felt as if it was far more than something platonic or pitying.

He desired her. Not just because he thought her lovely, but because he longed for the whole of her.

Prudence set aside the book to press a hand to her heart, though it couldn't keep her furious pulse at bay. Dr. Humphreys loved her—or was on his way to doing so. And as much as her instincts whispered foul little warnings about the fickleness of his feelings, her gaze drifted across the lines once more, relishing every word.

...

Rosanna didn't care for the library. Not that she disliked the written word, but there was so much more to do in the parlor. Prudence often retired here to get away from the noise and chaos that followed their siblings about the house, but Rosanna didn't understand the appeal of the silence. Solitude was not a comfortable thing.

But she remained precisely where Mama had told her to sit, for the sunlight streaming through the window to her right was perfectly situated to catch her golden curls. No doubt, Mama thought it was like a gilded frame for a painting, but Rosanna felt more like an offering served up on an altar.

Marry Mr. Courtney. That was for the family's good. For all that she had flirted with Dr. Humphreys, her duty had always been clear. There was no question, and perhaps that was part of the physician's appeal. What delight was there to be found in inevitability? Whether she cared for Mr. Courtney or not, Mama and Papa expected Rosanna to become Mrs. Courtney.

Mr. Courtney's vast coffers and connections would aid the family greatly. Francis and Katherine required assistance if they were to find suitable husbands. And though Prudence seemed on the path to becoming Mrs. Humphreys, the physician would fare better if he had a wealthy benefactor to aid him.

The Humphreys. The Courtneys.

Such great felicity, yet Rosanna's insides twisted as thoroughly as Grandmama's knitting. Pressing a hand to her stomach, she leaned over and tried to calm the roiling mess inside, but the sound of footsteps had her straightening immediately.

Muffled voices accompanied the sound, and then the door swung open, drawing Rosanna to her feet.

"Here she is," said Papa, sweeping in with Mr. Courtney at his elbow and Mama at his heels. Stepping around the gentlemen, the lady hurried to her daughter and pressed a kiss to her cheek.

"This is so wonderful, my dear!" she whispered.

Rosanna held onto a fragile smile as Papa swept the lady out, giving his daughter a wink before shutting the library door tight behind them. Mr. Courtney smirked and gave Rosanna an arched brow, and she fought against the blush threatening to emerge. And that was when she spied shadows at the door jamb. No doubt Mama had her ear pressed to the wood.

With a sigh and a shake of her head, Rosanna leaned forward enough to rub at her forehead. "I apologize, Mr. Courtney. My parents were born without even a smidgen of subtlety."

The gentleman huffed a laugh and came to stand before her. "As my intentions are obvious, it doesn't offend my sensibilities. I prefer it to subterfuge."

Rosanna straightened and gave him an arched brow. "You enjoy the chase, admit it."

"Certainly, but when it comes time to do business, it is best to be clear and concise."

"Business?" she frowned.

It was Mr. Courtney's turn to give her an arched brow. "Don't feign missishness now. You have played your role well, and I find myself entranced, but now, it is time to drop the pretense."

Rosanna opened her mouth to protest, but her teeth snapped shut as she realized she couldn't defend herself from such an accusation. Not entirely, at any rate.

"I have spoken to the vicar, and we have a date for a week from now," he said, tucking his hands behind him. "Your mother will be disappointed, no doubt, that there won't be more time for lace, flounces, and the like, but my business is concluded in Greater Edgerton, and I must return home. Besides, we'll need the time to get you properly outfitted for the coming Season."

He gave her gown a narrowed eye, though his expression lightened into another of his smirks when he met her gaze once more. "Your clothes are fine in the country, but even you shall require the height of fashion if you are to command attention. With you properly arrayed in the finest silks and jewels, you will be the envy of London."

The best gowns. Sparkling jewelry. The swirl of London ballrooms. The height of fashion. The center of Society. Granted, Mr. Courtney thought a bit too highly of his standing, for he was by no means a gentleman of such unlimited funds that he could command Society's attention or give as much as he promised, but it appealed to that greedy part of her heart, which longed to ignore the insights of the past few weeks and embrace the image of the vapid and vain young lady they all thought her to be.

Yet her heartbeat remained slow and sluggish. An ache settled in the back of her throat, and she tried to swallow, but it fought against her, leaving her mouth far too dry to be tolerable. Mr. Courtney kept reciting all the details of their forthcoming marriage, and despite the felicity of the moment, Rosanna couldn't help but wish the clocks would tick faster and move quickly on to the next hour when all would be settled.

That was what she wanted.

Wasn't it?

Mr. Courtney launched into the list of her duties to perform in London and at the family estate—all of which were no more strenuous than dressing in her best and standing at his side and smiling prettily, of course, and Rosanna saw the future unfold before her.

Forever standing on Mr. Courtney's arm. Desired solely because of her figure and face. And with each passing year, her power would diminish. For all that it had the strength to conquer strong-willed gentlemen like Mr. Courtney, it was a fleeting thing that faded with each wrinkle and gray hair.

Dr. Humphreys' words echoed in her thoughts, telling her she could be more than merely the ornament everyone wished her to be. Could she resign herself to a marriage where her husband would grow more and more bored with her? When the only thing she brought into the marriage faded from existence, would he be happy with her then? Would she?

Her stomach turned, and for all that she'd done a good job of ignoring it of late, the wretched organ felt like lead, dragging her down. This was not what a lady on the brink of matrimony ought to feel.

Chapter 40

"I anticipate children, of course," said Mr. Courtney with a wave of his hand as though they could simply send out to the grocer for offspring. "Once the heir is secure, you can amuse yourself however you wish. As long as you are discreet."

Rosanna stiffened, her eyes widening. Mr. Courtney spoke with such certainty that she would break her marriage vows, but then, it was clear from his tone that he fully intended to do so himself. But even as his words made the bile rise in her throat, Rosanna's thoughts turned to another gentleman who would not be so blasé about his affections. He never had been.

How had she been so blind to Dr. Humphreys? Her pulse thumped through her, stripping away any uncertainty she may have felt before, for her heart would not pain her so much if she didn't love him. The truth was clear. It thrummed through her veins, burning away Mr. Courtney's lukewarm affections, and left her with the knowledge that she would never find another man like Dr. Humphreys.

The life Mr. Courtney presented faded away into nothing, for Rosanna knew—positively knew—it would not make her happy. She didn't wish to be that frivolous woman, and if she accepted Mr. Courtney, that was precisely what she would be.

The gentleman droned on, clearly unaware that her attention had strayed far from his proposal (if one could call it that), and Rosanna's thoughts swirled with the possibilities. Her ribs tightened around her heart, squeezing it as she considered another unassailable truth.

Prudence loved Dr. Humphreys.

But she refused to be his second choice.

Despite the roiling feeling inside, Rosanna considered that with brows furrowed. Dr. Humphreys' affections couldn't have altered so completely in such a short time. Whether or not he wished to admit it, his first choice was Rosanna, and it would be cruel to allow Prudence to court a gentleman if his heart belonged to another.

What if Prudence were to marry the good doctor, only to discover he still harbored an attachment for her sister? That would be cruel. Unthinkable. Dr. Humphreys was entertaining the tendre simply because he didn't know that Rosanna's feelings had changed; if he knew the truth, he would choose his first love.

Being honest with Dr. Humphreys would be best for everyone involved.

With each thought, her heartbeat quickened, her thoughts spinning until she felt positively lightheaded. She forced her breathing to slow, and it felt as though her veins were filled with molten iron, warming her through and steeling her for what was to come.

Mr. Courtney's hand appeared before Rosanna, drawing her attention away from her tumultuous thoughts. Her brows rose as her gaze traveled up the arm to meet his. His brow was arched in that mocking manner of his, and Rosanna stared at it. How had she ever thought it attractive?

"Shall we tell your parents the news?" he said with a laugh in his tone.

Rosanna stared at him. "Tell them what news?"

Mr. Courtney huffed. "Do not be coy—"

"I am not, sir. As far as I can tell, you've come here demanding much but without actually saying anything of value," she said with a frown.

Folding his arms, Mr. Courtney stared at her for a long moment with half-lidded eyes. Then, in a monotone, he asked, "Miss Rosanna, will you marry me?"

"No." Rosanna rose to her feet and stepped around him, but he snatched her arm, pulling her to a stop.

"I am out of patience, Miss Rosanna," he said, a sigh heavy in his tone. "For all that these games have been entertaining, my time is short, and I cannot keep playing."

Rosanna glanced at his hand, holding firm to her arm. "I am not toying with you. I was uncertain before, but your 'proposal' has made it entirely clear we are ill-suited. I do not love you, and you certainly do not love me. I see no reason to marry."

Mr. Courtney smiled, a sharp laugh on his lips. "Ah, so I ought to spend more time complimenting and cajoling you, playing the part of the lovesick swain rather than admitting that this is a mutually beneficial arrangement?"

"Not at all," she replied with a shake of her head. "Marriage isn't an 'arrangement.' It's a lifelong commitment, and I will not bind myself to someone who only views me as a trophy—"

"Nonsense!" shrieked Mama as the library door burst open. Hurrying to Mr. Courtney, she took his hands in hers. "Do not listen to the girl. She is speaking nonsense. There has been illness in the house, and I am certain she must be feverish."

Rosanna stepped around the pair, and Mr. Courtney pulled free of Mama's hold, but the lady was like an octopus with arms to spare, seizing hold of him again as she babbled excuses for her daughter.

But above Mama's frantic ramblings, Mr. Courtney called out, "I am done with these games, Miss Rosanna. I shan't renew my addresses if you leave."

Pausing at the doorway, Rosanna looked over her shoulder at the gentleman. His eyes blazed with anger, and she held fast to her convictions, which grew stronger the hotter his gaze burned. And without another word, she went in search of an entirely different gentleman.

Pacing the length of the parlor, Parker ignored the pained sounds coming from the piano as Miss Katherine battled the keys. Mrs. Cora Leigh sat on the far side with her knitting, watching him cross the length of the room while he tried to ignore the elderly lady's shrewd looks. Thankfully, the youngest Leigh sister, Francis, was so occupied with reworking her bonnet that she didn't seem to notice the intruder.

Parker tried to sit, but he couldn't remain still with thoughts of that letter pulsing in his brain.

The thing had been a mistake. Not the words—he didn't regret a single one of them—but in the dark of night, it had seemed romantic to write Miss Leigh a proper note all her own. In the light of day, all Parker could do was question why he had thought to draw such a strong parallel between his present petition and his previous one.

Parker paused his pacing and pinched his nose. When a huff of laughter sounded from the sofa, he straightened to find Mrs. Cora Lee snickering from behind her knitting.

Turning away, he marched the parlor again, but kept his pace to more of a meander. Drifting around the circular table in the center, which was covered in all the accouterments a young lady required for fixing up a bonnet, and past the piano (which sounded as though the pianist were stabbing it), he reached the end of the room, turned on his heel, and returned to the far side.

How had his heart deceived him so much? Miss Leigh was superior to all other women in every facet. Miss Rosanna was a more obvious beauty, but Miss Leigh was lovely in her own right. She was stately with the strength and bearing of a queen. The sort of woman who only grew more appealing with age rather than fading when summer drifted into autumn.

Yet here he was again, comparing the Leigh sisters when there was no comparison.

Parker paused at the far edge of the room, his gaze fixed on the wall. He felt like banging his head against it, but the parlor door opened, and he spun on his heel, a smile quick on his lips. It died the moment his gaze rested on Miss Rosanna.

"You are here," she said, her voice little more than a breathy whisper.

"As you see." Parker shifted in place, his brows drawing close.

"It is a sign." Miss Rosanna stepped forward, and instinct had him stepping away while the gleam in her gaze had him glancing at the door, which was behind the lady sweeping toward him.

"Give us a moment, please," said Miss Rosanna, not looking away from Parker, though her tone made the words more command than request. The lady's grandmother huffed a laugh but rose and ushered out the younger Leighs. Parker moved to follow them, but Rosanna stepped in his path, and his stomach sank to his toes.

What was she doing?

"I was just going to look for you, but here you are, like a miracle from heaven. A sign," she said in a low whisper, her eyes aglow with something that had him flushing. And not for the right reasons. A slight sheen of sweat dampened his shirt, and Parker struggled to hold onto his smile.

"I was waiting for your sister," he said, frowning at the door as it swung shut, leaving the two of them quite alone.

Though Parker had hoped the statement might slow the lady's progress, Miss Rosanna strode towards him with a sultry smile that had him skittering backward and into the wall.

"I have thought of you quite a lot of late," she said, drawing up close to him.

Parker stared at her and said the only thing that came to mind. "Have you?"

"Yes," she whispered, leaning close. "Quite a lot."

His gaze darted to the door once more, but no rescue came, and his attention was jerked back to her when she brushed a touch along his waistcoat. Sliding away, Parker stepped around her and inched backward toward escape.

"That is interesting," he said, for he felt he needed to say something, and his thoughts were screaming all sorts of unhelpful things. What was Miss Rosanna doing? It seemed clear from her behavior, but it was too dramatic a shift for him to grasp.

And the far more important question was, what would *he* do?

Parker struggled to see past the strongest desire, which was to flee from the figurative Potifer's wife like Joseph of Egypt had without a backward glance. But this was his sweetheart's sister. Or his soon-to-be sweetheart. Surely there was some misunderstanding.

"I made a terrible mistake, Dr. Humphreys."

Ah, yes. See, she'd made a mistake just now. A silly little misstep that could quickly be forgotten. But Miss Rosanna kept following him as he wandered to the far side of the room.

"I was a fool to cast aside your letter," she added.

"Pardon?" Parker froze in place, his brows jerking into his hairline.

"I was blind and silly." Miss Rosanna winced, shaking her head as her expression crumpled. Shoulders drooping, she turned watery eyes to him. "You are the finest man I know, and I shouldn't have ignored your tender and earnest feelings. I should've realized what a prize you were."

With a wary eye fixed on her, Parker overshot the door and ran into the sofa, nearly losing his balance. But Miss Rosanna reached out and steadied him.

"I know this may come as a shock, but I realize what a mistake I made," she said, drawing flush to him. She gazed into his eyes, her own sparkling with unshed tears. Then, in a low whisper, she added, "Please tell me it is not too late."

Parker's eyes widened until they were liable to pop free from his head, and he stiffened, turning to marble as she jerked forward, her lips at the ready.

Chapter 41

Like many lovelorn souls, Prudence had imagined what love felt like—not the familial type, but that magical romance that bound two hearts together. And perhaps her feelings for Dr. Humphreys had not reached that level of attachment, but at present, her stomach was doing a lively and very determined country dance. Not precisely what she had anticipated "love" to feel like, but she couldn't help smiling all the same.

Running her hands down her skirt, Prudence turned before the looking glass and forced herself not to examine the imperfections to be found there. Dr. Humphreys cared for her as she was, and as much as she longed to primp and preen away, she refused to allow herself to dwell on that which she could not change.

Trust in him. That was all she could do.

A knock at the door had her jolting, and Prudence spun about as the maid entered with a bob.

"Dr. Humphreys is here to see you, miss."

"Thank you, Jane." Not bothering to give herself another moment to fret before the mirror, Prudence hurried into the hall, her footsteps fairly bouncing along.

A gentleman was calling on her. And not just any gentleman, but Dr. Humphreys!

Prudence felt like a will o' the wisp, untethered from the world and floating about on the breeze. She forced herself not to run down the stairs, for despite the zeal pushing her forward, she didn't want to seem too eager. Best not to frighten him away.

Pausing on the step, she considered that. As inexperienced as she was with courting, Prudence wasn't entirely certain how to go about it, but she knew well enough that many a beau or sweetheart skittered away when the object of their affection grew too adamant. Prudence didn't understand why that was. Did they believe all courting couples fell in love at the same pace? That one ought never to move quicker than the other? But she had heard of enough failed courtships that stemmed from too much zeal that she couldn't dismiss the sensible course of action.

Be engaging and encouraging but do not rush into the parlor like an untrained puppy.

Prudence nodded to herself and continued down the stairs, but stopped again when she heard tears and moaning coming from down the hall. With a wince, she crept along, avoiding the noisier floorboards as she snuck past. No good was to be found in asking Mama why she was distraught, for it could be anything from the foul weather to their impending doom, and Dr. Humphreys was waiting.

"There you are!" cried Mama.

With another wince, Prudence stared down at the landing, wondering if she might simply pretend she hadn't heard the lady. But there was little point.

Turning on her heel, she gave her mother a wary smile. "As you see, Mama. But I fear I have—"

"Have you spoken to your sister?" said Mama, hurrying down the stairs with her handkerchief fluttering about her.

"Not since—"

"You shall never believe what she has done!" Mama's hands

waved about, alternating between shaking her handkerchief at all the evils of the world and dabbing her cheeks. "She has turned away Mr. Courtney! Sent him on his way, despite how fine a match it would be. She shan't find another gentleman of his caliber in Greater Edgerton. She shan't!"

Prudence opened her mouth to reply, but her stomach clenched, and she paused to wonder why the news had her so uneasy.

"And now she has run off to who knows where, and Mr. Courtney has left, vowing he will never renew his addresses, and we are ruined!" Mama dropped onto the stair in a fit of sobs.

Backing slowly down the stairs, Prudence brushed away the niggling feeling that there was far more to the tale. Dr. Humphreys was waiting for her, after all. There was nothing she could do about Rosanna or Mr. Courtney—not that she had any interest in doing so. Rosanna's future was hers to decide, and she could marry as she wished. If anything, Prudence was pleased her sister hadn't chosen that pompous fool.

But Mama's cries followed Prudence along the stairs as she spun around and hurried down the last few.

Tingles ran down her spine, and she brushed them away. There was no reason to worry. There wasn't. Yet her steps moved quicker through the halls as the restlessness pushed her forward.

Reaching the parlor, Prudence paused to collect herself, but her hands moved without prompting, pushing open the door as Rosanna threw herself into Dr. Humphreys' embrace.

Everything inside her clenched as the blow struck her like a kick from a frenzied horse. Time slowed and that second stretched out into infinity as Prudence watched Rosanna reach for Dr. Humphreys' lips.

Pressing a hand to her stomach, Prudence felt the weight of her seven and twenty years press down on her with resounding clarity, and in a flash, she knew the truth—whenever the choice came between the Leigh sisters, everyone chose Rosanna. It was inevitable. The younger Miss Leigh was everything a lady should be. Graceful, beautiful, demure. With just enough fire to be coy and even a little cheeky at times. Rosanna Leigh was a light in the darkness that all gentlemen gravitated towards. Prudence was merely stalwart. A friend—

No!

Drawing in a deep breath, Prudence drew back her shoulders and banished those tainted thoughts from her mind, scrubbing the last of their filth from her. She was Prudence Leigh, and she had value as intrinsic as Rosanna's. And she loved the woman she was. Whatever may come, she was stronger than it—and she would not break.

Time leapt forward, speeding along as though making up for the lost minutes, and the world snapped back into focus. Dr. Humphreys twisted away from Rosanna, his smile growing more pained and brittle as she attempted to meet his lips with hers.

And that was when he spied Prudence.

"Miss Leigh..." His wide eyes darted between the sisters, his brows scrunched together as his gaze pleaded with Prudence. "I promise this is not what it appears to be."

"I know precisely what this is, sir." She crossed her arms, and a shaft of ice wove its way into her heart as Prudence stared at Rosanna, who remained pressed up to Dr. Humphreys, not moving despite the gentleman nudging her away. Rosanna finally cast a glance over her shoulder and had the courtesy to flush a little pink, though she remained plastered to the poor man.

"What do you think you are doing?" whispered Prudence.

Rosanna glanced up at Dr. Humphreys before turning a furrowed brow to her sister. "I did not want you to find out this way—"

"There is nothing to find out!" With more force, the gentleman pushed Rosanna back and hurried to Prudence's side. "I swear to you this means nothing."

"How dare you." Prudence fought to keep her voice even,

but a quiver broke through as she stared Rosanna down. "Is it not enough that every man we've ever met has fallen at your feet? For once, a gentleman favors me, and you must have him for yourself? Is it because you cannot bear to let a man off the hook? Or are you jealous because a man prefers your plain, sensible sister?"

Despite her best efforts, her voice rose. Fire burned in her veins, working its way to her heart, and the hot and cold battled together, filling Prudence to the brim.

Rosanna stood there, staring at her with wide eyes and a gaping mouth. "Prudence—"

"Can you not be happy for me?" she shouted. "Am I not allowed to have even a pinch of affection and admiration? You must steal it away for yourself?"

A jagged breath broke through her words, and Prudence pressed a hand to her mouth. Turning away, she curled in on herself, and Dr. Humphreys drew near, placing a hand on her back. But it was another hand touching her other shoulder that had Prudence freezing in place once more.

"Prudence, please..." whispered Rosanna.

"Do not speak another word!" Prudence whirled around, jerking a finger at her. "You knew how I felt about him, and you still threw yourself at him. Do not deny it!"

Those features that were so often praised to the skies were crumpled, and Rosanna's chin trembled, but when she opened her mouth again, Prudence turned away. Her eyes met Dr. Humphreys', and without a word, he took her by the arm and helped her out of the parlor, bundling her up against the cold as they escaped out the front door.

With all the strangeness of the last few minutes, Parker felt as though his head was about to spin clean off his shoulders. But then, it was not merely the last hour, day, or week. For one entire month, the world had upended itself every few moments, culminating in this entirely confusing and startling interlude.

But as Miss Leigh was clinging to his arm while he led her to his borrowed gig, Parker couldn't complain about it. Even if he wished it hadn't caused that dear lady so much distress.

Helping her up into her seat, he tucked her skirts in and draped a blanket across her lap; the weather was quite nice for their outing, but even the finest days were frigid with the air blowing through one's cloak. And Miss Leigh had only just recently risen from her sickbed.

Parker's hand rested atop her knee, and from this lower angle, he saw into her downturned gaze. Those dark brows were furrowed together, and her chin trembled. He longed for something to say, but what words could he offer at such a moment? His pulse still hadn't steadied, and for all that he liked staring up into Miss Leigh's gaze, he needed to move.

Stepping around the carriage, he climbed up next to her as he struggled to get himself under control. But his thoughts were not so easily guided as the horse, moving with the simplest flick of the rein. Eyes forward, Parker stared at the road and nearly lurched out the side when Miss Leigh slid her arm through his. Forcing in a deep breath, he drew close, allowing her warmth to seep in through his chilled skin.

What had just happened? Parker still couldn't comprehend any of it, and he struggled between watching the road and the lady at his side. She leaned heavily into him, and he hoped that was a good sign, but he still didn't know what to say. The moment played through his mind, though it showed the scene from her perspective, and Parker began to sweat anew.

His stomach clenched, and the worries of a few minutes ago surged up with renewed force, coursing through him. Staring beyond the horses, he let his gaze grow unfocused, which was not a wise thing to do when he was so inexperienced at driving through the middle of town. His left foot was perched on the ball, bouncing up and down like an overeager rabbit, but he couldn't make it stop.

Miss Leigh was at his side, so surely that was a good sign. But she remained silent, and Parker didn't know what to do.

Chapter 42

"I didn't know you owned a gig." Miss Leigh's comment was quiet, and a faint tremble belied the calm tone she affected.

Parker's gaze darted to her, and she finally faced him. Those dark eyes of hers were brimming with tears, begging for him to speak.

If a change of subject was what she wanted, he would gladly comply. Clearing his throat, Parker forced himself to focus on answering and guiding the horse through the thick of things. Thankfully, they would reach the edge of town in a few minutes, and he wouldn't need to exert as much effort on the latter task.

"I..." Parker's thoughts skittered for a moment before he gathered them into a semblance of coherency. "I don't. I borrowed this from my parents. As you are just recovering from an illness, and I want to steal away as much time as I can, I thought a drive would be best."

"You did?" she asked, her tone stronger than before.

His eyes moved to hers of their own accord. They truly were a lovely color, and Parker felt like preening when they warmed, a faint smile growing as she gazed upon him. The strain eased from his muscles, and for the first time since he'd written to her, Parker felt as though he could breathe.

"Of course."

"Oi, nitwit!" bellowed a man from an oncoming cart, ripping Parker from his daydreams

His arms jerked, his attention swinging back to the road in time to see the passing driver scowling and slinging more than a few colorful words in his direction. Parker guided the horse around it without too much trouble and winced, sending a silent prayer of gratitude as they drew up to the edge of town, and he was able to get them onto the emptier country lane with little trouble.

"I apologize, Miss Leigh. I fear I am not much of a driver. I suppose I ought to have simply taken you for a walk instead."

Sliding closer on the bench, Miss Leigh squeezed his arm. "A walk is nice enough, but at present, I prefer a drive."

The road stretched ahead, giving him a clear view. No coaches or carts were approaching, so Parker allowed himself to meet her gaze once more, and his heart lightened to see the shadows fading from her expression.

"I am sorry, Miss Leigh. I swear to you that I didn't intend for that to happen…" Parker frowned, struggling to know how to describe the incident. "I played no part in that…mistake." He stiffened. "Not that I made a mistake, for I did nothing to encourage. In any fashion. Whatsoever."

His racing thoughts immediately supplied all the many ways that phrasing might cause more trouble, but he couldn't think of what to say. "I—"

"I do not blame you, Dr. Humphreys." Miss Leigh sighed and shook her head, turning to stare out at the passing landscape. "I will admit that for a bad moment, I feared the worst, but that doubt had more to do with myself than you. Deep in my heart, I knew that you wouldn't behave in such a manner."

The strain of the past few hours faded away, leaving Parker feeling as light as the clouds dotting the sky above. Allowing himself a moment to bask in the beauty of that admission, he sent her a smile that he hoped conveyed all the gratitude and pleasure coursing through him with every contented patter of his heart.

But with a slight frown, he said, "This afternoon did not go as I had intended."

Miss Leigh turned in her seat, and though it gave him a better view of her, he didn't like the distance it forced between them. His leg and side felt all the colder for it.

"All things considered, this isn't how I imagined the afternoon, either," she said, a slight furrow creasing her brow. But as she met his gaze, her eyes warmed. "But I am happy nonetheless."

A ride in the gig had been a mistake—one Parker realized the instant he longed to take her hand in his but found both occupied with the wretched reins, and he didn't trust himself enough to attempt a one-handed grasp.

Despite turning a frown inward, Parker gave her a hint of a hopeful smile. "Might I hope that your appearance in the parlor..." He paused, shifting the conversation away from that terrible moment. "That my letter..."

But that caused his earlier fears to surface, gaining more strength after that interlude with Miss Rosanna. His hold on the reins slackened as he tried to think of how to ask the question he wished to ask without drifting toward unpleasant subjects.

"Did you come to the parlor...was it due to..." He stumbled and altered his approach, his words mixing into an incomprehensible mess. "May I be so bold as to hope? The letter? I meant every word I wrote. It wasn't as eloquent as I had hoped—I did try my best. But I wasn't certain..."

Parker pulled the horse to a stop in the middle of the road and turned towards her, stammering more apologies and excuses (though less coherently than before). Hazarding a glance in her direction, his brows rose at the sight of laughter in her gaze. Then she pressed her hand to his mouth, silencing his babbling.

"Calm yourself, Dr. Humphreys," she murmured, but that was hardly possible with her hand touching his lips. It made his heart pulse erratically and brought to mind hopes and desires that were far from appropriate at this early juncture.

Goodness! What fit of madness had spurred her to touch Dr. Humphreys in such a manner? The movement had seemed natural and easy, but Prudence's focus fractured when she began wondering just what his lips felt like. She both blessed and cursed her gloves; they allowed her the tiniest bit of self-control at that moment when her thoughts could think of little else but kissing Dr. Humphreys.

Their gazes met, their faces far closer than she had anticipated, and she felt the warmth emanating from his clear eyes. Such a look! Prudence had never expected to see such a thing directed at her, and it wove through her heart, erasing the last of her fears and doubts.

"This has been a wretched beginning, Dr. Humphreys. Might we try again?" Prudence's cheeks pinked at the breathy tone that sounded nothing like her. His brows rose in challenge, and she considered that before tacking on another, "Again?"

When she lifted her hand from his mouth, he grinned. "At this rate, Miss Leigh, we are bound to begin anew every few weeks."

Drawing herself up, she gave him a regal nod. "My name is Miss Prudence Leigh. I am the eldest in my family and far more of a parent to my siblings than those who begot us, and I love and loathe them in equal measure. I adore love letters written in indecipherable handwriting and drives or walks about town or anything else that allows me to spend time with my favorite physician."

"Even when he causes mayhem in your life?"

Prudence would've given a teasing response, but the seriousness in his tone made those words fade away. Holding his gaze, she smiled. "Even then."

Dr. Humphreys lowered his eyes, his lips pulling into a pleased smile that Prudence couldn't help but echo.

"Well, my dear Miss Leigh, I am Dr. Parker Humphreys, a physician of middling skill and minimal intelligence, and I tend to get myself stuck in awkward situations and still have not learned how to extricate myself without harming a lady who is exceptionally dear to me. Thankfully, she is silly enough to think me a catch, and I am determined to court her properly and make her fall madly in love with me before she realizes her mistake."

Prudence's lips twitched with a smile. "And what do you mean by a 'proper' courtship?"

"Long walks and drives on which I will lavish you with flowers, sweets, and various tokens of affection. Squiring you to every party, assembly, and gathering you wish to attend, and dancing with you as often as I am allowed. Haunting your parlor every evening you remain at home. Spending countless hours discussing any subject that crosses our minds in one never-ending discussion of everything and nothing."

Dr. Humphreys listed each without hesitation, rattling off every beautiful idea. With every addition, Prudence's heart expanded, stretching outward as though to embrace every opportunity.

"That sounds perfect." Those words were too small and simple, but Prudence didn't trust herself to say anything more, for the picture he painted was divine, as though he had plucked it from her dreams.

"Then we'd best get a move on," he said with a nod, turning back to the road before them.

But before he set the horse to walking, Parker Humphreys took her hand and lifted it to his lips; his eyes held hers as he pressed a kiss to her knuckles, lingering over it as though to savor every detail. She certainly did. Everything inside her stilled, and Prudence couldn't help but wish it wasn't her hand he kissed. Then he tucked her hand through his arm, drawing her flush to his side once more.

The gig lurched forward, and they bounced along the country lane, the movement making them sway together, their shoulders pressed close. For several long moments, they sat there, content to watch the scenery pass and bask in the beautiful now. Though this was by no means the end of their journey, the path here had exacted tolls on them both, and Prudence was quite pleased to simply revel in the bliss of the moment.

The lightness in her heart spread through her, drawing out a smile as they admired the rolling hills around Greater Edgerton while minutes and miles ticked away. Not even their eventual return to her doorstep ruined the beauty of the day.

No matter how Prudence preferred to remain precisely where she was, she reveled in the feel of his hands guiding her down from the gig. Heaven knew she was quite adept at doing so on her own, but her heart gave a happy skip as he aided her with all the tender care she had dreamed her beau would show.

But when they stood before one another, Parker did not release his hold of her hand. Holding her gaze, he gave her yet another of his smiles that was all warmth and laughter and raised her hand to his lips.

"Thank you for accompanying me," he murmured.

"Thank you for inviting me." Yet that did not come close to conveying all she wished to say. Staring into his eyes, Prudence wished she had the words to tell him how happy his letter had made her. As she couldn't describe it even within the safe confines of her thoughts, she wouldn't attempt it here and now.

"Thank you," she echoed, putting as much of her heart as she dared show in those two little words. Parker's gaze lightened, and he pressed another kiss to her knuckles.

But when she finally turned to leave, he snatched her arm up in his and gave her an arched brow. "Please allow me to escort you home, Miss Leigh."

"Certainly, good sir," she replied with a laugh as they climbed the few stairs.

He paused on the landing and swept into a bow.

"Might I be so bold as to ask if you would join me again tomorrow?" he asked.

"Tomorrow," she said with a nod. "And the next day?"

Prudence cringed at her audacity, but when Parker straightened and placed his hat back on his head, there was a laugh in his eyes as he said, "And any day you'll have me."

The pair lingered there on the threshold, smiling and staring at each other, and though Prudence didn't know what else to say, she couldn't bring herself to shut the door on him. Nor did Parker seem interested in being the first to turn away.

"There's a draft!" barked Grandmama from somewhere farther into the house, and the pair jerked from their ardent stupor and gave one last farewell before Prudence shut the door.

Chapter 43

With a sigh, Prudence leaned against the front door, certain her strength would give out. Yes, it was a bit dramatic, but she was feeling all sorts of dramatic at that moment. She glided up the stairs, giving a light chassé every third step, as though her feet were not content with simply marching along.

Parker Humphreys was courting her!

But the music in her heart ground to a halt at the sound of Mama's tears from down the hall. Prudence paused on the landing as gravity took hold of her once more, landing her firmly back in the reality of the day. Turning away from that sound, she crept up to her bedchamber door.

Her hand rested on the latch, and she stared at the wood, wondering what she would find in there—and hoping it was empty. Swinging the door open, she tugged at her bonnet strings and tried not to look at Rosanna's bed as she strode to her own and dumped her things atop it, but it was impossible not to notice her sister perched like a statue on the edge, staring at the far wall.

Flames sizzled through Prudence's veins at the sight of her sister, but for all that her anger attempted to settle into her heart, the pleasure of the past hour held more sway, turning the heat into something far more enjoyable.

Having deposited her things, Prudence turned to leave and strode to the door. And stopped at the threshold when Rosanna spoke three small words, so quiet that Prudence nearly didn't catch them.

"I am sorry."

Muscles tensing, Prudence gripped the door jamb and drew in a steeling breath before she turned to face Rosanna. With narrowed eyes, she stared at the young lady, though her sister's gaze remained fixed on nothing.

"You knew how I felt about Dr. Humphreys, yet you still threw yourself at him, hoping to catch him for yourself. Do you truly believe a small apology will make anything better?"

Rosanna shot from her bed, whirling to face her sister, her brows all twisted together, her eyes wide and pleading. "I am so very sorry for what I did. It was a horrid mistake, and I am so ashamed of my behavior, Prudence. I am!"

"Of course you are." Straightening, Prudence drew closer. Her ribs squeezed her heart tight as she studied her sister, the very picture of contrition. "You are so very sorry because you did not get what you wanted. But had he chosen you, would you feel so terrible about it? Would you have turned him aside out of guilt? Or would you have accepted your happy situation and felt only a niggling guilt that my heart had been broken in the process?"

As much as Prudence wished she could say for certain what Rosanna's answer would be, the past few weeks left her adrift. For all that she and her sister were very different people, they were the closest of friends. Or had been. It had been so for Prudence's part, but what friend—let alone a sister—behaved in such a manner?

Did she know Rosanna at all?

Pressing a hand to her stomach, Rosanna tried to breathe. A part of her longed to draw near and throw herself into Prudence's arms, but her insides roiled at the thought of coming any closer. Heaven knew she had no right to throw herself upon her sister's mercy.

No matter how many times she recalled the moment with Dr. Humphreys, Rosanna could not make sense of it. What had she done? What could she say to Prudence to defend herself? She certainly deserved no defense. Despite knowing the logic that had pushed her to act then, Rosanna couldn't make sense of it now.

The world blurred, and she stood there, chin trembling as she tried to think of something to say, but Prudence remained rigid and watched her with such cold eyes.

"I do not blame you if you never wish to speak to me again, but I feel wretched for what I did." Rosanna squeezed her eyes shut, and she shook her head with a wince. What word could she use for such a moment? How did one describe the shame and sorrow that accompanied such a betrayal?

"I have lived in your shadow for as long as I can remember," said Prudence, and Rosanna's eyes opened to see her dear sister staring at her with such a cold expression. Taking in a deep breath, Prudence held her gaze as she asked, "Was it truly so awful that someone might desire me above you for once? Could you not allow me this one shining moment?"

Rosanna stiffened, her head jerking back as she gaped. "For once, a gentleman looked at me and saw value beyond my features and figure. Not only that, he encouraged me to be better. Then the moment he comes to know you, he casts me aside and treats me like all the rest. He wouldn't even trust me to help care for you when you were sick!"

"Because whenever either of us gave you a task to do, you flitted off to pay calls or gossip with ladies in the shops, leaving me alone to manage everyone and everything!"

"What else is there for me to do?" said Rosanna, throwing her arms wide. "When I attempt to help, you give me meaningless tasks, 'managing' me as though I am of no more use than Mama. There is no need for me with perfect Prudence about."

With a scoff, her sister waved those words away and shook her head, turning to the doorway. "Spout whatever justifications you wish, Rosanna, but it doesn't alter the truth. If you wish to believe yourself the victim in this, that is your prerogative, but I shan't listen to you moan and complain about your perfect life as though being so admired and adored is such a burden."

"How dare you!" shouted Rosanna, tears blurring out the world, and though she knew she ought to guard her tongue, the whole of her feelings bubbled to the surface, refusing to hide away once more. The burbled and boiled, forced out her mouth before she could think better of it, bringing with them years of silence.

"You stand there, judging me as though my heartache is nothing at all, but you have no idea what it is like to constantly fall short of the paragon, Miss Prudence Leigh! My entire life, I have been compared to you—Prudence is so talented, so capable, so intelligent."

Adopting a snide tone, Rosanna mimicked all the many words she'd heard throughout her life. "'Oh, don't bother, dear. Your sister will manage everything, and you'll only get in the way.'" Shifting tone, she added, "'I am certain you do your best, but it's such a shame you haven't your sister's skills. Prudence is such a fine artist and musician, but you are a treat to look at. That is something.'"

Rosanna's chin trembled as the memories flooded her. "No matter what I do, I never measure up to you, and everyone is constantly reminding me of it. The only value I have in this life is my beauty, and that will fade, leaving me nothing but a useless husk with nothing to offer anyone. An object of pity."

The words erupted from her mouth, and Rosanna clapped a hand over it, though it was too late.

With wide eyes, Prudence turned to stare at her sister as Rosanna unleashed all her feelings in a torrent of words. And despite the ugliness of the moment and everything that had led to it, Prudence couldn't help but remain fixed in place, captured by the truth buried beneath all the pain.

Rosanna was jealous of her—not in some abstract manner, but in a very real way. Prudence stood there like a gaping fool as she tried to align that revelation with her view of the world. For one brief moment, her heart lightened, and a frisson skittered down her spine, settling into those broken parts of her soul that she hadn't even realized were fractured.

Rosanna was jealous of her!

Yet a chill came quickly upon its heels, fracturing her heart anew at the realization that her first impulse at Rosanna's confession was joy. Prudence's stomach soured, but she welcomed it, for that wretched impulse deserved condemnation.

Sightlessly, Rosanna shuffled backward until she hit her mattress and dropped down, her gaze focusing on nothing as everything within her deflated. Her sister was a lively soul, full of vigor and light, and at that moment, there was nothing left of it, leaving her that husk she predicted she would become. For all that her features did not change on any fundamental level, the vacant expression left her looking as haggard and worn as the heart beating in her chest.

Prudence's own broke at the sight.

Doubly so when Rosanna murmured, "Have you ever had a moment when you look at yourself and hate the person you are?"

Tears gathered in Rosanna's eyes, and Prudence's own couldn't help but follow suit. There was such pain etched in her tone, but more than that, there was such defeat and hopelessness rife in every syllable. And the phantom pains of the past made themselves known in Prudence's heart.

For all that she had thought she knew her sister, Prudence had never imagined Rosanna feeling such a thing. Miss Rosanna Leigh's world was filled with admiration and affection, freely given just because she existed. But perhaps that was the trouble.

True self-worth could never come from external sources, for one could not achieve such strength unless it originated from the "self." Having been cursed with such an obvious shortcoming as a plain face, Prudence had no choice but to wallow in despair or find her own strength, and she had learned that lesson long ago—even if she had to relearn it from time to time.

And while Rosanna believed Prudence was praised to the skies, those compliments had rarely been spoken to Prudence directly. The same voices so quick to commend Prudence to Rosanna were equally quick to do the reverse, rarely applying those sweet words to the person to whom they were speaking.

"I wish to be better," whispered Rosanna. "But I don't know how, and every time I try to do better, I fall short. And for once, someone looked at me as though I could be that person. He believed in me, and I wish I could say that I couldn't help myself, but that isn't true. I knew what I was doing. I don't know why I allowed myself to do it, but I did. All I could think was that if I ended up with a man like Mr. Courtney, I would never be better than the vapid little fashion plate he expects me to be—"

Rosanna's voice cracked, and she dropped her head, rubbing at her forehead as sniffling breaths wracked her. "I just—"

Although Prudence's heart had been suffused with stone just moments ago, no one listening to Rosanna's tearful words could believe her to be anything but sincere, and the hardened shell cracked. Gently, she came to sit beside her sister and took one of Rosanna's hands in hers.

"I am a terrible sister, Prudence," she said with shuddering breaths. "I know I am, and I am terrified of what the future will bring. Mama and Papa are going to be even more insufferable because I rejected Mr. Courtney, but I couldn't do it. I couldn't!"

Rosanna turned wide and watery eyes to her sister, and her whole being seemed to plead with her. "Please help me, Prudence. I do not want to be the trophy or the ornament, and I know I will if I am left to my own devices."

Clinging to her sister's hand, Rosanna fairly crushed Prudence's fingers beneath her steely grasp. Her breaths were jagged, her eyes pleading, and Prudence knew there was no other answer to give.

"There are times when you infuriate me, Rosanna, and I know I am quite capable of doing the same to you. We are two such different people that I can hardly believe we are as close as we are. But even as frustrating as you can be at times, I love you."

Prudence's voice broke on those last words. They echoed through her, resounding in the depths of her soul with their truth, even if she did not speak them as often as she ought. "That betrayal wouldn't have hurt so much if I didn't love you so."

"I am sorry, Prudence. I am. I cannot tell you how ashamed I am of myself. Once more, I have fallen short of the woman I wish to be." Rosanna's head dropped as fresh tears joined the old, and Prudence twisted closer to bring her arms around her sister.

"I cannot tell you how often I do as well, dearest," said Prudence as her sister's head came to rest upon her shoulder, as it so often had in the past. "All you can do is promise not to repeat your mistakes and try again."

Rosanna gave a small and very watery chuckle. "That is an easy promise to give. I am happy for you. Truly, I am."

In some hidden part of her heart, Prudence supposed she ought to be grateful for what had transpired, for if she'd fostered any doubts about Parker, they had been quickly erased at the sight of his panicked expression as he tried to untangle himself from Rosanna. But that was not something she would admit. Not at this time when the wounds were still too fresh.

"You shall find your own Dr. Humphreys one day," said Prudence.

Rosanna was quiet for a long moment after that. "I hope so."

But her tone sounded more like a wish than a belief. Prudence wished she had some advice or could foretell the future, but as Parker had been an unforeseen blessing, she had no assurances to give. What was to come would come, and they had no way of knowing what it would be.

"I am sorry, Prudence." Rosanna leaned heavily against her sister. "I love you."

Prudence wrapped her arms around her sister and held her close.

"Will you help me with Mama and Papa?" she whispered.

Puffing out her cheeks, Prudence sighed heavily. "I love you, but I do not know if I love you that much."

Rosanna gave a halting chuckle that ended in a sigh. "They are so angry with me."

"You made the right choice."

"Somehow, I do not think that will comfort them," she replied in a wry tone. Then she lifted her head, her brows pulling tight together and her gaze boring into Prudence's. "Will you help me be better?"

"It is something you shall have to do on your own, Rosanna."

"I know, but I have been trying on my own, and it has been a failure. I need assistance." Rosanna paused and considered that. "I need your help. Will you give it to me?"

Prudence's smile grew, her heart swelling as she held her sister close. "Of course, I will."

Chapter 44

One Month Later

Fantasy and reality were two very different things, and in most cases, the former was far grander than the latter, but in the weeks that followed Parker's second letter, Prudence was certain her new life outshined the dreams she'd constructed in days gone by. Her days as a courting lady were far more mundane yet so much more magnificent than anything her imagination could have conjured.

Parker didn't spend his days waxing poetic about her beauty or gazing at her with unabashed admiration, though there was plenty of that. No, Prudence simply hadn't imagined just how easily a gentleman could step into the role of friend and confidant. Life had not taught her to anticipate such a thing nor given any hint at how wonderful it was to have someone at her side, ready to shoulder her burdens and cheer her successes.

And that was far more wonderful than poetry and flowers. Though Parker managed plenty of that.

"What is that look for?" asked Rosanna, peering around her sister to meet her eyes in the dressing table's looking glass.

Prudence blushed—something that was becoming so commonplace she couldn't even feel a morsel of embarrassment at doing so. She only hoped one day she wouldn't be so easily flustered when caught deep in thought about her beau.

As the gleam in Rosanna's eyes made it clear that she knew the answer to that question, Prudence felt no need to answer it.

"Come now, we'll never have you ready in time if we keep dithering about," said Rosanna as she loosened the pins holding up her sister's hair. "We want you to look magnificent."

"That will take more time than we have," replied Prudence in a dry tone.

"What rubbish."

"Parker has seen me every day for the past four weeks—quite often in my work dresses and hardly looking my finest." But even as Prudence gave that protest, that young, romantic part of her heart quivered at the thought of looking her finest tonight.

Their first assembly together. They may have danced at the last one, but Prudence refused to give that any serious consideration. Besides, this was their first public gathering attended together with Parker escorting her. A lady ought to look lovely on such a night.

Shaking free of that thought, Prudence rose from her seat at the dressing table and strode to the wardrobe. "My blue gown is my finest, but I cannot wear the dark blue robe over it again. Though that one is my favorite, I wore it to the last assembly."

She sifted through the gowns and frowned. The lavender robe might do, but she didn't care for it over the blue gown, and a lady ought to wear her favorite gown for such a momentous event.

"Have you seen my white frock?" she asked, her hands on her hips as she stared at the meager offerings there. It was a shame she and Rosanna were not of similar tastes, or Prudence would borrow one. Of course, altering it to fit her lither frame would be a task, but the gold and pinks her sister preferred did not suit Prudence's coloring at all.

At the sound of a clearing throat, she turned away from the wardrobe to find Rosanna standing there with the missing gown draped across her arms to display the new adornments covering the white. Green ribbon circled the décolletage, and from that sprouted four columns made of the same material, outlining a string of diamonds along the sleeves, bust, and back in a diamond pattern, stretching down the skirts to the hem, which was now ringed in the same fashion.

The gown itself was a simple affair—one that Prudence usually wore beneath a robe—but with her sister's addition, the dress became something lovely in its own right. Understated yet with just the right embellishments to make it utterly unique.

"It is perfect," said Prudence, drawing nearer to feel the ribbon affixed to the fabric. Her throat tightened as she recognized the ribbons Rosanna had scavenged from one of her own gowns. "When did you do this?"

Rosanna lowered the dress and laughed, though Prudence didn't miss the faint sheen in her eyes, for it matched her own. "You have been quite occupied of late. It was an easy enough thing to manage when you were off making eyes at your Dr. Humphreys."

Taking the gown, Prudence laid it on the bed and drew her sister into an embrace. "Thank you."

"Think nothing of it," said Rosanna as they parted, though her voice wobbled just a touch. "You ought to look ravishing tonight."

Prudence's cheeks heated once more, and she couldn't fight the smile that spread as Rosanna made quick work of removing the day dress and replacing it with the newly made-over evening gown. The neck of the dress pulled at her hair, causing the last of her pins to pull free, and when she stood before the mirror, the straight locks hung free, draped over her shoulder.

Though green wouldn't have been her first choice for the decorations, the shade was perfect. It was the color of the forest when the foliage was so thick that the sunlight couldn't reach the ground, all deep and dark. If she were to choose a green, this would be the hue.

A knock at the door drew their attention, and Rosanna called for the maid to enter.

"Something's arrived for you, miss," said Jane with a bob as she drew up beside them with a bouquet in her hand. The girl stifled a giggle as Prudence took the offering, her smile broadening and her cheeks turning a deeper shade of red.

Not being much of a gardener, Prudence was not well-versed in the names of the blossoms, but it mattered little, for they smelled heavenly, and the colors were a blend of pinks and purples accented by rich green foliage. A note nestled amongst the velvety petals, and she freed it and leaned in to breathe deeply of the floral scent. It was perhaps the most beautiful arrangement she had ever seen, though its magnificence had as much to do with the sender as the gift itself.

It must've cost a fortune to procure such a lovely selection at this time of year, and though the knowledge dimmed the joy of the moment a touch, the loveliness of the gift and the sentiment behind it kept Prudence from fixating on the expense.

With her thumb, she broke the seal and found only two short words there.

Until tonight. — P.

Prudence clutched the note and inhaled the flowers' scent once more before tucking the missive into her side table drawer, along with all the others he'd secreted to her. Perhaps it was silly to make a keepsake of two words, but it mattered not. Prudence was going to keep this note safe and sound with all the others.

"We'd best get started or you shall never be ready in time," said Rosanna, ushering her sister towards the dressing table. With great reluctance, Prudence relinquished her bouquet, and Rosanna smiled at it and her. "These will do perfectly."

With quick fingers, she undid the bindings holding the flowers together. Prudence gaped, but Rosanna met her gaze in the mirror and winked. And with that, Rosanna and the maid set to work, binding up her hair with pins as they wove the blossoms into the locks, making up for the lack of curls with the flowers' vibrant colors.

Prudence straightened, glancing between the bouquet Jane and Rosanna were picking apart and her gown. Though Rosanna's alterations were not what Prudence would've chosen on her own, it was the perfect canvas to showcase the flowers—accentuating the colors rather than clashing with them. The rich green of the leaves matched the ribbons to perfection.

"Don't you dare cry. Your eyes will go red," said Rosanna, pausing as she studied Prudence in the looking glass.

"I am not going to cry," she protested, though the wobble in her voice betrayed her words. In truth, Prudence was finding it difficult not to be overcome by the tendernesses heaped upon her by Parker and Rosanna. "I am not feeling overwhelming fondness for my dear sister and my beau, who went to great lengths to coordinate a surprise for me. I am not."

Crouching beside Prudence, Rosanna put an arm around her shoulder and met her sister's gaze in the mirror. A smile brightened her face as she said, "You shall look your best tonight, Prudence."

Rosanna then straightened and brushed a casual touch under her eyes before putting the final touches on Prudence's hair.

Chapter 45

Curse all the broken bones, megrims, and apoplexies! Mr. Poole's gout had forced Parker to cancel his stroll with Prudence the day before, and now the Fowler family's bout with influenza had made him tardy to the assembly. Thank the heavens he'd been able to send Prudence the flowers before the Fowlers' summons had arrived. That was something.

Straightening his tailcoat, Parker hurried along the streets while cursing the societal dictates that required evening clothes. If not for that, he would've arrived tardy but not monstrously so. As it was, Prudence had been waiting for him for nearly an hour. Parker dodged around the piles of muck on the road, forcing himself to slow when he reached a particularly murky bit of road; it wouldn't do to go to all the trouble of polishing himself up if he then walked straight through something unsavory.

But the assembly rooms drew ever closer, and Parker weaved between the other patrons drifting towards the entrance, hardly slowing until he stepped into the main ballroom. His lungs burned, and he patted at his forehead, hoping the trickles of sweat were not noticeable. His gaze swept the room, darting from face to face as he hoped his own was not too flushed from the exertion.

And there she was. Parker quickly hoped he didn't look flushed for all new reasons.

Eyes were strange things. Though he hadn't made a thorough study of those organs during his schooling, Parker had enough experience to know they were flawed. The world had not altered, yet the images that moved from his eyes to his brain were entirely different from those which he had seen just a few weeks ago.

It was as though Prudence's features had rearranged themselves into something altogether new, though he knew that to be impossible, for she looked just as she always did. Only now, she was the most exquisite woman in the room with his flowers adorning her hair and bringing a rosiness to her cheek.

Her eyes met his, and Parker could hardly breathe at the sight of her heart shining within those dark depths. For a long moment, they simply held each other's gaze, and his heart thumped against his ribcage as her entire being brightened with a smile that stretched boldly across her face. Though others certainly noticed their marked attentions, Parker refused to look away as he forced his way through the crowd.

"Miss Leigh," he murmured, not trusting himself to say anything more. The brightness in her gaze warmed him and settled into his heart, making it expand until it was too big for his chest.

"Dr. Humphreys." Her reply was proper, as was her curtsy, but the softness of her voice set his blood pumping.

Nodding towards the dancers, he held out his hand. Prudence schooled her smile, though it did little good, for it shone in her eyes without restraint as she took his hand and allowed him to lead her into the dance.

Had Parker been wiser or had his mind been functioning at all, he would've waited to lead her into the fray, for the dance was far too quick to allow him to enjoy her company. Something slow that allowed him to focus on her entirely was preferable, but the only thought that had been running through his mind was his need to be near her.

Usually, dances allowed just that. Unfortunately, the reel had them moving back and forth, to and fro with such speed, and the steps were just intricate enough to force him to focus more on it than his partner. But when their gazes met, Prudence's face was aglow with the joy of the moment, and Parker threw himself into the movements with all his skill (poor though it may be).

Though a dance set could seem an eternity with the wrong partner, with Prudence at his side, the measures of the music sped by too quickly, and Parker couldn't help but wish that it would last another quarter of an hour. Or more.

With the last bow and curtsy, Prudence took his arm before he had the opportunity to offer it up to her, and Parker felt like preening as they strode away from the dancers. Such a little thing, her taking it so readily—so eagerly—made his chest expand, puffing him up like some swaggering fool. But when his gaze drifted to the lady at his side, he knew he had every reason to feel that way, for Prudence Leigh was his sweetheart. His treasure.

"I see you received my flowers," he murmured as his gaze lingered on the blossoms woven through her locks.

Prudence rather epitomized her namesake, for she was a practical person and not given to giggling or coyness, yet a giddy smile flitted on her lips, and she ducked her face away as readily as any flirtatious debutante. The difference being that her embarrassment was entirely authentic. And the sight of her discomposure added an extra bounce to Parker's strut.

"They are lovely," she said, "and I adore them, but they must have cost you a fortune. There is no need to spend so much—"

"Calm yourself," he said, resting his free hand atop the one that she had threaded through his arm. "I assure you I didn't spend a farthing on them. The flowers are from the Chorleys' conservatory and are something of an apology, to soothe their embarrassment at having called me out in the middle of the night when their emergency turned out to be nothing but a bout of indigestion. As much as I would've liked to buy you an entire garden's worth of flowers, I knew you wouldn't appreciate the expense."

Prudence straightened, her wide eyes darting to Parker's. He didn't know whether to be pleased that he knew her well enough to have surmised her preferences or panged at the thought that something as small as being considerate of economy was enough to shock her, but he focused on the former, feeling that bounce in his step once more at having given her such a perfect gift.

Weaving through the edges of the ballroom, Parker set them on an easy turn about the room, steering clear of any groups that might intrude on their private conversation. And that was when he noticed Mr. Leigh standing not fifty feet from them, his eyes narrowed as he studied his daughter's beau with a slight sneer to his lips.

"He will come around," whispered Prudence, though her tone spoke of more hope than faith that it was possible.

Parker smiled and sent her a covert wink. "Of course, he will."

Though he ought to know better than to lie, there were times when such little falsehoods were the better course. And Parker was certain Prudence knew it as well.

Having heard Mr. Leigh speak at length about Prudence's foolishness for entertaining the suit of a gentleman who couldn't provide for her as well as her father, Parker knew Mr. Leigh would never be content to see the family drudge pull free of their hold; then he might have to bestir himself to do more than hide in his library.

Giving the gentleman a nod, Parker turned them away; tonight ought not to be touched by that misery.

Thankfully, Mr. Leigh was easy enough to ignore. Unfortunately, Mrs. Leigh wasn't. She hurried towards them with wide eyes, fluttering hands, and all the excitement of a lapdog seeing its mistress after a long absence.

"What felicity!" she said, dropping into a bob. "I was afraid you wouldn't be able to attend, and Prudence has gone to such lengths to pretty herself up for you."

No matter how many times Mrs. Leigh blurted such bald statements, Parker would never be comfortable with them, most especially when Prudence blanched. As gratifying as it was to know that at least one of her parents was pleased with the match, he couldn't help but wish Mrs. Leigh was a little less pleased; dark and thunderous looks from afar were easy enough to avoid.

And having her mother elbow her way between you and your sweetheart was beyond the pale. Parker forced himself not to growl when Mrs. Leigh did just that and took them both by the arm, strolling along the ballroom side by side by side.

"I am so happy you came," said Mrs. Leigh. Peering at her daughter, she added with a nudge of her elbow, "Aren't we so very happy, Prudence?"

"Yes, Mama."

Parker never knew whether Mrs. Leigh didn't hear the sigh rife in Prudence's tone or ignored it, but as she never acknowledged her daughter's disquiet, he supposed it was the former.

"You look quite handsome tonight, Dr. Humphreys," said Mrs. Leigh, leaning close to Parker. There was nothing untoward about the action, but it made him cringe all the same. Prudence leaned back to meet his gaze from around her mother's head, and she mouthed an apology. As Mrs. Leigh rarely noticed anything beyond her own words, Parker didn't bother hiding the wink he sent in reply, and Prudence's gaze warmed, her lips pulling into a tender smile.

There was no doubt about it. Suffering through hours of Mrs. Leigh's awkward and invasive meddling was a small price to pay to court Prudence.

"You two looked splendid dancing together. Quite a fine couple. But I hope you aren't so impetuous as to drag her into another set so soon. You'll have to be patient, or you shan't be able to stand up with her for the rest of the evening. Three sets and people will talk, you know." Mrs. Leigh paused in her jabbering and gave him a sly smile. "Unless you wish them to."

"Mama!" Prudence winced, but her mother merely laughed.

"Don't be so missish, my dear. Dr. Humphreys understands my jests," said Mrs. Leigh.

Parker dutifully laughed alongside her, and the moment he could, he sent Prudence yet another wink, which discomposed her as easily as the first. All things considered, this was a rather entertaining game. If he did it a dozen times, would Prudence still blush? Parker thought so. And he expected Mrs. Leigh wouldn't notice a single one of them.

Perhaps he ought to test that theory.

Mrs. Leigh continued to babble on, and Parker darted a look at Prudence and gave her a wink with one eye and then the other. She ducked her head and pressed a hand to her mouth to stifle a laugh.

"Hello, there," called Miss Rosanna, hurrying to the trio. Flashing her sister a pained smile, Miss Rosanna came to their mother's side. "I was looking high and low for you, Mama."

Mrs. Leigh stiffened, lifting her chin as she turned her gaze away from her daughter. She didn't go so far as to ignore Miss Rosanna entirely, but ice suffused her tone as she replied. "Is that so?"

The young lady's throat clenched as though struggling to swallow, and the brightness in her gaze dimmed, though she held onto her smile as she nodded. "Mrs. Nott was just telling me a most titillating story about a certain young lady who recently went to Preston to visit family."

None of that made any sense to Parker, but he supposed that was the point, for Miss Rosanna infused enough insinuation into her tone that anyone listening would know the vague words signified something interesting but without actually spreading anything.

Mrs. Leigh required no more prodding; she dropped Parker's and Prudence's arms to take hold of Miss Rosanna's, and the pair hurried off—but not before the young lady sent her sister a significant look and nod towards the door. For all that Parker had once thought her an angel because of her beauty, Miss Rosanna now resembled those heavenly beings for an entirely different reason. There strode their savior.

Prudence snatched his hand, and as quickly as she could manage without causing a stir, she led him through the crowd and out the front doors and into the town square.

Chapter 46

Someone had lit a small bonfire to one side of the town square for those wishing for the air but needing a bit of warmth. With winter coming on fast, it was too brisk for many of the attendees, but after that rousing set and the heat of the ballroom, Parker welcomed the nip. More than that, he welcomed Prudence sidling up next to him, her arm wrapped snugly around his, and the fact that they were free to wander the area on their own without delving into scandalous behavior.

Music echoed through the windows, the rousing steps of the dances thundering in time as the people whirled, stomped, and clapped through the songs. Then the strains drew to a close, and many of those outside returned to the assembly rooms to join in the next set, leaving Parker and Prudence almost entirely by themselves. The last rays of sunshine dipped behind the horizon, shrouding the world in darkness. The bonfire provided a touch of light, but the square was filled with plenty of darkened corners in which to hide.

Just as Parker was about to offer up a belated apology for his tardiness, Prudence glanced at him and asked, "How are the Fowlers?"

Parker's brows rose, and she added, "I heard they weren't coming because they had fallen ill. As you are their physician, I assumed you were tardy because you were paying a call on them."

Such a little thing to say. So simple. So small. Yet her words struck him to the core. Buried within was a wealth of understanding and awareness, showing just how much she knew and cared for him. Just as when he'd had to cancel their outings in the past, there was no censure in her tone—merely concern for his patients and himself.

Clearing his throat (though it was surprisingly difficult at present), he said, "They are feeling poorly but it's nothing grave. The Fowlers will be on the mend before long."

"With your fine care, I am certain they will be healthy and hale in no time," she said, giving him a broad smile. Tipping her head back, Prudence looked up at the sky. The stars and moon were on full display, filling the darkness with their brilliant light. "Isn't it lovely?"

Parker readily agreed, though he couldn't turn his gaze from Prudence's face. Her pale skin shone in the moonlight, highlighting the elegant sweep of her neck. Then she dropped her gaze, meeting his, and despite the shadows, her eyes glowed with pleasure, lighting her up like a bonfire.

Even if he wrote a hundred letters and recited a thousand speeches, Parker was certain she would never fully understand just how much she affected him. He longed to take her into his embrace, to show her as no words ever could just how much his heart beat for her.

For goodness' sake! Would he not simply kiss her? Prudence was long past the point when such thoughts caused even a modicum of embarrassment, for that hope had burned within her for so many weeks now. And as much as she appreciated Parker's gallantry, she prayed he would give in to the moment and embrace her.

So many nights she fell asleep whilst thinking of his lips, carrying those thoughts into her dreams, and when she awoke, her mind never strayed far from Parker Humphreys. Holding his gaze, Prudence filled her eyes with all those dreams and longings—hoping beyond hope that he would see that she was quite ready for him to take that step.

Never was there a better moment. Though there was little true privacy to be found, Prudence had guided them to the one spot in which they could steal a few tender moments without being caught. Her cheeks still burned from the heat of the dance, but it was much more due to Parker's longing glances. Surely such a delicious moment ought to be punctuated with a kiss.

She poured all those feelings into her eyes, pleading with him to make his move. She did not wish to rush things, but how much more obvious could she be? Perhaps—

"I love you," he whispered.

Prudence's brows jerked upward; she'd imagined having a beau confess his affection for her, but rather than being calm and collected or giddy with delight, Prudence's jaw slackened and she stared, wide-eyed at him.

"Pardon?"

Parker let out a sharp breath and shook his head. "Perhaps it's too soon for me to say so, but I cannot help it. I wish I could say I always knew it deep in my heart, but we both know my heart is quite foolish at times. But I know it now without doubt or caveat. I love you, Prudence Leigh."

And still, she remained there, gaping and dumbstruck. While she'd hoped for some token of affection tonight, never in her wildest imaginings had she thought that she would hear such perfect words.

Her heart melted, searing through her veins like molten iron. Prudence loved him as readily as he loved her, yet words failed her. She couldn't think what to say that he hadn't already. What did a lady say at such a moment? Thank you? I feel the same? No combination seemed fitting, for the words could not convey the feelings burning through her.

An impulse flashed in her mind, and she refused to question it. Throwing her arms around his neck, Prudence pulled him close and brought her lips to his.

Parker drew his arm tight around her, pulling her flush as he delved into that kiss with all the feeling of his heart. He savored the rightness that settled into his soul as he lost himself in the sensation. His heart thundered in his chest, fluttering as though trying to break free of his chest—not slowing even as they broke apart. Parker couldn't help but grin at the dazed look in Prudence's eyes as she returned his smile.

"I have wanted to do that for some time," she whispered.

Parker chuckled. "I was trying to be gallant."

Her hands still rested at the nape of his neck, and a wicked glint sparked in her gaze as she leaned closer, her lips brushing his as she murmured, "I assure you—I've had enough gallantry."

Though he anticipated her closing the distance once more, Prudence paused and lowered one of her hands to rest against his chest, hovering above his heart. Suddenly, she seemed taken by a bout of nerves, for her gaze dropped away, her brows pulling together.

"I—"

"You needn't say anything, Prudence." Parker rubbed her back, matching his gentle tone to those tender caresses. "I did not say it expecting anything in return. I simply needed to tell you how I feel. The words were burning inside me, begging to be voiced."

Prudence's gaze darted to his once more, a hint of a smile tugging at her lips. "Do you think I often lure gentlemen into the shadows and kiss them soundly?"

"I certainly hope not."

That hand rose to his face, caressing his cheek. "I love you, Parker Humphreys."

Though her actions and behavior certainly hinted at what she was going to say, Parker still couldn't quite believe his ears. She loved him. He still didn't understand how he had managed to secure her affection after such a wretched beginning, but he wasn't about to question it.

Closing the distance, he swept her into another kiss. And though it may be a silly thing to think in such a moment, Parker couldn't help the thought that sprang to his mind, searing his mind with indelible truth and clarity.

Thank heavens for his poor penmanship.

Unlike ever before, Prudence understood why ladies were taught to guard their kisses. At that moment, any shred of decorum or sense was gone. It was such a heady feeling, and for the first time in her life, she felt giddy. Not merely happy but incandescently, insensibly, and irrationally joyous. Had the vicar or the busiest of busybodies strode upon them, she wouldn't have noticed or cared. Or stopped.

Not with the feel of Parker holding her so tenderly, his lips pressed against hers.

It was the sort of feeling that inspired one to the greatest heights of lunacy. At that moment, she was the loveliest creature in all of creation. Her wit and kindness were unmatched. Prudence was complete and perfect with the ability to drive any man to distraction. Yet as she lost herself in the sensation, she didn't want just any man: she wanted this one. Her dear Parker. If she was the best of women, he was the best of men. They were a perfect complement to each other.

And when they parted, they remained wrapped in each other's arms, and Prudence held his gaze, seeing the mirror of her feelings bright within his blue eyes. They were truly the finest eyes she had ever seen.

A gust of wind cut through the night, surging through all the many layers she was wearing, and for all that she felt ablaze with the feelings burning within her, a shiver tried to take hold. But Prudence refused to give in and surrender a single second of this moment with him.

"Come, you are chilled," he murmured.

Prudence sighed, though she couldn't fight the smile that emerged at that consideration. Day in and day out, he seemed determined to make up for her family's lack of care, and each little demonstration made her love him all the more.

Though she tried to distract him with another kiss (which he accepted readily), Parker led her back to the assembly.

"If you wish to be sensible, I suppose I shall have to be sensible as well," she murmured with a mock scowl.

With her arm tucked firmly in his, Parker smiled. "Might I have the next dance?"

She forced herself to remain firmly on the ground, despite her heart's best efforts to carry her away into the sky. "Of course."

"And the one after that?"

"Three sets and people will talk, you know," replied Prudence in a decent parody of her mother's tone.

"Let them talk. I want that dance, the next dance, and each one after that."

Prudence's heart might never survive Parker if he insisted on saying such delightful things. Leaning closer, she rested her free hand atop his forearm, her fingers drifting along the one bare patch between his gloves and cuff, allowing herself the freedom to touch as she had never done before.

"My dances are all yours," she whispered. "And they always will be."

Join the M.A. Nichols VIP Reader Club at

www.ma-nichols.com

to receive up-to-date information about upcoming books, freebies, and VIP content!

About the Author

Born and raised in Anchorage, M.A. Nichols is a lifelong Alaskan with a love of the outdoors. As a child she despised reading but through the love and persistence of her mother was taught the error of her ways and has had a deep, abiding relationship with it ever since.

She graduated with a bachelor's degree in landscape management from Brigham Young University and a master's in landscape architecture from Utah State University, neither of which has anything to do with why she became a writer, but is a fun little tidbit none-the-less. And no, she doesn't have any idea what type of plant you should put in that shady spot out by your deck. She's not that kind of landscape architect. Stop asking.

Website Facebook Instagram BookBub

Printed in Great Britain
by Amazon

27976953R00175